MW01707529

A Conflicted Love Story

Written by

M. Goyal

This is a work of fiction. Names, characters, places, and incidents either are the product of the author's imagination or are used fictitiously. Any resemblance to actual persons, living or dead, events, or locales is entirely coincidental.

Copyright © 2021 by M. Goyal

All rights reserved. No part of this book may be reproduced or used in any manner without written permission of the copyright owner except for the use of quotations in a book review.

First paperback edition January 2021

Book design by M. Goyal and Evelyn Roberts

ISBN 978-0-578-84502-9

Published M. Goyal

To Shri, without you this story would not exist.
To Sonali and Yash, without this story you would not exist.
Love you infinity, you cannot beat me!

Chapter 1

Talia and Mirlande's Luncheon

It was a beautiful sunny day in Williamsville, NY. The birds were bathing in the puddles from the rain the night before. "Sorry I'm late. Just as I was leaving, all of a sudden, it got so busy at the boutique. Before I left, I wanted to make sure my assistant was able to handle the customers on her own," Mirlande said as she greeted Talia with a kiss on her cheek.

Talia looked up from her laptop as she smiled, "I have been waiting for about forty-five minutes but that's alright I was able to get some work done."

Mirlande was relieved that Talia wasn't upset for making her wait. She pulled out her chair and sat across from Talia, "I see you ordered drinks and appetizers."

Talia zipped her laptop case. "The waiter brought them over seconds before you arrived. It didn't look nice for me to just sit here for half an hour not ordering anything." Mirlande felt bad for making Talia wait but she also knew her friend would understand.

Talia took a couple of grilled Cajun shrimps then passed the plate to Mirlande. "So what is it that you wanted to talk to me about and couldn't wait?" Before Mirlande could answer they were interrupted by the waiter.

"Here is your water ladies, I will return shortly to take your orders." The waiter then walked away to the table next to them.

As soon as the waiter left, Talia leaned forward, "So what is it that you needed to talk to me about so badly?"

Mirlande was about to take a bite of her shrimp but stopped. She was eager to share her excitement with Talia, "Ok, I am going to get right to it, I have been seeing this guy for about three months and I haven't said anything to you or Ally yet because I just wanted to make sure it wasn't going to be something which was just going to last for few weeks."

Talia was surprised to hear this. She smiled, "Wow that's great! Tell me everything about this guy, what's his name? How did you meet him?"

"Ok, ok jeez, I have never seen you get so excited about anything I have told you before! His name is Marcus. I met him at a merchandise show at the Convention Center. When I was looking at some of the clothes for the boutique he was looking for merchandise for his store that he owns and get this, it's not far from my boutique!!" Mirlande said excitedly as if she was a teenager who was in love for the first time.

Talia was excited too and wanted to hear more about how they met but the waiter interrupted them again...

"Are you ladies ready to order?" The two were so engrossed in their conversation that they both had forgotten to look at the menu.

Talia looked at the waiter and said, "I'm sorry we didn't get a chance to look at the menu as of yet, could you please give us a minute to decide, but you don't have to go. It'll really take us just a minute."

The waiter smiled and said, "Sure."

Mirlande and Talia quickly glanced at the menu so they could get back to their conversation. "Do you know what you want?" Talia asked, peering over at Mirlande.

"You go ahead and order, that will give me another second to choose," Mirlande replied, scanning the menu.

Talia looked up at the waiter, "I will have the tomato basil pasta please."

The waiter turned to Mirlande, who smiled and said, "I think I will have the same."

The waiter wrote down their orders, "Will bring your orders shortly" and walked away after he collected the menus.

As soon as the waiter left, the girls turned to each other, "Ok so continue," Talia said eagerly.

"Where was I? Oh yes, as I was saying, Marcus and I met at the merchandise show and it just so happened that as I was walking around looking at the products I kept running into him. He joked and said 'Looks like you are stalking me.' I smiled at him and replied, 'Maybe you are stalking me.' Then we both laughed and introduced ourselves and started to talk about the show and the consignments. Then he asked me if I owned a store and I told him yes and where it was. He then laughed and said, 'My store is actually two blocks away from yours.' I shook my head and said, 'It's a small world.' So from that point on we spent the day together. We were laughing and talking, liking certain items that were good and were making fun of certain items that were just weird. The show came to an end, we said goodbye to each other and parted our ways."

"Ok, so you guys didn't exchange phone numbers or anything? I don't get it?" Talia said with a puzzled look.

"Just wait, I didn't finish my story," said Mirlande with a smile and wink.

"Oh sorry. I just can't wait to hear what happened next," replied Talia excitedly.

Mirlande continued with her story…

"Couple of weeks went by and I was busy at the boutique helping customers when I heard someone behind me say 'Excuse me, I was wondering if you could help me?' I turned around and it was Marcus, standing there with a bright smile. I looked at him and said, 'Hey hi.' I asked him what he is doing at the boutique and jokingly said to him, 'Your store must not be doing well if you're here.' He laughed, saying 'I had been thinking about you and I remembered the name of your boutique so I thought I would stop by and say hello.'

"I didn't know what to say to him so I just smiled and said 'Ok.' I kept having customers come up to me so he said to me, 'I see that you are busy so why don't we get together and chat over dinner tonight if you are free?' I grinned, 'Yes sure but the only problem is that it will be really late by the time I lock up the boutique.' He said, 'That's not a problem I too have to close my store and it will be late also. What time is good for you?' He asked. 'I will be done by 10:30,' I answered. 'Perfect then I will come and pick you up from your boutique at 10:30.' I said to him, 'Ok that sounds great.' He peered mischievously and said, 'See you tonight' then left the store.

Mirlande was rambling on and on, Talia wasn't really interested in the mundane details and wanted to tell her friend to get to the point but she could see the excitement on her friend's face so refrained from saying anything…

"I was so excited the entire day that even though it was a very busy day I kept looking at the clock. Finally, it was closing time and I was rushing to get everything done so I could try to wash up and freshen my makeup but no such luck. There was this last customer in the store that was taking forever to just pick out what she wanted. I wanted to tell her just take anything and leave but you know I couldn't do that so instead I went up to her and politely told her that I am sorry but the store is now closed if she couldn't decide and needed more time, she could always come back tomorrow so she didn't have to rush. The lady looked at me very upset and said, 'I'll take this.' I personally didn't care at that time if I was going to lose a customer. ("Oh my God, she needs to stop with these details," thought Talia as her friend kept talking). I was finally going on a date with a guy! It had been so long since I had a date that I thought I was just going to become one of those bitter old women who die alone because they were so busy with their work and didn't bother to make time to find someone in life."

Mirlande winced at her friend, "Sorry Talia, I am not implying anything about you working all the time."

"Yeah sure. Go ahead continue with your story."

Mirlande smiled and was about to continue with her story but the waiter brought them their lunch. "Here you go ladies, is there anything else I can get for you?"

They both said in unison, "We are good, thank you."

Mirlande looked at her plate like a cat who was served a bowl of tuna, "I am starving!"

Talia twirled her fork into the pasta, "Me too."

They took a few bites before Talia asked Mirlande to continue with the story. Mirlande swallowed her bite and continued.

"Finally, the customer left and as I went to lock the door and turn the sign to close, I saw Marcus coming out of his car. He had parked his car right in front of the door. He beamed at me and I had a grin from ear to ear as I opened the door. He came in and asked if I was ready to go. I asked if he could give me just a couple of minutes so I could go and freshen up. He gently took my hand, looked into my eyes and said, 'You don't need to do that, you look beautiful.'

"I started blushing, of course you couldn't see my face turning red because of my chocolate skin but I sure was feeling the heat."

Talia laughed, "You and Ally always have something to say about your skin tone and ethnicity every time we talk. I find that hilarious and always wonder what people think of us when they overhear our conversation."

"Well, the problem is Ally and I don't have a problem saying anything about our skin tones or ethnicities because we are not saying anything wrong. The reason why people frown upon what we say is because we say what everyone is thinking but never have the nerve to say. Besides we are such good friends that we can talk about each other, our skin color, our culture, our religion because, at the end of the day, we know we love each other and we know we are not saying things to hurt each other. We are free to speak our mind!" Said Mirlande in a playful manner as she raised both of her hands in the air.

Talia shook her head as she smiled, "Speaking of Ally, does she know your story?"

Mirlande shrugged her shoulders like a little girl, "Ugh, nooo, why do you think I am telling you this first! I need for us to figure out how to talk to her about Marcus. You know how she is!"

"Yeah I know exactly how she is that's why I was asking you. She hasn't let you forget about your last boyfriend," replied Talia.

"Well, can I continue my story then we can figure out how to tell Ally?" Asked Mirlande enthusiastically.

"Yes of course, sorry go ahead continue with your story. So...what happened after you were done blushing through your dark skin?" Talia smirked.

Mirlande smirked back at Talia, "So, as I was feeling the heat on my face, Marcus was still holding my hand and I didn't know exactly what to do or say. He pulled me closer to him as he put his firm ass on the countertop near the cash register." She stopped, putting her finger to her chin and looked skyward. "By the way, did I tell you what he looks like?"

Talia shook her head no.

Mirlande leaned in, her eyes twinkling, "Well, then let me tell you before I continue my story so you can visualize him. He is tall, dark brown, not black but dark brown with a beautiful face, beautiful dark brown eyes and black hair. Did I mention to you that he is beautiful? He is not fat and not slender but just the right build. You can tell he works out but not to the point that he looks bulky. Imagine a tall dark brown- skinned guy, medium built with a yogic body. He doesn't do yoga but he has that body where it's firm just in the right places!"

Talia joked, "Wow! He sounds beautiful. You sure he is not gay?"

Mirlande smiled and gave a wink, "I can guarantee you that he is not gay."

Talia exclaimed, waving her finger at Mirlande, "You naughty girl!"

Before Mirlande could continue with her story the waiter returned and asked them how everything was? Both ladies looked up at him and replied simultaneously, "Great!" The story was getting too juicy to be interrupted. As soon as the waiter walked away from the table Talia gestured with her hands for Mirlande to continue her story.

"So where was I, oh yes, Marcus put his firm *brown* ass on the edge of the counter. Then he put both of his arms around my waist and pulled me closer. I couldn't move or say anything. Both of us were just silent. He then gazed into my eyes and told me how beautiful I looked. Meanwhile, apart from feeling the heat in my face, I was silently asking myself, 'Is he for real? Does he not see that I *am* a bit chunky?' For a second, I thought it was all a joke. I was thinking what if this guy was here to say all these nice things to me then start laughing at me because of my size? I was waiting for him to make fun of me. Why would a beautiful man like him find someone my size attractive? Thinking that started to make me sad. I really was waiting for him to laugh at me and say to me, 'You fat ass, did you ever think someone like me could actually be interested in you?' I got really sad and I guess he could see my mood had changed. He asked me what was wrong. I pulled away from him and said, 'You are being kind to me and saying that I'm pretty but I'm a bit puzzled, asking myself, doesn't he see how big I am?' She turned her head away, 'I'm waiting for you to make fun of me because of my size.'

"The reaction I got from him was unbelievable. He looked so hurt. He pulled me even closer to him. He whispered in my ear, 'I like big butts and I cannot lie' and then *he* started laughing." Mirlande recounted, her voice squeaking and her eyes becoming wide.

"I know he was just trying to lighten things up between us. Then he got serious and said to me, 'I'm just kidding! I saw this beautiful woman going from having a smile on her face to having this sad look. That bothered me. I believe in laughter being a healer of everything, that's why I joke in serious situations. I see you as a beautiful person inside and out. I know a lot of men go for slender women and I too used to do that because I too was very shallow when I was younger. But as I grew older and started to meet all kinds of women I realized that the women who look so perfect on the outside are very shallow and self-centered themselves. When I saw you and spent the day with you I could see your inner beauty. To be honest with you I am blinded by the purity of your heart. You may be a larger size but you have a very beautiful face and a beautiful soul and that is what I have been thinking about ever since the first time I met you. Any man would be a fool not to be with you.'

"I asked him, 'but you are gorgeous, you can have any beautiful woman, why would you even look at me?'

"He smacked the palm of his hand against his forehead and rolled his eyes, 'WOMAN! Didn't you hear a word I said to you?' I just looked at him with this 'deer in the headlights' look and then we both started laughing."

Talia interrupted, she put her hand on her chest, touched by what he said to her friend, "I think I am in love with Marcus just from what you told me about him. So what happened after that? I thought he was going to kiss you. Matter of fact, I'm pretty sure he was going to kiss you but you ruined the mood. From the story you were telling me it was as if I was reading a novel or watching a romantic movie. Seriously, you couldn't have picked another time to feel sorry for yourself?"

"Oh my God, you are so insensitive. Instead of saying something to make me feel better about myself you accuse me of ruining the mood!" Exclaimed Mirlande.

"Really, are we seriously going that way? How long have we known each other? We have been through this issue with you several times and at least I was nicer and I am still nicer to you than Ally. Wait until you tell her this story, I would love to hear what she has to say to you about that."

"Are you kidding me? I am not planning to tell her all the details of how I met Marcus as I am telling you. I am afraid of even bringing Marcus up to her," said Mirlande.

"Why? Marcus sounds like a fantastic guy unless there is something you will end up telling me that you haven't said yet? We know you have a history of picking some doozies but so far he sounds good," joked Talia.

"Oh my God, there you go again talking about the type of guys I pick," Mirlande replied exasperatedly.

"You know, I don't want to get started about your choice of guys because right now I am interested in knowing what happened next, besides I know Ally will take care of that part," said Talia as she laughed.

Mirlande squinted as she wrinkled her nose. "You know when I have friends like you and Ally, who needs enemies!"

"Oh you know we love you!" Laughed Talia as she blew a kiss across the table to her friend, with a smile.

"Yeah I know." Mirlande replied with an eye roll.

After a brief pause to take a few bites of their lunch, Talia demanded Mirlande continue the juicy story.

"Ok, so after our little chit chat Marcus said to me, 'I don't know about you but I'm getting very hungry. Should we go get something to eat?' I told him, 'Of course!' I locked up the boutique and we got into his car. He even held the car door open for me!

"It was pretty late and most of the restaurants were about to close so we decided to go to Jerry's 24 hour diner. We both sat there for hours talking and laughing. We were so engrossed with each other that the time went by fast and before we realized it, the sun started to come out. We both must have finished three pots of coffee!

"I gestured outside and said to him, 'Look! The sun is rising.' He looked out the window and said, 'Wow, we have been here all night and I didn't even get sleepy.' I said to him 'It must have been all that coffee we had,' and we both laughed. He paid the tab and then drove me back to the boutique so I could pick up my car. Of course we kissed," Mirlance smiled sheepishly and raised her hand, "but before you even ask, yes, the kiss was heavenly. It wasn't sloppy like some guys I dated. Marcus wasn't aggressive at all. He was slow and sweet, but, boy, could he use that tongue of his!" Mirlance closed her eyes and grinned, seeming to relive the moment.

Her eyes popped open, she could feel the blush coming on. "Anyway, I went home to get some sleep. I only had three hours before I had to open the boutique again. I didn't even change my clothes. I just went and laid down on my bed, but I found myself thinking about the night I just had. I thought about our conversation and how he made me feel. I don't think any guy has ever made me feel so comfortable the way Marcus did. It was as if I had known him forever. I kept thinking about him and couldn't sleep. Before I knew it, my alarm went off. So I got up, took a shower, had breakfast and went to work."

"Wow, so you didn't get any sleep?" Asked Talia.

"Nope, I was so happy that I didn't even feel sleepy."

"So what happened after that?" Talia inquired anxiously.

"Well, I didn't hear from him all day and I even left him a couple of messages but he didn't return my calls. So then I thought to myself, that's it, that's the end of that. I couldn't understand why he didn't return my calls and wasn't sure if I should stop by at his store. What if he didn't like me for some reason? I didn't want him to think I was a stalker. I started feeling sad and confused."

Talia was puzzled, "Why *didn't* you just go to his store to see him?"

"I told you, I didn't want him to think I was stalking him. I expressed my concern in the messages and I thought seriously what if he really wasn't interested in me after all? These thoughts crossed my mind so I just let him be. I knew it was too good to be true."

Talia felt dejected. "Aww, so what happened next?" She asked.

Before Mirlande could tell her, the waiter brought their check. They had been sitting there for some time so they split the check, paid for it, and walked out of the restaurant.

As Talia held the door for Mirlande to walk through, she said to her friend, "Well you know you need to finish the story."

"I know, but do you have time? I mean, you must have to get back to your work, right?"

"I've been doing my work all night to make sure I was caught up since I knew you and I were meeting today. I have another hour before I need to head back to work so let's hear the rest!!" Talia smiled, demanding Mirlande continue with her story.

"Ok, I will try to make the rest of the story brief. Do you want to go sit on a bench at the park?" Asked Mirlande as they were walking.

"Yeah sure, but hurry because I need to know!" Replied Talia eagerly.

"OK, OK!" Mirlande laughed.

Mirlande continued her story.

"So, like I said, I didn't hear from him for a few days and, no, I didn't go to his store. As much as I wanted to, I stopped myself. I actually did walk really, really close to his store twice but I stopped and turned around both times. I really didn't want him to think I was one of those psycho girls just in case he didn't want me anymore."

The two ladies sat down on a summer blue bench that faced the large fountain in the center of the park. Mirlande put her hand on Talia's arm and smiled.

"About a week later, he called me! I wasn't sure if I should answer the phone or not, I kept debating about what I would say to him or wondered why he was calling me after a week. I had so many emotions going through in my mind, then the phone stopped ringing. I waited to see if he would leave me a voicemail. I waited for about five minutes, then finally I checked my voicemail. Sure enough, he didn't leave a voicemail.

"I got heartbroken and became so melancholy. I somehow had convinced myself to get over him and then he calls out of the blue and doesn't even leave me a message! Most of my afternoon was wasted after that phone call. I wasn't able to concentrate on my work or even focus on the customers either.

"Finally, it was time for me to close the boutique. I was basically just dragging myself around tidying up the store and doing my normal closing routine. I was finally done with everything and went to the back office to get my stuff. When I returned to the front of the store, there he was, standing right outside of my door smiling from ear to ear and waving hello. I can't describe to you the burst of happiness that came over me when I saw him standing there. I waved back to him smiling ear to ear as I walked over to the door. I opened the door and he just came right up to me and held me close to him, like he had done the first time he came to the store. I looked up into his dark eyes to gauge his sincerity, 'Hello stranger, where have you been?' His eyes reflected genuine emotion and he said back to me, 'I am so sorry. I know I owe you an explanation of why I haven't called or anything after that beautiful night.'

"I just gave him that look that said, 'Yeah you sure do.' He sat at the edge of the counter holding me in his arms.

"He said, 'My apologies, beautiful, for not calling you this whole time. I did get your messages and you probably think that I'm a real jerk for not returning your calls but I do have a good explanation for all of this. That morning after I reached home, I checked my voicemail. I had turned my phone off while I was with you because I didn't want to be disturbed at all. When I checked my phone there were thirty messages all from my family. My grandmother had slipped and fallen down the stairs. They took her to the hospital and the doctor said that she had hit her head and there was swelling on the brain. He said she might not make it through the night. So my family was trying to get a hold of me. Just the night that I turned my phone off this had to happen. I tried calling my sisters but none of them answered the phone so I rushed to the hospital. When I got there, everyone was standing around her. I just made it in time to say my goodbyes to her. She passed away ten minutes after I got there. I was then busy preparing for the funeral and still in a lot of shock. I saw that you had called but I was just not in a mood to talk. I know it was wrong of me not to return your calls. I was really close to my grandmother. She had raised me and my three sisters after our parents passed away in a car accident when I was just three years old. I felt really bad that I didn't get the time to see her that day. I always used to stop by and eat lunch with her but that day I was just very busy after I left your store. The guilt was just killing me inside and I just didn't want to be around anyone. I hope you can understand and forgive me?' He just got this puppy dog look on his face and I could see that he was genuinely in emotional pain.

"I felt truly bad for him. I gave him a hug and told him that I was sorry about his grandmother and of course I understood. Then I joked with him a bit to lighten up the mood. I told him I thought I scared him away with my big butt. He just laughed, grabbed my butt in both his hands and said that he loved my big butt. Then he pulled me tighter in his arms and we started kissing. He asked me if I wanted to come over to his place. Of course I said yes. Then, ding ding ding, you can imagine what happened," Mirlande said with a devious grin on her face.

Happy to know that her friend wasn't mistreated, Talia joked, "You naughty girl, you jumped in his bed after seeing him only twice!"

Mirlande beamed, "Hey, it had been a while and there was a huge cobweb down there."

She then continued, "Ever since then for the past three months we have been inseparable. You have no idea how hard it has been to keep this secret from you guys whenever we were hanging out and I feel like now I really want you and Ally to meet him. I want to see what you ladies think of him."

Talia put her arm around Mirlande and squeezed, "He sounds like a great guy."

"He is! But you know how Ally is. I don't want her to scare him away so I wanted to meet you first and tell you about him before telling Ally. Actually, I wanted you to tell her about him, then I was going to talk to her after you told her."

"Seriously! Why are you scared of her? You know she only means well," said Talia.

"Yeah, but remember what happened with the last guy I was seeing?"

"You know what, I don't blame her for treating him the way she did, and I think you are forgetting…"

Talia was about to finish her sentence when her phone rang…

"Oh, I need to take this call," said Talia and answered the phone.

Mirlande nodded her head and waited for Talia to finish her conversation. Mirlande lifted her face to the sky and closed her eyes. Although the sun was still going strong and the temperature was high, there was a light breeze that blew through her hair and cooled her down.

After a few minutes Talia hung up the phone and told Mirlande that she needed to leave right away. She was in a hurry and Mirlande understood.

"You better call and talk to Ally about this soon, if I tell her instead of you she will be very upset with you," said Talia as she kissed Mirlande goodbye on her cheek.

"Ugh, I am afraid to tell her," replied Mirlande like a little girl who was afraid to tell her parents that she had done something wrong.

"Don't worry. Marcus sounds like a good man, I'm sure she will approve too!" Talia said as she grabbed her bag, "Ok I really have to go. We'll all get together this weekend. Plan it with Ally and let me know. I'm free Saturday night." Talia waved goodbye

"Ok, bye and wish me luck!" Mirlande called out to Talia, watching her friend walk back across the street. Talia smiled and waved again as she got into her white BMW which was in the parking lot.

Mirlande sat on the bench for a bit after Talia left, just thinking. As she sat there her phone rang and it was Ally! Mirlande was nervous about answering the phone but she knew she had to talk to her because all three of them were best friends and they didn't hide anything from each other. Besides, Mirlande wanted to introduce Marcus to both girls.

Mirlande finally answered the phone....

"Jeez, how long does it take for you to answer? I know you are not doing anything," said Ally.

"What makes you think I am not doing anything?" joked Mirlande.

"Talia just called me and said you guys had lunch together and there was something you wanted to tell me. By the way, thanks for inviting me to lunch!" Ally said sardonically. "Well anyways, don't bother saying anything to me about that because you'll probably try to come up with some lame excuse anyway."

Mirlande could hear Ally chuckle on the other end. "Actually no excuse, I needed to talk to Talia before I could talk to you about a guy because I know how you are when it comes to guys."

"Hmmm, which loser did you meet this time?" Mirlande could feel Ally's sarcastic tone through the receiver.

"Really? And you wonder why I didn't want to talk to you about this first!"

"What? I think you are forgetting about your so-called last boyfriend. No one could understand anything that guy was saying."

"Do you want to hear about this guy or not? I really like him and I want you and Talia to meet him soon."

"I have a couple more appointments today so I really can't talk right now but I'm free this Saturday. Wait, are we going to meet this guy on Saturday?"

"No, I thought the three of us could get together first then next time I will introduce you guys to him."

"Well, why don't you call me later today, in the evening, and tell me about this guy and then we can meet him this Saturday at my place for dinner? Now, I am very curious about him. I can't believe you told Talia about it first instead of telling both of us together."

"That's because Talia is nicer than you are," joked Mirlande.

"She's a lawyer. She's not supposed to be nice so she is being fake with you."

"Need I remind you that you are a psychologist? You're supposed to be caring and sensitive but you sure are not that are you?"

"Hey, I'm just honest about things and you guys know I'm a good judge of character. That's why you and Talia come to me, remember? I can't help it if you guys can't handle the truth and want to be pacified like a child. Don't I always tell you, it's better to rip that bandage off at once rather than doing it slowly which causes you more pain?"

"Yeah, yeah, yeah. Don't you have to get back to your crazy people?" Mirlande said laughing.

"Yep I do, so call me later and tell me about your new love," Ally said, laughing as she hung up the phone.

As soon as she hung up, Mirlande received a text from Talia asking her if she spoke with Ally and Mirlande responded to her.....

"Yeah, I did. Told her I want you guys to meet him but haven't told her details about him. Will be calling her later today and she said to bring him to dinner this Saturday at her house."

Talia: "Ok her house, this Saturday. Sounds good. I was thinking of meeting for drinks tomorrow in the evening, are you free?"

Mirlande: "Yes"

Talia: "Then I will ask Ally also. I think she had told me yesterday she was free tomorrow but I will confirm with her right now and will get back to you."

Mirlande: "Ok"

While Mirlande was texting Talia she was also texting Marcus regarding meeting the girls Saturday.

Marcus: "Ok that sounds good but I am getting a bit nervous meeting your best friends. What if they don't like me? Will you break up with me if they don't like me because I know their opinion means everything to you?"

Mirlande smiled after reading his text she thought it was cute that the girls made him nervous.

She then replied, "What is there not to love about you? Don't worry they will love you!"

While she was texting Marcus, she received a text from Talia confirming that Ally was free for drinks the following night.

Mirlande replied, "Fantastic!"

Then she texted Marcus, "I will not be able to see you tonight or tomorrow tonight because tomorrow night I am meeting the girls for drinks and tonight I am going to be at the store most of the night getting my inventory done since I will be busy Saturday night."

Marcus: "I can come help you tonight after I close my store?"

Mirlande smiled as she read the text and replied, "No, whenever you come to help me I never get anything done because you get naughty instead!"

She then texted lots of smiley faces.

Marcus: "Then I won't see you for two days and you know I need you to prepare me to meet the girls."

Mirlande: "You will be fine, it's only Thursday I am sure we will be talking before Saturday."

Marcus: "Ok, and I will get a bottle of wine and flowers for them. You know, to impress them a bit."

Mirlande: "Haha, if that will make you feel better but you don't have to. Just be yourself and don't be too hard. Ally can see through people very well. Just don't worry, be yourself and I just know they will *love* you."

Marcus: "Ugh, by saying that you're making me even more nervous. I'll be wondering what Ally is thinking of me the whole time. Who is harder on guys, Talia or Ally?"

Mirlande: "Ally is very hard on anybody. Talia is much nicer. I will fill you in on both of them a bit more when we talk later, k?"

Marcus: "k. have to go now. Someone needs my help."

Mirlande: "Call me when you are free."

After Mirlande stopped texting, she realized she should have just spoken to him on the phone since he sounded so nervous but she knew he would be around customers and he wouldn't have been able to talk.

Chapter 2

Drinks with Friends

Ally had just left her office when she received a text from Talia as she was walking to her car…

Talia: "Hey are you done with your work?"

Ally: "Yep, just finished, how about you?"

Talia: "I'm just wrapping up something, then will be heading out in about half an hour. Why don't we go together?"

Ally: "Ok, since you are still finishing up why don't you come get me from my house. I am done and heading out."

Talia: "Ok, will see you at your house in 45 mins."

Ally: "Ok."

Ally put her bag in her car and pulled out of the parking lot.

She reached her house in a short period of time since she only lived ten minutes away from her office. When she reached home she texted Mirlande letting her know when they would be at the bar.

Ally freshened up as she waited for Talia....

Talia arrived outside Ally's apartment and texted her to come out. Just as she finished texting, she saw Ally walking towards her car. She unlocked the car door and waved as her friend got in.

"Hi." Talia said.

"Hello. I texted Mirlande to let her know that we were on our way," said Ally.

"Good! So did Mirlande tell you about Marcus?" Asked Talia as she started driving.

"Yes, she did."

"Hope you are not planning to give her a hard time about this?"

Ally just smiled at her.

The ladies continued with small talk the rest of the way since the restaurant was not even five minutes from Ally's apartment. As Talia was taking a turn to park they saw Mirlande walking into the restaurant. "Do you want me to drop you at the door then go park?"

"No, let's go park then we'll go in together," said Ally.

As Talia was looking for an open spot, they saw a car pulling out of a parking space to their right so Talia waited for the car to leave and pulled into it.

They both grabbed their purses and walked towards the restaurant.

Both of the girls looked beautiful as always. Talia, a beautiful very tall, slender, blue eyed Jewish lawyer had her long blonde hair tied back as usual, and wore a black skirt with light pink tank paired with black Jimmy Choo heels and black Gucci purse. While Ally, a beautiful petite Indian woman with light brown eyes and olive skin let her silky brown hair down, and wore a lime green dress paired with golden Miu Miu heels and a red Louis Vuitton bag.

They both walked into the restaurant and saw Mirlande waiting to be seated.

Mirlande, a beautiful heavyset Haitian with a dark complexion and who was taller than Ally but shorter than Talia, had her black hair tied in a bun. She was wearing a black dress, red Prada pumps and carried a black Gucci bag. All three of them looked beautiful. The girls always dress well, they work very hard for their money and they also love spending it on themselves.

They all greeted each other with a hug and a kiss on the cheek.

"Our table is ready. The guy said to give him a minute and he will be right with us," said Mirlande.

The Maître d' walked over to take them to their table, "This way ladies."

"He is cute!" whispered Ally to Talia as they were following him.

"I was thinking the same thing," responded Talia with a bright smile and wide eyes.

The Maître d' seated the three friends, laid the menus in front of them and said, "Your waiter will be right with you ladies," and walked away.

"He is cute!" said Mirlande as she stared at his butt.

"That's what we just said!" exclaimed Ally and Talia and they all laughed a girlish laugh.

When the girls are working they are very professional and polished but when they are in each other's company they leave everything behind, they're even carefree and childish at times. It's their way of escaping from reality and seriousness of everyday life.

"I thought we were just meeting for drinks?" Talia said.

"Since when do we just meet for drinks?" Ally replied.

"I figured it would be a good idea to get a table since we always get into a deep conversation and end up asking for a table later in the evening anyways. Luckily, because it's a little early and it's not busy we were able to get one right away," replied Mirlande.

Talia stretched her arm across the table and gently rubbed Mirlande's hand and excitedly said, "I can't wait to meet Marcus tomorrow."

"I can't wait for him to meet you girls also!" Said Mirlande as she smiled ear to ear.

"Hope he isn't like that overgrown teenager," said Ally sarcastically as she wiped her nose.

Mirlande gave her a dirty look and just when she was about to say something Talia asked, "What overgrown teenager?"

"Oh, you don't know?" Asked Ally raising her eyebrows. Talia shook her head no.

"Well then, let me tell you!" Ally said excitedly.

"Oh my God! You will never let it go, will you?" Mirlande said as she clapped her palms on the table and leaned towards Ally.

Just as Ally was about to tell the story the waiter came over to their table. "Good evening ladies, my name is Mark and I will be serving you this evening. Would you ladies like something to drink?" he asked.

Talia asked him if he would get them their best bottle of wine. She was eager to hear the story so she didn't want to waste any time ordering any other drinks.

"Certainly, I will be right back with your wine and give you a moment to look at the menu," the waiter said and then walked away.

Talia turned to Ally and very curiously asked as she glanced at Mirlande, "So who was this guy and how come I don't know about this?"

Ally started telling the story as Mirlande sat there looking all embarrassed, "This was about, I would say, six months ago," she looked at Mirlande for assurance of the time frame, then she continued, "I think you were on a business trip at that time. I was at the mall shopping and ran into Mirlande with this…this so called man…" Ally was lost for words to describe the man, "he just didn't look right. I could tell she wasn't really thrilled about running into me but, you know me, I had to know so I walked over to her fast and asked her what she was doing at the mall. Of course I was staring right at the guy as I was asking her this. Oh my god, you had to see this guy. His hair was tied back and he was wearing baggy clothes with red sneakers. I just couldn't believe my eyes. He looked like an overgrown teenager, they just didn't look right together. Mirlande, a beautiful dark skinned Haitian who dresses well and he was just …" Ally shook her head and shrugged her shoulders as she couldn't come up with a positive description of him. "Anyways, I was waiting for her to introduce me to him but of course she was trying to avoid that. So what do you think I did?"

Talia said with a smile, "Let me guess, you asked her who he was?"

"You bet I did!" Said Ally as she laughed and continued telling the story…..

"It was a weekday and I was surprised to see her at the mall and not at her store. I was making a quick stop at the mall between my appointments because it was my cousin's birthday and I needed to get her a gift…Well anyways, so I asked her what was she doing at the mall and who the guy was…"

Ally was about to start her next sentence but was interrupted by the waiter....

"Here is our best bottle of wine ladies." As he poured wine in their glasses he asked them if they would like to order any appetizers.

Talia wanted Ally to continue with the story so she asked the girls, "The usual ladies?"

"Sure," Ally and Mirlande replied simultaneously.

So Talia ordered stuffed banana peppers and bruschetta. The waiter took the order and told them, "Will put the order in for you right away while you ladies decide what you would like to order for dinner," and walked away.

The ladies picked up their glasses and Talia toasted, "Here is to meeting Marcus tomorrow."

They all took a sip then Talia turned to Ally and said excitedly, "Ok, go on!"

Ally continued…"So where was I, oh yeah, so she wasn't going to introduce him to me so I said: 'Hi Mirlande, what are you doing at the mall and who is this?' Before she could say anything, he introduced himself to me and said that they just started dating... and he said something else I could not understand. I just looked at her and said, 'dating!' I was shocked!" Ally feigned disbelief. "We always tell each other everything but this was news to me. She was just standing there like she forgot to talk or something and the guy was answering me and I couldn't understand a thing he was saying. I just kept looking at Mirlande. So, I pulled her to the side and said to her, 'what the hell is wrong with you? Why aren't you saying anything to me? And what is this guy saying?' She then told me that she would explain everything to me and asked if we could meet later that night. I told her I had to go to my cousin's birthday party and should be free after 10 pm. We planned to meet after I returned from the party that night…

"After my cousin's party I went over to her house. To make everything short, she told me he had come into her store one day to buy a gift for his female "friend" and had started talking to her. He had asked for her number and they went out a couple of times, so when I ran into them, it was their third date. I asked her, 'So what kind of female 'friend' was he shopping for?' She said he told her that they were good friends and he was buying her a gift. Then I asked her, where did he take her on a first date? She told me he had two jobs so he could only meet her in the afternoon around lunch time so they had a lunch date. Matter of fact all of their dates were during lunch. Something didn't seem quite right to me so I kept probing her. Well anyways, apart from him speaking a language I could not understand. It turned out that this guy actually had a girlfriend. That female 'friend' he was shopping for turned out to be his live-in girlfriend and Mirlande was the one who ran into him and his girlfriend. I mean seriously, I couldn't believe how gullible she was."

Mirlande became flush with embarrassment while Ally told Talia the story and Talia's jaw just dropped as she was listening. Talia just turned to Mirlande...."Seriously, is this true? How did you even go out with a guy like that?"

Mirlande was mortified, "I know I know. I am …" She was about to say something when the waiter returned to the table…

"Here are your appetizers," he said while placing the platters in the center of the table. "Are you ladies ready to order dinner?"

"Sorry we didn't get a chance to look at the menu as of yet, could you please give us a few more minutes?" said Ally.

"Sure take your time," the waiter replied and walked away.

After he left, Talia asked Mirlande, "So what happened to you?"

Mirlande continued, "I know I know, I am not really proud of that. You know I just felt, and still feel like I am getting older and I am not finding anyone. I'm scared of being alone and dying alone. I know I have you guys but I feel very lonely that I don't have anyone to go home to. I work so hard and for what? So I can just go home to an empty house? When I go home I want someone to ask me how my day went. I want someone to have dinner with every night instead of me sitting there with my TV on or checking my emails while I am eating.

I want someone to hold me when I go to bed and wake up next to me in the morning.

"I am just afraid of being alone. It's hard to find guys. I feel like all the good ones are already taken. I'm not slender like you two and don't get the attention both of you get from men. I get so excited if a man actually comes up to me or wants to date me. I know I may not be choosing the right type of guys but you know how the saying goes, 'Beggars can't be choosers.' Talia, you are alone because you choose to, not because you can't find a decent guy. Ally, you too are alone out of your choice but it's not like you can't get guys. So, now, I found someone who actually likes me and seems to be a decent guy but knowing my luck, I am scared after you meet him you'll see something off in him that I don't. I'm afraid there may be something wrong with him also."

Mirlande's eyes began welling up with tears. Ally and Talia tried to comfort her...

"Look Mirlande, first of all, you are a beautiful woman in every way and any man would be so lucky to have you. I'm not just saying that because we're friends. For as long as I have known you, you have always had a beautiful heart," Ally said in a compassionate voice.

She continued, "And what makes you think I don't want someone in my life? I know exactly what you mean when you say you don't want to die alone. I feel that way too. I also want someone in my life just the way you do. It's actually harder for me to find a guy than it is for you."

"What are you talking about? If you can't find a guy then your family will try to find someone for you," replied Mirlande as she wiped her tears.

Ally looked at Mirlande shockingly..."Are you kidding me?! You don't have to worry about whether or not the guy will be accepted in your family. For me, for my family, religion is very important. They will not accept anyone who is not of the same religion. You know how they have been trying to arrange me with Muslim guys! You also know my fear of marrying a Muslim guy!"

"What is wrong with marrying a Muslim guy?" Interrupted Talia, raising her eyebrows.

Ally looked at Talia, "I am not saying all Muslim men are bad it's just that knowing my luck I will end up with a Muslim guy who may not be religious at first then might become religious later, as I've seen happen to too many of my friends and family. They are fine with becoming religious but you guys know I don't believe in that. I believe religion is a very personal thing between an individual and God. I don't believe I need to show the world how religious I am. I have seen so many religious people from different religions that go to mosques, churches or temples to pray and lecture people on what's good and evil then behind closed doors they definitely are not doing anything that is even close to being religious.

"Tell me which God tells people to rape young boys or girls? It happens a lot among the Catholic priests. Which God tells people not to talk or touch a human being just because he or she is a beggar who is not of a same status or cast? Hindus believe in that. Which God says it's alright to kill innocent people in the name of religion? We watch on the news how certain Muslims are doing just that.

"My argument with my family is people pick and choose what they want to follow about Islam at their own convenience and I don't believe in that. People interpret religion based on how it benefits them at that time. I don't think if I marry a guy that is not Muslim but is a nice person I will go to hell. What is the use of being religious when you intentionally hurt someone whether it's physical or emotional? Do you think that's ok with God? No, I truly believe deep down in my heart that if an individual who is a good human being, who means well for others and helps others rather than someone who is pretending to be religious and hurts others, will go to heaven. I don't care what religion the person belongs to as long as he is a nice individual. But if I choose someone of different faith then that would mean my family will disown me. So, if I find a guy from a different religion and if he doesn't convert then I have to choose between him and my family.

"See Mirlande, it's not as easy as you think it is for me to be with someone. Life is hard for everyone we just have to be strong and whenever or whatever is meant to happen it will happen. We cannot change our destiny. I truly believe that before we were born our destiny has been written out for us by God. So, my dear, the right person will come into all of our lives when it's destined to. Don't be sad or scared, you will not die alone. We will all meet our Mr. Right when it's time,"

"Wow, you know, that was deep!" said Talia.

"Shut up! You are ruining the moment," replied Ally with a smile and a little laugh.

They all laughed…

The waiter returned to the table. "How were the appetizers?

"Delicious as always," replied Talia.

"Are you ladies ready to order?" he asked.

Talia made a gesture with her hand to indicate a small amount. She gave the waiter a pleading look and responded, "Just give us 3 more minutes please."

"Yes, of course," the waiter nodded and turned his attention to another table.

Talia said to the girls, "Lets pick out what we want to eat before the guy comes back, then we can return to the topic at hand."

"Sounds good," both Ally and Mirlande replied simultaneously.

Talia said, "I don't know about you guys but I am starving even though we just ate those appetizers."

The girls had finished glancing through the menu when the waiter returned after a few minutes.

"Are you ladies ready?"

The three of them looked up from their menus and replied "Yes," nodding their heads.

Ally took the initiative of ordering, "Should we order a few things then just share as usual?"

"Yep," said Talia.

"Sounds good to me," replied Mirlande.

"Veal Rib Chop sounds good," said Ally.

"Yeah I saw that too. Let's get that along with Eggplant Napoleon," Talia suggested.

"Should we get the homemade ravioli also?" Mirlande asked.

"Yes," the other two ladies replied in unison.

"I think that should be enough food for all of us to share," said Talia and then she asked the waiter if he could bring three extra plates so they could share the entrées family style.

"Yes of course, I will put the order in for you ladies right away," replied the waiter as he gathered the menus and left the table.

"So Mirlande, how does Marcus feel about meeting us tomorrow?" Asked Ally in a friendlier tone.

"He is excited and also nervous at the same time. He knows how important you guys are to me and is scared because he feels if you guys don't like him for whatever reason then I won't see him anymore."

"Aww, tell him don't be nervous. From what you have said about him he sounds like a good guy and I am sure we will like him," Talia said as she gave Ally the "look."

"What? Why are you looking at me like that?" Asked Ally.

"Don't you have anything to say?" Asked Talia.

"Look, I know you guys think I am always tough on the men but you two have to understand that there are a lot of strange people out there and I feel like I need to protect the three of us. See, when we're in a relationship sometimes we really can't see what others can see in the guy. We get so blinded by having someone in our life that we can't see if the relationship is healthy or unhealthy for us. I have had clients who were getting abused emotionally but they never saw that. After listening to them for a while I actually had to ask them if they felt that their relationship was a healthy relationship and the answer was always the same, 'yes'. I couldn't believe it! A few times I gave them the same scenario but, instead of them, I put someone they cared about in their situation and asked them if they felt the person they cared about was being treated well in the relationship? As an outsider they could see what was wrong in the relationship but not when they were in it. My point, ladies, is that, when we are involved in a relationship, we don't see what others are able to see. If I am a bit tough it's because of my nature. Isn't that only going to help you?"

Ally gazed at both of them to see if they understood what she was trying to say. She then continued…

"If or when I start dating someone I would expect you guys to tell me something you see that's wrong in someone that I can't see."

"Yeah I guess you are right. But I guess I am just afraid of knowing the truth because of the fear of being alone again. I know that sounds stupid but that's really the truth," responded Mirlande.

"I know that's hard but it's better to find out about the person sooner rather than later, right?" Said Ally.

"Yes, you are right but I just can't help being scared," replied Mirlande.

"Well, hopefully this guy is exactly what you think he is and there won't be any surprises. I actually can't wait to meet Marcus tomorrow. Does he know we are really crazy when we get together?" Ally asked, hoping to make Mirlande feel better.

"Oh, he knows how crazy my sisters are!" Said Mirlande with a smile.

"Should we do take out or should I cook?" Asked Ally.

"Can you make Indian food? I haven't had your home made food for a while," said Talia.

"I was thinking the same thing and Marcus has never had Indian food and wants to try it," agreed Mirlande.

"Ah, so we have a black guy who lacks some real spices in his life. Well, if he's planning to be part of our team, he needs some spice in him," joked Ally and they all laughed.

"Have you told Marcus how politically incorrect Ally can be?" Joked Talia.

"Hey, it's not just me! You guys are like that too," responded Ally.

"True, but not as politically incorrect as you are, and, besides, you were the one who influenced us," Talia pointed out.

"You mean I taught you guys to say what everyone thinks but is afraid to say?" Said Ally.

"She is right you know. If we all could just speak our mind I feel like people wouldn't be as fake and maybe, just maybe, it might loosen people up a bit in this world," commented Mirlande.

Just as Mirlande finished her sentence the waiter brought their dinner to the table...

After having a very serious conversation, the girls enjoyed their night with lots of drinks and laughter.

Chapter 3

Meeting Marcus

The girls had a late night but Ally woke up early as usual. Instead of getting out of the bed she just stayed there in her red silk pajama set, reading the news and checking her emails on her laptop. As she was glancing through the emails, she received a text from Talia asking her to give her a call when she wakes up.

Ally called her, "Hey, how come you are up so early?"

"I had some work to complete this morning so I'm not stressed about it later," replied Talia.

"Are you done with your work now?" Ally asked.

"Almost done, maybe another half an hour or so. I wanted to ask you if you needed any help cooking dinner tonight."

"Sure, thanks. I'd definitely love some help. I was going to have breakfast, get dressed, then go grocery shopping. Do you want to come?"

"Yeah, I will be able to come over as soon as I am done."

"Great!" Exclaimed Ally.

"Ok, see you soon," Talia replied, then hung up.

After ending the phone call, Ally got out of bed and went into the bathroom to brush her teeth. She then went in the kitchen and made a light breakfast for herself. She fried a couple of eggs, grabbed a clementine from the fridge and a glass of water then sat down to eat her breakfast as she made her grocery list.

The phone rang and it was Talia, "Hey, what are you doing?" She asked.

"I was just having my breakfast," replied Ally.

"I'm walking into my office right now, I just have to get something. My neighbor was doing a coffee run so I asked him to drop me at the office, I figured you could just come pick me up from here so we can go shopping together," Talia said.

"Sure, I am almost done so I will see you in a few," Ally confirmed.

After she got off the phone, she finished her breakfast, then washed her plate. She took a shower, changed her clothes, put on lip gloss, grabbed her keys and purse from the table and walked out of the door. As she stepped out, she saw her neighbor, Jeff.

"Hello my vicious vixen! Where are you off to this early on a Saturday morning instead of relaxing at home?" He asked.

"Good morning Lawson, I'm going to meet Talia at her office then we are going shopping. Mirlande is coming over for dinner with her new boyfriend so they asked me to make dinner."

"Making Indian food I take it?"

"Yep, you want me to bring you some?"

"Hey you know I don't eat all that spicy food."

"Yeah I know, maybe one of these days I am hoping to convince you to try some. You need some spice in your life," Ally said with a grin.

"Just having you as my neighbor and friend is spicy enough for me," replied Jeff as he smiled.

Jeff always joked around with her…

"Alright young lady, you go ahead enjoy your day with the ladies. Come over for coffee or a drink with me one of these days. We haven't done that in a while."

"Yes, definitely will do that," Ally stated as she waved bye to him and got in her car.

Ally and Jeff, who was a very tall, light-skinned black male in his 60s, became friends the day Ally moved next door to him. Jeff not only was a very good friend of hers, but he was also like a father figure in her life. When she needed advice she went to him because he understood her and was very open and honest with her about everything. He didn't sugarcoat anything and he told her things as is and that was what she liked the most about him. She usually talked to him about things that she was not able to talk to her own dad about.

Ally arrived at Talia's office in no time. She parked her car right in front of the building. Instead of waiting in the car, she decided to go meet Talia in the office.

As she walked towards the elevator she saw a man busy texting on his phone as he waited for the elevator. Ally looked at him and her heart just sank. She decided not to take the elevator, instead she took the stairs. As she reached the fifth floor, just as she was about to pass the elevator, the doors of the elevator opened and the man that she had seen downstairs stepped out. Their eyes met, and he seemed surprised to see her. For a second, they both froze and then....

"Hi Ally, hi Ary," said Talia as she walked towards them.

"Ally, this is Aryan, but everyone calls him Ary...Ary this is my best friend Aliah but everyone calls her Ally."

Ally and Ary said hello to each other awkwardly. Talia thought that was strange but didn't say anything. Ally then turned to Talia...

"We better catch that elevator before it goes down."

"Yes, let's go. Bye Ary, will chat with you next week," Talia said as she and Ally rushed into the elevator before it went down.

When they got into the elevator Ally asked Talia...

"How long have you known him? What does he do?"

"He moved from New York about seven months ago and started his own consulting firm. I actually ran into him the day he was moving into his office, which is right across from mine. He has an MBA and Law degree from Syracuse University so he is combining the two and doing compliance consulting for small businesses. After graduate school, he worked in Investment Banking for a few years in New York City. I think he didn't like banking. (He said he lived in Buffalo for a few years and did his undergraduate here) so he left New York and returned to Buffalo for some personal reason. He didn't tell me everything and I didn't want to get into his business at that time. He and I have become good friends in the past few months but I never really asked him what that personal reason was. He is really nice, we meet for lunch now and then," replied Talia.

"He is handsome. How come you didn't hook up with him?" Inquired Ally inquisitively.

"I don't think I am his type. We have been friends for a while now but he never showed that kind of interest in me.

Hey maybe I can hook you up with him!" Exclaimed Talia with a bright smile.

"Nah, he is Hindu. Wouldn't work out since I am Muslim."

"How do you know he is Hindu?" Asked Talia puzzled.

"By his name."

"Oh. I forgot you know all that stuff. So, what are we doing first?" Asked Talia.

Ally looked at her watch…

"We have about half hour before the Indian store opens, want to grab coffee?"

"Sure," replied Talia.

They both got into the car and Ally drove off…

"What dishes are you making for tonight?" Asked Talia.

"You mean what WE are making tonight! You know you are helping me cook, right? Don't be thinking you are just going to be chatting my ear off."

"I think you are forgetting that I don't know how to make Indian food."

"Well I will teach you, who knows what if you find an Indian guy in the future," said Ally, chuckling.

They reached Café Aroma, and found a space right in front, and parked the car. The café is located in the village of Williamsville, a very quaint suburb of Buffalo. They both walked inside. It was a small place surrounded by windows. It was very cozy with a fireplace on one side. It was the girls' favorite place to hang out whenever they wanted to just sit and chat. Ally loved their pecan bars.

"You want to grab a table while I get coffee for us?" Said Talia.

"Sure, I will have my usual," replied Ally.

"Ok, see you at the table," said Talia, then went to get the coffee.

Ally found a table near the window. She sat at the table looking out the window as she waited for Talia. Talia returned with the coffees…

"I can't believe how busy it is already," she said as she put the coffee on the table.

"I know, I got lucky with the table. As I was walking around I saw a couple putting their coats on so I grabbed it quickly."

As they both sat and chatted, Ally pointed outside to a man and woman with a child.

"Look out there. I have been watching that couple and the child who just refuses to listen to the parents."

Talia turned her head and looked out the window.

"Do you think we will ever be able to have that?" Asked Ally.

"What, a bratty kid?" Responded Talia.

"No, I mean a family, with the right person. Every time I am at a party, people, especially my parents, are always reminding me that I am not getting any younger and I need to find someone. They even go to the extent of trying to set me up with men."

"Hey! Speaking of that, what's going on with you and the Indian doctor your parents were trying to set you up with?" Asked Talia.

"Oh, I completely forgot to update you and Mirlande about that. So this guy is my parents' friends' son. He is finishing up his fellowship. He is a very nerdy guy but nice. I've met him about two times now for dinner. We are very different in our personalities. He is a very reserved guy and you know exactly what I am like!" Ally said with a naughty smile.

"So do you think it is going to go somewhere? When are we going to meet him?" Asked Talia enthusiastically.

"Hold on to your panties, I have no clue! I don't know if I'm at that point right now."

"Since you were setup with him by your parents, is he religious?"

"That's the thing, I'm not quite sure as of yet and I didn't want to just come out and ask him. Whenever we've met it has been for a very quick dinner since our schedules don't match. I would say, we must have spent maybe a total of three hours in our last two meetings. He really seems to be a very nice guy. He doesn't seem like someone who might have had any girlfriends at all."

"That's odd," said Talia with a weird look on her face.

"Well, I said he seems like he never had any girlfriend that doesn't mean I know for sure. I won't know unless he tells me right?"

"So when are you meeting him next?"

"I don't know, it depends on our schedules," Ally said, looking at her watch. "Oh look at the time, it's almost lunch time. We were so engrossed in our conversation we forgot about our grocery shopping."

The girls threw their trash out quickly and headed out to get the groceries.

"Hey look, the family is still sitting there on the bench," said Ally as she pointed to the young couple and child they saw earlier.

"The guy is cute!" Talia elbowed Ally, as they both walked to the car.

The ladies arrive at the Indian store (Spices of India), Ally looked at the list on her phone to see what she needed to buy first. Talia walked around the store, taking in the smells of all the spices around her.

"I love the smell of these spices. I wish I could learn to cook Indian food."

"You are a typical white girl," Joked Ally, who continued to shop for her groceries. As Ally was picking out her groceries, Talia was picking up packets of different spices and smelling them like a curious little girl…

"I hope you're planning to make my favorite. You know I love your mango dessert!"

Ally smiled as she was picking out the tomatoes.

"Yes, I know you love that desert and yes I am making that."

Talia gently clapped her hand in joy like a child whose mother said yes she might buy her candy if she was good. Ally smirked at her friend and asserted…

"You can be such a kid at times!"

She then continued to pick out the tomatoes. A lady came up right next to Ally and looked at her…

"Hello beti." (Means daughter in Hindi)

Ally turned to her right to see who was talking to her…

"Oh hi auntie, how are you?"

"I'm doing fine, how are you? How is it going with Sameer and you?" She asked inquisitively.

"We are just getting to know each other auntie," replied Ally politely, but trying hard not to roll her eyes.

"Do you think we'll see a wedding anytime soon?"

"I don't know, we will see." Ally forced a smile on her face.

She was getting annoyed by all the questions coming from her nosy auntie and just wanted to end the conversation and move on. Talia saw that Ally looked very uncomfortable so she walked over to the two ladies…

"It's getting late, are you ready to go?"

Ally looked at Talia…

"Yes, I'm sorry. I didn't realize the time."

She then looked at the fat nosy lady…

"Ok auntie, I have to go."

The lady replied with a puzzled and annoyed look on her face as if she wished the white girl would just disappear…

"Ok beti, hope to hear some good news soon."

Ally said bye to the lady and rushed to check out her groceries. As soon as they walked out of the store she whispered to Talia, putting her arm around her friend…

"Thanks for coming to my rescue."

"Yeah you looked like you could use some help. Who was that lady? Why was she calling you beti? Is she your aunt?"

"She is my mom's friend who set me up with Sam and she wanted to know if I was getting married to him soon. Beti means daughter. Even though I am not her daughter, in our culture the elders tend to call girls, beti and boys, beta, which means son. On the reverse, she is not my aunt, but, again, in Indian culture a woman or a man that is your parents' age are called auntie or uncle out of respect."

The girls put the groceries in the car. As Ally pulled off, Talia continued to question her.

"Didn't you guys just meet? How does she expect you to get married so fast?"

"Are you forgetting how arranged marriages work? Remember I told you in the olden days the parents of the boy would come meet the girl with their son and within a day or two they used to decide if the marriage was imminent. If both sides agreed then they set the wedding date with a fast engagement ceremony in between. At least now they are allowing me to get to know the guy only because my parents know I refuse to just marry someone out of the blue."

"You know, I really think I like this idea. At least they go find potential guys for you and you can say yes or no and if you say no then they go find another guy, I can't even find one guy. I don't even know where to go look for one."

"It's not that simple. You have no idea the pressure that is put on the girl and if the girl keeps rejecting boys then they all give her this attitude as if she is a slut. Trust me it's not as easy as you think."

"Wait, isn't Sam (that's what everyone called Sameer) like the fourth guy your parents have set you up with?" Asked Talia with a puzzled look on her face.

"Yep!"

"So the people in your community must think you are a real slut then!" Joked Talia as she elbowed Ally and laughed.

"I am glad you are having fun at my expense! I told you it's not that easy, I am under a lot of pressure," said Ally with a stressed look on her face. Talia saw her look.

"Seriously then, what if it doesn't work out with you and Sam? Is there a time limit as to how long you can get to know him? I mean, I am sure they are not going to wait for couple years for you to decide right?"

"Couple of years?! Are you kidding me! The only reason they haven't harassed me for an answer as of yet is because they know Sam has been very busy and we haven't been able to meet as much. I haven't told my family that he does call me whenever he gets a chance. But I know very soon my parents and their friend will want an answer."

"Wow! I really didn't realize the pressure they put on you. Ever since I met you, you have always talked about the guys your parents are setting you up with. Did you ever date anyone before that? I mean when you were in college I'm sure you must have liked someone?"

Before Ally could respond they arrived at her place. Ally parked the car and the girls took the groceries into the apartment. They put the bags on the kitchen counter. While Ally took the groceries out of the bags, Talia went to use the bathroom. When she finished unpacking the groceries, Ally looked in her fridge to see what she had for them to eat for lunch.

Talia returned to the kitchen. Ally looked up, taking a container out from the fridge.

"I have some pasta salad. Do you want to have it while we cook dinner?"

"Sure, that sounds good, I'll grab the bowls for us."

Talia went to the cabinet to get the bowls, but stopped when she looked at the clock on the microwave…

"Did you see the time?" Talia asked as she handed the bowls to Ally.

"Yes, I saw the time when you were in the bathroom. I can't believe how fast the day is going by and we only have a few hours to get dinner ready. Indian food takes time," Ally replied while she filled a bowl with the pasta salad and handed it to Talia.

Talia took a bite of it.

"Yum, this is really good! Did you make it?"

"No, Mrs. Olson had a party couple of days ago. She had invited me but I couldn't go so she brought food over for me," Ally replied, as both standing against the island in the center of the kitchen, devouring their food.

Ally lived in an expensive luxurious apartment in Williamsville. Her kitchen was beautiful. It was very spacious and brightly lit. The walls were white and gray but she had a few very colorful décor pieces on the counters and wall that stood out. Ally loved bright colors.

"She is a good cook, you are lucky you have neighbors that are always bringing you things. I wish I had neighbors like yours," Talia said as she sat on a chair at the center island, enjoying the pasta salad.

Ally didn't want to waste time so while they were eating she started to gather everything she needed to start cooking. She then turned to Talia…

"Would you mind cutting the onions, then tomatoes, then the cilantro as I start sautéing so it can get done fast?"

"No problem! We have three hours to get the cooking done and then clean up and get ready."

"Yeah I know that's why I asked you to cut while you are eating."

The girls worked fast as a team and got everything done right on time.

"Why don't you go wash up and change while I clean up the kitchen, then I will get ready," said Ally.

"Why don't I help you clean up the kitchen so it can get done fast then we both can wash up?"

"I only have one bathroom and it will get late, right?"

"Yeah that makes sense but I'll help you clean a little bit then go get ready," Talia snapped her fingers. "Oh…I think I left my clothes in your car. I will get them after I help clean."

After Talia finished loading the dishwasher, she went to get ready.

Meanwhile, Ally continued cleaning. She looked over at the clock and started cleaning faster. As she was cleaning, her phone rang. She could hear the phone but she was not able to find it. By the time she found the phone, it stopped ringing. After a minute, it started ringing again. This time she answered it before the ringing stopped. She looked to see who was calling but it said 'private number' so she decided to answer, it appeared that someone was trying to get hold of her. There was no response, so she hung up. It rang a third time. She answered, and again, there was no response. She was getting annoyed. She needed to get her work done. She went back to cleaning. The phone rang again, this time she didn't look to see who was calling and just answered it…

"Hi Ally."

"Hi Sam, did you call me earlier?"

"No, this is the first time I am calling you today, why?"

"Oh, someone called earlier then didn't answer. Well, anyway, I'm surprised to hear from you today. I thought you were working?"

"I am at work at the moment but I will be able to get off early tonight so I thought maybe we could meet for dinner if you are free?"

"Oh I am sorry, I will not be able to tonight. I have plans with the girls tonight, I would love for you to come with us but Mirlande said she needs to talk to me and Talia."

"That's alright, I called just in case you were free. We are meeting in couple of days anyways. Well, I have to get back to work. I will call you tomorrow, ok?"

"Ok sounds good bye."

After she hung up the phone she turned around and saw Talia standing at the kitchen entrance. Talia had heard Ally's conversation with Sam.

"Why don't you invite him over tonight? That way we can meet him and Marcus."

"No. I told you I'm not ready for that yet."

"Ok, why don't you go change now they will be here any minute!" Talia said, as she grabbed the broom from Ally's hand.

Ally looked at the clock…"Oh yeah, I didn't realize the time. Can you please just take out wine glasses for me?"

"Sure, go hurry!" Talia pushed Ally out of the kitchen.

After Talia finished sweeping the floor she opened the cabinets to get the wine glasses. As she was busy getting the glasses out, the doorbell rang. Talia went to unlock the door but before she went she knocked on the bathroom door to let Ally know that they were here. Then she buzzed Mirlande and Marcus in…

In no time the guests arrived at the door just as Talia opened it. Mirlande introduced Marcus to Talia. When Marcus kissed Talia hello on the cheek, she got a puzzled look on her face as if she has seen a ghost. Then Talia gave Mirlande a hug and the three of them walked into the living room. At that moment, Ally came out of the bathroom, adjusting a loose strand of hair and gave Mirlande a hug.

Mirlande then introduced Marcus to her. Marcus gave Ally a kiss on her cheek as well and handed her a bottle of wine.

"It finally is a pleasure to meet the two of you." Marcus sounded nervous.

Talia and Ally just looked at each other with a puzzled / shocked look on their faces.

"Why don't you guys have a seat while I get wine for everyone and turn the stove off," Ally said, finding a reason to leave the room.

"I'll come help," Talia added.

"It smells really nice in here Ally. I am getting hungry just smelling the food," said Mirlande

"It certainly does," Agreed Marcus.

Ally thanked them then she and Talia rushed into the kitchen. As soon as they both entered the kitchen, they just look at each other in shock.

"Oh my God, is it my imagination or is it Marcus that we saw outside of the café with the woman and kid?" Asked Talia with a disbelief on her face.

"It's him! He is wearing the same clothes as he did earlier so we are not mistaking him for someone else. I don't understand. I hope there is a good explanation for what we saw," stated Ally, shocked.

"Seriously, what will he tell us? He can't say that was his sister the way he was touching her. Poor Mirlande, I feel really bad for her," said Talia perturbed.

"Let's just wait and find out before we jump to any conclusions. Although I don't know how we could not jump to the conclusion that we already have," stated a perplexed Ally.

As they both were talking, Mirlande and Marcus came into the kitchen walking hand in hand.

"We decided to join you guys in here," said Mirlande with a smile

Talia and Ally had this awkward smile on their faces. They really didn't know what to think of Marcus from what they had seen in the morning. They just wanted to come out and ask him but they knew they couldn't. They were trying to think of ways to ask him without Mirlande knowing what was going on. Poor Mirlande, she thought she had finally found the right guy. Ally and Talia needed some time to process the whole thing but they also needed to keep a straight face for Mirlande's sake.

"Are you guys ready for an appetizer?" Asked Ally.

"Oh yes, I have been feeling hungry ever since I started smelling all the spices," said Marcus.

"What did you make? It all smells so good?" Asked Mirlande.

"I made chicken keema samosa and chaat for appetizer. Chicken keema samosa is ground chicken cooked with different spices and stuffed in a home-made pastry, then fried. Chaat is a snack that is made of potato and chickpeas topped with spices, yogurt and chutney," explained Ally.

"That sounds so yummy, it's making my mouth water," said Marcus.

Ally was disgusted with Marcus, and, at that moment, she was wondering why she and Talia bothered being nice to him. She really had been trying very hard to control herself for her friend's sake. Thinking if Mirlande wasn't at the state of mind that she was in, they would have sorted out the matter right away.

Talia saw Ally's face and she could see that she was really trying hard to control herself so she poured wine for Mirlande and Marcus and asked them to go sit at the dining table while she and Ally brought in the appetizers.

"Why don't I help you guys?" Said Mirlande.

"No, that's ok. Ally and I can handle this so go keep Marcus company, we will be right out," Talia stated with a smile as she walked Mirlande and Marcus out of the kitchen.

"Are you ok? You look like you wanted to kill Marcus?" Talia asked as soon as she turned around.

"I don't know about you but I am so disgusted with him right now! I have no interest in going ahead with this dinner. We really need to get to the bottom of this. I don't know if I can control myself. This is so hard seeing what we have seen and not knowing the truth. Are you not bothered by it as much as I am?" Questioned Ally infuriated.

"I am but..."

"I think I am going to just ask him. I don't want Mirlande to be wasting her time or be lied to. She doesn't deserve this and if he does come out and say he has a kid then it's better for her to know. His having a kid is not my concern, it's the way he was with that woman. The way he was holding her!" Interrupted Ally angrily.

"Listen, you know we can't do that. Let's just take a step back and handle this delicately. You are a psychologist, you should be able to handle this calmly," Talia was trying to be the voice of reasoning.

"Yes, you are right, but right now I am not reacting as a psychologist but rather as a friend I guess..."

"We better go before Mirlande starts wondering what's going on," interrupted Talia.

"Ugh, yeah I suppose we should go," Ally agreed shrugging her shoulders.

As soon as the ladies walked into the dining room door Marcus got up to help them with the dishes in their hand.

Mirlande breathed in the smell of the food and smiled.

Ally served the appetizers to everyone and they all picked up their glasses to make a toast.

"To friendship," toasted Talia, as she glanced at Ally and Mirlande with a smile.

"So Marcus, Mirlande tells us you also have a boutique like her. Do you feel like there is competition between the two of you?" Asked Ally with a forced smile.

"No, not at all. I don't mean it in a bad way, I mean I love her so I don't even think of her business as a competition for me. I am surprised we didn't meet sooner since we are just couple of blocks away," responded Marcus as he held Mirlande's hand.

"So have you ever been married or have any children?" Asked Ally as she just couldn't help herself.

Mirlande just turned and looked at her and Talia gave that, "yep that's Ally" look.

Marcus sort of ignored the question by saying...

"Wow these appetizers are so good! I love the spices that are in here. You must teach me how to make them."

Ally and Talia looked at each other shocked. Now both of them got even more upset because now it proved to them that he is trying to hide something. Mirlande didn't seem get the drift of what was going on because for her Ally asking him that question didn't surprise her. For her, it was Ally being herself.

"Yeah sure I can teach you how to make them. So, have you been married or have any kids?" Ally asked him again, but a bit more firmly this time.

Marcus laughed a nervous laugh and looked at Mirlande and joked...

"You weren't wrong when you said to be prepared to be interrogated. I can see how much you ladies care for each other."

Ally and Talia could see Marcus was doing whatever he could to avoid the question but Ally being Ally then joked…

"Yeah we all care for each other and it is our job to make sure our friend isn't getting involved with anyone that is wrong for her. I'm sure you understand and don't mind us asking you questions. You can't get into our club until you pass the test."

She then laughed sarcastically, but winked.

Marcus laughed also and agreed with Ally.

"You guys should have a questionnaire for the guys to fill out before they meet you," he said jokingly.

Talia was starting to lose it a bit, she chimed in…

"Nah, we like to ask the questions in person so we can see the reactions."

"Yeah that's the best part, the expression on the face is the best. But you haven't answered my question yet," said Ally slyly.

"Jeez, this really is a team game," remarked Marcus as he looked at Mirlande and held her closer to him as a child holds a teddy bear to comfort himself in a stressful situation.

Mirlande looked at him with a smile…

"I told you to be prepared to answer questions."

She then looked at the girls…

"Give him a break you two, he really was nervous meeting you guys. I warned him about your questions."

"But he hasn't even answered our first question!" Exclaimed Ally.

"Don't you think he would have told me by now if he had been married or had children? So why don't you ask him the next question," said Mirlande obliviously.

"Hey our job is to ask, his job is to answer. How can we approve if he doesn't even answer our first question?" Ally laughed but inside she was getting very upset by the fact that he was avoiding her question and Mirlande was not helping by getting in the way.

Ally and Talia gave each other a disapproving look, which Mirlande got the glimpse of and started to wonder what was going on. Now it seemed like the matter was getting a bit serious between the girls and Mirlande could really sense that. It actually started to get a bit awkward for everyone.

"I'll get water for everyone," said Ally as she got up from the table.

"I will help you," said Talia.

The two of them left the dining room. As soon as they entered the kitchen they both turned to each other and simultaneously exclaimed, "He is avoiding the question!"

While Ally and Talia were in the kitchen plotting their next move, Mirlande could see Marcus was very uncomfortable with the situation so she tried to make him feel a little comfortable. She held his hand and smiled…

"Jeez those two are something huh? They probably are in there coming up with more questions to ask you. Don't mind them they really are nice and mean well for me."

"I know they care about you, women in general make me nervous let alone two best friends like them," said Marcus as he took a sip of his drink trying not to appear nervous.

"Can you excuse me for a minute, I will tell them to go easy on you," said Mirlande as she got up from the table.

Mirlande walked into the kitchen and found the two of the talking to each other.

"Hey you two! You are really making the poor guy very nervous. Can you please not give him the third degree?" Begged Mirlande, as she clasped her hands together.

"Mirlande, we just asked him one question and he avoided answering it. So, is he married with child or not?" Asked Ally.

"Why are you asking him that question? Don't you think if he was married or had a child I would have known about it? I really don't get it. What is going on? You two have been acting a bit weird ever since we got here. I didn't want to say anything but I feel like there is something," stated Mirlande a bit frustrated.

Talia saw Marcus' shadow on the floor outside of the kitchen and realized that he was listening to their conversation.

"You guys, Marcus is alone in the dining room so why don't we go join him so he doesn't feel like we are ganging up on him," said Talia.

She just needed an excuse to see what he was up to.

"Good idea," said Mirlande with an angry tone as she walked out of the kitchen.

As soon as Mirlande left Talia turned to Ally, Ally said…

"I don't like this at all. I don't know why won't he just answer us?"

"Not only that, when you were talking to Mirlande I saw his shadow, I think he was listening to use," said Talia.

"Are you serious? Something just isn't kosher about him. We better go in there and see what's going on."

When they both walked into the dining room they didn't see Mirlande or Marcus. They both then walked into the living room and they didn't find them there either but noticed that the door was a little open. As they both walked out of the apartment they saw Mirlande and Marcus standing and talking. As they started to walk over to them they saw Marcus getting into his car and then he left. Mirlande was very upset with them.

"What happened? Where did he go?" Asked Talia.

"What do you mean? You guys made him feel very uncomfortable so he said maybe he is not ready to spend time with you guys yet," said Mirlande very upset and confused.

The three of them came inside the apartment. Mirlande just sat on the sofa and asked the girls,

"I don't understand what happened tonight. Why did you guys make him so uncomfortable? I don't get it. Are you guys not happy to see me happy? Just explain to me why couldn't you just let it be?"

She started crying. She was very angry with her friends. She just couldn't understand why they were giving Marcus a hard time.

Talia was about to tell her what they had seen in the morning but Ally gestured her not to, so Talia stopped and instead said,

"You know we just asked him a simple question and I don't understand why you can't see that he avoided the question?"

Mirlande got very upset and decided to leave…

"I just need to go home right now!"

Talia tried to stop her but she didn't listen. She grabbed her purse and walked out.

"Wow, she doesn't get it! Why did you stop me from telling her what we had seen?" Asked Talia.

"Just think about it for a second. You know she is going to talk to Marcus at some point and if we tell her that we had seen him, she would tell him, and that will give him a chance to come up with a story and she might not get to know the truth. Well, at least for some time. But if we don't tell her and he doesn't know we had seen him, we will know if he comes out and says something to her. Do you get what I am trying to say?" Said Ally.

"I think so. So you are saying that if he doesn't know we had seen him, either he will come out and tell her the truth if he truly loves her or he will continue to lie to her, right?" Clarified Talia.

"Exactly!" Exclaimed Ally.

"Then when will we tell Mirlande about what we had seen?" Asked Talia.

"We will have to wait and see if he tells her and if he doesn't tell her and she continues to see him then after she is emotionally stable we will have to let her know why we had asked him that question and then we will be able to question her as to why he hasn't talked to her about it after the question had been brought up," said Ally.

"Ugh, I don't know about you but all of this has given me a headache!"

"Yeah, tell me about it. We went through the trouble of cooking for this guy and it turned out like this. Mirlande and her never ending guy dramas. I thought maybe she finally found the right guy," said Ally.

"We have so much food, what are we going to do with it all?" Asked Talia.

"Well, we can sit and enjoy the dinner ourselves and whatever is left over you take some home and I will keep some. We both won't need to cook for a week!"

"That's fine with me, you know I love your Indian food! Want to go for a movie after dinner?"

"Sure, we definitely need something to get our mind off of this whole thing."

"Should we call Mirlande to see how she is doing?" Asked Talia.

"No, let's give her some time to calm down and I am sure she will call us when she is ready to talk to us. If we call her now she will just get upset again. Besides, I am guessing she might be with Marcus. Come on, let's have dinner then go for a movie."

The two of them cleaned up the dining room that had the dishes from the appetizers then sat down to eat dinner.

Chapter 4

The Call

It was early Saturday morning and Ally was up having coffee. She was in a thoughtful mood, sitting in her comfy chair, her feet stretched out on the ottoman with her computer on her lap. She had a hiking date with Sam. It was actually his idea. She didn't really want to meet with him but she had committed to it so she had no choice but to go. They had planned to meet for lunch then go hiking afterwards.

Ally was up early finishing up some work that she didn't get to complete at her office the day before. As she sat on her bed doing her work, her phone rang. She looked at the clock and wondered who could be calling her so early in the morning. When she looked at her phone it read "private caller." She found it really strange that, lately, she had been getting calls from a private caller but whenever she answered the phone there was complete silence on the other end. She decided to ignore it thinking it might be a wrong number. She continued doing her work. A couple of minutes later the phone rang again. Although she suspected it was the anonymous caller, she looked at her phone. She was right but she answered it anyway. She said hello and, yet again, no one responded on the other end. She waited for a bit but the person didn't respond so she hung up the phone.

After ten minutes the phone rang again. It was that same person calling. Ally was seriously annoyed so she answered it one more time, regretting that she didn't turn her ringer off. Silence, again. This time, she didn't wait to respond, "Whoever this is I am about to hang up the phone. If you want to talk to me please say something or else I will hang up the phone and next time you call me I will not pick up the phone. Not because I don't care it's because it seems like you don't want to talk to me. So please say something."

She wasn't sure if it was a person who was in need, perhaps in crisis, and didn't have the courage to talk. Then she thought to herself, why would someone be calling her on her private phone and not at her office? She didn't want to take any chances because of her profession. She needed to be polite and not get upset. She waited a few seconds but still no answer then she said,

"Ok, I guess you don't really want to talk to me then I am hanging up now and I will not be answering my phone if you call again. I gave you few chances to talk but you choose not to so there is nothing I can do and if you really are in need of help please call my office when you are ready."

As soon as she finished her sentence the caller said, "Hi Al."

She took in a sharp intake of breath and almost dropped the phone. She knew that voice and only one person called her that.

"Sorry I have been calling and hanging up, I wanted to talk to you but I knew I wasn't allowed to call you."

Ally was in shock, her heart was beating so fast as if she just ran a marathon. She could feel the heat in her face and her cheeks were turning red. The voice was too familiar and gave her the comfort that she had been longing for but…she wished she hadn't received the call.

"Why are you calling me? How did you get my number? Never mind I think I know how you got my number....but you are not supposed to call me!"

"I know I wasn't supposed to call you but I just couldn't help myself. I want to meet you, please meet me today."

"I am sorry I can't, I won't!"

"I beg you, just once then I won't bother you after that. I just want to talk to you." Ally could hear the desperation in his voice.

"Whatever you want to say, say it now. Why meet?"

"Please just meet me, just for a few minutes."

The person begged her so much, after a few minutes she didn't know what else to say…

"But but…ugh… Ok, I will meet you but this will be the only time I will meet you. I don't have much time today, I have plans so I only have a few minutes."

"I'll take those minutes! Can you meet me now?"

Before Ally could say anything she got another call. It was Talia so she asked the man on the other line to hold for a minute and answered Talia' call.

"Why did you give Ary my number?"

Ally was so upset that she didn't even say hello. She just answered the phone with a question.

"Oh, he called you?"

"Yes, he is on the other line right now and wants to meet me today and I have plans with Sam. Why did you give him my number?"

She asked her again in an angry tone.

"Jeez, why are you so upset? I thought maybe you would be happy."

"Well I am not happy! What made you think I would be happy?"

"You thought he was cute and he was asking about you so I thought if things didn't work out with Sam you had another option."

"Hold on, let me just hang up with him then I will tell you why I'm so angry."

Ally switched over to the other line to end the conversation with Ary…

"Like I said, I really don't have that much time today."

"So meet me now!"

Ally looked at her clock on the table then said…

"I can meet you in an hour at the café close to your office."

"Perfect, I will see you then," he said excitedly and hung up.

Ally then switched over to Talia' call.

"I'm back. I'm meeting him in an hour."

"Oh that's great! So, why are you upset that I gave him the number? What is the story you want to tell me?" Asked Talia inquisitively.

"Remember you had asked me if I had dated anyone?"

"Oh yeah, you never answered me."

Ally continued…

"Well, before you and I became friends I had been dating someone for a few years and that was Ary."

"What? No way! What a small world, so what happened?!" Interrupted Talia.

"Well, Ary and I met as undergrads. I actually met him the summer after freshman year of college. He was taking summer classes and I was working on campus. He had just moved to Buffalo from India with his mom. His dad had passed away in a car accident a year before he came here. He had no plans to come to Buffalo for college. He was accepted at another college but due to his father's unexpected death and his mom falling ill they both came here for her treatment. They picked Buffalo because his aunt, his mom's sister, lived here and she was going to help with his mom's treatment. He started taking summer classes to catch up since he had taken a year off before starting college.

"I was on my lunch break at the library and that's when I ran into him. I don't know why I ended up saying hi to him but I did and we just started chatting. After a bit, I had to get back to work. The next day I saw him again during my break. I felt like having fries to eat so I was going to McDonalds to get some fries so I asked him if he wanted to come for a drive. He said yes, so we went through the drive thru. I got the fries for myself and asked him what he would like. He said he didn't want anything but the Indian in me forced him to get something so he picked chicken nuggets. I treated of course. We came back to the campus with our fries and nuggets and sat in the courtyard and ate. I went back to my work and he went to his class.

"Throughout the summer we met every day for lunch. I loved eating bagels and cream cheese, and sometimes I would force him to have some with me, even though he didn't like bagels or cream cheese.

"We became very good friends in such a short period of time. He and I were very different people from very different backgrounds, yet we were similar in so many ways. I came from a conservative Muslim family and he came from a political Hindu family.

"So, the summer went by really fast and he was done with his classes before the fall semester started. He gave me his number but I didn't give him my number because, like I said, I'm from a very conservative Muslim family and I still lived with my family. They didn't allow me to have friends that were boys. Yes, even at that age I couldn't have male friends but little did my family know that most of my friends were guys. I have always gotten along with guys better than girls.

"Well, anyways, for a month I didn't see him and, one time, I picked up the phone to call him because I missed talking to him but and when someone answered, I think it was his aunt, I hung up. I didn't want his family to get any wrong ideas about us. In an Indian family whether it's Muslim or Hindu, friendship between a guy and girl means marriage. Things are changing but not fast enough and tradition is still very strong in my culture.

"A month went by and it was time for college to start. For the first week of the semester I didn't see him. We had different majors so we weren't in the same buildings. Then, I saw him when I was with my friends (most of them were guys). It was really awkward between us. I think he didn't like the fact I was surrounded by so many of my male friends and he seemed a bit upset he wasn't getting a hundred percent of my attention like he used to during the summer. Anyways, after a week or so, we were back to being friends like we used to be and then he moved into the dorms for whatever family reasons. His mom helped settle him into the dorms then she went back to India. He had told his mom about me, I was his Muslim Indian female friend. She was fine with that and surprisingly she didn't think anything of it. Maybe because we were of different religions or it could be because her son said we were just friends? It could have also been because she was a mother of a boy, so it didn't matter to her but if she was a mother of a girl (like my mom) she might have flipped out. That's why my family never knew about any of my male friends. As far as they were concerned all my friends were girls.

"Ary and another male friend of mine, Nick, had become good friends. They both would hang out together even when I wasn't there. One day, they both were drunk and had a bet as to who was going to ask me out first (Ary or Nick) and who I would say yes to. I guess Nick told Ary that I would say yes to him, meaning Ary. Ary thought I would say yes to Nick because he was much better looking and Italian. I liked Italian men.

"Then, one day when Ary and I were in the library he asked me out, even though, earlier that day Nick had already asked me out. Ary was a very good friend of mine and I never saw him in any other way. He had said to me that if I say no he was going to transfer to another college because then he wouldn't have any reason to stay. I really liked Ary's personality and he was a good friend of mine. I told him to give me a few days to think about it. I needed time to think because he really was a good friend and I didn't want to lose his friendship if I said no but I also was concerned that if I said yes, what if it didn't work out? I would lose him as a friend either way. I was in a catch-22.

"Another big reason was our different religious backgrounds. There was no way my family would accept him if we dated. So for a few days I really was contemplating. Then I finally gave him an answer. I knew because of our religious differences it wasn't going to work out and I figured just like others, even if I said yes most likely it would just last for a couple of months then fall apart. I really didn't want to lose my best friend so I said yes to him. After I said yes he told me he was so sure that I would have picked Nick because of his good looks.

"So, since, he had asked me out and we were more than just friends, we both thought, now what? He never had a girlfriend and I had never really dated anyone. I had guys ask me out but I never went on a "date" with anyone because of my family. So, from that point on, we had planned to meet early every morning before we would head to our classes and meet for lunch and whenever we could. Remember, I couldn't meet him at night or my family would find out. After my classes were over, I was expected to be home. I know for anyone who is not from the same culture that's hard to understand. He couldn't even call me at home. Can you imagine a boy calling me at home? My parents would have freaked out!

"So I would sneak and call him whenever I could. The semester came to an end and we had winter break. I couldn't see him at all during the break but called him as much as I could. I guess I kind of gave him a hard time. I was a little distant from him emotionally because of my family and the religion thing. I was afraid of getting too close to him and not having it to work out between us because of my family.

"Then the second semester started and we were hanging out again. A month after college started, he got a phone call from his aunt saying that his mom was sick, remember I told you his mom went back to India after she settled him here? His aunt said his mom was sick and needed surgery. So, he booked his flight to India. He told me about it when I came to see him in the morning before I went to my classes. He told me he would pick me up at my class after it's over and asked if I would help him pack his suitcase?

"After my class, I was expecting him to pick me up but he didn't come. Instead, his roommate came to get me. I asked him where Ary was. He really didn't answer much and just said he was waiting for me in the room. When I got to their room, Ary was very upset. He found out that his mom wasn't going to have surgery but rather she had passed away and his relatives didn't want to tell him until he landed in India. I felt so bad for him. By the age of 19 he had lost both of his parents and was all alone in this world. I cannot tell you how bad I felt for him. His parents were very young, both were 43 at the time of their death. I didn't know what to say or do so I just held him tightly for a little while. Then I helped him pack fast because his uncle was coming to take him to the airport. It didn't take long, and then he was gone.

"He was in India for a few weeks and when he was there I did call him from his room like he had told me to whenever I wanted to talk to him. He came back after the funeral. I had actually missed him and I think at that point that's when my feelings for him changed. Until then, I didn't realize how much I liked him and cared for him but when he came back he did notice a difference in my behavior towards him. He told me he was planning to end whatever we had because he believed that I didn't feel the same way about him that he felt about me.

"When he came back to school and saw me, he knew things were different for me. I wasn't distant towards him anymore, the boundaries that were put up by me were coming down slowly. So, we developed a good relationship despite my family's restrictions and a few years passed by and towards the last semester of our undergrad my father found out about us. He had seen us going somewhere in my car. He was so upset to know that I was dating him. If he was a Muslim boy he would have been fine with it but the fact that he was Hindu, it was a big no no! He asked me several times not to see him anymore unless he was willing to convert. I told my father that Ary would not convert.

"By this time, Ary and I were very serious in our relationship. My father was really stressed about it and he would watch my every move and make sure I wouldn't see him. He was so stressed out he had a heart attack. Of course, the heart attack was blamed on me. My mother never failed to constantly remind me that I was the cause of my father's ill health. It really hurt my feelings every time my mom would bring it up and blame me. She didn't see me as a human being with a heart. She just saw me as a selfish daughter that didn't care about them. But I would try to make myself feel better by saying that it wasn't my fault. My parents had a very unhealthy lifestyle and their genetic predispositions didn't help. No matter how much I tried to convince myself, my mother always knew which button to press to hurt my feelings…"

"Didn't your siblings try to help you?" Interrupted Talia, all upset and sad.

"My siblings? Are you kidding me? Let me tell you about them. You know, I'm the youngest in the family and they are much older than me, right?"

Talia nodded.

Ally continued, "My sister, who was married to a guy of my parents' choice, was and still is my parents' perfect daughter. So, she would call me, checking up on me. She would try to tell me how what I was doing was wrong and that I shouldn't hurt our parents like that, etc. So, that's my sister. Now my brothers, they were my father's spies. They were keeping an eye on me like a hawk, as my father had asked them to do. Even to the point where my one brother actually showed up on campus one time to check up on me. I didn't see him but he left his business card on my car's windshield to let me know that he was there.

"That wasn't the worst thing that had happened. One morning, I was walking out of my house to go to my classes like I always did and the three of them, my father and my two brothers just blocked my way to the door and demanded that I hand over the keys to the car. They didn't want me to go to college anymore because they knew I would meet Ary. Somehow they were able to snatch the keys out of my hands. Just imagine, I was literally being wrestled to the ground to stop me from leaving the house. At that point, I was so scared and hurt by what they were all doing to me. I had that fear of what I used to hear / watch on the news about what Muslim families were doing to the daughters to protect their honor. I fought hard and walked out of the house with my purse and backpack. I didn't have my car keys to go so I just walked fast to the nearest bus stop. Not knowing what bus to take to get to the campus or how much it even cost. I got on the bus and asked the driver how much it cost and how far does the bus go? I had to take two different buses and walk for a bit to get to the campus.

"So now you tell me, you think my siblings were on my side?"

Talia gasped in disbelief. "Wow, I just can't believe what I am hearing! In this day and age, here in the USA, this actually happens?!"

"Yes, unfortunately it does happen in certain households. There was a part of me that understood what my family was doing. From their perspective they were trying to make sure I didn't go to hell after I die by being with someone who is from different religion. I get it that they meant well but, for me, what they wanted was not what I wanted. I understood no matter what religion people follow a belief is a belief and people will do anything to follow that belief. What scared me was that I felt like I was going to become a prisoner in my own home.

"That's exactly what happened. After I finished my undergrad, I was pretty much a prisoner in my own home. I wasn't allowed to go anywhere unless someone in my family accompanied me and when I started working, they kept a close eye on me. My father had my work schedule so I was expected to be home straight from work. I couldn't go anywhere and I couldn't see Ary. This went on for a year…"

"Why didn't you leave or move out since you had a job?" Interrupted Talia shockingly.

"I didn't make enough money to do that. It was a job that helped me determine what I wanted to do but not a job that paid a lot of money."

Ally's voice changed a bit as she tried to control herself from crying. She then resumed her story…

"One day I was at the mall with my cousins and I saw Ary walking hand in hand with another girl! As I looked at her, it turned out to be a friend of mine. That just broke my heart! I loved him so much and he did this. I mean, I guess I should have tried to understand that I couldn't even see him but I used to talk to him every day. I would be sneaky and call him yet he never said anything about dating her. He pretended like he and I were still together. I know he was all alone and didn't have me there anymore but he didn't even tell me. It broke my heart!"

At this point, Ally became sad and felt like she was reliving what she had put behind her. Her voice was cracking as she was trying her best not to cry….

"Ugh, well anyways, so for one year I was pretty much locked in my house. I mean I could go to work and anywhere else my family went but I could never go anywhere on my own. All this stress made me really sick and that is when my autoimmune disorder was triggered and will have until it kills me. I would get angry at my parents when I thought about my illness. Because of them, I have developed an illness, but they never saw what they had done to me. I would then say to myself that they are my parents and they mean well for me and they just don't know that what they want is not what I want in life.

"After a year, I woke up and realized I needed to educate myself further so I can be on my own two feet and not depend on my family. I wanted to be strong and not be like any other Muslim girl that was in my situation, who gave up and did what her family wanted. I needed my family because I couldn't afford to live on my own and, even after all that's happened to me, my parents were still my parents and I did love them. So, I had made a promise to my father that I will not have anything to do with Ary if he allowed me to go to graduate school and live on my own. Surprisingly, he agreed...

"I had seen Ary with a friend of mine and when I had asked him about it (I snuck behind my parents backs and called him) he completely denied it. He knew I knew but he didn't tell me the truth. So, I told him from this point on I would have nothing to do with him and he will never hear from me again. It was really devastating for me. Not only had I lost someone I loved but I also lost my best friend (he was my best friend). That's why I didn't have a problem making a promise to my father to not see him if it meant I could educate myself to the point I would never be dependent on anyone.

"All of this made me a very strong person. I used to be a very simple and naïve girl but life changed me. I had lost my innocence. I became very strong mentally. All the protective walls that Ary had brought down with his love went up all again after his betrayal. I didn't know if I could ever trust anyone ever again and, 'til this day, I don't. I decided to go become a psychologist and those were the days when I met you.

"I did find out that Ary went to Law School in Syracuse. I never bothered to find out anything else about him because, after what he had done, he wasn't worth it for me to fight with my family and lose them from my life also. So I moved on. Well, I moved on with the motions of living but emotionally I never moved on completely. The pain has always been there with me and that is one of the major reasons why I haven't found anyone else. My first love and betrayal has been very hard to forget.

"At this point, I only see guys that my parents try to arrange for me because I know most likely it will not work out. They get the pleasure of me agreeing to meet men of their choice and I get the freedom of living away from my family and doing what I want…So this is the story about my life that I never told you or Mirlande."

"Oh my God, wow! I just can't believe in this day and age and in this country you have gone through this. I didn't realize Ary turned out to be a jerk who cheated on you and lied to you, I am so sorry I gave him your number."

Talia was very sad to hear her friend's story. She wished she was there to give her friend a hug.

Ally could sense her friend's sincerity. "No, I actually don't blame him. Yes, even today I am heartbroken. But I've come to realize that losing his parents was devastating for him and then he lost me from his life so what was he to do? I'm sure he needed someone in his life so he didn't feel alone in the world. He didn't have anyone in this city. I don't think I'm upset but just very hurt by him and upset with God for putting me through this. If he and I were not meant to be then we shouldn't have met. That's what I am really upset about. Trust me I try my best to like the guys that my parents set me up with but it's just that Ary was my best friend and my first true love, and I really miss him even today. When I met him that day in your office building, all those feelings came back to me. I cannot tell you how hard it was for me to pretend he was a stranger to me. Since that day I ran into him at your office, I have been trying my best not to think about him or ask you any questions about him. Imagine how difficult it is for me now that I know where he is and know how to get hold of him. I am trying my best to get him out of mind," Ally stated with a slip of a cry.

"Oh Ally, I can feel the pain in your voice. I can sense the love you still have for him. You can't tell me you don't still love him, I can sense it."

"No, I am not going to deny the fact that there is a part of me that still loves him but there is nothing I can do about it. He probably has someone else and, even if he doesn't, don't forget about my family. If I choose him then I will really hurt my parents and most likely they will never have anything to do with me. That's why I am seriously thinking about spending more time with Sam and get to know him better instead of trying to avoid him as much as I have been. This way, if things don't work out at least I will still have my family."

"But Ally the way your parents treated you is not normal. I understand it's a cultural thing but it's not normal or healthy for you."

"Yes I know, I know all that, trust me I do. I know what that has done to me emotionally which no one can understand but at the end of the day they still are my parents."

Talia argued, shaking her head, "I don't understand you! You try to tell Muslim girls not to be submissive and don't let any man try to control them like that. You try to tell them to educate themselves so they can stand on their two feet and do something with their life and here you are doing exactly the opposite! You are educated and are really independent but you are not willing to fight for what you want and just relent or capitulate. You just give in to the bullshit. So isn't that being submissive? For goodness sake, do what you want and if your parents truly love you they will be happy for you."

At this point Talia was a bit angry with her friend for not being strong…

"You don't get it Talia, for my parents religion is everything. They are getting older, so, as you know, when people get older they have nothing to do but think about life after death. My parents believe if you are not a good Muslim and follow what is asked of Muslims then you will go to hell. In their mind, if their daughter marries a non-Muslim then she is going down the wrong path and they feel that if I go on the wrong path then I will go to hell and as parents they can't see that happening. They won't care what race a guy is as long as he is a Muslim. Besides, what makes you think Ary wants to be with me? It's been a few years and I'm sure he has someone in his life. Maybe he is still with that girl, who knows."

"Why would he want to meet with you then? What if he doesn't have anyone in his life? Would you start where you guys left off or start over again?" Asked Talia a bit frustrated and a bit excited.

"I honestly don't know." Ally sighed.

"Well, I will pray really hard that he doesn't have anyone and you guys end up together!"

Ally was very sad...

"You know life is not like a movie. Stories like this usually don't have a happy ending in real life."

"Well, whether it happens or not I will still pray for you both to be together." Talia suddenly burst out, "Oh my God, you have ten minutes to go meet Ary. Get off the phone and go! You better call me as soon as you leave the café!"

"Don't hold your breath, it probably will not be what you are thinking," replied Ally disappointingly.

"You always tell everyone to be positive in life and now look who is so negative? Be positive and go!" Said Talia rushing Ally to get off the phone and go.

"Ok, ok I am leaving, jeez!"

"Don't forget to call me right away, bye!"

They both hung up the phone and Ally rushed to get ready to go. She was a bit excited but also very nervous meeting him. She had butterflies in her stomach…

Meanwhile, Ary had arrived at the café. He looked at his watch, he realized he had gotten there a few minutes early. The café was actually busy so he nervously waited for a table to clear up. He looked across the room at the table where he and Ally used to sit when they were in undergrad. He went up to the people who were sitting there and asked if they will be a while. The men looked at him and told him they were actually going to be leaving in a few minutes. Ary was glad and thanked them, he really wanted to sit at their usual table. In all these years the café hadn't changed at all. He kept looking at his watch nervously and realized it was time and Ally hadn't come. The men cleared the table and let him know that he can have it. He thanked them again and sat down at the table, looking out the window hoping to see her. As he sat there, all the memories from the past were going through his mind. This is where he and Ally used to hangout every day. It was a small cozy café which had a few tables and couches set in front of a huge fireplace.

She was now fifteen minutes late and he was getting even more nervous thinking maybe she would not come. He was thinking to himself that she was not going to come. He was thinking that she was still so upset with him after all these years, why would she want to come? He thought of texting her to see if she was coming then thought to himself that she said she will come. But then he thought, what if she changed her mind? With all these thoughts going around in his head, it almost made him dizzy.

"Ugh, Al please come!" He muttered under his breath as he looked at his watch again.

Forty-five minutes had passed and still no Ally. He frowned. "I guess she is still upset with me. Looks like she may not be coming after all. She did say she didn't have that much time today and had other plans," he muttered as if he was talking to someone else.

Ary looked out the window hoping to see her but he didn't. He gave up hope and decided to leave. Just as he walked out of the café, he heard someone from behind calling him. "Ary!" He turned excitedly and saw it was a friend of his. "Oh, hi Carrie." He said disappointedly. He was hoping it was Ally but sadly it wasn't. He continued walking without saying anything and Carrie, Ary's friend's wife, could see that he wasn't in a mood for any conversation. Ary was noticeably upset and kept wondering why Ally didn't come? He was so engrossed in his thoughts that he bumped into an elderly lady out walking her dog. He was very apologetic for bumping into her, she understood and told him not to worry about it since she and her dog were unhurt. Ary continued walking, got his phone out to call Ally to find out why she didn't come meet him and to see if she was alright but then he thought she must be still very upset with him and that's why she didn't come. He kept staring at his phone contemplating if he should call or text. After a few minutes, he put his phone back in his pocket, thinking that if she cared and wanted to she would have come or at least called to tell him she wasn't.

Meanwhile, back at home, Ally was in her room sitting on a chair crying with her phone on the table. She kept looking at it in hopes that Ary would call her. The phone rang and Ally got excited and looked at the phone, it was Sam calling. She didn't answer and let it go to her voicemail. Ally was in two minds about Ary. There was part of her that wanted him to call her and there was a part that didn't. The phone rang again, she looked to see who was calling and it was Talia. This time Ally answered, Talia didn't even say hello…

"Oh my God! I have been waiting for you to call me and since you didn't I decided to call you. So how did it go?"

"I didn't go."

Talia could hear the sadness in her tone and the voice sounded a bit raspy.

"What? Why? Have you been crying?"

"I didn't go because I couldn't do it," replied Ally crying.

"What do you mean you couldn't go? And why are you crying? You still love him don't you?"

"I don't know, I'm so confused. He hurt me really bad by cheating on me. There is a part of me that, I guess, still cares about him but there is also a part of me that hates him. I can't discount the fact that he cheated on me. I have something going on with Sam and hope that it works out. That way it will make my family happy and it will not make things complicated in my life."

"But Ally, will you be happy with Sam?"

"I don't know, I'm guessing I will," replied Ally with a confused tone.

"Listen, if a client of yours was telling you what you are telling me what advice would you give them?"

"I knew you would ask me that sooner or later and, to be honest, I know what I would say but I can't do that because this is personal to me. I can advise others as an outsider but, right now, I am not able to follow my own advice. The pain just doesn't allow me to.

"Don't you think you're harming yourself by trying to please your family?"

"You are assuming Ary is not in a relationship. What if he is and he just wanted to meet with me to see how things were?

It's not like he even bothered to call or text and see why I didn't come. The Ary I knew would have called me."

"You just stood him up! If he did that to you would you have called him to ask?"

"You didn't know our relationship. Yes, we both would have done that. The fact that he didn't shows me that he's not the same person anymore."

"Shouldn't you at least have the decency to call or text him to let him know why you didn't come? Don't you think you owe him that much? I don't blame him for not calling you, he is not at fault here, and you are. I actually feel bad for him and feel like calling him myself which I just might do.

Although Talia was angry with Ally, she could feel the pain in her friend's voice and wanted things to work out between them. She was trying to be the voice that Ally is to everyone else. She didn't want to give up on her.

"You just don't understand."

"I guess I don't but I am trying to understand your situation Ally, I really am. I guess the part I'm having a hard time comprehending is that just because he is of a different religion you are going through this for your parents. I am sorry, this is just making me very upset. I really thought you were a strong woman. How can you go around lecturing other young women about educating themselves and making themselves strong enough to stand on their own feet and not have anyone control them when you yourself are not doing that? You are allowing your family to control you? Ugh, you know what? I think I'm done talking to you right now. This is just really frustrating. You need to call him and apologize to him. If you didn't want to go, you should have let him know that instead of just not showing up. If you don't want to see him that's fine, that's your choice but at least call him. I know you have to go meet Sam later today but I know you, you are not mentally going to be ok if you don't call and let Ary know the reason you didn't meet up with him. He shouldn't have to call you. You need to call him. Ugh, I have to go to my office to finish some work. When I'm done, I will call you to see what happened. Will you call him? Please say you will, at least do that!"

"Ok, ok I will."

"Good! I will call you in a bit to make sure you did. Do you want to meet for lunch before you meet Sam?"

"I'm supposed to meet Sam for lunch. He left me a voicemail. Let me see what he said before I agree to anything. I'm hoping he canceled. I have a headache and I really am not in a mood to hang out right now. I will text you. Go finish your work, bye."

She hung up then checked her voicemail. Sam was just confirming that he will be able to meet her as planned. Ally wasn't sure what she wanted to do. She thought Sam was really a nice guy but with Ary being back in the picture she was really confused. She texted Sam saying she got the message and will meet as planned.

She then texted Ary…

"I am really sorry I didn't come. I know it was wrong of me not to call or text you. I was ready to come see you but at the last minute I just couldn't do it. It was really hard for me when we parted. It took me a long time to get used to not having you in my life. I'm pretty sure you have moved on as you had when we broke up. I'm not quite sure what you want from me now so I thought it was best for me to not see you. Again, I do apologize for not calling or texting you."

She read her texts a couple of times before she sent it. She then went to lie down on the bed. She wasn't feeling that great and wanted to rest and try to clear her mind before she met Sam. As she lay there she kept checking her phone. She wanted to see if Ary texted her back and every time she checked she was disappointed. She fell asleep waiting for him to return her text.

After a few minutes her phone rang, she woke up quickly from her nap and answered the phone. It was Talia...

"So did you call or text him?" She asked without even bothering to say hello.

"Yes, I texted him but he hasn't returned my text as of yet."

"He must be upset and I don't blame him. What are you doing? Did you want to meet for lunch?"

"Oh, sorry I forgot to text you. I can't, I have to meet Sam for lunch. He had left a voicemail that we were still on as planned so that means he isn't running late and I will be meeting him for lunch."

"Ok, shouldn't you get ready as he will be there shortly?"

"Oh shoot, I didn't even realize the time. Thanks!"

"So what are you going to do with Sam?"

"What do you mean?"

"I mean, you know you still are in love with Ary and you really haven't gotten him out of your mind. How will you be able to go ahead with Sam?"

"I am going forward with Sam because there is nothing between me and Ary. What part of that can you not understand? Seriously, Ary has moved on and I really can't have anything to do with him if I want my family in my life. I am not even sure if I still have those feelings for Ary. I am sorry but I really need to wash up my face and go."

"Fine, you go but at least stop lying to yourself about your feelings towards Ary."

"I am not lying to myself about anything, I know what I am doing, and at least, I think I do. Sorry I really need to go and will call you later."

"Ok go, bye," replied Talia a bit upset.

Ally then hung up the phone and went into the bathroom to get ready. The doorbell buzzed. Ally got a bit nervous, "he is here already?" She thought to herself as she walked over to buzz him in. She didn't even bother to ask who it was as she knew it would be Sam. She then walked over to the door and opened it, looking down and fixing her top.

"Sorry, I am not quite ready yet..." Just as soon as she finished what she was saying, she looked up and got a shocked look on her face.

"Ary! What are you doing here? How did you know where I lived?"

She just questioned him without even saying hello.

"Hi Al. Talia gave me your address. Sorry I came without calling you. I didn't want you to avoid me again and Talia said you were home right now."

Ally didn't know what to do. She was expecting Sam at any moment and she couldn't believe Talia told Ary that she was home, knowing that Sam was coming to get her.

"May I come in?"

"Yes, sure," she responded not knowing what to do and part of her wanted to call Talia and yell at her.

"Could you excuse me for a moment? I was in the middle of washing my face. I was actually getting ready to go out. Sit, I will be right out," Ally waved toward a chair in the living room.

As she was talking to him, she grabbed her phone from the table without Ary noticing and went into the bathroom. She looked at the time and that's when she realized that Sam would be arriving in 45 minutes. She didn't know what to do. She couldn't just walk out on Ary. So she texted Sam saying that she was running late, that she was at her office finishing some work and will text him when she gets home.

While she was waiting for Sam's response, she texted Talia: "Why did you tell Ary where I live and that I am home?"? He is here and you know Sam will be coming over soon too. I am so upset with you right now!!"

Talia responded right away with a smiley face: "I am sure you will thank me later!"

Sam hadn't responded, Ally nervously walked out of the bathroom. Ary was looking out the window as he waited. He turned when she came out of the bathroom and smiled at her.

"I missed you," he said as he walked towards her...

At that moment, Ally forgot about everything. She became very weak. He came over and hugged her, Ally felt the comfort that she had been missing for what seemed like centuries to her. She too put her arms around him, Ary held her tight.

"I missed you so much!" He quietly exclaimed.

"I missed you too," said Ally as she put her head on his shoulder.

The comfort that the two felt in each other's arms was indescribable. Ary slowly kissed her neck and she held him tighter. He kissed her again, just making sure she was ok with it. She held him tight. He slowly kept kissing her neck then slowly kissed her ear then her cheek. Ally looked him into his eyes and then he kissed her on her lips. They were only kissing for a few seconds when Ally stopped him and pushed him away slowly. He knew that was his cue to stop so he did.

"I am sorry I didn't come today. So why did you want to see me?"

"I know we have been away for a while and I know you didn't want to see me anymore. After I ran into you and you pretended as if we were strangers, I played along but from that moment on I couldn't stop thinking about you. Don't get me wrong, I have always been thinking about you all this while. I didn't have your number and I didn't even know if you had gotten married. I actually figured you would have gotten married because of your parents. Then, after I saw you, I found out through Talia that you weren't married and you lived on your own. Seriously, living on your own! How did you manage that with being under your parents' control?" Ary asked with a wry smile on his face.

Ally smiled back. "I had made a deal with my parents that if they let me live on my own without being married I promised them I would never have anything to do with you. Last time when I saw you, you were with 'her' and, since you didn't tell me, I guess that made it easier for me to hate you and think about freedom for myself. There was not a day that went by that I didn't think of you. You were my true love, my best friend. I spent time with you every day for so many years, then you hurt me and the religious issue with my parents, all this just broke my heart and I fell really ill to the point that I developed an autoimmune disorder caused by stress and I have to live with it until it kills me!"

She had tears streaming down her cheeks as she couldn't control herself anymore. Ary couldn't stand to see her cry so he held her closer in his arms. As he held her, all the memories, the heartache came back to her and she started to cry uncontrollably. Ary looked for a box of tissues around the room and spotted a box on the table nearby. He took a tissue and tried to wipe her face. He then sat her down next to him on the sofa.

"I am sorry for hurting you. I hadn't seen you for so long and I became lonely. When you wouldn't come over to see me or even talk to me because of your parents, I really became very lonely. I didn't know what to do without you. After my parents died, you were my world but I couldn't see or talk to you. I cannot tell you how lost I felt in this world..."

"So you cheated on me?! You could have just told me instead of cheating on me!" Interrupted Ally angrily.

"I am sorry, it was wrong of me. I didn't know what to do. I needed someone in my life. I wanted you but your family didn't allow that."

"So why are you here now? I am guessing you are still in a relationship since you can't be alone?!" She asked in a very angry tone through the tears, "Answer me, you are in a relationship aren't you?"

Ary nodded his head slowly and said softly, "Yes, I am in a relationship."

"Same person or someone else?"

"Same."

After hearing this she became furious. She could feel blood rushing into her face. Part of her wondered why they weren't married but part of her thought that it didn't matter, the fact that he was still with her said something.

"Then why are you here?" Asked Ally sardonically.

"After I saw you, I just couldn't keep myself away from you. I really missed you, I really missed my best friend."

"So that's it? You missed your best friend and that's why you are here? What do you want from me when you have someone in your life? Shouldn't she be your best friend now?" Said Ally furiously.

"No, no one could be the friend you were to me. You were more than my best friend, you were my family. I felt so secure in this world knowing you were always there. My parents were dead and I didn't have any family but I always had you. We would have never separated if your parents didn't have an issue with my religion. We would have been married and lived happily ever after. I didn't want anyone else when I had you. You have no one to blame but your parents for all this," responded Ary angrily.

"You have moved on and you know we can't have anything between us so, like I've asked multiple times, what do you want from me now?" Asked Ally sadly, turning away from Ary.

"I want my best friend. You make me feel so safe and secure when I am with you. Why can't we stay friends?"

"I don't think I can be friends with you. It's too painful for me, especially when I know you have HER in your life. I can't believe how selfish you are being!"

Ary replied in a jealous tone, "Talia told me you were seeing someone. A man your parents set you up with so you can marry him."

"So, are you saying to me that you want me to be friends with you even though you have a girlfriend, and she will be ok with this?" Asked Ally sarcastically.

"I don't know how she will be."

"Well let me tell you, she is not going to be happy with it and I am pretty sure she will tell you not to be friends with me. Besides, if I get serious about this person I'm sure he will not be happy about that either, so no!"

She was trying to make him jealous and it was working. She could see it on his face. There was part of Ally that was so angry with Ary but there was also a part of her that still loved him. Then she would just get angry knowing he was with someone else. While the two of them were in middle of their conversation, Ally's phone was buzzing. She looked at the phone on the table' and ignored it. Ary took notice of this and looked at the phone.

"I really don't think it's going to work out. I don't think we can be friends…"

The phone vibrated again as she was talking to Ary. Ary interrupted in a jealous manner…

"Why don't you answer the call I am sure it's your boyfriend calling."

Ally looked at Ary, stood up, grabbed the phone, and answered it while walking away. It was Sam. Ary was getting angry and jealous as he watched her talk on the phone. He was trying very hard not to show it but Ally knew what he was truly like and knew it bothered him. Ally returned after a very short conversation.

"Your boyfriend I take it? It's funny I couldn't talk to you when we were seeing each other and look, he can call you whenever he wants," he said sarcastically.

Ally knew him very well and knew his facial expressions when he was upset so she played along with it to hurt him like he had hurt her.

"Yes that was Sam. We have planned to go hiking so I will have to leave soon if you don't mind."

"Oh, so Sam is his name! Well fine I will leave and let you go fuck him!" Exclaimed Ary angrily acting as if they never had parted all those years from her.

"What is your problem? Why are you upset when you and I don't have a relationship and you have a girlfriend?"

"I don't understand why you have a problem staying friends?" Asked Ary as he started losing his patience.

"No I can't! I am sorry but I need to get ready to go."

"Ok fine, I will go but think about it," replied Ary as he walked towards the door. He then turned around…

"I really want my best friend. I have a girlfriend and you have a boyfriend. What if we don't tell either one of them about our friendship? Think about it. Will you think about it?"

Ary was becoming desperate. He didn't want to show his anger for fear of her not wanting to see him again. Ally needed him to leave at that moment so she told him she will think about it. Ary got excited and smiled for a second thinking that she finally agreed at least to think about it, he then said goodbye and closed the door.

As he walked away, he had a smile on his face thinking of Ally being back in his life but also got angry at the thought of her being with someone else even though he had a girlfriend himself. He was also very curious to see who this guy was that she was going out with so he sat in his white Ferrari waiting. He waited for a bit then he saw an Indian looking guy coming out of a black Audi across the street and going towards Ally's apartment. Ary was not able to see his face to well because he was looking the other way. He was getting angry again, more of a jealous feeling than anything else because he couldn't see anyone else with Ally. After Sam entered the building Ary drove away frustrated because there was nothing he could do and couldn't afford to make Ally mad if he wanted her in his life again.

Meanwhile, Talia called Mirlande to see how she was doing. Mirlande hadn't called her or Ally since that dinner night with Marcus. Talia and Ally had decided to leave her alone until she was ready to talk to them and sort things out with Marcus. The phone rang for a while and, just when she was about to hang up, Mirlande answered.

"Oh hi, I was just about to hang up. The phone rang few times and you didn't answer so I thought you might be still upset with us. How are you doing?"

"I don't know how I am," replied Mirlande sounding overwhelmed.

"What's the matter? Were you able to talk to Marcus and find out the truth?"

"I haven't heard from him since the night of the dinner. I left him several messages but he never returned my calls. So I just let him go. Maybe you guys were right, he probably has a wife and child and was lying to me. Why do I always find the wrong guys?" Asked Mirlande with a very sad tone.

"Oh honey, I am sorry. It really isn't your fault that there are so many jerks out there. At least it's better for you to find out about him now rather than after you had invested so much time into the relationship. Why haven't you called us?"

"I didn't know what to say to you guys. I felt bad I walked out on you guys so angry that night and, since Marcus hadn't returned my calls, I just didn't know how to face you guys or didn't know what to say. I didn't want you guys to laugh at me."

"Oh sweetie, we are your friends and we do mean well for you. We don't want to see you get hurt. All of us are there to look out for each other not to point fingers or laugh at each other."

"Thanks Talia, that means so much to me. You guys are like family to me and it's been hard not being able to share my feelings with you guys."

"Hey, if you are not busy, want to grab a coffee and chat? I also want to fill you in on what's going on with Ally."

"Yes I'm free right now. What's wrong? What's going on with Ally, is she ok?" Asked Mirlande very concerned.

"She's fine but there is a very important part of her life that she had never shared with us so I want to fill you in on it so we can help her."

"Oh my god, of course! I can't wait to meet you so why don't you start telling me on the phone as I drive over to the café?"

"Ok I will because it really is a long story then when we get there we can figure everything out."

Mirlande lived a little further away so she left the house before Talia did. Meanwhile, Talia was at home on the phone telling Mirlande about Ary and Ally as she folded her laundry.

Chapter 5

Hiking

Ally and Sam arrived at the hiking trial……

"What a beautiful place. I have never been here before," said Ally in an admiration.

"Isn't it? I come here often when I just want to relax and enjoy the scenery. There is a nice diner here, I thought it would be a perfect place to eat before we start walking," said Sam as he pulled into the parking lot.

"That sounds great. I am getting kind of hungry."

Sam parked the car then they both start walking towards the diner which was located on a small hill surrounded by trees. It actually looked like a cabin. The diner was very busy so they both had to wait to be seated. Sam gently took Ally's hand and pulled her closer to him, smiling down at her. She looked at him with a smile and was very surprised he was holding her hand. He had never touched her before. He stood there holding her as they waited to be seated. Ally didn't know what to do so she let him hold her. The waiter came up to them to let them know their table was ready.

Ally and Sam walked over to their table and sat down. The waiter told them he would be right back to take their order as he handed them their menus, then he left.

"Can you order me a coke when the waiter returns please? I'm just going to use the restroom?" Said Sam.

"Sure," replied Ally.

She waited for Sam to walk away few feet then she opened her purse and pulled out her phone. While they were waiting for a table Ally could feel the buzzing in her purse, she had a text. She couldn't check it because Sam was holding her. Now that Sam was not there she took the opportunity to check to see who it was. It was a text from Ary. It read, "I was just thinking of you. I'm glad I came to see you today and glad you agreed to stay friends with me. You must be out with your future husband? So enjoy yourself!"

Ally knew Ary very well and she could sense that he was jealous. He was trying to distract her from Sam. On the way to the hiking trial, Ally had been thinking about her meeting with Ary. She was very upset with him for hurting her and didn't really want to be friends with him but there was a part of her that still had feelings for him. Thinking about the fact that he had someone else in his life made her hate him. She didn't want to be friends with him but she also wanted to seek revenge. She decided to make him think that she wanted to stay friends with him so she could make him very jealous. Her plan was to try to make him get closer to her again then dump him even if it is just as a friend so he could feel the pain she had felt and somewhat was still feeling. She knew that it disturbed him that she was out with someone else. As she was staring at his text, she got another text from him. It read…"hi it's me again" and had smile faces. Ally smiled as she read it but didn't respond to him because she knew it would bother him even more. She saw Sam returning, so she quickly put the phone back in her purse.

Sam sat down. "Sorry it took me so long. It was busy in there."

"Oh no problem. Since it's so busy, the food must be good here then!" She commented.

"Yes, it is," responded Sam.

The waiter walked over and asked what they would like to order in a very abrupt tone. Sam looked at Ally and said, "You should try their burger it's the best!"

Ally smiled then turned to the waiter, "I guess I will have the burger."

"And you sir?" Asked the waiter turning to Sam.

"I will have the same," he replied.

The couple provided the waiter with how they wanted the burgers and what they wanted on them. Since the burgers came with French fries, they didn't order any appetizers.

"What would you like to drink?" Asked the waiter.

Sam gestured Ally to order…" I will have coke please."

"I will have the same," said Sam.

"I will bring your drinks right away and put your order in," said the waiter, brusquely, as he put his pen in his pocket. He collected the menus and walked away.

"Very friendly isn't he?" Joked Ally.

"Yeah, unfortunately that's the down side of this place. The food is great but their service is really bad."

"I guess they don't care to train their servers since they are so confident that people will keep coming back for their food," said Ally with a smile.

"Probably," agreed Sam with a smile.

There was silence for a few seconds then Sam held Ally's hand from across the table. "I just wanted to say that I really enjoy spend time with you. I know it seems like I am always so busy but all that is about to change. I will have more time since my fellowship is coming to an end. My parents have been asking me about us and I am sure yours have been too. I wanted to ask you a question." Ally nodded in response.

Sam gave Ally a sincere look. "How do you feel about us? I mean do you think…I mean would you like to marry me?"

Ally could see that he was very nervous and she was also very shocked that he asked her to marry her. She thought they were still getting to know each other but then again it was a semi arranged marriage situation so it's expected to happen soon. She just stared at him for a second with a nervous smile on her face.

"Are you asking me to marry you? Or are you asking me if I am considering marrying you? I'm not sure what you are asking?" Questioned Ally, a bit frazzled.

"I am sorry if I put you on the spot, maybe it's just not coming out right. I am a bit nervous because I don't know how this is supposed to be and I am sure you don't either, or maybe you do, I don't (he rambled nervously). What I am trying to say is, I like you, I enjoy the time that we spend together. I guess I can see myself spending the rest of my life with you. I wanted to know if you feel the same about me," clarified Sam.

Ally took a deep breath and just stared for a second, just when she was about to say something she was interrupted by the waiter. "Here are your drinks, the burgers will be here shortly," he said, then quickly walked away.

Sam looked at Ally waiting for her to respond. Now Ally didn't have a choice but to answer him. She smiled at him, "I really like you as well and yes my parents have been calling and asking me about us as well. I…I just feel like I need a little more time. I mean, I…uh…I want for both us to be really sure about each other because you know how our parents are? I feel bad that you have this definite answer and I am saying this to you, I just need a little more time."

Sam smiled at her. "Sorry, I am not trying to add more pressure on you. I just wanted you to know where I stand on this...I guess you can call it a relationship? I don't know…I don't know what this set up is called but I just wanted you to know that I want you in my life…forever. If you need a little more time to figure it out that's not a problem. I guess I thought girls usually want to know if a man is ready for marriage."

"Most normal girls would love to hear that BUT I am an outlier, I guess!" Ally joked to lighten up the atmosphere between them then they both started laughing.

Just then the waiter returned with their burgers…"is there anything else I can get for you?"

"No, I think we are good." Replied Sam as he looked at Ally to get assurance. She smiled and nodded her head yes. The waiter left the table and the two of them started eating.

"Did you know your parents have invited my family for the party they're having?" Said Sam.

Ally just looked at him with shocked and said, "No. My mom didn't say anything to me about that."

She really wasn't ready for the families to be hanging out as of yet since she is not even sure about Sam.

"Will you be able to come or are you working that night?" Asked Ally, hoping that he says he's working.

"I am working but I'll try to see if I can switch my shift with someone else," replied Sam.

Ally was relieved for a second when he said he was working but became nervous when he said he'd try to switch shifts. For Ally, this was going too fast but she was also aware that this is how it is with arranged marriages. Matter of fact, they happen even quicker than this. Ally was able to take her time only because of Sam's fellowship or else they would have been married by now.

She thought to herself, 'If her parents invited his family for the party he must have given some indication to his family that he wants to marry her and his mom must have said something to her mom.'

This was stressing Ally internally....

As she was sitting there eating lunch with Sam, she could feel her phone buzzing away to glory. She pretended to take a tissue out of her purse just so she could see who was texting her. There was a text from Talia and there were five texts from Ary. Of course, she couldn't check any of them at the moment but she could tell that Ary was passed anxious and straight into neuroses.

They both finished their lunch and were waiting for the waiter to come with their check, "is there anything else you would like?" Asked Sam.

"No, I'm stuffed. You were right, their burgers are really good!" Exclaimed Ally.

Seconds later the waiter arrived with the check. Sam looked at the check and took cash out quickly as the waiter was picking up their plates. "I'm sorry but we are in a bit of hurry so here is the money. You can keep the change."

"Sure no problem, thank you," replied the waiter, taking the money from Sam.

Sam and Ally then got up and walked out.

"I didn't want to wait for the guy to return for the money. Who knows how long it would have taken him," explained Sam when they stepped out of the diner.

"Yeah I know, it's very busy in there," agreed Ally.

Sam excitedly grabbed Ally's hand. "So, ready for our hike?"

Ally was seeing a different side of Sam. She had never seen him be so excited before.

"Yes, I am!" She exclaimed enthusiastically.

Sam grabbed his backpack from the trunk of his car and led the way. They both walked into the woods as they admired the beauty of the nature. They came to a stream surrounded by rocks.

"Want to take a break?" He asked.

"Sure," replied Ally.

Sam sat on one of the rocks as Ally gazed at the stream.

"This is so beautiful," Ally said, as she looked at the sky.

"Yes it is," Sam agreed, as he grabbed Ally's hand and pulled her closer to him. She was a bit nervous. He put his arms around her waist as he sat on the rock and Ally stood close to him. He then stood up, looking at her as he held her tighter in his arms. Ally was uncomfortable at first but then she put her arms around him. He started kissing her behind her ear and down her neck. She felt the gentle touch of his lips on her skin. This made her feel weak in the knees and she experienced a tingling feeling all over her body. She held him tighter as he continued kissing down her neck, to her shoulders, and then back up. In the heat of the moment, the weakness was overcoming. Then he kissed her on the lips. She kissed him back. Everything around them became silent as both of their lips locked, their tongues melding. He slowly moved his fingers lightly down her neck and to her collar bone, then shifted his hands to inside her t-shirt, up her back and unstrapped her bra. He slowly lifted her t-shirt and started kissing her breasts. Ally felt the chills on her back as he kissed her stomach and then unbuttoned her shorts. He put his hand inside her shorts. Ally became weaker and weaker with every touch. She could feel his member through his shorts getting harder and harder. She couldn't resist...she started unbuttoning his shorts and then massaged his pulsing member. He sat on the rock and pulled her closer to him. He pulled down her shorts and panties then pulled his shorts down. She then sat on him gently. She felt the warmth of his manhood going into her slowly. He held her tighter as he thrusted his shaft deeper and deeper into her. With each thrust, Ally moaned in pleasure, tossing her head back. She was enjoying the pleasures of being rocked back and forth... "Doc sure paid attention to his human anatomy class!" She thought....

She suddenly heard someone in the woods. She gestured him to stop. He was really into the moment, enjoying himself, and didn't understand what she was trying to say. Then she whispered in his ear, "I think someone is coming."

He immediately stopped. Neither one of them would want to get caught having sex in the woods. They both stood up and quickly zipped their shorts. While Ally was fixing her t-shirt the rustling of the branches got louder as if someone was right behind them. Sam and Ally looked at each other as she tried to fix her bra and Sam was standing in front of her to cover her. He could see and hear the branches bending and then out comes a grey squirrel. Sam and Ally slowly looked at each other and then started laughing. The squirrel was startled at the human presences and darted away.

"This thing is what killed the mood!" Exclaimed Sam.

"At least be glad it wasn't anyone else," said Ally, through her laughter.

"Ugh, just when it was getting good," said Sam as he grabbed Ally at her waist to hold her.

"Should we continue?" He asked as he looked into her eyes.

"I think the squirrel kind of ruined it," said Ally with a smile, as she put her bag on her shoulder.

"Oh well, then I just might have to spend the night with you tonight," joked Sam, picking up his bag.

"We'll see," said Ally flirtatiously.

As they started to walk Ally could feel her phone buzzing. She didn't want to check it but it just wouldn't stop buzzing. Sam could also feel the buzzing as his arm was around her.

"Your phone is buzzing a lot, maybe you should check it," he said concerned.

Ally didn't want to, thinking it may be Ary. "No, it's ok. I'm here with you and whoever is texting can wait," she replied.

They continued walking with his arm around her waist. The phone kept buzzing, "I really think you should answer. It's ok. What if someone really is trying to get hold of you?" Said Sam.

Ally really didn't want to check but she agreed. "Ok." She said as she nervously opened her bag and looked at her phone. She had several texts and calls from Mirlande. There were voicemails also.

"That's strange," Ally said, looking concerned.

"What's wrong?" Asked Sam.

"It's my friend Mirlande. She's the one who's been texting so much, asking me to call her. Let me check my voicemail." Said Ally as she started listening to the voicemail. As she heard her friend's message, the look on her face transformed into extreme worry. She took the phone away from her ear and she started walking fast, with tears coming down her cheek.

"Sorry but we have to get back, I need to go to the hospital!"

Sam kept pace with her. "What's wrong?" He asked very concerned.

"I don't know what's wrong. Mirlande said Talia is in the hospital!" Exclaimed Ally…and then they both started running

They both reached the car in no time.

"Which hospital?" He asked.

"The Suburban," replied Ally.

Sam started driving while Ally tried to call Mirlande. She kept calling but there was no answer. Sam tried to comfort her by holding her hand. The phone rang. It was Mirlande.

"Is she ok, what's wrong?" Asked Ally without even saying hello.

"She's not conscious right now and I really don't know what happened to her…" Before Mirlande could give further details, she told Ally that she had to go and hung up quickly.

This made Ally even more scared and nervous. "I wonder what happened!"

"What did Mirlande say?" Sam asked, trying to keep his eyes on the road but wanting to also comfort Ally.

"She doesn't know what happened to her. All she said was that Talia was not conscious and will tell me everything when I get there. She had to go so hung up the phone. She was crying," Ally replied with tears rolling down her cheeks.

Sam was feeling bad and wanted to pull over to console her but he also needed to drive fast so they could get to the hospital.

After a long car drive, Ally and Sam arrived at the hospital. They both ran to the elevator…

"Why don't you go see Mirlande in the waiting room and I'll go speak to the attending physician," Sam said as he rushed out of the elevator.

Ally entered the waiting room and found Mirlande pacing back and forth. As soon as Mirlande saw Ally, she came over and hugged her.

"So, what happened to her, is she ok?" Asked Ally.

"I don't know. She and I had planned to meet at the café. Initially, we were going to drive separately and meet at the café but then I called her and told her that I had to stop at the post office to pick up my package so I would just pick her up on my way. It was busy at the post office so it took me longer than I expected. I called Talia to let her know that I was going to be a little late but she didn't pick up the phone so I left her a message. It took me an hour by the time I got to her place. I called her from the car letting her know I was waiting for her outside but she didn't pick up the phone. I waited a couple of minutes and called her again. Again, she didn't pick up. I found that to be strange, especially when she knew I was picking her up. So, I went to her apartment and rang the doorbell. She didn't answer I rang it a couple more times and, when she didn't answer, I pressed other doorbells hoping someone would buzz me in. I got lucky when someone did. I went to her apartment and found her door was opened slightly. I called her name as I opened the door, my heart was pounding. I found her passed out on the floor all bruised and bloody like she was beaten. I checked to see if she was breathing and, thank God she was, but barely. I immediately called 911 and tried to see if there was anyone in the hallway who could help.

"I was following the ambulance to the hospital when I called you."

Mirlande started crying profusely, looking down. "It was my fault, I took too long to pick her up. If I had been there earlier maybe this wouldn't have happened."

Ally grabbed Mirlande by the shoulders and looked her in the eyes, "Listen to me, this wasn't your fault! Whatever happened to Talia, we both need to be strong for her! Do you have any idea who did this to her?"

Mirlande nodded and wiped the tears from her cheeks. "No, the police asked other tenants in the building if they had heard anything or seen anyone but most of the tenants weren't home and those who were said they hadn't heard anything," she replied.

"Who could have done this to her? I don't remember her saying anything about any of her cases being really bad to the point she was being threatened or feeling her life was in danger. Did she say anything to you?" Asked Ally.

"No, I haven't talked to either one of you since our dinner," replied Mirlande.

"Have you seen her yet?" Asked Ally.

"No, they're still working on her so they won't let me see her."

"Sam came with me and he works here. He went to talk to the attending doctor so hopefully he will come soon and let us know what's going on."

They both then started pacing, not really saying anything to each other. Ally looked at her watch then texted Sam. After a few minutes, Sam came into the waiting room. Ally rushed up to him and Mirlande followed.

"Did you see her? How is she?" Questioned Ally.

Sam put his arm around Ally shoulders. "The doctors are still doing some tests and she is still unconscious. It looks like she had been hit on the head a few times which led to a subdural hematoma and loss of consciousness. She's having a CT scan done to see how bad the damage may be," Sam replied in a concerned tone.

"Oh my God! I wonder who could have done this to her?" Said Ally furiously.

Sam continued to hold Ally but turned to Mirlande. "You must be Mirlande? Hi, I am Sam. Sorry we had to meet like this," Sam pulled away from Ally and gave Mirlande a comforting hug.

Mirlande just let him hold her as she was unable to speak. Just then the doctor walked in, "I have some good news...your friend is up but she is still a bit confused as to where she is. You may go see her. It might help her to see familiar faces but just don't ask her too many questions right now. Give her some time to gain consciousness properly. Normally I wouldn't allow visitors so quickly but because you ladies are friends of Sam, I am allowing it," the doctor related.

Ally, Mirlande, and Sam followed the doctor to see Talia. When they got to the ICU, Sam told Ally and Mirlande to go see her while he talked to the doctor. The two ladies walked over to Talia, both on either side of their friend.

"Hey, Talia, it's Ally and Mirlande," Ally said as she took Talia's hand and Mirlande held the other.

Talia shook her head a little, unable to speak as she was still groggy and unsure of what was happening. Talia opened her eyes for a few seconds then closed them again.

Sam walked over to the girls. "She's not completely awake yet. Give her some time to get her bearings," he said.

"Did the test results come back?" Asked Ally.

"Not all but the best news is that the MRI looks good so we don't have to worry about any brain damage," replied Sam.

"Oh, thank God!" Exclaimed Mirlande.

"So she should be able to recover quickly then right?" Questioned Ally.

"Not sure as of yet, we need to still wait for the other test results to come back to see if she has any other internal damages. She was beaten badly," Sam answered.

Both girls were happy that she didn't have any brain damage but concerned that there may still be other injuries.

"I'm going to go home and take a shower. I switched my shift with the doctor that will be coming in tonight. That way I will be able to keep an eye on her all night," said Sam. Ally nodded her head ok and thanked him for doing that.

After Sam left the room, Mirlande looked over at Ally and said, "He is really nice."

"Yes, he is," agreed Ally as she admiringly watched Sam as he walked away.

The girls turned around and looked at Talia who was continuing to wake up. Gradually, her eyes opened, then she saw the girls standing next to her. Mirlande and Ally smiled at Talia.

"Hello," they both said in unison.

Talia tried to smile and say hello to the girls but her face was a bit swollen.

"How are you feeling?" Asked Ally.

"I don't know," replied Talia, still a bit dazed.

"Who did this to you?" Asked Mirlande.

"My ex-husband," replied Talia.

"What?!! You never told us you were married!" Exclaimed Ally, shocked by the news.

"I guess, just like you, I too have a past which I wanted to forget. But it finally caught up with me," Talia said.

Just when Ally was about to say something, the doctor came over and asked the ladies if they would wait in the waiting room for a few minutes while they perform some more tests on Talia. The girls told Talia they would be back, squeezed her hands, and then walked away.

"I wonder who this bastard is who did this to her!" Exclaimed Mirlande angrily as soon as they stepped into the waiting room.

"I am sure we will get all of our questions answered soon and as soon as we know about him then we will make sure he pays for what he has done to her," said Ally, very upset.

Mirlande sat on the chair holding her head, thinking.

"I need to use the bathroom, I will be right back," said Ally.

Mirlande nodded her head ok.

Ally walked into the restroom which was on the other side of the waiting room. After she entered the restroom she turned her phone back on to check her messages. She had turned off the phone when she had entered the hospital. She then washed her face as she waited for the phone to get turned on. She heard texts coming through. It was Ary asking her to call him. Ally just stood there, looking at her image in the mirror. She was not very strong when it came to Ary. The mixed feelings she had for him were getting the best of her. As she was standing there thinking, her phone rang and it was Ary. She debated whether to answer or not...she answered.

"Hello," she said.

"Hey, where have you been? I called and texted you several times and you didn't any of them! Let me guess you were busy with your boyfriend?" Said Ary sarcastically.

Ally could sense that he was jealous but she really didn't want to deal with it at this time.

"I'm at the hospital right now. Talia' ex-husband physically abused her and she is in bad shape."

"Oh my god, is she alright?! I didn't even know she was married," Ary said, very concerned. He and Talia had become good friends especially after Talia found out about him and Ally.

"She just regained consciousness. The doctor is doing some tests so I'm waiting to go back in to see her."

"Which hospital is she in? I want to come see her."

"She is at Suburban hospital but I think you should give her sometime before you come to visit her. Maybe tomorrow will be a better day."

"Ok, if you say so. How are you holding up?"

Before she could reply, Mirlande knocked on the door letting her know that they can go back to see her now.

"Ok, will be right out," Ally called out to Mirlande.

"I have to go now, will call you when I get a chance." She hung up the phone and left the bathroom.

She and Mirlande walked over to Talia's room. As they walked closer to Talia they could see her waving them hello and smiling at them. They both smiled back as they approached her bed.

"Did the doctor say anything?" Asked Ally.

"No, just said they need to wait for some more blood work," replied Talia.

"We are so glad you are ok, who did this to you?" Mirlande said as she started crying because she could no longer hold back her tears.

Talia was bruised horribly all over her body. She even had cuts on her eye brows. Her upper lip and right eye were swollen. Her left leg was broken and was in a cast. Her left arm was in a sling but it wasn't broken, she had a dislocated shoulder.

"Hey, I am alright, please don't cry," said Talia looking at Mirlande.

"So, Talia, you said something before about the person who did this to. You said it was your ex-husband. Who is this guy and why did he hurt you?" Mirlande asked, shaking with outrage.

"My doorbell rang so I assumed it was you since you were on your way to pick me up. When I opened the door my jaw just dropped, it was my ex-husband."

Mirlande and Ally stood in shocked silence, not knowing what to say.

Talia looked at Ally. "As I started saying before, just like you, I have a past which I never want to think about and just want to forget. I left that life behind and moved here to begin again," Talia continued, "Matt and I met when we were just teenagers. His parents knew my parents so that was just perfect. My family also loved him because he was Jewish. It was their dream come true. They always wanted me to find someone who was Jewish (just like your parents want you to find a Muslim guy) and I did. We dated for couple of years then we got married at a very young age. I was very happy, he was happy and of course our families were happy.

"Our life was great, more than great, it was perfect and one day he and I were out shopping, he was looking at clothes in the men's section and I was in the women's. A man came up to me and needed help finding the right size for his wife. He was buying a gift for their anniversary and he wasn't sure if the size would be right for her. Matt saw me talking to him and came over. By that time, the man had walked away. Matt asked me if everything was ok. I told him that the man asked for my help to find the right size for his wife. Matt joked and said 'how do you really know he has a wife? You don't know men, they will come up with something just so they can talk to a pretty lady.' He said. I really didn't think anything of it and thought it was cute that he was jealous. There were few other times where he showed his jealousy. I just kept thinking it was cute.

"Then, one day we were at a party, a few of us were sitting at a table and talking about old movies. Someone mentioned the movie Indecent Proposal. A friend of Matt's asked him what if someone offered him money to sleep with your wife. I don't know exactly what happened with that conversation because I was busy talking to a friend of mine and all of a sudden I saw Matt getting into a physical fight with his friend. From that day on, I started to pay more attention to him. I didn't find his jealousy to be cute any more. He started becoming very possessive of me. I was afraid to talk to any man for the fear of him hurting the person. He started keeping an eye on everything I was doing and he started becoming more religious.

"I told my parents about it and they thought it was great he was becoming religious. They were really happy about it but they just didn't hear what I was saying about him being possessive. He then would only hang out with Jewish friends and not anyone else. I was feeling so claustrophobic in my marriage. I didn't know what to do, who to talk to since my parents wouldn't listen.

"One day I went to talk to his mom, who was really a sweet lady. When I told her how her son had changed it didn't surprise her at all. It turned out that Matt's dad was the same way. She told me she married him at a very young age and had kids right after their marriage so she didn't get a chance to educate herself. She advised me to leave her son. I couldn't believe that his mother was telling me to leave her son when my own mother didn't even hear what I was saying. His mom told me if he was anything like his dad then I needed to be afraid of him and leave him. She said that she would never want any girl to go through what she had gone through. She hoped her son didn't get his dad's genes but my telling her about him made her realize he did. She said it's too late for her to leave his dad. She had learned to endure through her experiences because of her children but I was young and didn't have any kids so it's easier for me to walk away. She told me she would help me anyway possible. I told her I would ask for divorce. She said not to make that mistake. She told me to leave the city, go far away somewhere he wouldn't know where to find me. Then from there to file for divorce.

"I was really scared and didn't know what to do. My parents were just not listening, yet, I was glad I had his mom on my side. I thought and thought hard for weeks of where I would go and how I would file for divorce. One day it just came to me. I decided to go to law school so I started studying for my GREs without him knowing about it. I also started saving money slowly without him suspecting anything. His mother also helped me by giving me money without her husband knowing about it. I then started applying to different colleges. I didn't care which college as long as it was away from where he was. I opened up a P.O box so he wouldn't know what I was doing. It was a very long year for me and with his mom's help I came here. I asked his mom to explain what her son is like to my parents and make them understand but not to do that until I leave. I didn't want to take any chance of them screwing it up for me while I was still there. I filed for divorce shortly after I arrived here. It was a long and hard process for me but the divorce finally came through," Talia looked down at her hands. "I don't know who would have told him where I was. That's the question I am asking myself since I woke up in the hospital. I hope his mom is ok, I am worried about her.

"So, you see Ally, just because you marry someone of the same religion doesn't mean you will marry a nice guy. When you told me about how your parents were towards Ary I couldn't stop thinking about my life. I just couldn't make myself tell you about my life because I wanted to forget it but now I can't. Now I will fuck his life over and he won't know what hit him."

Talia was justifiably very upset while telling her story.

"Did you tell the doctor who it is that did this to you? I'm sure they asked," Questioned Ally.

"No, they haven't asked me yet and I need to play this correctly to make sure he gets what he deserves," Talia replied, the lawyer in her coming out.

While the girls were talking, Sam came over to see them. Ally formally introduced Sam to Talia. "It's nice to meet you but I wish it wasn't under these circumstances," he turned to the other ladies. "Talia needs to rest and you ladies need to go home and get some rest also. You can come and visit her tomorrow. Don't worry I will be here for the next 48 hours so I will make sure she is well taken care of," he said.

The girls thanked him. They we very tired and they knew she was in good hands, so they took his advice and decided to go home. They both said goodnight to Talia and told her if she needed anything to have Sam call either one of them. Sam walked the girls out of the ICU.

"I'll get the elevator," Mirlande told Ally, realizing that she needed to give the two of them some alone time.

After Mirlande walked away, Ally turned to Sam and thanked him again.

Sam smiled and hugged her. "You don't need to thank me. Get some rest and don't worry about Talia. I will take extra care of her," he said then he kissed her on the forehead as he heard the bell for the elevator ring. The two ladies got into the elevator and left the hospital.

Ally went in Mirlande's car since she came to the hospital with Sam. On their way home, Ally finished telling Mirlande the story about Ary and her. Everything that Talia was going to tell Mirlande but didn't get the chance to.

Chapter 6

Long Evening

After a long busy day at work, Ally was going to the hospital to visit Talia. She wasn't able to call Sam to get a report on Talia because she had a full schedule. She had texted Sam earlier in the morning asking him how she was doing and letting him know that she wasn't going to be able to talk until she was done with her work. She didn't receive any response from Sam so she figured he may be busy at work.

As she was leaving her office she noticed that she had a missed call and a text from Sam asking her to call him. Unfortunately, she hadn't been able to check her phone until she was done with all her appointments. She became very concerned and called Sam. He didn't respond. She then texted Mirlande letting her know that she was leaving for the hospital. A Few minutes later, Mirlande responded stating that she was at the hospital already. Ally called Mirlande, but her friend didn't pick up the phone. When she reached the ICU she saw Sam talking to another doctor. He waved hello and gestured her to wait as he finished his conversation with his colleague.

He came over after he finished his conversation, gave her a kiss on the cheek.

"How is Talia doing?" Asked Ally.

"I need to talk to you about her. I'm sorry I haven't been able to respond to you all morning. I did receive your texts and did eventually respond but I'm sure you were busy too. Last night Talia had some complications. She developed a blood clot and went into a cardiac arrest. She was operated on and she is doing much better. When you didn't answer this morning, I called Mirlande to inform her and we also informed her family. They should be arriving soon," Sam revealed.

Ally felt so bad that she didn't know all of this had happened. "Why didn't you call me when it happened?" She asked.

"It actually happened around 3am and we had been working on her until I had the time to reach out to you. When you didn't pick up I called Mirlande. Luckily, we had gotten her family's information from her before this happened to be able to contact them," Sam said.

"How is she doing now? Can I go see her?" Asked Ally petrified.

"You could see her but she is not awake yet. Mirlande is in the waiting room and is very stressed out. Why don't you go see her first then both of you can go see Talia? I have to go see another patient and as soon as I am done I will come to see you."

"Alright, thank you, I will go see Mirlande."

As Ally entered the waiting room she saw Mirlande sitting there massaging her forehead. When she saw Ally, Mirlande stood up and hugged her friend. "I'm so glad you came. Talia went into cardiac arrest…"

Before Mirlande could finish telling her, Ally interrupted… "I just saw Sam and he told me. I feel horrible. I was so busy with my work that I didn't hear about it until just now."

"There was nothing you could have done even if you were here earlier. I came here after Sam called and I haven't been able to see Talia. Her family is on their way here too. I just want to kill her ex-husband for doing this to her," said Mirlande, clenching her fists.

"Yeah I know. I do too!" Exclaimed Ally as she clasped her hands to her chest.

"I want to go see her." Ally turned to pick up her purse from the chair.

"Ok, we'll go together. She is still not awake though," said Mirlande as they both walked out of the waiting room.

They made their way into the ICU and saw Talia hooked to different machines.

"I hate seeing her like this." Ally shook her head and gently took Talia's hand. She bent forward and softly whispered, "Hello Talia, can you hear me?" She didn't receive any response from Talia.

"Don't worry she will be up soon," Sam quietly said from behind them. "There's no place for anyone to sit here so let's go into the waiting room, the nurse will come get us when she wakes up."

Ally nodded her head yes then the three of them went to the waiting room.

In the waiting room Sam made the girls comfortable on the sofa… "You guys had a long day, I will go get you ladies something to eat from the cafeteria."

Ally smiled and thanked Sam. She knew he was tired too since he worked all night but didn't express it. Sam left the girls alone.

"He's very nice." Said Mirlande.

"Yes, he is." Agreed Ally.

"So why do you want to have Ary around in your life when you have found someone who is so nice?" Questioned Mirlande.

"Revenge my friend, revenge!" Exclaimed Ally.

"What do you mean?" Asked Mirlande, a bit confused.

"I want to get back at him for what he did. I want to …" before she could finish her sentence she saw Ary coming towards the waiting room.

"Speaking of the devil," said Ally as she pointed towards him.

Mirlande turned and saw him coming. "That's him? What is he doing here?" She asked.

"I am guessing he is here to see Talia," replied Ally.

"Hmm, maybe Talia is an excuse?" Said Mirlande.

"Who knows, I don't care," said Ally, shrugging her shoulders.

"Hey what about Sam? He is going to be back soon. Are you going to be ok with both of them here?"

"Oooh…I completely forgot about Sam for a second there…"

Before Ally could finish, Ary walked into the waiting room and greeted Ally with a kiss. "Hi Ally, the nurse told me you were here."

"Hi Ary." Ally pulled back and gestured toward Mirlande, "This is my friend Mirlande."

"Hello Mirlande, Talia has told me so much about you," he said as he took her hand and warmly shook it.

Mirlande smiled and said hi. For a second Mirlande forgot about being upset with him as she was flourished with his charming personality. It only took a "hello" from him for Mirlande to realize why Ally fell for him. There was something about him that women liked. It wasn't his looks so it may just be the way he carries himself. He does have such a smooth voice that could make women swoon.

"How is Talia doing?" He asked.

"She went into cardiac arrest last night and isn't awake as of yet. We are just waiting."

As Ally was talking to Ary, Mirlande saw that Sam was coming back with a tray of food. She then quickly interrupted their conversation, "Why don't I take you to see Talia?" She suggested, as she raised her eyebrows to Ally and grasped Ary's elbow.

Ally was a bit confused but then saw Sam coming down the hall. She quickly said, "Yes, why don't you guys go see her. I will stay here since there is not enough space for the three of us in the ICU." Mirlande quickly walked out of the room with Ary.

Ary was hoping to go with Ally but he obviously couldn't say that to Mirlande. That would have been too rude. The girls actually didn't even give Ary a chance to say anything.

As soon as the two left, Sam walked into the waiting room, "I have some great news! While I was at the cafeteria I got a call from the police. They tracked down her ex-husband and arrested him!" He exclaimed.

"Oh my god, that's great! I wish I could go beat the shit out of him for hurting Talia," said Ally angrily.

"Yes, we all would like to do that but unfortunately we can't. I guarantee you, he will pay for what he has done,"

Assured Sam as he put the tray of food down on the table and hugged Ally, and just stood there holding her.

Ally melted into his arms. "I just want to thank you for taking extra care of Talia. I was able to sleep last night knowing that you were here watching her. I am so glad you are working when all this is going on. I wish it had never happened but at least I am glad you are here at the right time. I knew I was going to introduce you to my best friends but never thought it was going to be under such circumstances." Ally said as she held him.

Just then Ary rushed into the room and saw them holding each other. His face turned a bit red with jealousy seeing the two of them locked in arms. Ally left Sam's arms and turned as she heard the door open.

"Talia is awake." Ary said, looking at Sam angrily. Ally's and Sam's faces lit up as they hurried out of the room.

Ary followed them with a scowl on his face. He knew he had no right to say anything to Ally because he too had someone in his life but, as a man, he couldn't help himself being upset to see Ally with someone else. There was a part of him that felt like Ally was still his possession, even now. The chauvinist pig in him thought it was alright for him to be with another woman but how could she be with some other man?

All three walked into the ICU. Usually this many people were not allowed in the ICU at one time but because of Sam being the doctor they were able to get away with it. Mirlande looked at Ally all happy but Talia was still very groggy. Ally gently held Talia's hand and smiled at her as Mirlande stood on the other side holding Talia's other hand. Talia tried to smile and say hi but couldn't. Ally looked at Sam with a questioning look.

He knew that look. "Give her just a little more time as she's trying to wake up."

Meanwhile, Ary was standing there feeling very awkward and angry. At this point, neither Ally nor Mirlande were paying attention to the dynamics of the situation. They were engrossed with Talia status. After some time, Ary turned to Ally, "I think I will take off now."

Just then, the nurse came over to Talia's bedside, "Excuse me doctor but I need to draw some blood and check her vitals."

Sam nodded and made a gesture toward Talia "Yes, go right ahead…in the meantime, we will be in the waiting room." He escorted the girls to the waiting room for the second time.

After they entered the room, they turned to each other. "What do you think? How does she look to you?" Ally asked Sam.

"She is still very groggy but she will be more, if not completely, awake in a little while. She should recover in no time with the right support and treatments," replied Sam.

Ally sighed in relief but her anger flared up again. "I am so glad the police caught the bastard!"

"They did?!" Mirlande and Ary asked simultaneously.

"Yes, they did and he was arrested. I'm sure he will be punished for what he has done," replied Sam.

Sam looked at Ary, offering his hand. "I am sorry. I don't think we have met?"

"Oh sorry, Sam, this is Ary. Ary, this is Sam," Ally introduced the two men, without mentioning her relationship with the two of them. Ally continued, "Ary has a business on the same floor as Talia's so they became friends." Both men shook hands.

Ary wanted to strangle Sam but he kept his cool. He looked at the two ladies, "I think I will take off now. I will come see her again tomorrow when she is feeling a little better and is up for visitors. Please let her know I stopped by and will come see her tomorrow."

"Ok, thank you for coming," Ally said.

"Let me know if there is anything you need, I am just a phone call away," said Ary.

Ally smiled and replied, "I will and thank you again."

Ary then purposely kissed Mirlande and Ally on the cheek, nodded at Sam and walked way. He wasn't happy seeing Sam and, of course, Ally could see that but that wasn't a problem. Her attitude was, if he can be with someone else why can't she?

Sam received a page, he looked at Ally. "I have to go. It's getting late and Talia needs to rest so why don't you ladies go home and get some rest also? I will be done with my shift in an hour and I will check on Talia before I leave. I'll let the doctor on duty know to call me directly if there is a problem."

"Ok," Ally responded to Sam as she looked at Mirlande for confirmation. Mirlande agreed, so all three of them walked out together. Sam went to answer his call and the girls went to say goodbye to Talia.

Chapter 7

Mom's Phone Call

It was early one morning, after a long week of work and checking in on Talia. Ally had just finished making her breakfast and, as she sat down to eat, the phone rang. "Salam Ammie (hello mom)," Ally said as she answered the phone.

"What is going on with you? You haven't called in few days?" Inquired her mom.

"I have been very busy at work and Talia was in the hospital so I was busy with her also," Ally replied.

"Is she ok? What happened?"

"It's a long story. Will tell you about it later but the short version is that she had an "accident" and, at the moment, she's trying to recover," explained Ally, knowing that her mom was asking just for the sake of asking.

Her mom couldn't beat around the bush so she got straight to the point of why she called, "What is going on between you and Sameer? Haven't you made your decision yet?" She didn't even pause for a moment. "His mom tells me that he is ready to marry you but it's you who is taking your time. You know, you really are embarrassing your family. Both of your brothers and sister married whomever we picked out for them and they only met them the night of their wedding. I can't believe your father has allowed you to get to know Sameer for such a long time. Enough is enough, I am not listening to your father or you anymore. You need to say yes now and that's it. You are not getting any younger. You should be lucky you are able to get a decent boy at your age. There are much younger girls he can choose from but he is all right with you." Her mom was sounded really angry.

"You know, Ammie, this is my life and it's a big decision, I really want to make sure we are right for each other," Ally responded exasperatedly.

"What do you mean? Why can't you be like your siblings? Why do you always have to be difficult? It's your father's fault you are like this, he has spoiled you too much." Her mom scolding her.

"What do you mean, be like my siblings? You mean I should just let you pick whomever you think is right for me? Have you not seen their marriages? All three of them have problems! Both of my brothers don't get along with their wives and would have gotten a divorce by now if you guys had not interfered and forced them to stay married. They are not even happy together and fight all the time but yet you are happy because they stayed married. And my sister? She is married to a controlling freak who doesn't give her any freedom to do anything. That's alright with you?" Questioned Ally angrily.

"What's wrong with your sister, she has never complained?" Replied her mom.

"What are you talking about? When he gets angry with her he stops her from calling you or coming over to see you. She keeps her mouth shut because you have put it in her head that once a girl leaves her father's house no matter what she can't return and should do what the husband wants. What is that? Even in this day and age you believe that. She is so insecure about herself that she can't even say anything to her husband. He has become so religious and forces her and the kids to follow a certain life style which she doesn't want." Ally paced back and forth, waving her free hand.

"What are you talking about? She is happy following Islam. At least she is following God's path and will go to heaven. What about you? Do you even know how to read your namaz (prayers in Islam)? Because of you, your parents are going to go to hell. At least we did something right with your sister. She hasn't shamed her parents like you have. I can't believe you had gotten involved with a Hindu boy. A Hindu! If he had converted we would have been fine with it but that wasn't the case. Now you have this chance, hope you didn't say anything to Sameer about your past? I don't want anyone to know about your past. It will make it hard for us to find you someone. Sameer and his family will be coming for the party tonight so come over before the guests come. I really wanted to have your engagement ceremony but of course you still have to think about it. In my times girls didn't get a choice. The families met and if they liked the boy or the girl that's it, an engagement was done then the wedding followed shortly." Her mom ranted all in one breath without even giving Ally any chance to say anything.

"Well, are you there? Do you have anything to say?"

"Yes, I am still here. What do you want me to say? You are not letting me say anything," replied Ally being fed up with the conversation.

"Listen, your father is getting stressed out. He already had a couple of heart attacks because of you. If anything happens to him again you will not have a family," her mom stated coldly.

Ally was about to say something but she got another call. It was her sister.

"Are you getting another call?" Her mother squawked.

"Yes, it's Appa (that's what Ally called her older sister)," replied Ally.

"Why don't you answer it, I have to go anyways and make sure you come before the guests arrive," her mom demanded and then hung up the phone.

"Hello Appa," said Ally as she answered her sister's call. She really didn't want to talk to her because it was never good when her mom and sister called around the same time. It usually meant they were cooking up something.

"What are you doing?" Asked her sister, named Zara.

"I was just talking to Ammie," replied Ally, knowing for fact that her sister was aware of their mom calling her.

"Oh, why don't you finish talking to her then call me back?" Said Zara.

"No, she is done talking." Ally sighed.

"You are coming for the party tonight, right?" Zara knew for a fact she was.

"Yes, I am." Ally rolled her eyes since she knew the game Zara was playing. In Zara's mind Ally was her little sister who needed to be told what to do. She always felt like she was smarter than Ally but that wasn't the case. Ally was much smarter than her. There was a part of Ally that felt bad for

Zara because of the way her life turned out, so she let her sister believe that she was oblivious to everything.

"So, have you made a decision about Sameer? I really want a wedding in our family."

Bam! That was the question Ally was waiting for her sister to ask. She knew sooner or later in the conversation it was going to come up. She knew their mom put her up to this.

"No, not yet," replied Ally thinking of ways to end the conversation with her sister.

"What are you waiting for? I heard he is nice boy. I am really surprised Ammie and Baba (their father) actually are letting you get to know him. When they set up your brother-in-law with me all they said was that they spoke to his parents and they all agreed to the marriage. Ammie and Baba asked me if I was ok with their decision. I was young and didn't know what to say. I figured they were my parents and they knew what was best for me so I said yes," said Zara.

The conversation was making Ally uncomfortable. She could sense the jealousy in her sister's tone but she had to appear as if she was the perfect one and did what she was told to do by her parents.

"And are you happy with your life?" Asked Ally sarcastically knowing the truth.

"I got used to him and I have kids now," replied Zara.

There was a seven years age difference between Ally and Zara. Although Zara had always been nice to Ally, they didn't spend much time together. By the time Ally had become a teenager and lost her "babiness", her sister was married. Ally actually grew up like an only child because of the huge age difference between her and her siblings, who represented a different generation. Ally was always treated like a little princess and was taken care of by her siblings. But things were different after she started dating Ary.

"You didn't answer my question, are you happy with your life?" Ally asked again trying to prove something to her.

"Ok, I have to go now. Just called to see if you were coming tonight. I heard Sameer and his family are coming tonight. Maybe you can surprise everyone with your decision," Zara said, dodging her sister's question.

"Alright, I'll see you tonight." Ally took this as an opportunity to end the conversation and hung up the phone.

Ally knew exactly why her sister called. Zara was their mom's puppet. Mommy dear was trying to have the sister assist Ally in expediting the decision making process. They still thought of Ally as a kid and were in denial of the fact that she was an adult now and that they could not manipulate her. Most of the time, Ally played along with it unless it was something that affected her. It was hard for Ally to take any advice from her sister because as nice as her sister was, she felt Zara was very insecure as a person.

"Zara never stood up for herself and was a people pleaser. She strived to be the perfect daughter, sister, and wife so she did things just so that people didn't think badly of her. Ally didn't respect her at all. She didn't like Zara letting her husband control her life. Ally always believed there was a difference between doing things for your significant other out of love and care than because of fear. Ally's brother-in-law didn't ask for her sister's opinion on anything in their marriage nor could she even question him about what he did or said. For those reasons, she can't trust her sister's opinions, especially regarding relationships.

"One night, before Ally had ever met Ary and she was still living with her parents, her sister had stayed over at their house when her husband was out of town. She told Ally that she would never wish her life onto anyone and that she would make sure her daughters' lives would never be like hers. Ally had felt bad for her then but couldn't understand why she wouldn't become strong enough to leave her husband. At that time, Ally was young and didn't know that their parents would have never supported Zara's decision of leaving her husband, especially because she had kids.

"In the Indian culture, it is difficult for a divorced woman to remarry, let alone a divorced woman with kids. So her sister remained in a marriage that existed without any respect or love from her husband. Well, for whatever reason that was the choice Zara had made but Ally wished her sister would stop listening to their mother and be the sister, and friend, that she really needed. Now, Ally had Talia and Mirlande in her life to fill the void, but there were things in her culture that they could not understand.

Just as she was sitting on her bed thinking about all of this, she started crying. Thinking how alone she felt even though she had people in her life. She wished she had someone who really understood her and her desires. Just then the doorbell rang. She wiped her tears and went to answer the door, puzzled at who it could be. She asked who it was on the intercom and to her surprise, it was Ary.

"Hi Ally, sorry I came without calling, something just told me to come over so…here I am."

"Come on in," said Ally as she buzzed him in. There was part of her that was actually glad to see him, for that one second she forgot about everything.

"Are you ok? Looks like you were crying?" Asked Ary as he walked into the door a minute later.

"No, I am fine, I'm not crying." Ally felt her cheeks, checking to make sure she didn't have any tears on either.

"I may have been away from you for some time but don't forget I am the only person in this world that knows you extremely well just like the way you know me and you can't fool me," said Ary with a smile, softly stroking her cheek.

Ally smiled back in agreement. "I was just talking to my mom and sister…"

Before she could finish her sentence Ary held up his hand…"Say no more! Let me guess, they were lecturing you about getting married and how you have shamed them by not getting married yet?!" Ary was being sarcastic. He couldn't stand her mom and sister because they didn't support Ally when she wanted to be with him.

"Listen Al (that's what he always called her), your mom and sister are very old fashioned minded people who don't want to move on with the time, especially your sister. I don't know why you let her get to you? You know what kind of life she has and she probably doesn't want you to have a better life than her so her attitude is "bitch my life is a hell, how could yours be better."

Ally smirked. "Oh stop it!"

Ary always knew how to cheer her up by telling the truth but in a way that made her laugh and made her understand what her family really was like. He could see she was feeling sad so he held her in his arms as if no one else existed in the world. Ally felt so comfortable in his arms that she too forgot about everyone. She put her head on his shoulder and they just held each other for few minutes. The two immersed in the comfort of one another's arms. He then slowly started kissing her on the back of her neck, she just closed her eyes and felt his lips touch her soft skin. He moved to her ears and then her cheeks. He gently kissed her on her lips while she moved her hands up his back. He pulled her closer and tighter. She could feel that he has aroused. He slowly picked her up and laid her down on the sofa as he continued kissing her. He gently slid his hand on to her breasts, holding them gently not know how she may react. She slowly moved her hands down his back and down to his butt. He pulled her top up, as he kissed her breasts. Ally closed her eyes in pleasure. He slowly moved down as he kissed her stomach. She sucked in her stomach as she felt the soft touch of his lips tickling her. He then unzipped her pants and pulled them off, Ally took her turn to help Ary take off his t-shirt. He turned her onto her stomach, kissing her butt as he gently fondled her breasts. He unzipped his pants, pushing them off, and slowly inserted his stiff member into the heart of her femininity. Their bodies became enjoined as one. Their movements reminiscent of an undulating wave. The comfort they both felt with each other was nothing like any other people they had been or were with. They forgot about everything and were lost in their one world together.

Just as they both were reaching climax, Ary's phone rang. He ignored it. The phone kept ringing, he stretched his hand out and turned off the ringer as he continued thrusting. The sweat of their bodies glistened like dew. Ary burrowed his face into Ally's neck as she arched her body to allow him to go deeper. She dug her fingers into the cushions beneath them. Their movements accelerated as Ary's thrusts quickened, explosive energy filling their minds. They reached climaxed together and collapsed into the sofa. Ary pulled his slowly shrinking organ out of Ally and flipped her on her back so that they faced each other. They laid on the sofa holding each other tightly.

Ally's phone started to ring just as Ary's phone started buzzing.

"Looks like someone really is trying to get hold of you," said Ally sarcastically.

Ary knew exactly what and who she was referring to and responded, "I guess so, and it looks like someone is trying to get hold of you as well." He then leaned in and gave her a kiss. He joked with a sideways grin, "friends with benefits!"

Ally laughed coyly and repeated, "Friends with benefits." They decided it was time to separate from each other and got up from the sofa. They went into the bathroom together to clean up. Ary sat on the toilet as Ally went to take shower. He stepped into the shower, "want some company?"

"Sure." Ally smiled, making room for him.

By this time, Ally had forgotten all about her problems with her family. Ary knew how to make her feel good, in more ways than one. After they cleaned off the smell of intimacy, they both came out of the shower and helped each other dry off, then put their clothes on. Ally checked her phone while Ary was using the bathroom. She had three missed calls from Sam and a text saying, "I am on my way to take you out for lunch." This text was fifteen minutes ago, she panicked and rushed to the bathroom, "Sam is on his way here, you need to go!" She exclaimed.

Ary became a bit jealous and upset. "I guess you would like me to leave now?" He said sarcastically.

"Yes, please!" Exclaimed Ally, as she tried to rush him out.

"Ok, ok I'm going. So, I take it you want to marry this man since your parents approve?" He asked, his tone a bit more angry.

"Listen, you are getting angry as if I was the one who cheated on you. Don't forget you have someone in your life and I am guessing you are going to marry her?" Said Ally, frustrated.

Just as they were both beginning their same old argument, the doorbell rang.

"Shit, he's here!" Ally became panicky.

"What are you going to do now?" Ary laid his head on her shoulder, looking up at her sheepishly.

"Hey! If you want us to continue being friends you better not do anything stupid. Stay in here until I figure out a way to get you out of here." Ally pushed Ary's head away and tried to tidy up the room quickly.

The doorbell rang again. "You better answer the doorbell before your husband-to-be gets upset." Ary laughed, enjoying the moment.

"You are an ass, you know that! Stay here until I come get you." She said as she closed the bathroom door. She then went to buzz Sam into the apartment.

"Hi, I called and texted you," Sam said as he kissed her.

"Yes, I just saw that. Sorry I was in the shower," Ally nervously replied.

They both walked into the living room. Sam held Ally in his arms tightly and hugged her. Ally was looking towards the bathroom over his shoulders and saw Ary through the cracks of the bathroom door making inappropriate hand gestures. Ary gestured jerking off as he silently laughed and pointed to Sam. Ally was getting angry. She didn't want Sam to catch him in the bathroom but she was also trying not laugh. That's the quality that she loved about Ary, as serious as he may appear he was also very boyish.

Sam was hoping to get some but it was too late, Ary had taken care of that. Ally quickly pulled away knowing what Sam's intentions were based on where his hands were moving, "I am starving, let's go for lunch!" She desperately tried saying it in a bright tone.

"Okay." Sam replied in a disappointing tone, hoping for something else at the moment.

"I'm just going to go use the bathroom quickly then we can head out, ok?" Ally ignored the look on Sam's face. She grabbed her purse and went into the bathroom, closing the door behind her.

"Aww, the poor guy was hoping to get lucky, now he is just standing there with his dick in his hand," whispered Ary, laughing softly.

"You will never change! We are going to go now, here is an extra key. Wait at least ten minutes after we leave then you can go. Just make sure you lock the door. I will get the key from you later," She whispered back to him.

"Whoa, you are giving me your key? Guess I can come over whenever I want now." Ary slyly grinned.

Ally pointed her finger in Ary's face, "Don't get smart, it's just this one time. I will be taking it back from you so don't get too excited." Ally then walked out of the bathroom, closing the door.

She grabbed Sam's arm and practically dragged him out of the apartment. "We could have just ordered in if you wanted?" Sam said, thinking of how horny he was at the moment.

"Oh that's ok, I actually would like to get some fresh air so I don't mind going out for lunch," replied Ally.

Poor Sam…he really wanted to get laid but in his mind he was thinking Ally was not getting any of his hints when in reality that's exactly what she was trying to avoid. Besides she was done for the day.

"What would you like to eat?" Sam asked, finally coming to terms that he wasn't getting any today.

"How about Chinese? You ok with that?" Suggested Ally.

"Chinese sounds great," replied Sam.

"I am sorry but I have to make it a quick lunch because my mom wants me to come early to help before the party," said Ally.

"Sure, we can eat quickly," Sam replied. In Buffalo, NY everything is within twenty minutes' drive.

A short time later, Sam and Ally are sitting across from each other in a local Chinese restaurant…

"So how is Talia doing since she has been home from the hospital?" Asked Sam as they both enjoyed their Hot and Sour Soup.

"Actually, her parents took her back home with them so they could take good care of her. As you know, she needs time to recover and her parents were not able to stay here for long so they thought it best that Talia recuperate with family around. They felt very bad for not understanding what she was going through in her marriage and they also realized how wrong they were about her ex-husband. Her mom said that much when she saw Talia's injuries and was thankful that she was alive. I want to thank you for taking such good care of her when she was in the hospital. It made me feel so much better when I was at work and couldn't be there with her all the time," Ally relayed, touching Sam's hand.

"No need to thank me, it's what I do. She is your best friend so of course I would give her more attention. I am just glad she is doing better and, yes, it will take her some time to get back to feeling like herself again. It's good that she is with her parents where there is someone with her all the time. That's what she really needs, she is not able to take care of herself right now." responded Sam.

Just as he finished his sentence, a little old lady brought their meal. It smelled so delicious that Ally couldn't stop breathing in the aroma.

"The food here is so good this is my favorite place to eat!" Said Ally as she smiled at the grandma.

The grandma spoke in her Chinese accent, "glad you enjoy it so much and I enjoy making it for everyone. My children are all grown up and all are so far away. I don't get to see them or cook for them any more so now I cook for the children of Buffalo. Enjoy your lunch now and let me know if you need anything else." She smiled and walked into the kitchen.

As they both served themselves Ally said, "I wonder if she really is as sweet with her kids as she is with us or she is like our moms who are so controlling and pushy."

Sam grinned. "Aren't Indian and Chinese parents the same? I mean, I think both cultures push their kids to succeed and want to make sure they don't screw up their lives. I guess in some ways we need to be thankful for them. I wonder if we would be as successful as we are today if they weren't the way they were."

"I know, but I also think that they don't allow us to grow as individuals. It has to be what they say, they don't let us make mistakes and learn from it. I understand they want to protect us and want us to be successful in life but they also control every part of our lives. They truly believe what they think is right for their kids. They think they know their children but in reality they only see what they want to see in their kids. They don't try to understand what their kids like or what they desire because they don't believe in that stuff. See, for you, it's a bit different because you are a guy. You have the freedom to go out and do whatever you want. You may not have chosen to go out but at least you had the choice. For me, being a girl, my parents were very strict.

"When I was really young, I could play with friends but as I got older and in high school I was expected to go to school and come straight home, no extra circular activities were allowed. They didn't believe I needed that for my future. I wasn't really allowed to hang out with friends either. I remember one day I wanted to go to the movies with a girlfriend of mine. My parents sent my brother to go with me.

"Even when I was in college my father made me give him a copy of all my class schedules and room number. He would time how long it would take me to travel from college to home so every day he kept an eye on my schedule to make sure I got home on time and not a minute late. He had retired early so he had the time on his hand to keep an eye on me. One day I was late because my class ran late and I had not called so he showed up at the college looking for me," explained Ally.

Sam was struck by what Ally said. "Wow, that's rough! You're right, it wasn't like that for me. Being a girl is harder in our culture. You know, to be honest, what you just told me had never occurred to me. I guess my parents had trained me like a dog to listen to what they say without questioning anything or else I would have been punished. I used to see my older brother getting in trouble and fighting with my parents all the time because he just wanted to go party with his friends. I didn't want that happening to me so I just did whatever they asked. I think, even for marriage, I probably would have just said yes because they think you are the right person for me even without getting to know you.

"I have been able to understand who you are as a person only because you asked your parents for more time to learn about me. I know it's weird that I'm like this, as a guy, but I guess I just didn't want to deal with my parents. They sheltered me so much and because I didn't want fighting in the house all the time I just buried myself into books. In a way, it turned out fine for me because now I am a doctor and I will never have to worry about not making enough money in life. The negative side is that I never got to grow and know what I truly wanted for myself or who I really am. So maybe I need a strong woman like you in my life?" Sam shrugged his shoulders, looking a bit confused about himself.

"Oh great, so you are looking to go from one woman who has always thought for you and made decisions for you to another woman who will think and make decisions for you? Is there any part in your life where you are planning to think for yourself?" Ally poked fun at Sam, becoming a little concerned with what he said but not wanting to show it. She didn't want to be a mother to him. Although, he may be a perfect husband who will do anything she says without any argument since he is not used to arguing with anyone.

Just as she was finishing her thoughts the little old lady returned. "Is there anything else I can get for you?" She asked in that beautiful Chinese accent.

"Actually, we're all done. The food was very delicious as usual. Could we please have the check?" Ally waved at the empty plates in front of her.

"Oh yes of course, I will be right back." The lady cleared the table then left.

"I am sure you didn't mind me asking for a check since you are used to your mommy making the decision?" Ally asked as she laughed jokingly.

Sam too laughed. "Nope not at all, I might as well get used to it coming from you now."

Ally giggled half-heartedly as her heart sank a bit at the thought of what he just alluded to.

The old lady returned with their check, "I am guessing you will be paying for this young man?" She asked as she handed the check to Sam suggesting that he should pay for it and walked away.

Ally turned to Sam as soon as the old lady walked away. "See I told you she is just like our mothers! She basically told you to pay for it, ha-ha-ha! And, of course you are ok with that because you are used to it," Ally joked.

Sam grinned, nodding his head. "Great! I am going to hear about this from you all the time now, aren't I?" Sam proclaimed while he put the money with the tip on the table and they both walked out as they laughed.

They both got in the car, with Sam driving. "Our lunch date went by so fast. See, we got to learn a bit more about each other and got to know how we were raised by our parents. Don't you think it is important for us to get to know each other to see if we are compatible or not?" Ally asked.

"I suppose I agree with you but you know how our parents are? Their attitude is once we get married we have our entire life to get to know each other and that's how you learn to love each other. According to them, it will take years by the time we get to know each other and by that time, we end up having kids. They say when people date each other once they have a fight they end the relationship, walk away, and move on to the next without even trying to make things work out. Whereas, in an arrange marriage, if a couple has a fight it's not that easy for them to walk away. It forces them to work on their relationship for the sake of their families and kids," replied Sam.

"Yes, I know, that but they don't see the part where if two people are not compatible and don't get along from the beginning. Their families put guilt trips on them and force them to stay together. Sometimes the parents even suggest to the couple to have kids thinking that will make things better between them, not realizing that's the worst thing to do. I know a few marriages where the women want to leave their husbands because of their controlling or abusive nature but put up with it for the sake of their kids. There are women in our culture who are forced to get married at a young age and don't even have a college degree so when they want to leave their husbands they can't because they are not able to support themselves. The sad thing is that they feel they can't go back to their parents because they are told by their mothers that no matter what happens when a girl leaves her father's house and enters her husband's only her dead body comes out of her husband's house. I know this seems so surreal in this day and age but this does happen. Yes, there are some families that are a bit more modernized in India but amongst most Muslims this is still true. We read about honor killings even today and makes you wonder if these people will ever change..." Ally was tired of the discussion and took a deep breath. "Sorry, I think this conversation is getting way to deep, all this just makes me very angry. Anyways, I think I better go in now. I'll see you later?"

Sam had already pulled up outside of her apartment and was waiting for her to finish. He could tell she was all worked up about the topic so decided not to say anything else about it. Instead he just gave her a kiss on the cheek, and said, "Ok I will see you soon."

Ally said bye and got out of the car. Sam watch her go into the building. As he sat there he was getting very horny noticing her ass in a short tight dress. After Ally went into her building he drove away, still horny of course!

Chapter 8

Right Match

Ally was busy putting her laundry away when she received a text from Mirlande.

Mirlande: "Hey, what r u doing?"

Ally: "I was putting my laundry away."

Mirlande: "I needed to talk to u, r u free to meet?"

Ally: "I've got a couple of hrs. Want to come over or want to go grab some coffee?"

Mirlande: "I could use some coffee. Meet u at the usual place in 10 mins?"

Ally: "make it 15, need to finish up here."

Mirlande: "ok, sounds good c u in 15."

Ally: "ok."

Ally quickly put the clothes away. She got out the outfit she was going to wear for the party this evening. Since she was going to her parents' house for the party that meant she needed to wear Indian clothes. Ally didn't feel like wearing them but when her parents have a party it is expected that everyone wears Indian clothes. So she too had to wear culturally appropriate attire or else she will have to hear from her mom for the entire evening and then some. Ally pulled out a yellow and green churidar suit. A churidar suit consists of long leggings, a long shirt that goes down to the knee called a kurta, and a matching scarf called dupatta. It's easier and faster to wear the churidar suit compared to a sari which is a very colorful drape that varies from five to nine yards and is wrapped around the waist, with one end draped over the shoulder baring the midriff. A blouse, which is fitted and cropped at the midriff, is worn with it. Ally loved wearing saris but she only loved wearing them in a sexy way, which meant she liked her navel showing and her blouse short and sexy. She couldn't wear her sari like that at her parents' house so she just never did. Since her family is Muslim they are not allowed to show any skin. Although there are some Muslims that do like to wear their saris in a sexy way, she came from a very conservative and religious family so they didn't allow that. Along with the churidar suit, she took out matching bangles, gold earrings, and a necklace set. Indians tend to wear mostly gold Jewelry which is made of 22 karat gold; anything below 22 karat is considered for the poor.

She laid everything on her bed so when she returned after hanging with Mirlande she didn't have to rush getting ready. Ally looked at her phone to check the time. She noticed there was a missed call from Ary but no voicemail. She didn't bother to return his call. She really didn't have much time and needed to meet Mirlande. She grabbed her purse and a sweater along with her keys which were on the table near the door. She was putting her sweater on as she walked out of the door.

Meanwhile, Mirlande had arrived at the café and was waiting for Ally. While she waited, she ordered a dark coffee and got some pecan bars for herself and Ally. The café made the best pecan bars and Ally loved them. As she walked towards the table to sit, Ally came right up behind her.

"Hey, sorry I'm a little late," Ally said.

Mirlande turned around as she put the pecan bars on the table. "Hey, hi! That's not a problem. I got a dark coffee for myself and pecan bars for the both of us. I know how much you love them and they looked fresh! But I didn't get you a coffee because I wasn't sure what you wanted."

"Oh thanks! They look so good and are so fattening, but I don't care! You sit and I'll go get my coffee," Ally said excitedly, no matter what kind of mood Ally was in, pecan bars always made her feel good.

Mirlande placed Ally's plate on the bars on the table across from her and took a sip of her coffee. Just as she closed her eyes and took in the aroma of the pecan bar, Ally returned with her coffee.

"Smells good?" Asked Ally with a smile when she saw Mirlande smelling the bars.

"As always!" Exclaimed Mirlande, her eyes still closed.

"Surprisingly, it's not that busy here today." Ally looked around the café.

"I know, right?" Replied Mirlande.

Both women paused to take a bite of their treats, savoring the mix of pecans, honey, and phyllo dough.

"So what's going? How come you wanted to meet right now?" Ally questioned Mirlande after licking her fingers of the sweet stickiness.

"With everything going on between Talia's and your situation I didn't get a chance to talk to you about Marcus and needed some advice from you before I meet with him again," replied Mirlande.

"Meet with him? Really, you guys are together again? What happened about the situation?"

"Ok, ok…I have all the answers for you and a dilemma too," said Mirlande.

"Alright, shoot," Ally said as she took another bite of her pecan bar.

"Well, Marcus finally called me a while back and, like I said, with everything that was going on I really didn't want to deal with him but he was persistent. I finally talked to him."

Mirlande took a pause and held up her hand in a stop motion, "But first, I have to tell you what happened right before Marcus called me." She put her hand down and took a deep breath. "Marcus' ex-wife, Natacha, called me!"

"What?! How did she know your phone number?"

"Well, she told me that Marcus had mentioned me to her when they last met and that I owned Marigold Boutique. She took a chance and called me there. She said that Marcus would be very upset if he found out she talked to me so she made me promise not to say anything. I said I wouldn't tell him. She didn't have much time to talk so she just wanted to let me know that when Marcus told her about me and she could tell he had such strong feelings about me. She said he looked like a man in love. She didn't go into her marriage with Marcus or why they split up but she did say that Marcus will always have a special place in her heart and she just wants to see him happy. That's why she called me, because she spoke with him recently and he told her what happened with you two. She wanted me to give him another chance. That was pretty much the conversation."

Mirlande sat back but continued her story...

"Anyway, back to Marcus. We actually met at my boutique one night and so I heard him out. I was very good at not giving away my phone call with his ex. Well, he first apologized to me about not telling me everything about his life. Before I could ask him anything he asked me not to say anything until he finished telling me everything so I just sat there listening to him.

"He said he got married about three years ago and the person he married, Natacha, already had a baby girl about a year old, the one you and Talia saw. He had met Natacha at his friend's birthday party. When he met her, he didn't know she had a little girl. He said the woman didn't tell him about the baby for a few months because she was afraid he wasn't going to even give her a chance to get to know her if he found out that she had a daughter.

"They dated for a few months and he really liked her so when she saw that he was getting serious about her she told him about her daughter. He had no clue because whenever he was at her house she had her mom watch her daughter. So when he got serious about her she finally came out and told him about her daughter and she didn't say anything to him all this while because she wasn't sure if it was going to work out and she wanted him to get to know her first as an individual but not as a mom to a little girl. She told him that she had seen her friends who were divorced with kids have a hard time getting any dates once they found out they had baggage so she didn't want that to happen to her.

"The woman told him that she took a risk of dating him and not telling him about her daughter keeping in mind that he may leave her when he finds out about her daughter. The woman felt that if he leaves her at least she will get to know that he didn't leave because of her but rather because of her having a daughter. He said he met her daughter when one day he went over to her house and she actually had her baby at home. When he saw the little girl, he became confused but then his girlfriend explained everything and pleaded with him to spend time with her daughter so that maybe he would stick around after seeing how lovable she was.

"After he got over the initial shock, he did get to know the little girl and he just fell in love with her. He and the little girl developed a good bond. So a not far down the road he asked the woman to marry him and, of course, she said yes. Marcus said the first few months of their marriage were great then, out of nowhere, all the drama with the baby's father began. This man wanted to be able to see his daughter and Marcus felt it was only fair since he truly was the baby's father.

"To make a long, long story short, Marcus said there was so much drama that was going on between his wife and the girl's father that he just couldn't take it anymore. He said he put up with it as much as he could and one day he decided that he couldn't deal with it anymore so he decided to divorce her. He also felt that there was more to his wife's and her ex's relationship than just their daughter. He felt that they both might still have had feelings for each other.

"He said that the day you and Talia saw him was the day the divorce was finalized and his ex-wife just wanted to meet him for the last time to say goodbye. She was leaving town for good with her daughter's father. He said that night he walked out of the dinner because he became very nervous after you guys started questioning him and because he hadn't said anything to me about his life. He just didn't know what to say, he was afraid he was going to lose me. He was dealing with one friend who was a shrink and the other one who was a lawyer. He got intimidated and scared. So he just shut down and walked away." Mirlande took a sip of her coffee.

"Wow!" Exclaimed Ally, not knowing what to say.

"So what do you think? Based on what I just told you, do you think he is lying and made that story up?" Asked Mirlande.

"No, I don't think he is lying. He knows Talia and I would do anything to protect our friend, which may mean finding his ex-wife and asking her. You know that divorces are a matter of public record? But since she already spoke to you that would be a moot point now." Ally assured her friend.

"Well, what do you think I should do? Should I give him another chance?" Asked Mirlande hoping she says yes.

Ally sighed, shook her head in disbelief. "I can't believe you are asking me for advice on this matter after finding out about my dilemma. I am surprised you actually would trust me on this subject!"

Mirlande held Ally's hand across the table. "Of course I trust you! It's easier to look at another person's adverse situation and declare it to be right or wrong when it's not you. But when you are going through a similar circumstance yourself, you get blinded by feelings which makes you think irrationally.

"In your case, you have put your feelings aside for the sake of your parents. I may think it's wrong but I do understand your dilemma. Isn't that what you always say to us? What is it that you always say to Talia and me regarding life? 'Everything happens for a reason. We may not know it at the time and may not like it but whatever is meant to happen will happen and we can't change that.'

"Isn't that what you tell us all the time? In my case, all I want to know, given my wonderful history of picking the guys that I do, is if you think Marcus is lying to me or not? I didn't ask you if I should have a relationship with him. That's the choice I have to make," said Mirlande as she smiled at Ally.

Ally smiled. "It doesn't sound like he's a bad guy. I think I can honestly say to you that you actually picked a nice guy this time."

They both started laughing. At that moment, Mirlande felt tremendous relief. She felt that for the first time she didn't pick a loser and this actually is coming from Ally, who is great at judging people. Just at that moment Ally's alarm on her cell phone went off.

"What's that for?" Asked Mirlande.

"Oh, your session is up," joked Ally. "Just kidding, I actually set the alarm so I wouldn't lose track of time. I have to go to my family's house for a party tonight and I can't be late since my mom has lectured me about it already. Hey, you want to come so I don't get questioned too much about my decision of getting married?" Ally gave Mirlande a wishful look.

"Well, as great as that sounds, I told Marcus I would meet him tonight to discuss the situation. I wanted to talk to you first about it before I make any decisions about him," Mirlande said as the two friends got up from the table and started to walk out the door.

"Okay fine, I guess I have to deal with it myself since you won't help me," Ally said woefully yet hugged her friend goodbye anyway, with a smile of course.

Chapter 9

The Party

Ally was on her way to the party. She was running a bit late because she ended up taking a shower again to calm her nerves. She was very nervous about her parents and Sam's parents expecting an answer about the marriage. She wished he and his parents weren't coming. That would have made it easier but there was nothing that she could do about it. She thought, "It is what it is." Because she was running late, she had several missed calls from her mom since she had asked her to come earlier. Ally figured she would just have to come up with something to explain to her once she got there. She wasn't worried about her mom being upset as much as she was worried about giving them an answer that night. She really wasn't ready to make that commitment just yet. She knew they were not going to understand that and it really didn't help the fact that Sam had told his parents he was ready to spend the rest of his life with her. As she was driving, she got a call from Ary again. He had called her earlier in the day and she hadn't gotten back to him. She decided to answer the phone hoping to get her mind off of everything else.

"Hi, Ary."

"Hey, I called you earlier but you didn't return my call."

"I know, I just had so much going on. What's up?"

"I wanted to stop by and return the key to you."

"Well, I'm on my way to my parents' house right now. Remember I told you I had to go tonight?"

"Oh yeah, I completely forgot.'

Which was a lie…he was just jealous that Sam was going to be there and he knew the families were expecting to agree to marriage.

"So, I guess you'll be an engaged woman tomorrow, huh?" He said sarcastically, hoping she didn't see it that way.

"I guess you'll know tomorrow then, right?" Ally responded in the same tone, knowing exactly what Ary was trying to do.

She pulled up to her family's driveway but didn't see many cars. "Hey I have to go now, I'm here," she said nervously.

"Ok, I will be going out tonight maybe on my way back I will swing by the apartment and if you are there I will drop off the key," he said.

Ally's mind was racing with the pending event which distracted her, so she really didn't pay attention to what he said and just told him, "Ok, that's fine, I have to go now."

She then hung up the phone, took a deep breath, got out of the car, and grabbed the baked goods from the back of her car seat that she had bought for the party. As she got to the front door her sister, Zara, opened it.

"Hey, you were supposed to be here a little earlier. The guests will be coming any minute!"

"Well, I am here before they are so I guess that counts as me being here early." Ally walked into the house. They both went straight into the kitchen where their mom was.

"Where have you been? I called you so many times and you didn't pick up the phone?" Her mom was definitely upset.

"I was really tired so I fell asleep. When I woke up I realized it was getting late so I jumped in the shower really quick. You must have called when I was in the shower and I didn't hear the phone. I was in a hurry to get ready so I didn't bother to check my phone." Ally lied.

"Let me see the jewelry you are wearing." Her mom examined Ally's earrings and necklace as if her daughter was still a little child.

"Why didn't you wear a bigger set than this?" Asked her mom. She was always concerned about what people might think. For Indians, the weight and the size of gold jewelry represents the wealth of the family.

Before her mom could say anything else Ally exclaimed, "Oh, you made mirchi pakoras (hot green chilies stuffed with spices then dipped in chickpea flour then fried nice and crispy)!" She grabbed a few in her hand to eat them.

"Those are not for you! Yours are in the bowl next to them!" Her mom swatted her hand away. Everyone knew that Ally loved mirchi pakoras but she didn't like them stuffed with any masala (spices) so her mom always fired plain ones and kept them separately for her. Ally put the ones in her hand back onto the plate and took the ones in the bowl, then began eating her hot and crispy mirchi pakoras. Just when her mom was about to ask her something, the doorbell rang. Ally sighed in relief. She knew exactly what her mom was going to ask but she was saved by the bell. Just when her sister was approaching her to ask what her mom couldn't, their cousin walked into the kitchen.

"Ally! I haven't seen you in a while! Where have you been hiding? Why didn't you come to the wedding last month? It was a lot of fun!" Her cousin queried, as she took a pakora from Ally's hand.

"A friend of mine was in the hospital, in critical condition so I couldn't make it," Ally replied, still eating her pakora.

"Oh, what happened? Is your friend ok now?"

"Yes, she is better and out of the hospital."

Meanwhile, Zara was waiting to talk to her sister but Ally was doing her best to avoid that so she took her cousin's hand and walked out of the kitchen while her cousin continued talking.

Ally's mom walked into the kitchen just when Ally left. "Zara, did you get a chance to ask your sister if she is ready for the marriage yet?"

Zara shook her head. "No, Ayesha was talking to her then they both left the kitchen."

"Your sister is very clever at avoiding the question. Make sure you get hold of her soon and ask her. Actually, you need to tell her she needs to make a decision tonight so we can announce it at the party since everyone is going to be here. It is so embarrassing that Sameer's mom can proudly say that he is ready for the marriage and it's my daughter that they are waiting for. I know she is implying that her kids listen to her and mine don't," said her mom with a pretentious smile as she looked at others across the kitchen, which was very large with a large island in the center where she had set all the food. It was an open kitchen with a sitting area at one end and a dinette on the other. The dinette side led to the family room, which was also very large and the sitting area led to the formal dining room which seated about twenty people....She then walked away to greet more guests.

The doorbell rang. Ally was in the family room talking to her cousin and looked over her cousin's shoulder to see who it was. Her heart was pounding. She was very nervous as she stared across the room....Sam and his parents entered the house. The moment that she was dreading was finally here. She excused herself and went upstairs to the bathroom and locked the door. She could feel the heat in her face as it was becoming flushed. She just stood in the bathroom, staring in the mirror. Both families were expecting an answer but she was not ready to give it. She was very confused.

She lifted her left hand and thought, "There is Sam on one side, a very nice guy who would treat her well." She then lifted her right hand, "and there is Ary on the other side, a guy with whom she doesn't have a future with because of the religious differences and also because he has moved on to someone else." There was a part of her that felt like she should just say yes and get it over with but then there was also a part of her that was really scared. What if she was making the wrong decision? But, then, she also felt like she had no other option. She realized that she was not getting any younger and what other choices does she really have? What if she doesn't find someone who is as nice as Sam?

Just as Ally stood in front of the mirror trying to gather her thoughts, her phone started buzzing. She opened her purse to see who it was, Ary was calling. She was about to answer the phone when there was a very firm knock on the door which startled her. She quickly put the phone back in her purse and opened the door. It was her older brother.

"Ammie is looking for you," He told his sister while his youngest son pulled him away from the bathroom. Ally watched her brother being dragged away. She saw her sister coming with Sam.

"Shit!" She muttered to herself as she waved at Sam. "Look who was standing and pretending not to be looking for you," joked Zara.

"Hi." Ally feigned a smile.

"He is a perfect guy for you. Everyone is expecting to make it official tonight," Zara whispered in Ally's ear and then she walked away.

Ally could feel her heart beating faster and faster. "Can you excuse me for one minute?" She said to Sam then closed the bathroom door as Sam waited for her outside. Ally was so scared that she felt like crying. She knew she couldn't delay this much longer but she was too mixed up. She just closed her eyes and said in her mind, "Please God help me, I don't know what to do. Help me choose the path that is my destiny and I will not fight it. If Ary is not my destiny then give me the strength to say yes to Sam. I am a human being. I don't know what my future holds for me but you do. So, please God help me choose the path that's destined for me." She then opened her eyes wiped the tears, blew her nose and flushed the toilet to make Sam think she had used it. She then took a deep breath and opened the door.

As the door opened, Sam turned to her. He could see the sadness on her face that she was trying to hide.

"Are you ok?"

"Yes, I'm just a bit nervous because everyone is expecting an answer from me tonight."

"No pressure, right?" Joked Sam and that made her smile a bit. "Hey listen, I told my parents not to ask your parents whether you have made your decision. I told them we were still getting to know each other, so don't worry about it," Assured Sam.

Ally smiled at him. "Thank you but that doesn't mean my family will be alright with me not giving them the answer tonight I just hope you understand that my reservation about the marriage really has nothing to do with you. You are a great guy, I just mentally am not ready for the family drama. .."

Just as she was explaining, her aunt walked by with her son in her arms. "Hello you two, standing here away from everyone? Don't worry you will have plenty of time to be with each other once you get married." She said annoyingly. She then looked at her son, "Baby do you need to go potty? I think I need to take him to the potty, excuse me." Her aunt then pushed passed the two to enter the bathroom. She closed the door on them.

Ally started laughing. Sam looked at her. "What's so funny?"

Ally laughed uncontrollably and although she finally took a deep breath, she still couldn't control her laughter. She was finally able to get her words out, "My aunt thinks her son needs to go to the bathroom because he farted but in reality I had too many of those mirchi pakoras." She burst into laughter again and then Sam caught the laughing bug.

"That stink bomb was you? That poor kid…his mom is going to make him sit on the toilet until he does something. You are bad!"

"I can't help it, those mirchi pakoras do it to me every time." Ally was still trying to control her laughter.

"I'll have to remember to make sure you don't eat them when we are out." Sam pointed out in jest.

During their moment of hilarity, Ally's mom walked over. "Sameer, your mom is looking for you and it's also time to eat dinner."

"Ok, thank you auntie." Sameer winked at Ally and was just about to go find his mom when she walked up to them.

"Here you two are." Sam's mom said.

"Salam (hello) auntie." Ally nodded to his mom.

"We are actually thinking of doing a little ceremony after everyone finishes eating," said Ally's mom to Sam and her.

Sam looked at Ally and he could tell she was very surprised about the ceremony and didn't know what to say. "Come on, let's all go have dinner now before it gets cold," said Ally's mom.

Both the moms walked together while Sam and Ally were a few steps behind them. Ally just looked at him like a lost puppy. Sam whispered to Ally, "I know you are not ready for this. I think I know how to help you out. You go ahead, I'll be there in a minute. If my mom asks, tell her I had to take a call." He then walked away into a room.

Ally appeared a bit confused, not sure what to think. When she entered the dining area, Sam's mom asked her, "Where did Sam go?"

"He had a call so he went into the bedroom to answer it." Ally reported what Sam told her to.

"Oh, ok." His mom shrugged her shoulders and turned back to talking with Ally's mom.

Ally's sister came over to her. "Did you hear? They have planned a ceremony for you guys. Are you ready for it?" Zara even surprised herself with the news. She thought their mom was going to wait for Ally to give an answer but it seemed like their mom had other plans.

"I don't understand what the ceremony is when I haven't even made my decision," said Ally angrily.

Just as her sister was about to say something, Sam came over and asked Ally in front of Zara, "Would you mind driving me to the hospital? They just called me and I have to run over there. I came with my parents in their car so I don't have one."

"Sure!" Ally wanted to hug Sam at that moment.

Sam then walked over to his mom who was standing next to Ally's mom. "I need to go to the hospital for a bit. They just asked me to come in because they are short of staff, and for some reason, its busy there today. I asked Ally to drive me there since you are eating."

"Ok, how long will you be?" She asked.

"I am not sure…as soon as I'm done we'll be back." Sam leaned in and gave a peck on his mom's cheek.

"But beta (son), you guys haven't eaten anything, why don't you eat something first then go?" Ally's mom pleaded.

"I have to go now but we can grab something to eat in the car on our way there," replied Sam as he looked at Ally and then his mom.

"Ok beta, I guess you don't have a choice, it is your job." Ally's mom, dejected, packed some finger food on a plate for them.

Sam and Ally said their goodbyes to their moms and other guests, then left. Ally's mom then turned to Sam's mom. "Hopefully, they will be back soon so we can have the ceremony."

"I hope so too but whenever he gets called to the hospital he doesn't come back for hours." Sam's mom was disappointed too.

Meanwhile, in the car, Ally peeked over at Sam. "Do you really need to go to the hospital or was just an excuse?"

"Told you, I would help you out." Sam winked with a smile.

"Oh. Thanks! So, what do you want to do now?" Ally was all smiles.

"Want to go out for dinner?" He asked.

"Well I really need to change my clothes before we decide to do anything or we can just eat at my place? I think my mom packed enough food for three people."

"Sounds good." Sam grinned.

"Thank you for helping me out but I really don't want you to think I don't like you and that's why I am not giving an answer," Ally said, genuinely feeling grateful but guilty at the same time.

"Yeah I don't get it, I am such a perfect guy why wouldn't you want to be with me?" He nudged Ally with his elbow.

They arrived at her apartment. As the two of them were walking into her apartment they ran into Jeff. "Hi, my lovely, you look very beautiful." Jeff greeted Ally with a bow.

"Hi Jeff, this is Sam. Sam, this is Jeff, my confidant." Ally made introductions.

"So this is the young man who has been trying to take you away from me?" Jeff eyed Sam in a teasing way.

"Yes sir I am, if she allows me to." With his arm around Ally, Sam shook Jeff's hand.

"Want some Indian food Jeff?" Asked Ally.

"As good as it sounds, you know that spicy food and I are mortal enemies."

"Yes, I know but I figured I'd ask you just in case today was the day you decide to become friends with spicy food," Ally said slyly.

"Well, you two go enjoy your spicy dinner while I go and enjoy a drink."

"Ok, you go enjoy yourself too."

"It was nice meeting you," Sam said.

Jeff nodded his head to Sam and went into his apartment. Sam and Ally then went into hers.

"Hungry?" She asked, as they entered the apartment.

"A little bit," replied Sam as he set the food on the table. "Do you mind if I use the bathroom?" He asked.

"Yes I mind," she joked, "but I will go change my clothes while you do your business."

Sam went into the bathroom and just as Ally was about to go into the bedroom to change, there was a knock at the door.

She was puzzled at who could be knocking on the door now. When she looked through the peephole, she saw Ary. For a second she panicked then she glanced behind her to see if Sam was there. He wasn't so she opened the door quickly.

Ary put his hand on the door to open it up. "Hey, I was going past your neighborhood and I saw your car so I thought I would stop by and give you the key."

"Now is not a good time. Sam is here. I will get it from you later," whispered Ally, hoping to get rid of him before Sam came out of the bathroom.

"Over for a nightcap?" Ary commented sarcastically with a jealous look on his face.

"Now is not the time Ary!" Ally asserted in a firm tone and just then she heard the bathroom door open. "Look, you need to go now. I will get it from you tomorrow," She said and closed the door quickly on Ary, hoping he doesn't do anything stupid. She was really upset that he came over without calling.

Sam saw her closing the door. "Going somewhere?"

Ally smiled coquettishly. "No, it was just Jeff asking if we wanted to join him for a drink. I thought maybe you and I could spend some quiet time together so I told him maybe some other night."

"Good thinking," he said as he came close to her and pulled her into his arms. She wrapped her arms around him, nervously, hoping Ary was gone.

"To be honest, I think I'd rather spend time with you like this than be at the party," Sam said.

"Yes, definitely!" Ally exclaimed. Ally was so glad she didn't have to give an answer tonight but she couldn't let Sam know that. "Are you hungry? Want to have dinner?" She asked.

"Sure."

Ally took the bags from the table and they went into the kitchen holding hands.

She was getting the plates out of the cabinet while Sam got the food out of the bags Ally's mom had packed.

"Want some wine?" Ally asked.

"Yes, please."

"Do you want to pick out the wine you would like? It's in that cabinet over there," she asked him as she got the wine glasses out of the cabinet.

Sam walked over to the cabinet and picked out a bottle of wine that would go well with their meal, a Chardonnay. "Maybe you should have taken some of this wine to your family." He let out a chuckle.

"Oh my god, can you imagine what my parents' reaction would be if they found out I drink?" Ally covered her face, shaking her head.

"You want to find out next time?" Sam continued teasing.

Ally was glad that even though Sam has done everything his parents had asked him to all his life, he somehow enjoyed drinking alcohol. At first she wasn't sure if he drank since he still lived with his parents and he was so influenced by them. When she went out with Sam for dinner one night he had asked her if she would like a drink. At first she thought maybe he was testing her to see if she drank and he didn't since it is not allowed in Islam, but then he told her this is probably the one thing he does that his parents would disapprove of. From that point on, day by day she seemed to grow fonder of Sam. At times she felt like she was starting to fall in love with him, which she never thought she would again after Ary, especially since he came back into her life. Maybe not in the way she would have wanted him to but nonetheless he was there.

"I hope the food isn't too spicy for you? Everyone eats spicy in our family." Ally handed Sam a plate of food.

"No, it's fine. I don't think I can eat the mirchi pakoras like you can but everything else is just fine." Sam took the plate graciously.

"Yeah, mirchi pakoras are my weakness but don't worry I won't eat them tonight since I already had them and now you know what they do to my stomach." Ally laughed.

While both of them were enjoying their dinner, Ary was still outside of her apartment in his car. He was jealous and upset that Sam was with her instead of him so he sat in the car contemplating whether to go back and ruin their evening. He had been sitting in the car for a half an hour thinking but he couldn't take it anymore. His feelings of jealousy got the best of him so he decided to go back to the apartment, not knowing what he would say to her or Sam. He got out of the car and walked into the building. He had the key so he didn't need her to open the building door. He walked into the building and looked at the key in his hand, then decided maybe it would be better if he knocked instead. He was afraid he would see something they could be doing and lose his mind, then regret his actions later.

Ary had a bad temper when he was jealous. As he was about to knock on the door, his phone rang loudly. It startled him and reached into his pocket to silence the phone. It was his girlfriend calling him. Then it dawned on him that he had left her at the grocery store which was a minute away from Ally's apartment. He had told his girlfriend he was going to run a quick errand and meet her back in the store in five minutes. He needed an excuse to see Ally but then he lost track of time after his interaction with her. Now he had no choice but to leave.

He answered the phone as he was walking out, "Hey sorry I am late. I ran into a friend. Will be there in a minute..."

Meanwhile inside the apartment Ally heard the phone ringing outside her door. She recognized the ringtone and realized that was Ary. She became nervous and started wondering what he was still doing outside her apartment. She was afraid of him using the key and walking in. What would she say to Sam? Just when she was feeling like things were heading in the right direction in her life, she couldn't understand why this was happening to her with Ary. She sat there affecting a smile at Sam but, inside, she couldn't understand why things always had to be so complicated for her. Like others, why couldn't she just move on with her life without her past coinciding with her present and future? In her mind she couldn't understand why God made things so difficult for her. She felt as if God liked to tease her by bringing good people in her life then taking them away from her. She couldn't understand why God was so cruel to her. She was so scared of Ary walking in, she became more and more anxious. She waited for the bad news to walk in but it never did. She then realized he wasn't coming. "Is he gone?" She thought to herself. After a few minutes, she sighed in relief realizing he was not going to barge into her place. She needed to find an excuse to see if Ary was still out there but how could she go out there? What if Sam came with her? She decided to text Jeffery and ask him to check for her.

"Can you excuse me for a minute, I need to go use the bathroom?" She grabbed her phone from the table on her way without Sam realizing it.

As soon she got into the bathroom she texted Jeff. "Hey, can you please do me a favor and check to see if Ary is outside my door please? Long story, I will explain later." She sent the text then she closed the toilet seat and sat on it as she waited for Jeff to answer.

She sat there waiting impatiently staring at her phone. A couple of minutes went by but there was no response from Jeff. She started feeling edgy, "What if he was sleeping?" She thought. She looked at her phone again and still there was no answer. She was about to call Jeff then Sam knocked on the door concerned.

"Are you alright in there?" He asked.

"Yes, I'll be right out," She answered. She couldn't take the chance of calling Jeff now, she was afraid of Sam hearing her. She disappointedly put her phone in her pocket then opened the bathroom door.

"Everything ok?" He asked, looking concerned

"Yes I'm fine, I saw a little dirt in the corner of the wall so I was just cleaning it." She smiled, but nervous as hell on the inside.

"While you were in the bathroom my mom texted me asking what time I would be done and if I needed to be picked up from the hospital? I told her I might be at the hospital most of the night, I wasn't sure and that I dropped you at your house and kept your car since I didn't know how long it was going to take me at the hospital. I didn't want you sitting and waiting for me. I told them to go home after the party and you will drop me off whenever I am done at the hospital. They were planning something if we were returning to the party soon. So I thought this might be the best answer so we don't have to go back, was that ok?" He proffered.

"Yes, perfect! Does this mean you will be staying over tonight?" Ally asked with a naughty and flirtatious grin.

"If that's alright with you?" Replied Sam, in the same flirtatious manner.

They both then went back to finish their dinner. Ally was still very anxious to hear from Jeff just then she felt buzzing in her pocket. She needed to check her phone without Sam noticing.

"I'm going to get water for us."

She got up and walked over to the fridge which was on the other side of the kitchen, behind Sam. As soon as she reached the fridge, she checked her phone hoping it was Jeff but instead it was Ary. She panicked as soon as she saw his name then she quickly read the message.

"Hope you are enjoying your night, I will give you the key the day after tomorrow."

That made her feel relieved. It also confirmed that Ary wasn't outside! She happily filled two glasses of water then took it to the table smiling.

Sam noticed her face was glowing. "You're all smiles," he said.

"Yes, just excited about being able to spend time with you like this instead of running around all the time.

They both enjoyed their dinner as they joked, laughed and talked about other people. They finally finished eating...

"Would you like to pick out a movie to watch while I clean up the table? If there is nothing on TV, I have some DVDs on the shelf you can see if there is anything that you like," She said.

"Why don't I help you clear the table so it gets done faster?" Sam offered.

"No, it's not a problem. You go pick out a movie and I will clean up quickly. There really isn't much to clear."

Sam got up from the table and headed into the living room where the DVDs were kept while Ally cleared the table. She was in the kitchen putting the dishes in the dishwasher when she got a text. The phone was on the counter near the sink so she peeked to see the text, it was Ary. Ally dried her hands and read the text.

"I am sorry I came over without calling you. I was in the neighborhood so I stopped by to return the key."

Ally knew exactly why he had sent that text. He couldn't imagine her with Sam and wanted to ruin the evening for her. This just made her more upset with him. She deleted the text and went back to putting the dishes in the dishwasher. After she finished she walked into the living room where Sam was picking out a movie. He had a few DVDs in his hand.

"I didn't know you like James Bond!" He exclaimed excitedly because he was a diehard James Bond fan.

Ally smirked. "I do like James Bond but I wouldn't say I am a diehard fan like you."

"Really? You could have fooled me, you have the whole Bond collection," Sam said in surprise.

"They actually belonged to my friend from college. I was supposed to mail them back but I guess I just forgot about them." Replied Ally…the truth was that when she and Ary were together she had bought the collection for him for his birthday because he loved James Bond. When she found out he had been seeing someone else she didn't give them back to him and just forgot all about them.

When she saw the DVDs, old memories of how she and Ary used to watch them together came back to her and made her a bit sad but she hid her emotions very well.

"You want to watch them with me?" Sam asked.

She really didn't want to but she also realized she had to let go of her past and move on. Ary was not the only one who liked James Bond, many guys do, she thought. This was another step she had to take in order to keep moving forward. She hadn't seen James Bond in a long time because it always reminded her of Ary.

Ally and Sam cuddled up on the sofa and started to watch James Bond. As they were sitting there watching, Sam held her closer to him then started kissing her. She kissed him back with a passion. He then unbuttoned her top and slowly traced her curves from her neck to her stomach, his tongue flicking out at times that drove her crazy. He reached her navel and unzipped her pants, then pulled down her pants and panties. He circled her belly button with his tongue and continued down to her between her thighs. He spread her thighs like pedals of a flower and enclosed on her core. Ally laid there writhing in pleasure until she could no longer hold back and cried out in ecstasy. Sam moved up to face her but Ally had other plans. She reached down and unzipped his pants, stripping them off of him and throwing them on the floor. She made him switch places with her so that she was above him and maneuvered down to his manhood. She took hold of his engorged organ and encircled it with her lips. She played with her toy until Sam begged her to stop.

He picked her up from the couch and carried her into the bedroom. There, he gently threw her on the bed and flipped her onto her stomach. He guided his member into her pool of moisture and thrusted ever so vigorously. Ally let all her thoughts go away and was enjoying Sam as Sam, and not the man who most likely will be her future husband…..

He climaxed quickly since he had been waiting to have sex with her all day and all that energy burst forth in a moment of time.

They both just held each other and lay on the bed for a while.

Sam looked at Ally. "So…ready to be my wife?" He asked in the heat of the moment.

"Wow, wife!" She exclaimed looking at him with a feigned shock look on her face.

"So, is that a yes?" Sam challenged her again.

"Hmm, you must have really enjoyed yourself!" Joked Ally, still trying to avoid answering the dreaded question. Sam smiled and kissed her hand.

"I think I need to use the bathroom." Ally pulled herself out of bed and walked out of the room.

Sam realized that she was avoiding his question but at the moment he didn't mind it because he believed that since she slept with him the answer must be yes. It's just a matter of time when she will actually come out and say it. "Why else would she sleep with him if she doesn't want him?" He thought to himself. He was really an innocent, easy going guy. He looked at the clock then realized that it was getting late and he had to get up early for work. He got out of the bed and started putting his shirt on, Ally walked into the room.

"I'm sorry but I need to get going. It's getting late and I have to work early in the morning," Sam explained.

At first, Ally thought maybe she may have hurt his feelings by not answering his question but then she remembered that he had told her earlier in the evening that he had work early the next morning. In a way, she was glad he was leaving. At least for now she didn't have to give him an answer. She wanted to say yes to him, he really seemed like he would be a good partner in life but there was something that was stopping her. She really couldn't understand why she was not able to come out and just say yes. Could it honestly be because of Ary? But how can that be when he was in a serious relationship with someone else? Besides, even if it was possible she could never be with Ary if she didn't want to lose her family. Poor Ally, why couldn't her life be normal like everyone else's? Well, anyways...she drove Sam home. They both were quiet for the most of the car ride and there were a few awkward moments. Although Sam's house was only fifteen minutes away it felt longer to the both of them.

After she dropped him at his house, on her way back she decided in her mind that enough time had gone by and she would give him an answer by the end of the week. She felt she wasn't being fair to him. There was no reason for her to prolong her decision when she already knew what it was but, before doing that, she felt she really needed to say goodbye to Ary. It wasn't for his sake but rather it was for herself. She needed closure on their relationship. Even though it had ended many years ago, by him coming back into her life it made things a bit complicated for her, especially when she slept with him again.

After she returned home she was feeling really bad about Sam. She texted him as she lay on her bed.

"Hey, I just wanted to say thanks for rescuing me from the family tonight. I really had a good time tonight so maybe you can come over again but this time stay all night?"

She waited for a few minutes to see if he would respond but there was none so she went to take a shower. After she came out of the shower she checked her phone to see if Sam had responded yet but he hadn't. She thought to herself, either he is upset with her or he may have fallen asleep since he had to wake up early for work. She too then went to bed. She was mentally, and physically, very tired. All this stress was starting to take a toll on her health which she could feel now.

She had developed an autoimmune disorder called ITP (idiopathic thrombocytopenia purport), a bleeding disorder in which the immune system destroys platelets that are necessary for normal blood clotting. People with the disease have too few platelets in the blood. When she is under stress, whether physical or mental, her body destroys the platelets it produces thinking it's a foreign substance in the body. When this happens to her she gets severe migraines and becomes very irritable. If her platelets drop very low it is very dangerous because she can have hemorrhaging from any part of her body and it can kill her. She monitors her platelet count very closely by regular blood testing and, if they are very low, she needs to go for treatment right away. She received this lovely gift from her family when she was in a relationship with Ary. She was normal until she went through that stress, which triggered the autoimmune, and is something she will live with for the rest of her life. As long as she keeps her stress under control, she is fine.

Chapter 10

Answer for Sam

It was early in the morning when Ally's phone rang. She put the pillow over her head because she just was not in the mood to wake up, which was very unusual for her since she was the type of person who felt if she woke up at 7am she had wasted most of her day. She sighed and reached for the phone to see who it was. Mirlande.

She answered it, "Hi Mirlande! Can't believe you're up early!"

"Yes, I woke up early before you could get a chance to plan your day." Mirlande sounded bright and chipper in her response.

"Wow, you sound like you are in a great mood, what's up?" Ally asked, raising up on one elbow.

"Yes, I feel wonderful and I have so much to tell you. Please tell me you are free to hang out with me today?" Mirlande inquired eagerly.

"Yes, I'm free and can meet you but it would have to be at the mall because I need to go gift shopping."

"That's fine with me, I'm up for doing anything you want."

"Ok, how about I meet you right when the mall opens. It'll give me enough time to get ready."

"Sounds good, see you in a bit!"

The girls said bye to each other and hung up the phone. Ally rolled out of bed, put coffee on for brewing then went into the bathroom to brush her teeth and shower. Ally usually didn't spend too much time showering, ten minutes was all she needed. After a nice hot shower she walked into the kitchen and poured herself a cup of coffee. Then she sat on the sofa, took her laptop out and checked her emails while she enjoyed her morning cup o' joe.

A couple of hours later, having replied to the majority of her emails, she looked at the clock and realized she needed to get ready to meet Mirlande. While she was getting ready the phone rang. Ary was calling her. She ignored him since she needed to get ready and if she started talking to him she knew she would be late. Besides, she was trying to do her best to distance herself from him as much and as soon as possible. She needed to give Sam his answer very soon and having Ary in her life increasingly made things complicated in her life. She had thought of meeting him before saying yes to Sam to have closure for herself but Ally was going through so many mixed emotions that she didn't even know what to do anymore, which was very unusual for her.

Ally arrived at the mall and as she was walking into the mall she heard someone say to her "Hi sexy, wanna walk with me?"

Ally smiled and turned around. "Hi Mirlande."

They both hugged each other as if they were seeing each other for the first time in years. They both had so much going on in their lives that at that moment, as the two friends hugged all their troubles seemed to have disappeared.

"For some reason I feel like I haven't seen you for ages," said Mirlande.

"I know what you mean, it does seem like that. So, what's going on with you? How are things with you and Marcus?" Ally asked, as they both walked towards a bench and sat down. Mirlande looked at her and started giggling like a little girl, then she extended her left arm and flashed her hand.

"Oh my God, is that an engagement ring?" Ally looked gleefully shocked, grabbing Mirlande's finger to get a closer look.

"Yes!, I know this seems so crazy since Marcus and I haven't known each other for that long but he and I have been spending a lot of time getting to know each other and we have become so comfortable with one another that we want to spend every second of our lives together. He surprised me with a ring last night and of course I had to share my happiness with you and Talia. I called Talia after I spoke to you this morning and told her. She couldn't believe it."

"Oh, I am so happy for you!" Ally hugged her friend tightly.

"You are not mad or think I'm crazy?" Mirlande asked.

"Are you kidding me, not at all? If you had done this a few months ago and asked me this I probably would not have agreed with you but I think at this point in my life I can understand. You are able to do something I am having a hard time with. I have found a perfect guy but I am not able to make myself say yes to him," Ally replied, looking away in sadness.

"What's wrong Ally, it's not like you to be like this? You are always so sure of things and you're the voice of reason for everyone. Seeing you like this bothers me."

"You know me, I'll be alright! I just have to figure things out for myself I guess." Ally was trying not to make this moment all about her. She turned to look back at her friend and glimpsed Ary with his girlfriend across the mall. Ary's girlfriend had gone into the store while Ary remained outside on the phone.

Ally, putting her hand on Mirlande's arm, said, "Wait right here, I will be right back. She then stood up and walked towards Ary.

As she approached him, he saw her and hung up the phone. Ally said hi to him then hugged him tightly. While she was hugging him, she saw his girlfriend looking at them from inside the store. That was exactly what Ally wanted.

"Hey, I saw that you called me. Sorry I couldn't call you back, I was in a hurry this morning. Did you call me for something?" She asked sweetly, still keeping an eye on his girlfriend out of the corner of her eye. She could see his girlfriend was trying to get through the checkout line quickly so she could pay and get back to Ary. Ally could see that the girlfriend was not happy Ally was talking with her boyfriend. Ary didn't want to engage in a serious conversation with Ally because he was afraid his girlfriend would see them together. He had no idea his girlfriend already had seen them hugging and talking.

Acting nonchalant, Ary shrugged his shoulders. "I called to see if you wanted to meet me for dinner tonight?"

Just then, Ally saw the girlfriend heading toward them.

"Your girlfriend is coming this way, you better come up with a good story," She whispered into his ear and gave him a kiss on his cheek, walking away with a smile on her face. As Ally was walking away, Ary slowly turned around and saw his girlfriend approaching, with fury in her eyes.

Meanwhile, Ally strolled towards Mirlande, smiling devilishly. Mirlande sat there shaking her head since she watched the entire show.

"You are very bad, you know that, right?" Mirlande said to her friend, waving her finger back and forth.

"Payback is a bitch!" Ally vehemently uttered.

"What do you mean?"

Ally explained, "You don't know what a bitch his girlfriend is so let me tell you the entire story. His girlfriend and I used to be friends when we were in college, her name is Mona. She loved partying and sleeping around with whomever she wanted. One day, she and I were out shopping and we had gotten into a conversation about men. We were talking about different men, etc. and in that conversation, in not so many words, she wanted to know how he was in bed?

"As you know, I am not the type of person who talks about my personal life nor did I feel like it was her business so I just made a joke and said he needs to work on that. So she says to me, 'maybe I need to teach him a thing or two, once I get done with them they tend to get good.' She thought she was being smart and pretending to joke about it but I knew what she was like. She was just curious to know why I was with him and how he must be in bed. She couldn't understand why I was with him and not with someone else. I personally thought she had low self-esteem. She needed attention from guys and, of course, by sleeping around she thought she was getting that attention. She didn't realize that guys don't care, they will sleep with anyone.

"Well, anyways, it became a challenge for her. She wanted to see if she could break us up by sleeping with him. She never really could stay in a relationship because the guys knew she was really easy and constantly needing other guys' attention. She didn't like the fact that Ary and I had a very tight relationship and became jealous of our relationship. It's not that she liked Ary in that way at all, she just couldn't see me happy with him. That's when I truly realized she wasn't a good friend. So when Ary and I were having issues because of my family and I couldn't see him at all, she took advantage of it and went after him when he was lonely and vulnerable.

"So now she thinks she has won because she was able to take him away from me. I'm not making any excuses for Ary. Yes, he did fall for it and, ever since then, I have felt like he truly never really loved me the way I loved him. I'm pretty sure that she is cheating on him because she is not the type to be with one guy and, besides, he really isn't her type. I guarantee you that when they are not hanging out together she is out with someone else."

"So why would she be with Ary all this while if she knows she has broken you two up and has won?"

"For security, her parents will want her to get married and she knows Ary is the type of guy that can give her the security while she still screws around."

"If Ary isn't that type of guy, if he is such a committed type then why did he sleep with you while still in a relationship with her?"

"Same reason why I slept with him even though I may be getting married to Sam. We were each other's first and we had a great relationship. We might not have broken up if it wasn't for my family. I'm pretty sure even Mona wouldn't have been able to break us up either. He probably feels the same way about me as I do about him when I see him, I forget about everyone and everything in his presence."

"So what is your point then? I mean if you are going to get married to Sam then why play these games and break up his relationship? I guess I am a bit confused about this entire thing about you getting revenge against Ary and his girlfriend."

"Okay, let me try to explain it to you," Ally took a brief pause, then continued, "I am really upset that Ary did not wait for me and jumped into a relationship so quickly. I know, I know…I couldn't see him because of my family and I had picked my family over him. But there is a part of me that continues to be very resentful of him, that I feel like he needs to experience the same pain I have felt all these years. I also want to get back at Mona for going after him when we were friends. I feel if I break them up it'll be a win-win for me. I would be getting back at Ary and her. Besides, if they do break up and even if I am not with him he is better off without her because she is not someone who is going to be true to him so in a way I am doing him a favor.

"I also sometimes think that if I let him be with her then when he ends up marrying her and he will find out that she is sleeping with others and that will hurt him. I don't think he has found out what a slut she is as of yet because, if he did, I know he wouldn't be with her. I don't know…I do know…I may be babbling and not make any sense to you but I am just very angry and I just want to get back at both of them for what they have done. I just don't know how much more I could explain these feelings to you so that you'd understand."

Mirlande could see the frustration and pain in her friend's eyes. She felt so sorry for Ally knowing she is such a strong person who is always there to protect her and Talia from getting hurt but this time it is she who needs to be protected and Mirlande didn't know how to help. Talia was not there to help Ally either. Mirlande felt helpless and sad, but she decided to voice what she believed may be the only thing she could think of to say, "Ally, I understand that you are in a lot of pain on the inside but don't you think it's best for you to just let him or them be and you do what's best for you? Or are you really hoping that somehow it works out between you and your family so you can end up with Ary?"

"I know that's not possible. You know I would have to give up my family if I wanted to make it work out with Ary. At this point, I don't know if I want Ary. Like I said, maybe I'm just very upset with him and want him to feel the pain that I did," Ally replied, shrugging her shoulders and still very confused about her feelings.

"But what makes you think he didn't feel that pain when you stopped seeing him and picked your family over him? Maybe by being with someone else was his way of dealing with it. He obviously still has some feelings for you since he finds reasons to see you. Think about it...he is here with his girlfriend but yet he still talked to you. He could have ignored you or walked away when he saw you for fear that his girlfriend would see you. Maybe he wants to get caught with you?" Mirlande was trying to be the voice of reasoning.

"No, trust me he doesn't want to get caught with me. He really thought his girlfriend couldn't see him because she was in the store. You should have seen his face when I told him he better have a good story because his girlfriend just saw us. He knows he can't be with me so why would he want to ruin it with her? He doesn't like being alone so he would have made sure she didn't see us," Ally said, gesturing toward where Ary was standing.

Mirlande sighed, then said, "I don't know Ally, I think you might be hurting yourself more by trying to get back at him. I can completely understand the pain and the anger you may have for him but I really think it's best for you to just walk away from him if you know you can't be with him. I really don't think you are upset with him specifically. Maybe you are just upset with the situation in general? I mean, I think, if I were in your shoes I would be more upset with God for making me go through this. I think I would be just angry with life. If someone came to you with this problem what advice would you give that person?"

"To be honest, at the moment I couldn't tell how I would advise someone because my feelings would get in the way of my thinking. I guess you're right, I think I may be just upset with life or God in general. I feel like it's not fair that others are able to be with whomever they want so why can't I without any consequences? You, for example and please don't take this in a wrong way, don't you think I am upset or jealous of you for being able to be with the person you want to be with? Why can't I?" Ally started getting teary eyed.

Mirlande hugged her friend and held her tight for a few minutes. She could see that Ally was still very much in love with Ary and seeing him with Mona just made her upset even more. Mirlande felt like telling her friend to just forget about the family and be with Ary but she knew how important family was for Ally so, instead, "You know Ally, you always say to us that everything happens for a reason and maybe all of this is happening to you to test your love for Ary? Maybe it's a test for both of you to see how much you both may care for each other. I know your family is very important to you and, because of that, you would never give up your family over him so why don't you try to talk to your dad again and see?"

Ally looked at Mirlande. "If I try to talk to my dad about this, first of all, he would know I'm still in touch with Ary which negates his deal for me that I don't see Ary ever again in order for me to live on my own. Secondly, my father would say he would be fine with me marrying Ary so long as Ary converts. And, you know, I would never ask Ary to do that because I don't think it's right and also I don't follow my own religion so how can I ask him to do that? Ugh, you know what? Don't worry about this. I am sure I will figure my life out. I think I am just very upset after seeing Ary and Mona together. Let's talk about your exciting news! So when are you guys planning to get married?"

Mirlande didn't know what to say to her friend but after Ally started talking about her engagement and marriage she got excited and started to behave like a little girl.

"Well he actually wants to get married as soon as possible. He feels like there is no reason to waste time. We were actually thinking of getting married next month!"

"What? Next month? How is that going to be possible to arrange everything that quickly?" Asked Ally, shocked.

"I know it is so soon but Marcus' friend owns a restaurant with a banquet hall at the back and he said that it's slow season right now so he has a lot of dates available and we can pick any that we want. Marcus said he has many friends in every type of business that can make this happen!" Mirlande replied with a squeaking voice and a big smile.

"Wow, he has really thought about everything! Seems like he really loves you and wants to be with you. That really is great!" Ally said excitedly.

Mirlande became serious and looked at Ally in a pleading way. "Would you be my maid of honor?"

"I would be honored!" Ally emphatically hugged Mirlande.

"I hope Talia can come to the wedding. I know she is still recovering and I know psychologically it is difficult for her to be in this city right now. Do you think she will come?" Mirlande asked hopefully.

"I honestly don't know. I know she would love to be here but we also have to understand what she has gone through. I spoke to her couple of days ago and she was telling me that she seriously is thinking of not returning to this city. Apart from recovering physically she really needs to recover emotionally. That monster really has done great harm to her both physically and mentally. I really don't blame her for wanting to be with her family and she really is dependent on them right now. She's not able to walk without her mom's help. Apart from us, she doesn't have anyone in this city to help her and, since we work, we can't be there to take care of her 24/7 like her mom. She was telling me how terrible her mom feels for not believing her when she told her mom about what she was going through while married to that guy. I guess her mom cries everyday thinking how badly she was beaten and almost died.

"Talia was saying, apart from her mom being a great help to her, it is also helping her mom psychologically. Her mom partly blames herself for not protecting her daughter and now that Talia is there with her she feels like she can protect her. She was telling me her mom even sleeps in the same room as her. Her dad, of course, feels the same way about it and does whatever he can to be there for her. He told Talia that if her ex-husband wasn't in jail he would have beaten him to death and wouldn't have cared if he went to jail for it."

"I can completely understand how her parents feel. There is a part of me that still feels like it was my fault…if I had been there on time she wouldn't have gotten hurt," Mirlande somberly insisted.

"Like I have said to you several times already, it wasn't your fault! What do you think would've happened if you had gotten there earlier? He would have hurt you too. Her ex is a big man and very strong, on top of the fact that he had all that anger inside him. Trust me, he would have put you in the hospital also. I understand that you feel bad she got hurt but there is no way it was your fault. I really hope you understand that. This is a happy time for you now so stop thinking like this and let's just be very thankful that we have Talia in our life and do try to understand if she is not able to come to your wedding," Ally decided to change the subject. "So…tell me, when do we start planning for your wedding since we only have a month? Hope you are not going to make me wear a horrendous dress?" She joked, trying to make Mirlande feel better.

"Hey I need to look good so yes you will be wearing an ugly dress," Mirlande laughed.

Ally joined in the laughter then they both got up from the bench and started walking.

"So did Ary tell you why he called you this morning?" Mirlande asked.

"Yes, he wanted to know if I would like to have dinner with him tonight."

"And? Are you going to meet him for dinner?"

"Before I could answer him, his girlfriend came out of the store and towards us so I didn't get the chance. I'm guessing he will end up texting or calling me later today."

"You still haven't answered my question, whether or not you will be meeting him for dinner? You know what else I can't understand? I know you meet him often at night so where is his girlfriend? I thought they lived together?"

The ladies were deep into their conversation that they were oblivious to the goings on around them.

"No they don't live together. I told you she is a slut and, yes, I meet him often at night. She is most likely out screwing someone else at that time. There is no way she will live with him unless it is absolutely necessary. It just makes it easier for her to screw around."

"I don't get it, if Ary has been with her for a few years why wouldn't he want to live with her? He just found out about you living in the same city recently, I would think he would have been living with her all this while. I seriously don't get it?" Mirlande shook her head in puzzlement.

"Well, he could have asked her to live with him and maybe she came up with some excuse or maybe he never asked her because he may not be ready? I really don't know but I am sure I will find out soon!" Ally raised her brows, adding a devilish grin.

"Hmm, I know that look, you *are* going to meet him for dinner tonight aren't you? I think you should just forget about Ary if you know for a fact you are not going to be with him and just give Sam an answer. You and I can get married around the same time. I know you are upset at both of them but who cares, just let them be unhappy together and you move on and have a happy life with Sam." The two friends walked into a store.

Ally knew what Mirlande was saying was correct but she just had so much anger towards Ary she didn't know what else to do about it. She wasn't even sure if the anger was towards Ary or life itself. Whatever it may be she was very upset with life and admired those who could be with the ones they loved.

"I can't tell you how lucky you are, Mirlande, to be able to be someone you love. You have no idea what I would give to be in your shoes right now," Ally realized that she was changing the subject again and didn't want to make their time together a downer so she moved in a new direction. "So, when can I meet Marcus properly? Last time was a disaster!"

"Actually, I was going to ask you the same question! Marcus felt like you guys got off on the wrong foot so this time he wanted to take you out for dinner. He was hoping Talia could come also but he realizes right now that's not possible. I told him about you and Sam, and he said to ask you about brining Sam along so that he can meet him too."

"Well, we can meet tonight for dinner if you guys are free?"

Mirlande smiled. "I thought you were going to meet Ary for dinner tonight?"

Ally shrugged her shoulders, gesturing with her hand. "I am sure I can change my plans for my best friend."

"Actually, tonight will be fine if you don't mind doing a late dinner? I will be going to his store tonight to help him close then we can meet you after that?"

"That's fine with me, I will text Sam and ask him if he is free and if he would like to join us." Ally pulled her phone out of her purse. When she was about to text Sam she noticed that there was a text from Ary that read, "You didn't answer me about whether you will be meeting me for dinner tonight?"

Ally thought for a second then replied to him making sure Mirlande couldn't see, "I can meet you for a drink in the evening, then I have to meet Mirlande for dinner."

After she texted Ary she then texted Sam asking him if he was free at night to have dinner with Mirlande and her fiancé. Just as Ally was in the middle of the text to Sam she received a text from Ary confirming their drinking date for the evening.

Mirlande saw her texting Ary out of the corner of her eye but didn't say anything to her. Ally then put her phone back in her purse and the two of them entered another store, since the last store didn't have what they wanted.

"So, who are you buying a gift for this time? I think you are the only person that I know who is always shopping for gifts," Mirlande said to her friend while eying a pretty bracelet at the counter.

"It's my cousin's birthday so I need to buy her a gift and I also want to buy something for Sam. I feel like he deserves a gift for putting up with me."

"What are you thinking of buying for Sam?"

"I am not sure, maybe a shirt, what do you think? I really don't know much about him in that sense. I am still getting to know him so I figured I would play it safe and get him a shirt."

"Yeah I guess a shirt would be the safest thing and you have good taste so I'm sure he will like what you pick out. I think I might get Marcus something too."

Just as the two ladies were picking out shirts for their men Ally received a text from Sam, "I might be free tonight but are you sure you want me to come for dinner with your friends? Wouldn't that give people the wrong idea about us?"

Ally's face dropped after she read the text. Mirlande saw her friend's face change and asked, "Is everything ok?"

"It's Sam, I think he is upset with me," she replied as she showed Mirlande his text.

"Ouch! Yeah he does sound upset with you, what happened between the two of you?"

"I think he's upset because I'm avoiding the marriage thing. He told me he understood and to take my time but I really think he, along with his parents, are frustrated with me. I think he's confused as to why I don't have an answer for him."

Mirlande understood where Sam was coming from but she also understood her friend's feelings towards Ary and the confusion she was experiencing.

She gently tried to explain to Ally again, "Just move on, Ally. Let Ary go if you know for a fact it will not workout with him. Sam is a great guy, I would hate for you to miss out on a chance to be happy. I saw you texting, I know you are going to meet Ary for drinks this evening so why don't you tell him you are going to marry Sam and that it's your last meeting with him. Then when you meet Sam tonight, tell him you will marry him and we can celebrate both of our engagements tonight."

Ally knew she couldn't keep avoiding Sam's question. "You are right, Mirlande. I can't prolong this anymore. If you don't mind, I think I will go home now and think things through since this a big decision of my life. I just want some time for myself to accept everything and decide how I am going to do this. I will definitely meet you and Marcus for dinner and it seems most likely Sam will come with me so reserve a table for four and I will see you guys tonight. Text me the time and place after you make the reservations and, thank you, for pushing me to make my decision. Do you want to walk to the car with me or are you going to stay and get something for Marcus?"

"Think I am going to shop for Marcus. You go ahead and I will talk to you later." Mirlande gave Ally a quick hug.

Ally said goodbye to her friend and, as she walked to her car, she texted Sam "let's meet for dinner tonight with Mirlande and Marcus and I will let you know my answer as well."

Sam replied to her text right away, "Great! I will come pick you up after I am done with my shift."

"Sounds great, see you tonight," replied Ally

As she was driving home from the mall, she started thinking about her life, specifically her relationship with Ary. All the good memories came back to her and she just started crying. From silent tears rolling down to her cheeks to a wail of agony and pain that anyone who saw her could feel her emotional distress. She had stopped at a red light and a woman who was next to her in the other lane rolled her windows down and asked her if she was ok. However, Ally didn't notice the other driver at all nor could she hear the woman since her windows were closed. The lady was quite concerned for this aggrieved stranger so she honked her horn to get Ally's attention.

The noise startled Ally, who looked in the direction of the other driver but only rolled her window down slightly. The woman asked her again if she was alright and if there was anything she could do for her. Ally gave the woman a feigned smile and shook her head, letting the woman know she was ok. Just then the light turned green and Ally drove away, giving the other woman a brief wave. The interruption did not stop Ally from crying as she thought about her past and future. When she reached home she parked and sat in her car for a couple of minutes trying to gather herself together. She took a deep breath, wiped her tears, and then exited out of the car. As she was heading to her apartment building she ran into Jeff, who was on his way out. When Jeff saw her he could tell that she was suffering.

Being worried, he approached his neighbor, "What's the matter my vicious vixen? Why so sad and why were you crying? Is everything okay?"

Ally just couldn't control herself and started crying again as she tried to cover her mouth with her hand. Jeff gave her a hug and said, "You know I'm here for you whenever you need me. Right now I'm running an errand and there is someone waiting for you at your door. I will not be out for too long so why don't you attend to your guest then come to my place and we can talk?"

Ally was very surprised, who could be outside her door? She wiped her face with a tissue, said goodbye to Jeff and walked quickly to the entrance. When she entered the building she saw Ary standing there against the wall with his legs crossed. He looked up when he heard the door open and saw her. He gave her a big smile. As she got closer to him, he could see that her eyes were puffy and red. He tentatively moved towards her, with a concerned look on his face.

"Hey, are you ok, what's wrong?"

Ally gave Ary a surprised expression. "What are you doing here so early?"

"I called you and you didn't answer so I called Mirlande to see if you were still with her. She told me you were on your way home so here I am. I really needed to talk to you and thought since the weather is nice we could go to our favorite place, Old Fort Niagara."

"I am not sure if it's a good idea right now."

"Oh come on…it's beautiful out. Instead of having drinks at home, let's go out by the water and we can have drinks in Lewiston. Then take a walk at the Fort and you can tell me why you've been crying."

"I wasn't crying." Ally opened her apartment door.

"Come…hurry and wash your crying face so we can go quickly before you change your mind!" Ary dragged her to the bathroom.

Ally had no idea what he was up to but his presence helped her forget her troubled thoughts. She even forgot that she had to tell him that she was planning to marry Sam. She washed her face quickly, as Ary waited for her at the bathroom door. Then she applied lip gloss and was ready to go. She grabbed her purse and they both left her apartment.

As they were leaving, she ran into Jeff again…this time he was returning home. He could see that she was feeling much better and looked better too.

"Hi Jeffrey, this is Ary and Ary this if Jeff, my neighbor and a beautiful friend." Jeff and Ary shook hands.

"I will see you later young lady." Jeff said, putting his hand on her shoulder.

"Thanks, Jeffrey." Ally gave her neighbor a grateful smile and walked away with Ary.

"Lets go in my car," Ary said, directing Ally towards his Ferrari. Ary opened the passenger side door for Ally and then got behind the wheel. It was a beautiful spring day, not a cloud was in sight. The sky was a beautiful clear blue with lots of sunshine. The temperature was higher than normal for this time of the year in Buffalo. They both seemed to be so happy in each other's presence. The chemistry between the two of them was something to celebrate.

"Did you have lunch yet?" Ary asked.

"No, I haven't." Ally realized her stomach was growling.

"Ok good, I haven't had my lunch either. So why don't we get lunch first? Do you want to go to the restaurant where we used to go in Lewiston? I'm being you today and forgetting the name?" Ary winked at Ally.

Ally was always bad at remembering names of people, places, movies etc. and Ary was always good at making fun of her for that but this time he couldn't say anything. This is not like him because his memory is like an elephant's.

"Wow, you actually forgot the name of the restaurant, what is wrong with you?" Ally feigned shock, laying her hand on her heart.

"Well for two reasons. First of all, last time I was there we were dating and, secondly, I really have a lot on my mind right now." Ary's words took on a serious tone.

"Oh? What's going on?"

"I will tell you about it later but right now I am interested in knowing what made you so upset earlier?" Ary pivoted the conversation.

Ally took a deep breath and contemplated for a minute whether to tell him now or later about her decision to marry Sam. Then she thought to herself that she should just tell him and get it over with since she has to tell him before she meets Sam later that night. "I…aah…I have decided to marry Sam and I'm planning on telling him tonight when I see him," She blurted it out.

Ary wasn't expecting to hear that from her, at least not at that moment so he just shut down. There was an awkward silence for a few minutes.

Ally couldn't stand the quiet and was now worried, "Why are you so quiet? I'm sure you knew this day was going to come sooner or later? I wanted to tell you before I told him. I don't know why I wanted to tell you first since it's not like you had told me you were going to start dating Mona. It's not like I owed you anything or hurt you in any way like you did," Ally was starting to jabber, using her hands to emphasize the emotions spilling out of her. "I can't believe you started dating her when I was having problems with my family. I loved you so much and was going through so much with my family for you and...and...you, you just didn't seem to have the same feelings, which I thought you did, as I did for you. You had no problem moving on. Then you show up in my life again after so many years while you are still with her. I mean, the nerve of you to do that! I never once heard you apologize to me for what you did and expected me to be your friend as if nothing happened. I am even surprised you are here with me instead of being with her. I am surprised you had the nerve to come out after she saw us at the mall. I know what she is like and I am pretty sure she gave you hell for that. Heck I would have too if I was in her shoes. What happened, you had a fight with her so you had nothing better to do than to come hang out with me since I have always been the stupid one to still talk to you?"

Ally just let all her feelings and emotions come out in one breath without even thinking about it. She had a lot of anger and it seemed like she just wanted to let him know everything that was built up inside of her for so many years and now she just couldn't hold it in anymore. Who knows this might have been the last time she was going to be able to let him know how she felt so she let everything out without even giving him a chance to respond. She spoke nonstop for twenty minutes and Ary just sat there driving and listening to her, in shock. He really wasn't expecting this from her at all. She finally stopped talking then turned to him with tears in her eyes.

"Don't you have anything to say to me?"

Just then, they had reached the restaurant. He pulled into the parking lot and parked the car, then turned to her. "If I hurt you so much then why have you been hanging out with me all this while? You always say that people have choices right? So, if I am so bad why did you choose to sleep with me again or hang out with me when I asked? You could have said no. I didn't force you to be with me, did I?"

She became even angrier at him. She thought, 'this is what he had to say to me after what he had done?' She was livid and told him so, "You are right, people have choices and, yes, I chose to hang out with you but, now? I am done hanging out with you! Don't call me or show up at my door ever again. From this day on, you are no one to me! I want nothing to do with you, I don't want to be your friend or anything because this is what I am choosing to do now! Take me home, I am done with it!" She yelled.

It was very visible to Ary that Ally was furious with him and he felt bad that she was crying so much again so he tried to put his arms around her to console her but she kept pushing him away as if she was disgusted by him. He just wanted to calm her down but she kept pushing him away then finally he just held her tight in his arms and said softly, "Shh shh....I can see that you are very upset with me but there is something important I want to talk to you about so can you please just relax?"

After a few minutes resisting him, she finally calmed down and stopped crying. He then slowly pulled himself away from her and peered into her eyes, "Listen to me. There is something I really need to talk to you about which is why I got you out of your house so that no one could disturb us," He took a tissue from his pocket and wiped the tears from her cheeks. "You look drained. Let's go to the restaurant so you can wash your face and we can get something to eat. I am not telling you to not be upset with me but please hear what I have to say. I listened to you now, it's time for you to listen to me."

Ally just couldn't get herself to stop hating him but she also didn't have a choice. She knew he wasn't going to take her home until she listened to him and she had no other ride. She went into the restaurant to wash her face in the restroom while he was getting a table for them. She wasn't in the mood to eat or anything but at this point she just wanted get this over with and go home. She wanted to leave her past life behind and this was the closure she needed before she could start the next chapter of her life.

By the time she came out of the restroom, Ary had been seated and was waiting for her. He smiled at her as she walked towards him but of course she did not return the smile. "Feeling a little better after washing up?" He asked.

"I am not in the mood for this. Just say what you need to and take me home!" She said angrily.

"I am not going to say anything to you until you change that frown on your face." Ary wanted to cheer her up but, at the moment, he was at a loss as to how to do that. He wasn't going to give up though and decided on a tactic. He had gotten a nice table out on the patio in a corner near the trees where they could have some privacy for themselves. Ary gazed out at the beautiful landscape and evergreens that made up the natural enclosure. "Hmmm, haven't been here for so many years. Remember how we used to sneak away from your family and come here? I always loved being here with you." With fond memories escaping his lips, Ary peeked over at Ally with hooded eyes.

Ally gave a sarcastic snort, "I am sure you brought your girlfriend here."

"No I didn't…this place had so many memories of you, of us, I couldn't come back here. Remember how we used to walk down the harbor eating our ice cream and watching the jet boats? The beauty of this area is breathtaking." Just as he was about to say something else he was interrupted by the waiter. "Can I get you something to drink?" The waiter asked.

Ary looked at Ally. "What would you like?"

"I will have a Virgin Mary, please," Ally conveyed to the waiter.

"I'll have an extra spicy Bloody Mary," Ary gave his order.

"Are you ready to order or would you like some more time?" The waiter asked.

"Could you gives us a few more minutes please?" Ary replied.

"No problem, I will get your drinks while you guys decide." The waiter then walked away.

"Let's pick out what we want before he comes back then I will tell you why I brought you here." Ary opened his menu and looked at the selections. Ally did the same.

"Seems like they have changed the menu a bit but everything sounds really good, doesn't it?" Ary asked, trying to redirect the awkward silence between the two of them.

"I guess." Ally shrugged her shoulders, still looking at the menu and avoiding eye contact with the man next to her.

"Look…they have your favorite, fish and chips," Ary pointed to one of the choices under "finger foods".

Ary nodded her head. "Yeah, I just saw that. I think I will get it. Hey, they have the grilled chicken sandwich you always liked too."

"Yep, I was thinking of ordering that."

"Looks like you haven't changed about ordering boring items to eat...thought by now maybe you would've wanted to try different things." Ally finally looked up at Ary.

"Hey, leave me alone. You be as adventurous as you want to be...I like to play it safe. I can't be like you, trying new and weird things. I like my things just right!" They both smiled at each other.

The chemistry between them still hadn't changed. Both of them always picked on the other one and joked around all the time. Ally seemed to have forgotten for a second that she was supposed to be angry with them. Ary looked across and saw two elderly people walking down the harbor.

He chuckled and subtly pointed towards them. "Look, I think that lady is wearing Depends."

Ally turned her head towards the elderly couple and then back at Ary. "Oh my God! You will never grow up will you? You are so insensitive! One day when you are old, someone young will point and say the same thing about you! And knowing you, you will be a grouchy old man walking with a walker with tennis balls attached to them and wearing your Depends." Ally started giggling.

"I think you are thinking about your future. I will be the dashing gentleman with all the ladies while you will be a nasty old Depends wearing hag, with wrinkles and everything heading south." Ary gestured with his hand in a mocking way to emphasize his perspective of the future.

This is how the two always teased each other....

"Ah, so your maturity level stayed at the age of a 15 year old. I thought by now your girlfriend would have changed you," Ally countered caustically.

"Apparently, you haven't reached adulthood with those biting remarks either."

Before Ally could reply, the waiter returned with their drinks. "Ready to order?" The waiter took out his pad and pen.

Ary and Ally both gave their orders to the waiter, who wrote them down.

"Will that be all?" The waiter inquired.

"Could I have a glass of water please?" Ally replied.

"Certainly. I will be back shortly with your meals." The waiter gathered the menus and went to put the couple's order in.

After the waiter walked away, Ally turned to Ary, clasping her hands on the table in front of her. "Why are you out with me on this beautiful day? Shouldn't you be spending time with your girlfriend on your day off? So, what is it that you needed to talk to me about?"

Ary was silent for a second and then took a deep breath, "After she saw the two of us talking outside the store, she became very upset. She asked me if I was in touch with you again so I told her that we ran into each other a few months ago. She was clearly very unhappy and wanted to know if we were still friends. I told her we were. Then she asked me if I had slept with you recently and, obviously, I didn't want to say anything to her so somehow I was able to dodge the question. She chose that moment to bring up marriage.

"She said that, since she and I have been together for so many years, it was time for us to get married. The catch is that she will only marry me if I agree to stop seeing or speaking with you and move out of this city. She told me she could not live in the same city as you. She didn't want me to see you at all and felt we would somehow continue to be friends forever. She doesn't like the comfort that I have with you and is afraid I won't be true to her if I remained in communication with you. So she asked me if I would agree to these terms before getting married. At that moment, I didn't think about her at all......"

Just then, the waiter came over with their order and placed the dishes in front of the guests, "OK, here is your lunch. Fish and chips, and a grilled chicken sandwich. Is there anything else I can get for you?" He asked.

"Thank you, I think we are good for now," Ary replied.

"Let me know if you need anything and enjoy your meal." The waiter turned to leave, stopping only to pick up something from the floor.

Ary looked at Ally and continued...

"As I was saying, at that moment, I wasn't even thinking about her at all. All that I thought of was you, the thought of not being able to see you ever again made me feel a bit sick to my stomach. You were my best friend who had always been there for me whenever I needed you.

"For a couple of years, when I was away from you things just weren't the same. I always missed you and when I needed to talk to someone you weren't there for me so I kept everything inside of me. Yeah, Mona was there but I never felt comfortable sharing any of my deep feelings with her. You were always a voice of reasoning for me and I didn't get that from her. She was always into going out, having fun but when it came to serious stuff I felt like she really wasn't there. I mean, I just felt that she couldn't understand me the way you always understood me. I never had to say much to you and you knew what I was talking about. I could be open and be myself with you without worrying about being judged. With her it wasn't like that then and still isn't today. You were there for me when my mom died and I was left alone in this world but you never made me feel like I was alone.

"When you were in my life, I felt that no matter what happened you would take care of me and would never let me fall. I just never felt like that with her. I could always trust you with everything and I knew you would never do anything to harm me but with her, that isn't the case. My relationship with her seems more pretentious than genuine. Yeah, she's a party animal, likes to have fun but she also constantly needs to be told how beautiful she is. You are more secure about yourself…you don't need someone to tell you how you look.

"Whenever Mona and I had a fight, Mona would have no problem going out with her friends and her reasoning was that's how she dealt with things. You and I used to have fights but you still cared and I always saw that. So, now, when she told me if we get married I could never see you ever again, I just couldn't do it, I told her that's not possible."

After Ary stopped talking she looked at him and with teary eyes she softly asked, "What makes you think I will be friends with you forever?"

"What do you mean you won't be friends with me?" Ary looked at Ally shocked.

"I mean, I most likely will be getting married to Sam soon and he doesn't know anything about you and I am pretty sure he wouldn't like me to be friends with you knowing our past relationship. No matter who I marry, no guy would be alright with me being friends with a guy I used to date. Would you allow your wife to be friends with her ex-boyfriend? I know you…you wouldn't so I don't see why you think Sam would either."

He looked down at the table, then he looked up at her, "You didn't let me finish. I know that no guy would want you to be friends with me. Just like whomever you marry would not like to see you with me, I cannot see you with someone else..."

Ally interrupted him a bit confused but guessing what he may actually be thinking, "What are you saying?" She asked.

Ary took a deep nervous breath and said, "What I am trying to say is that…I can't imagine my life without my best friend. I can't see you with anyone else either and it became obvious to me that I really don't care for Mona the way she wants me to care for her. What I am saying is, screw your family, and screw the world where religion means more than a human being, I want to marry you. I want to marry my best friend and from the sadness from your eyes I can see that deep down, inside your heart it is me you want to be with.

"Come on, only you and I can put up with each other. No one can understand our sense of humor the way we understand it. Do you honestly think you can be open and talk to Sam the way you do with me? Do you think you can actually fart in the grocery store isle and jokingly blame him for doing that? You can only do that with me! He is a doctor. Imagine you looking at old people walking by and trying to guess with him who is wearing depends and who is not! He is going to look at you and think how insensitive you are and not see the sense of humor in it. For a girl, you have a warped sense of humor like I have and no one will be able to see that because you will have to learn to be polite, and trust me I know you very well that is not going to last that long. You can only handle being polite for so much after that you will want to scream. Only I know how crazy you are because I am crazy like that. I know your family will never accept me but will you accept your life and be happy with Sam? Will you be happy pleasing your family?"

Ally controlled herself from crying then said, "You cheated on me! How do you think I felt? I was going through a rough time with my family because of my relationship with you and what did you do? You started seeing that slut! Did you know that you and I are just a game to her? I know her. She wanted to break us up and she won…and it's because of you that she won. I am hundred percent sure she slept around behind your back, those times you were talking about when you guys had a fight and she went out?

"Well, I guarantee you that she was out screwing around but I am pretty sure you saw none of that. I can't believe you now want to come to me after she made certain demands if you were to marry her. Why didn't you try coming back to me before that, even if my family had an issue? Why didn't you try to fight for me? I didn't see that, I just saw you going off with someone else when things got rough. You have no idea the pain that I felt in my heart. I thought I was going to die because of the emotional pain. No one, not even my family could feel my pain. Forget them, you say. If you have this thing for me then why did you hurt me? Can you just answer me that? You think you can come and go out of my life as you please? Well, you can't. Now you can feel the pain that I felt all these years. I can choose my family over you because I can't trust you! How can you guarantee me that if I fight for you, that you would never hurt me again?"

Ary didn't expect her to say everything she just did. "You have to trust me. Whatever happened in the past was because of your family. They took you away from me and I was left alone, no you and no family. Then Mona came along. Whatever her intentions you say there were at that time, she came along and I wasn't feeling alone anymore. Don't blame me, blame your parents. If it wasn't for them, I would have never been with anyone else. Why can't you think of this as a life's lesson or test to see how truly we really love and care for each other? Think about it, she wants to marry me and I walked away from her. I'm here because I can't imagine myself without you. I know you are that person I can trust with my life, and with our future kids…."

Ally interrupted him, putting her hand up. "Well that's just it, you trust me because I never gave you a reason not to but I don't know if I can trust you. I don't know if you are worth fighting with my family. This will be the last time we will meet in life because, from this point on, I never want to see you again. I want to start a new life with someone I can trust, not with someone who doesn't wait for me. Now please take me home, I am done. I really can't do this to myself," She then gestured to the waiter to come over. When he neared the table, Ally gestured to the plates. "Could you please pack this for us and bring us the check? We have an emergency and we need to leave right away," she said

"Certainly I will return in a moment," the waiter replied and left quickly to retrieve the check.

"Ally, I can't imagine my life without you, and I can tell that you too want to be with me so why are you fighting it? Why can't you let the past be a growing experience and accept our present and future as fate? You always say everything happens for a reason so, think about it, we were away from each other for so long and, yet, here we are. Don't you think maybe it's meant for us to be together?"

Before Ary could say more, the waiter came back with the check and boxes for the leftovers. Ally took the check from the waiter to pay, she didn't want to wait so she got money out of her purse and gave it to the waiter, "I don't need the change back, thank you."

She then put the food in the boxes, grabbed her purse and started walking out as Ary followed her, careful not to draw attention to herself. They both walked out of the restaurant and towards the car. Ary was lost for words. He was so troubled and scared of losing her. He knew her very well and once she had made up her mind about something it was impossible to change it but this time he wasn't about to give up. Deep down inside he was hoping he could somehow make her change her mind.

As they approached his car he grabbed her hand and turned her to face him. "Wait, Ally, I can't let you go. Please, just give me a few more minutes then I will drive you home and do whatever you want me to do but please just spend more time with me."

"What is it that you want to say that you haven't said already? Why do you want to make this more difficult for me than it is? I told you it's not possible for us to be together. I can't give up my family for you."

"Let's take a walk in our favorite place and talk," he pleaded, really not wanting to let go of her.

As angry as Ally was, there was a part of her that didn't want to let go of him but then what other choice did she have if she wanted her family in her life? She felt life was just not fair to her. She couldn't understand why Ary was ever injected into her life if he wasn't supposed to be part of it forever. She didn't want to regret anything and as hard as it may have been for her, she decided to go for a walk one last time with her true love in their favorite place. She figured she would probably never walk in that area ever again with anyone else so she nodded her head yes. That made Ary smile and it might even have given him a false sense of hope. They both walked down the harbor holding hands. Ally loved the comfort of his touch and thought to herself about how much she will miss it. She didn't resist. On one side of them were beautiful flowers and the other side jet boats were zooming by at high rates of speed. The couple never got tired of watching the fast boats.

As they were walking hand in hand, Ary looked at her and said, "I am sorry for what happened in the past. I really don't know what happened. One minute you were there in my life and the next you were gone, and I was left alone in this world. After my dad passed away, my mom and I held onto each other, comforting one another through the loss but then *she* died. I was all alone. I lost my entire family until you came into my life and you changed the way I felt about life. I really thought you were always going to be there with me. Never did it ever cross my mind that you weren't going to be there but, then, one day you were gone!

"At that time of my life, I was very upset with God. He took away everyone that I loved and left me bereft of warmth so when Mona came into my life I really didn't have any feelings left in me. She was just someone who was there physically for me. I don't think I really had strong feelings for her at all. She was just a body for me to hang onto. I don't think I ever had the love or care for her the way I always had for you. I became very cynical about everything.

"She and I hung out whenever we could. I never asked her to move in with me nor did she ever ask me either, which made it easier for me I guess. I never thought of getting married to her or anything. I guess, in a way, I liked my relationship with her because my emotions weren't there. Those emotions that could hurt me the way I had been hurt, first the loss of my parents then the loss of you. I did always wonder what happened to you. I figured your parents would have arranged a marriage with some loser they thought would be good for you. I never bothered trying to find out because I guess I was afraid.

"The day I ran into you and came to find out you weren't married. You have no idea how happy I was to see you again. I would try to find every excuse to see you and then when I found out you were being set up with that guy. You have no idea how angry and jealous I was! I wanted to jeopardize whatever you had going with him but then I didn't want you to hate me so I held myself back. Now you are telling me you are going to marry him. How do you think I feel? When Mona said we should get married and said I could never see you again, I just couldn't do that. I had no problem telling her because, like I said, she didn't mean anything to me like that. It didn't bother me even once at the thought of not ever seeing her, but the thought of never seeing you, I just couldn't bear.

"Please don't leave me, don't marry him. You are the one person in this world that I know who genuinely cares about me and who I can trust, who I truly love. I think, if you still said no, I would just hate life and God so much." Ary's voice cracked and Ally could feel the power in his grip as he begged for her to agree to be with him.

She started crying. "I don't know what to do. If only you were of same religion things would have been so much different. I couldn't and I wouldn't ever ask you to change because I respect who you are and you are a good person, religion is something that has to come within. I never believed a person should be forced to convert. Religion is a very personal thing and how can anyone convert if they don't truly believe in it. Not only that, it's not like I am a religious person either but if I choose you I have to prepare myself to say bye to my parents and my family. What if things don't work out between us for some reason, then what? Then *I* will be left alone in this world."

Ary looked at her puzzled then responded, "Why do you think we won't be together in the future? How do you know what the future holds?"

"Is there a guarantee we will be together forever? I have seen so many people who were in love for so many years, who were married for twenty plus years then end up in a divorce. I guess there are no guarantees in life and I also feel really bad doing this to my parents."

Ary became a bit exasperated. "I understand they are your parents but do they even care that they have stressed you out to the point that you now have an illness that could kill you? It's something there is no cure for, and they blamed you when your dad suffered a heart attack not realizing it runs in the family. Come on, I don't understand!" He lifted his free hand in frustration.

He was clearly very upset but poor Ally, she was torn between him and her parents. She just didn't know what to do. She stopped walking and hugged him. "I admire those people who can marry whomever they want I just don't understand why God has made it so difficult for me!" She said.

As angry as Ary had become he also could feel the pain in her voice, they both were so stressed out. They both sat down on a bench and just sat there staring at the water, holding each other.

Ally realized the sun was going down a bit and that Sam will be coming to pick her up very soon. They have to meet

Mirlande and Marcus in only a couple hours. She became very nervous and felt sick to her stomach and started to cry even more trying not to show it to Ary. She kept wiping her tears, and then her phone rang. Her heart just dropped thinking it might be Sam calling her. She ignored the phone but a couple of minutes later it started ringing again. She ignored it again but whoever it was wouldn't stop calling. Ary became annoyed and he tried to get the phone out of her bag to answer it himself.

"Oh my God let me guess it's that guy calling you!" He exclaimed angrily.

"No Ary! No don't answer the phone!" Ally pleaded.

"Then you answer the phone and tell him you don't want to be with him or else I will let him know that!"

"You know I can't do that."

Ary snapped, "Fine! I guess I don't mean anything to you! You want to be with him and not me then let's go. I will take you back and you could live happily ever after with him since you think if we get married we will end up in a divorce. Go, go be happy with him!" He was furious.

He then grabbed her hand and started walking towards his car. She didn't say anything but just cried. When they got to the car he opened the door for her then slammed the car door after she settled in the seat. She didn't say a word, she had never seen him that angry before. Ary then got into the car and quickly drove off, tires screeching.

On their way home neither one of them spoke a word to each other. Ally sat quietly crying and Ary seething. The half hour ride seemed much longer since they weren't talking to one another. They didn't want to say goodbye and, as they rode in silence, they could only think of each other. They finally reached her apartment. He abruptly stopped the car out front and waited for her to get out. She sat there for a minute not knowing what to say. Finally, she just hugged him and said goodbye to him. He didn't say a word to her but when she looked at him, she noticed his eyes were red. She sighed and then left the car. After she walked a few steps, she could hear the car's engine rev and scream off into the distance. She turned to look, but he was already gone.

Jeffery was outside throwing his garbage in the bin. He saw everything that went on. When she came close to him he could see she had been crying. With a sincere look on his face, he lifted her chin with his finger. "You know where I am if you need me."

Then he walked away. He wanted to give her some space and let her decide when she was ready to talk. She always went to him for advice so he knew she would come to him when she was ready. He could tell this had to do with the love triangle but he didn't want to say anything until she asked him for advice. Ally just nodded her head and went into her apartment.

She had a really bad headache from crying so much. She wasn't in any mood to meet Mirlande and Marcus for dinner but she couldn't stand them up. This was a very special time for Mirlande and she wasn't going to take that attention away from her friend, so she decided to go ahead with the dinner plans. She had just enough time for a quick nap and shower before Sam was supposed to come over to pick her up.

Meanwhile, Ary had arrived home, sat in his big chair and stared out the window. His heart was aching dreadfully. He had his phone in his hand, contemplating whether to call Ally or not. She had made it very clear to him that she no longer wanted to see him but he didn't want to give up so easily and he also knew her very well. If she makes up her mind about something no one but herself could change her mind.

Ary knew there was the greatest possibility that he had lost her for good, his best friend, the one person whom he could trust and who was always there for him, will no longer be there. Yes, for a few years he had lost touch with her but, through their mutual friends he always knew what she was doing. Perhaps, he too didn't get married knowing that she wasn't. He decided he couldn't sit around anymore and needed to try to convince her again. At this point, he felt he had nothing to lose so he didn't care if she told him not to ever get in touch with her again. He got into his car and went as fast as he could hoping to stop her before she met with Sam and give him her answer. Since he didn't live far from her, it would not take long to get there. As he drove he also tried calling her but she wasn't picking up. He kept redialing her number until he reached her apartment but there was never an answer.

He had become very anxious by the time he reached her place. He rang the doorbell. She didn't answer. He leaned on the buzzer for several minutes to no avail. Just when he was about to walk away from the door Jeff came out. When Ary heard the door, he turned to see if it was Ally but it wasn't. Jeff recognized the young man by the door so, as he walked past Ary he leaned towards him.

"She's not home. She left a few minutes ago." Jeff kept walking, not looking back.

"Oh, ok, thank you." Ary's tone turned to dejection.

He wanted to ask Ally's neighbor if she left alone or with someone but he didn't know Jeff well enough to ask him that. So he just got back into his car and sat there in a somber mood, contemplating whether he should sit there and wait for her to return or just go home. He thought to himself what good is that going to do to wait for her if she has made up her mind. Then he had an evil thought of waiting for both of them to return then approach her to jeopardize her relationship with Sam but then, he thought, that's not going to get her back, instead it will make her hate him even more, so he left.

Chapter 11

Dinner with Mirlande and Marcus

Mirlande and Marcus were seated in the restaurant, waiting for Ally and Sam to arrive. Both were sitting across from each other, holding their hands. They appeared very happy and in love to other restaurant goers.

The waiter approached them, "Would you like to order your drinks now or wait for your guests?" He asked, filling up the glasses with ice water.

Marcus looked at Mirlande. "Should we order a bottle champagne for everyone? They should be here anytime now."

Mirlande nodded in agreement. "Yes, that sounds good and Ally is always on time so I am guessing they should be here any minute."

Marcus turned to the waiter. "Could you please bring us your best champagne?"

"Certainly." The waiter left to get the champagne.

Just as the waiter walked away, Ally was seen walking towards the table. She was wearing a beautiful red V-neck chiffon dress with a black belt just above her waist and a pair of black and red open-toed heels. Her hair billowed down as she walked, holding a black clutch in her hand. She smiled at them. Marcus noticed how beautiful she looked tonight.

He turned to Mirlande and whispered, "Wow! She looks stunning. Sam is sure a lucky man."

Mirlande smiled at Marcus in agreement, knowing that her friend is a beautiful young woman with a perfect naturally tanned skin tone. There was a part of Mirlande that was jealous of how she always presented. Ally may not be a tall woman but her curvy, petite frame was desired by many. She worked very hard to keep her body in good shape, although, it was harder for her to do that since she had a small physique. Gaining even one pound would easily show on her petite figure. As she approached the table, Marcus and Mirlande stood up smiling at her. Ally and Mirlande gave each other a big hug then Ally turned to Marcus and gave him a sweet kiss on the cheek. She grabbed Marcus' hand as well as Mirlande's, beaming at them and hiding any signs of her earlier experience.

"Congratulations! I am so happy for you guys."

"Thank you so much!" Marcus grinned ear to ear, like a kid with a new toy. He pulled out the chair for her so she could sit.

"Is Sam still parking the car?" Mirlande asked while the three of them were getting comfortably seated in their chairs.

"Actually he wasn't able to come. He texted me earlier saying that it was really busy at the hospital and he wasn't sure when he'd be able to leave. So, he asked me to apologize to you guys and said he will make it up to you," Ally replied.

Mirlande caught a glimpse of something in Ally. "Are you feeling ok? Your eyes look very tired."

"Actually, I had a really bad migraine earlier so I took a nap before coming here. I am not used to taking naps but it felt good." Ally half-heartedly feigned a smile.

"Aww...too bad Sam couldn't make it but I'm glad you were able to come." Mirlande did not catch the lie.

"You know I wouldn't have missed this special dinner for..." Just when Ally was in the middle of her sentence the waiter arrived with the bottle of champagne and four glasses.

"Your champagne sir," The waiter said as he poured a bit for Marcus to taste.

"It's delicious! Good choice." Marcus nodded to the waiter. The waiter started pouring the champagne into the glasses but Marcus held up his hand. "My apologies but there will only be three of us tonight, not four." The waiter gestured his understanding and proceeded to fill three glasses with the bubbly.

"Are you ready to order any appetizers?"

Marcus was excited. "If you ladies don't mind, I would like to order the appetizers for us and I am sure you will like it!"

Mirlande and Ally looked at each other delighted. With smiles on their faces, they both spoke in unison, "Sure!"

The waiter smiled at them then started to write down the order.

Marcus started, "How about pot stickers, bruschetta, calamari…."

Ally interrupted him before he could say anymore, "I think that's enough don't you? What are you planning to do? Order everything on the menu?"

Mirlande laughed. "It seems he's a bit too excited. I agree, we won't be able to eat our dinner if you order so many appetizers."

"Are you sure it's enough? I certainly want to make sure *I* get enough." Marcus emphasized himself with a rub of his belly.

"Honey, they is more than enough. Look at Ally…does she look like someone who eats a lot!" Mirlande laughed.

Marcus looked at both of the ladies and threw up his hands. "Ok, if you ladies think it's enough then I guess it's enough."

"I will be back in a few minutes with your appetizers and then take your dinner order," the waiter said and turned away, almost running into a coworker. He was able to avoid the collision and walked toward the kitchen.

Marcus picked up his glass of champagne, focused his gaze on Mirlande…"I would like to make a toast to my beautiful very near future wife. I can't wait to spend the rest of my life with you."

Mirlande and Ally both lifted their glasses and gave a cheer.

"So did you guys decide on the date?" Ally asked.

Marcus and Mirlande looked at each other and smiled. Mirlande turned to Ally with a gleam in her eyes. "Yes. Exactly one month from now!"

"Wow, that's great! Will you guys be ready with all the planning and everything?"

Marcus held Mirlande's hand as he put his glass down on the table. "Everything is already set. My friend owns a restaurant with a banquet hall and, since it's not busy this time of the year, the hall is available for us next month. He and I have already planned the menu, music, décor etc. My aunt owns a bakery and she said she will make the wedding cake for us as a wedding gift..."

Mirlande chimed in, "His aunt also sews so she said she will also make the wedding dress for me!"

"Wow, you guys are really lucky to have so many connections and can have everything done in such a short period of time. How about the flowers?" Ally asked.

"Talia is actually gifting us with the flower arrangements for our wedding. She said she knows a florist very well who is a client of hers and they told her they could do the arrangements without a problem. Apparently, it's a slow time for the florist also," Mirlande said.

"I guess you guys have picked the right time to get married. Then what's left for me to help you with? Wedding invitations?"

"Well, since we don't have that much time to get them printed Mirlande and I will be making calls to friends and family. We actually started doing that as soon as we decided on the date," Marcus replied.

"Wow! You guys are really amazing! I don't think I've known anyone like you two who could organize a wedding so fast..."

Their waiter approached the table and placed their appetizers in the center.

"Here are your appetizers. Are you ready to order dinner?"

Marcus spoke up first, "I hope you ladies will allow me to select your dinners as well? I have tried everything on this menu since I come here often. The lobster with pasta is absolutely out of this world. I know both of you like sea food so, trust me, you will love this and, if you don't, we can always get something else."

"Well, I guess this is a great test for your future husband to see if he has the same taste as we do. If you pass, then you are part of our gang and, after that, no questions asked," Ally joked.

The waiter smiled as he wrote down the order then he turned to Ally. "For this dish, you get to select the lobster you like from the tank before it is cooked."

"No thank you! I don't want to see any of our food alive so if you don't mind just pick what you think is best!" Ally shook her head using her hands to wave no and then Mirlande agreed with Ally, "Same here! I don't think I can eat it if I see it alive either."

"Very well, I will select the best three. Anything else?" The waiter asked.

"I think we are good. The lobster dish comes with so many side items I don't think these ladies will have any room for anything else," Marcus replied.

"You guys enjoy the appetizers while I go pick out your lobsters," The waiter said and then walked away.

As the night wore on, Ally was trying her best to be focused on Mirlande and Marcus but she couldn't stop her mind from wandering and kept thinking about everything that had happened with Ary earlier in the day. She had agreed to meet Sam after dinner since she had promised him she would have an answer for him by the end of the night. She knew he was eagerly waiting to meet her later. He had texted her several times during dinner expressing his eagerness and somewhat fearfulness about her answer. Ally really wanted to get some advice from Mirlande and Marcus before she finalized her decision but wasn't sure if it was the right time to ask. She really didn't want to dampen the mood they both were in but she was afraid as the night went on that her emotions would become transparent to Mirlande since her friend knew her very well.

Then again, she thought to herself that maybe Mirlande will not notice as she and Marcus were so engrossed with their wedding plans. Ally tried to remain focused but then she received two texts from Ary which distracted her. Every time her phone buzzed with texts she would be very discreet when she checked to see who was texting her. Luckily for her, Mirlande and Marcus were still focused on their wedding that they didn't notice she was checking her phone. The restaurant was very busy so their dinner had arrived late.

The waiter had apologized to the trio. "Sorry about the delay. For some reason it has been very busy tonight and we are short of staff. The manger didn't expect it to get this busy and did not schedule enough staff."

Marcus certainly understood the issue. "Not a problem at all, it is expected if you guys hadn't planned it to get this busy."

Throughout their night together, Ally had thought to herself how nice Marcus really is and understood why Mirlande was so fond of him. She also liked the fact he took charge of things to make sure everything was going well. She found herself comparing him to Sam, who seems to be more passive and expects her to make most of the decisions. It wasn't that Marcus seemed controlling, it was just that he appeared to be very aware of others' likes and dislikes. He paid attention to people and their personalities whereas Sam seemed to be more reserved and let people make their own decisions and, at times, have others help him make decisions for himself which drove Ally crazy. Sometimes, he made her feel more like his mother than a woman whom he maybe marrying.

For Ally, it was very refreshing to see a man take charge of things and show some love and care for others. She loved how Marcus is so detail-orientated, especially when it comes to the wedding planning contrary to Mirlande, who sometimes misses the details. Ally then realized that most couples she knew had at least one individual who was passive. She thought that maybe it's just nature's intention. She had many thoughts crossing her mind and, yet, she somehow managed to stay engaged in their conversation.

"You were so right Marcus…the appetizers were very delicious. If your taste is like this I can't wait for your wedding dinner!" She exclaimed while Mirlande kissed Marcus so proudly.

"Does this mean I'm part of the gang now with no questions asked?" Joked Marcus.

"I guess you are part of our gang now!" Ally gave a chuckle.

"Well, since now I've got the seal of approval and am officially part of the club and that gives me the right to test your doc to see if he is good enough for our group," Marcus teased.

"Yes, now you have the authority to approve or disapprove a new member." Ally winked back.

At that moment, Mirlande excused herself to use the rest room. Ally decided to join her. Both ladies made their way towards the restroom together. As they were walking Ally tilted her head and ran her fingers through her hair, just as she was doing that she saw something that made her stop and look in shock but continued walking to the restroom. When they entered the restroom they both gasped.

"Wow!"

"Oh my God, this is a bathroom?! I would love for my bathroom to look like this!" Mirlande exclaimed.

The ladies room looked like a luxurious spa room. It had a beautiful red and white lounge area and smelled like roses. The wall had an antique mirror on it, the wooden floor was covered with a red mosaic rug. Both of them just went straight to a couch against the wall and sat down. Mirlande completely forgot she needed to use the restroom after she saw the lounge.

"I don't think I am going to be leaving this room anytime soon. It just makes you feel so wonderful!" Exclaimed Ally.

As they both sat there, Mirlande gave Ally a questioning look. "So, do you really like Marcus now?"

"Yes, I really do. I feel bad how it all started with us. He truly seems to love you and I just love the fact that he pays attention to every little details of the people in his life. He is completely opposite of you!" Ally laughed.

Mirlande smiled in a delight. "I guess that's what relationships are supposed to be made of. Like the saying goes, opposites attract! But seriously, can you imagine if we both were the same? I think life would be very boring if we both thought and acted alike. We would also probably drive each other crazy trying to one up on the other so we can make everything just perfect. You know, if you are comparing Sam to Marcus, then don't! As much as you like the idea of your other half taking charge of things, I know you, you will not like that all the time. You have an alpha personality and you usually like being in charge of your life. I understand sometimes you get tired of it but you will not like having your spouse be alpha also, at least, not as strong as you and that's why Sam is perfect for you.

"Actually, you should be very happy you found someone like Sam. I think any woman would love to have someone like him, who is very easy going and doesn't like to be in control of everything. Think about it, he will do everything just as you like it without any arguments! I understand at times that can be tiring for you but overall I think you will like it that way. Listen, I know you very well and I love you. I am saying all this to you because I suspect that's what is on your mind by the way you were talking to Marcus. I can also see that you haven't been completely yourself tonight. I mean, you are physically here but your mind hasn't been with us. So, would you like to tell me what is going on?"

Tears started to flow down Ally's cheeks. She tried to control herself but she couldn't. "I am so sorry. I really didn't want to do this. It's a very special moment for you and I didn't want to take that away from you and Marcus. Today is your day and my problem can wait until another day. We better get out of this luxurious lounge before Marcus starts wondering what happened to us." Ally wiped away her tears and forced a smile on her face.

"I completely forgot I needed to use the bathroom!" Mirlande exclaimed, walking into the stall. Ally rinsed her face and freshened up her lipstick.

After a few minutes, the ladies left the bathroom. As they were walking back to the table, Ally glanced over to the table they had passed on their way to the restroom, then turned back towards Mirlande. When they reached their table, Marcus stood up and joked, "I thought someone kidnapped you guys and was about report it to the police!"

"You should go see the ladies restroom. It's like an opulent lounge. Very beautifully decorated. Ally and I completely forgot that we were at a restaurant and were about to just sit around and chat then remembered you were out here waiting for us!" Mirlande giggled.

"If that room made you that happy and relaxed maybe I should go see what it looks like so I can make one of the rooms like that for you at home. Then, you and I can spend lots of time in that room, if you know what I mean." Marcus winked at his fiancé.

"If you guys really need a room, we can end our dinner now and you guys could go ahead." Ally laughed.

Mirlande just blushed and didn't say a word as they all sat down again.

"I took the honor of ordering all of us dessert. I know you ladies like to watch your figure but tonight I don't want to hear that you are not going to eat any dessert," Marcus said.

"How could it be that you order dessert and we not eat it? After the delicious dinner you ordered for us I can't wait to taste the dessert," Mirlande said, as she smiled at Marcus.

While they were waiting for their dessert, the three of them were laughing and enjoying each other's company even though Ally was still a bit distracted but she was trying very hard to stay focus on her company. The waiter rolled over a cart filled with different desserts. They were all decorated beautifully and looked so irresistible.

Mirlande's eyes opened wide and her jaw dropped. "Don't tell me you ordered all those desserts!"

The waiter smirked. "Yes, all these are for you guys."

"Are you kidding Marcus? If you haven't realized it, there are only three of us here, not fifty!" Ally shook her head in disbelief.

Marcus smiled. "I ordered all these desserts so we can taste them and decide the best one for our wedding. After seeing the dessert menu, I just couldn't decide. They all sounded so good and I thought it would be a good idea to try them so we can have lots of desserts for our wedding. I don't know about you ladies but most people I know are more interested in the dessert than the dinner. If the dinner doesn't turn out to be what people like, having a selection of many types of desserts will please everyone and people always remember what they had for dessert, especially when it's really good! Having a good dessert makes everything look so perfect. Think about it, how do we make ourselves feel good when we are stressed or upset about something? Eat sweets, right? It is the most important day of my life and I want everyone to remember that day, and talk about it for years to come."

Mirlande held Marcus' hand tightly as Ally had the look of awe on her face. The three of them sat there trying out thirty types of desserts. It took them over an hour just to try them all. Although they were very full, they couldn't resist trying all the desserts because they looked and tasted so delicious, and the three of them were really enjoying every minute of it.

"I think I just gained twenty pounds eating all these desserts!" Ally indicated the larger size with her arms.

"You and me both! The only difference is you could afford to gain it, I can't!" Mirlande joked.

"Oh come on ladies stop complaining. Before we started tasting them I told you not to think about that. It's for a good cause." Marcus looked around the table at the half empty dessert plates. "So, do you ladies have any favorite ones? I can honestly say to you that they all are so good I can't decide which one to pick."

Mirlande agreed, "You're right, they are all so good. I think it's going to be hard to pick just a few."

"How many desserts are you planning to have, Marcus?" Ally asked.

Marcus shrugged his shoulders. "I was thinking about fifteen of them."

"Good luck narrowing them down to fifteen, honey!" Mirlande patted Marcus' arm.

"Why don't each of us pick five desserts we like so that way it covers different taste palettes of different people and if we pick any of the same ones then we choose that many different ones?" Ally suggested.

"That's a great idea!" Marcus was impressed.

All three of them then wrote down desserts they liked the best. Ally was enjoying this task so much that she actually forgot what had been on her mind the entire night. All three of them were eating, drinking, laughing and were just having a great time together. The restaurant had actually closed now but the owner didn't disturb the three of them because he knew they were busy selecting desserts for the wedding and of course that meant more business for him. The waiters were cleaning up the restaurant and the owner came over to their table.

"Hello Marcus. How is the selection process going?"

Marcus stood up and shook his hand. "Hello, Jon. meet my lovely bride to be Mirlande and our dear friend Ally, the girls smiled. These desserts are absolutely delicious and we're finding it very difficult to select fifteen from the thirty you have here. They're all so good! But I think we finally have narrowed it down to what we want. How will these desserts be presented at the wedding?"

"We could present them however you like. We could present them on rose peddles, small horse carriages etc. the options are endless," Jon explained.

"The little horse carriages sound really nice!" Mirlande excitedly clasped her hands together.

"Wow, you actually picked something out for our wedding without me asking you! So little horse carriages is what we will get," Marcus responded to his future wife. Mirlande blushed while Ally nodded her agreement, giving two thumbs up.

Jon wrote down all the information he needed for the wedding and gave each of them an extra complementary dessert to take home. It was very late at night, all of them were having so much fun that they didn't realize the time.

"Hey, let's go to the wine bar. I am having so much fun with you ladies and I'm just so happy that I don't want the night to end. I know it's late but who cares…lets have fun! Let's go dancing!" Marcus suggested, excitedly.

"I'm in and you better be too, Ally." Mirlande pointed her finger at Ally.

"Yes, of course you can count me in," Ally assented. She could see how much Marcus genuinely wanted to just go out and celebrate, and she didn't want to dampen the night.

"Hey why don't you call Sam and have him meet us?" Mirlande proposed to Ally.

"Actually, I don't want to wake him up just in case he had a really rough day and needs to work tomorrow."

"Yeah, as much as I would like for him to come out with us, I don't want to disturb the doc." Marcus conceded.

"Let's all go in one car. I don't want you to drive alone so late at night especially after drinking. Since your place is not far from here why don't we drop your car off and then go?" Mirlande recommended.

"Sure, that's sounds like a good idea." Ally agreed.

They all left the restaurant and got into their respective cars. Marcus, with Mirlande beside him, followed behind Ally. In no time, they reached her place. She parked her car then dashed to Marcus'. As she was opening the car door her eyes caught sight of Ary's car parked nearby. She got into the car quickly hoping he didn't see her. As Marcus drove away, Ally turned back and looked at Ary's car but the windows were tinted too dark so she really couldn't tell if he was looking at her or not. She then checked her phone to see if there were any texts and sure enough there were texts from him and Sam. They both were looking for her and, of course, she had not checked her messages since earlier in the night at dinner.

Ally sat in the back of the car watching Mirlande and Marcus interact with one another, admiring their relationship. As she sat there she thought to herself that she too could have a relationship like the two of them have. She has found someone who really likes her and who will treat her nicely. She finally realized that she needed to let the past be past and shouldn't try to compare people. She also realized that she is destined to be with Sam and there is nothing that she or anyone could do to change that destiny. She always told others whatever is meant to happen will happen and they always listened to her but now she had realized it's time for her to listen to herself. She decided to text Sam…

"Hey r u up?"

To her surprise he responded right away…

Sam: "Yes was worried about u, u didn't respond to any of my texts so couldn't sleep".

She grinned then texted…

"Sorry I had a very bad migraine n slept. Mirlande n Marcus just showed up at my door n now we r going drinking n dancing, can u join us?"

Sam: "Sure, I don't have work tomorrow so that'll be nice n I get to spend time with u ☺"

Ally: "That's great, meet us at Darcie's…we just got on the road so leave now!"

Sam: "Leaving as I text u!"

Ally: "Great, see u soon"

Sam: "Can't wait!!"

Just as Ally finished reading her texts Mirlande turned around and asked, "You're very quiet, everything ok?"

"Yes, I was just texting Sam to see if he was up and wanted to come out with us. He said yes and is on his way there also but, listen, I need you guys to do me a favor and not tell Sam that I went out to dinner with you guys. I had a very bad headache and wasn't going to come out for dinner. I told him I wasn't going to dinner with you guys and just go to bed early tonight but I really didn't want to cancel this special dinner with you, I just didn't want to … I don't know how to explain it.. Uh, I just wanted to spend the time with you guys…I know it sounds weird, I just don't know how to explain it, I…" Ally was struggling to explain the situation.

"Don't worry about it, glad he can join us tonight," Marcus interrupted realizing that Ally was in a "word jam."

"Thank you Marcus." Ally sighed, as if her life just got saved.

They arrived at the place. It just had started raining so Marcus stopped the car in front of the door so the ladies could go in without getting wet, then went to park the car. Parking in that area was a bit difficult since the parking lot wasn't that big. While he was out parking the car, the two women went inside to get a table.

The environment at Darcie's was very cozy with soft lighting. It was one of those places where you can drink, smoke cigars and dance if you so desired. Darcie's was set like an old house with many rooms that consisted of soft sofas and tables, as if you were in your living room. All the rooms were draped with colorful sheer curtains, the curtains gave you privacy if that's what you were looking for or they could be tied if you wished to have the view of the bar and dance floor. There were two floors, bottom for non-smokers and top for those who wished to enjoy cigars with their drinks. They also served finger food if anyone were in a mood for late night munchies and most likely than not, people enjoyed having something to eat with their drinks and cigars. Actually, Darcie's was known for its finger food even if you were not hungry…just the smell of the food made you want to eat. It also was a great place for people watching!

There was a wait of fifteen minutes to get a table and ten minutes had already passed as the girls waited for a table and Marcus. Just as they were looking out the door to see if Marcus was coming, instead to their surprise they spotted Sam walking in. Ally waved her hand to get his attention. He saw her and walked over.

"Hey, how did you get in here so fast? Did you find a good parking spot?" Ally asked as she hugged him.

"I got really lucky, as I pulled into the parking lot someone was walking towards her car, so I waited for like a minute, that's it!" Sam related, snapping his fingers.

"Wow, you really lucked out. We've been waiting here for more than ten minutes and Marcus still hasn't made it in. Looks like he may be parking really far from here." Mirlande smiled at Sam and gave him a hug.

Just then Marcus walked in. "You won't believe how far I had to go to find a parking spot," Marcus declared.

Marcus had not met Sam as of yet so Ally introduced the two men, who shook hands, and then the waiter came to seat them. The two couples followed the waiter to their sitting area. They had put their name on the list for a smoking area since they did enjoy having cigars occasionally so they were seated on the second floor. Actually, the second floor was great for people-watching too. You could see all around the bar, including the dance floor, from there and something interesting always occurs. The second floor was just as interesting as Alfred Hitchcock's "Rear Window". If you were a fan of that movie, then you would definitely be a fan of Darcie's best kept secret. Ally, Mirlande and Talia always chose to sit on the second floor even if they weren't in the mood to smoke cigars. They often came to Darcie's late at night after their long busy work week and just enjoyed drinks and snacks and of course watching people.

The four were really enjoying the night together drinking, smoking cigars and snacking. The music was blasting and people were being loud as they danced. The twosomes were dancing and having fun themselves. While they were all were dancing, Mirlande's eyes caught someone approaching them. Mirlande nudged Ally to get her attention. Ally looked at her and then in the direction that Mirlande motioned. Ally turned her head and froze…it was Ary.

Ary looked very upset and he was walking towards them! Ally motioned him not to come but he didn't seem to care. Ally became nervous since she was with Sam and she was afraid Ary might make a scene so she gestured him to meet her at the restrooms. She quickly excused herself. Sam offered to walk her to the bathrooms but she insisted she would be fine and that he didn't need to walk her there. Sam wasn't comfortable with her going alone so insisted on coming with her but then Mirlande chimed in and rescued her by offering to accompany Ally because she too needed to use the restrooms. Sam felt better so he nodded to girls and walked back to their seating area with Marcus.

As the girls were walking towards the restroom, Ally thanked Mirlande profusely for intervening. Mirlande was about ask Ally something but then they both ran into Ary. Mirlande said hi then excused herself and went into the ladies room. Ally demanded to know what Ary was doing at Darcie's. Ary tried to stay calm and keep his composure but he was very jealous seeing Ally with Sam and upset she might have already agreed to marry him.

"I don't know why you won't marry me but instead want to marry him?!" Ary tried to keep his voice down so as to not attract attention.

"You know exactly what you have done and why I will not marry you," replied Ally frustrated.

"I am sorry I hurt you and I know there's nothing I could say to you that will make it right. All I know is that you are truly the one I love and care for. I just can't imagine my life without you. When you were not in my life for the past few years, it was never the same for me. I hated your family for not seeing me as a human being and not letting me be with you. When you came back into my life things haven't been the same for me either. I am not able to move on and I don't want to move on without you. I feel like I am talking to a wall, repeating the same thing over and over and you are just not hearing what I am saying!" Ary through up his hands.

"You know what? Fine...this is what you want? Then go marry him. I know you, once you make up your mind about something there is nothing anyone could say or do that will change your mind but I thought maybe this time it would be different. What was I thinking? You will never change!" Ary abruptly turned and walked away as Ally stood there staring after him.

Mirlande was standing close by and heard the entire conversation. She came up to Ally.

"You know he really sounded very genuine. I can feel the pain in his voice. I hope you haven't answered Sam yet so you can really think this through. Your decision will effect three lives..."

Mirlande hadn't finished talking when she saw Sam and Marcus coming towards them so she ended the conversation and walked over to meet the boys.

"Everything ok with you ladies? Sam here got very concerned because you two were taking so long. He didn't believe me when I told him there was no need to worry and that you ladies mostly likely were just chatting as usual," Marcus teased as a cover for Ally.

"I wasn't worried...I was just wondering where you ladies were since this place will be closing in ten minutes," Sam countered embarrassingly.

"Is it time for it to close already?" Mirlande asked in a surprising tone.

"We all can go to my place and have some coffee and chat," Marcus suggested.

"That would be great but I am getting a bit tired. If you guys don't mind can we get together for coffee another day?" Sam declined.

"Of course doc, that's not a problem. I'm glad you were able to join us tonight. It was great meeting you and hanging out." Marcus offered his hand.

Sam shook it. "It was great meeting you as well. We definitely should get together before you guys get married. You all look like you're tired also so why don't I take Ally home and you two get some sleep," Sam proposed.

Mirlande and Ally looked at each other and smiled. Ally then grabbed Sam's hand.

They all walked out together. They stopped near Sam's car since it was close by.

"Why don't I drive you guys to your car since its parked so far away?" Sam teased.

"Alright doc, just because you got lucky with the parking spot no need to take a dig at me," Marcus laughed.

The four of them got into the car and Sam drove to Marcus' car, which was about four blocks away. Mirlande and Marcus thanked Sam as they exited his car and said goodnight. Sam and Ally watched their friends get safely into Marcus' car.

There was some silence as Sam and Ally were driving home. The sky was starting to get lighter with the morning sun peeking through the clouds. They both were very tired and, at one point, Ally even fell asleep. Sam let her sleep until they reached her place. He parked the car and then gently ran his fingers down her cheek. Ally slowly opened her eyes not realizing they had reached her home.

"Had a nice nap?" Sam asked softly.

"Sorry, I didn't realize I fell asleep," Ally replied, as she pushed her hair off of her face.

Sam got out of the car then opened the door for her. She was still very sleepy but was trying to pretend she wasn't. Of course he could tell. He had his arm around her, holding her up, as they walked into her apartment. As soon as they entered her apartment he started kissing her and she reciprocated. In no time, Sam picked Ally up and carried her into the bedroom. Their kisses became fervent as he laid her upon the bed, their hands groping and eventually tearing off each other's clothes. Their passion grew as love-making overwhelmed their thoughts. Ally was finding a new side of Sam that she had never experienced before. This made her want him more and with every touch, with every movement, their bodies became a symphony of pleasure. Their bodies entwined like snakes in a mating ritual, undulating to the music coming from outside. Who was playing the music so loudly, they did not care. Sam's increased momentum carried them both to a climax with a brilliant cacophony of lights and the sounds of ecstasy. They collapsed in each other's arms, where they fell into a deep sleep, the day's activities finally catching up to them.

A few hours later, dawn already having broken through, Sam's pager from the hospital began beeping repeatedly. He went into the bathroom with his phone so as not to disturb Ally. After he was done with the call, he returned to the bedroom, put a note on the pillow next to hers, gently touched her cheek, and quietly left. Just as the door closed, she woke up and found the note he had left next to her.

The note read: "Sorry I am leaving like this, I have to go to the hospital text me when you are up, will try to call you when I get a chance. Thank you for a great night! I really loved waking up with you in my arms and I hope this is how I wake up 'til the day I die."

Ally had a big smile on her face after she read the note and she just lay there holding it to her chest.

Chapter 12

Making New Friends

It was a Saturday afternoon and Ary had gone to his office to do some work. As he was unlocking the door he heard someone say, "Hello stranger!" He turned around and saw Talia. He was really shocked to see her so he gave her a hug. "Hey, how are you? You look great!"

"Thanks!" Talia smiled and hugged him back.

Ary invited Talia into his office. Opening the door wide, he gestured for her to enter ahead of him. "Come on in." He closed the door behind them and gestured for her to sit on the sofa next to the window. "How have you been? I haven't seen you since the day you were discharged from the hospital."

"I'm actually doing very well. I feel like myself again." Talia replied as she sat down.

Ary sat in the chair opposite to Talia. "I am so glad to hear that. You scared all of us and, of course, I miss seeing you here every day. There were times I wished you were here so we could talk. I missed that too. So are you back for good?"

"I'm in town for the wedding next week. I thought I would stop by the office and clean everything up since I *am* planning to come back for good next month," Talia explained.

Ary displayed shock, "Wedding next week?"

"Yep. I'm sure Ally might have told you about it, right?"

Ary shook his head, still in disbelief.

Talia continued, "I'm so sorry it didn't work out between you and Ally. I wish I had been in the right state of mind so I could have helped you guys."

Ary was shocked to hear about the wedding. He felt weak in the legs and like his life had come to an end. "No, I am not aware of the wedding next week. So Ally is happy with Sam then?" He asked sadly.

"I'm not quite sure if she *is* happy with him. I think we both know that, in a perfect world, she would have loved to be with you as you would have with her but I feel like she compromised for the sake of her family. Sam is really a nice guy but I think she would have been much happier with you. What can we do? She's made up her mind. After she told me about her decision, I tried to talk her out of it but she seemed determined to go through with it. She was really upset with you for not waiting for her. That made her feel like you didn't love her as much as she loved you. She also said she was afraid to fight with her family or even give them up for you out of fear that you could leave her in the future...so she settled for Sam. I would still love to tell you to fight for her until the day of her wedding but I don't know how feasible that is." Said Talia.

"I would love to fight for her but she refuses to answer my texts and calls. I have even stalked her outside of her apartment and that just made her even more upset." Ary became very melancholy.

Meanwhile, as Ary and Talia were discussing ways to change Ally's mind, Ally had returned home from her office across town. She had a lot of paperwork she needed to catch up on so she had gone to her office at 5 in the morning. Since she was hungry and very tired she had picked up Chinese on her way home. As she walked towards her apartment there were boxes all over the hallway and also blocking her door. She was looking around to see who the boxes belonged to so she could ask that person to move them. When she didn't see anyone she decided to move the boxes out of her way herself. She placed her take out bag on the floor near her door.

Just as she was trying to push the boxes to the side she heard someone say, "Oh I'm so sorry for blocking your door." Ally stopped and looked up.

The voice came from a casually dressed, very handsome, tall, thin, olive-skinned man. He looked like one of those models from GQ magazine. Ally just stood there for a second not saying a word, she was so mesmerized by his looks. He repeated again, leaning toward her, "I am so sorry for blocking your door. I didn't realized I had done that."

Ally came back to herself and instead of getting upset she just smiled. "It's quite alright. I didn't see anyone so I decided to move the boxes out of my way."

The man then introduced himself, "Hi I am Zain, I guess I'm your new neighbor."

"Hi Zain, I'm Ally and I guess you're my new neighbor," Ally responded, echoing Zain as they both shook hands.

"Here, let me move those boxes out of your way," said Zain as he put his Grande cup of coffee on top of one of the boxes. After he made space for her he grabbed her bag of food that was on the floor.

"That smells delicious," he said as he handed her the bag.

"It's Chinese, why don't you come in and have some with me, I have plenty," Ally offered.

"Oh thank you, but I don't want to interrupt you with your lunch," Zain replied.

"No not at all! Seriously come on in. I promise you will love this Chinese food. It's the best in town and we can get to know each other bit since we are neighbors now."

Zain was actually happy to make a new friend in the building so he agreed to join her.

"Can you give me one minute? I will be right back." He held up his index finger and went into his apartment.

Ally opened her door and entered her apartment, leaving her door open. She set the food on the table. Just as she was getting plates out of the cabinet there was a knock on the door.

"Come on in!" She called out.

As she turned around, as Zain and a strange female entered her apartment, with a bottle of wine and a brown take-out bag. Ally was surprised to see the female or perhaps was even disappointed since Zain was very handsome and she could've fixed him up with a friend.

Zain introduce his friend, "This is Lulu." The girls nodded to each other.

"We brought wine and, you will not believe this, we also had ordered Chinese from the same place," Zain said, carrying a bag from the local Chinese restaurant. They all laughed.

"There was no need for you guys to bring the wine and food but please have a seat." Ally gestured to the dining table.

They all sat down. Ally figured they were husband and wife but she didn't see a ring on either one of their fingers so she then thought to herself they might be dating or living together but for some reason their body language didn't appeared as if they were in a relationship. She also thought to herself, from their names it appeared as if they may be Pakistanis or even Indian Muslims, either way she was surprised they were able to live together considering their religion. All these thoughts were going through her mind. She was very intrigued and wanted to ask questions but since she just met them she wasn't sure if that would be appropriate. Of course, being who she is, she just couldn't help it and had to know.

"So where did you guys move from?" She asked.

Zain smiled and replied as if he was expecting the question, "Lulu's and my family originally are from Pakistan but the two of us were born and raised in the US…in Chicago, to be exact. We have been married for two years but now we are in the process of a divorce."

"Oh, sorry to hear that! But you guys don't seem like a couple who's getting a divorce?" Ally said surprised.

Lulu looked at Zain with a wink and began, "Well, there is a story behind our relationship. We would have stayed married but…"

Lulu was about to say more but Zain interrupted, "Well you see, Lulu and I kind of had an arranged marriage. I wasn't really finding anyone and, as you may know how parents are in our culture, they sort of 'arranged' for us to meet. After the two of us went out a couple of times, we both agreed on getting married. In less than three months we were married. Lulu is a great person and we get along very well. We had no issues except for when it came for sex. I loved hanging out with her but I just didn't want to have sex and this caused tension between the two of us.

"As time went on, I realized I was gay. I mean, I always knew it but because of the family and culture I always pretended I wasn't. There was a part of me that wasn't happy at all. Then Lulu started to notice I was the happiest when I was around a friend of hers, who happened to be gay. She tried to talk to me about it but I would avoid her. In the middle of the night, while I was pretending to sleep, I could hear her crying next to me in bed. I just hated the nights because of what she was going through. I was sure she that way all the time but I think the nights were worst because I couldn't give her the intimacy she was yearning.

"I slowly started avoiding her and I could tell she was getting lonely. I felt very bad for her and like I was ruining her life. Our parents would come over and our moms would ask us when we were going to give them a grandchild. Since we both just finished our residencies, we're both surgeons, they felt we didn't have an excuse anymore. Every time they asked I would get very angry and walk away, and the conversation just made Lulu sadder. One day, I finally decided to have 'the talk' with Lulu. After we discussed our situation for what seemed like hours, we finally decided that it was best for us to get a divorce but telling our families was the most difficult thing!

"We first talked to my parents about it and that didn't go so well at all. Matter of fact, my father doesn't talk to me at all. He thinks being gay is a white people thing and, of course, our religion doesn't accept that. Apart from not being able to face his family and friends, he fears his son will going to hell. My mom is trying very hard to be supportive but I think she still is having hard time accepting the fact that their only child is gay and she too fears that I'm going to hell. I feel really bad for my parents but I couldn't live a lie and I just didn't think it was fair for Lulu to suffer.

"Then we went to tell her parents. Her parents just said so much because they felt bad for their daughter. It wasn't their daughter's fault that her husband turned out to be gay. They liked me and wished that wasn't the case. They too tried to explain to me how it was haram (forbidden) in Islam to be gay but because I wasn't their son their reactions were still different compared to my parents. They were just upset with me for marrying their daughter when I knew I was gay and ruining her life. But Lulu, she was good about it that she tried to explain to them that it was hard for me to come out and accept who I was, and even harder to tell everyone.

She and I have become great friends, I respect her a lot! I don't think anyone in her situation would have reacted the way she has and I am very grateful for that. She came here with me to help me get situated in this city. I found a job at Millard Fillmore Hospital..."

Suddenly, there was a knock at the door. It opened and a young handsome Caucasian man with blonde hair and yogic body in jeans and a t-shirt peeked from around the door, a grin on his face... "I thought I heard your voice here."

Zain got up and motioned for him to come in. The young man came into the apartment. Zain introduced the new arrival to Ally. "This is Ethan, my boyfriend. Ethan, this is Ally, our new neighbor." Ally got up and shook Ethan's hand then asked him to join them.

"I'm guessing you have already told Ally your life story? Ever since he had the courage to come out he blurts out his life story to anyone who asks," Ethan joked.

"I don't blame him for wanting to share his story with everyone. What he has done is very courageous and, of course the support, he received from Lulu is very admirable. I must say your, story definitely is something you could write a book about and I'm sure it would become a best seller," Ally lauded the couple.

"Please don't give him any ideas!" Ethan chuckled, slapping his palm to his forehead.

They all sat down at the table and enjoyed their lunch. Ally couldn't help but admire Zain for being able to have the courage to standup for his life with his family. Of all the people in this world, she definitely knew how difficult it was to do so. As she sat there watching the three of them, she started thinking about her life. She wished she had the courage to stand up to her family for what she wanted in life but she figured it was too late for her now.

"So. . what do you do Ally?" Zain's question shook her out of her reverie.

"I'm a psychologist," She responded.

"Oh now I see why it's so easy to talk to you. There is something about you that makes people feel comfortable and welcoming," Zain said admiringly.

"Yes, you have that aura about you that is very approachable," Ethan chimed in.

Ally beamed. "Thank you! You guys are very sweet. So what do you do, Ethan? Lulu and Zain are doctors, are you as well?" Asked Ally.

"No. I can't stand the sight of blood! I'm an investment banker. I actually work in New York City and come home on most weekends. I am hoping to transfer my job here but will have to see how that goes. Zain didn't want to live in the big city. He hates commuting long distance and getting stuck in traffic. Then, he saw a job opening here so he decided to apply. When he had an interview, I came with him and he just loved how everything is at most half hour away here! Since we're from Chicago the cold doesn't bother us so we weren't afraid of the Buffalo winters that everyone talks about. I don't mind traveling to New York and back. Yet here we are making great friends already!" Ethan said.

"Well, I am glad you guys picked Buffalo and picked this apartment complex or else I probably wouldn't have met all of you," Ally expressed with a smile.

They all finished their lunch and seemed to have connected very well. Lulu looked at the two men. "Okay, you two, now that we took a nice long break and made a great friend I think we need to get back to our unpacking. Ethan and I have a flight to catch tomorrow or else you will be unpacking all by yourself, Zain."

"I guess we should get back to unpacking!" Zain responded sarcastically.

The three of them helped Ally clear the table and, just as they were leaving, Talia was walking towards Ally's door.

"Hey you!" Ally exclaimed, surprised to see her.

"Look at that, perfect timing. Going out?" Talia asked, hugging her friend.

"Nope. Meet my new neighbors, this is Lulu, Zain and Ethan. We all just had lunch and they were just going back to their apartment to finish unpacking. This is my best friend Talia," Ally said as she grabbed and squeezed Talia' arm.

"Hello," They all replied simultaneously, gesturing with waves.

"It's nice to meet you, Talia. You just missed a great lunch. Next time, we will have to get together," Zain offered.

"Yes, definitely," replied Talia.

The three new neighbors picked up a couple boxes and went into their apartment. Talia followed Ally into her apartment.

"Oh my God, those two guys are so good looking!" Talia exclaimed.

"Yes, they certainly are but keep your panties on…they are gay." Ally smirked.

"What? A Pakistani Muslim guy gay?!" Talia voiced in a shocking tone.

"First of all, gayness doesn't have any cultural boundaries and, secondly, I am impressed you knew he was Muslim and Pakistani just by the name!" Ally winked at her friend.

"Hey! For how many years have you been teaching me about how to tell if someone is Hindu or Muslim and Paki or Indian? Also, hanging out with someone who politically isn't that correct really helps too," Talia countered, teasingly.

They both laughed then sat on the sofa.

"So, really, they're both gay? And what about Lulu, who is she to them?" Talia inquired.

"Well, to make a long story short, Zain and Lulu have been married for a couple of years and she helped him come out. They are from Chicago, settling here now. Zain's dad doesn't talk to him because he is going to hell for being gay, 'you know, the religious stuff' and Lulu is such a great person that she is helping Zain settle in. They both are in the process of a divorce but they both will continue to stay friends forever. Zain is a doctor, so is Lulu. He got a job here at Millard. Ethan is a Banker who works in New York and comes home on the weekends. That's pretty much their story," Ally divulged in one breath.

"Wow, that's unbelievable. Learn something from him, he came out *and* he is a Muslim!" Talia urged.

"Yeah but the father doesn't talk to him at all."

"Okay, but he looks so happy. It doesn't look like he is bothered by that."

Ally knew where Talia was going with this conversation so she decided to change the topic. "So, how did it go with cleaning your office? Are you ready to move back?"

"You know after coming back to Buffalo I realized how much I like it here. I actually missed this city. People are right…everyone complains about the weather in the winter but there is something about this place that you miss and makes you want to come back. As horrible as the winters are here the life here is great. I really missed all the great restaurants and, well, just everything. I feel so comfortable…I don't think I'm going to wait for a month to move back. I think I am mentally ready. I am not going back to my parents place. I am going to tell them I will come get my stuff from them when I get a chance. It's not like I need those clothes. I still have my apartment and my belongings here so I don't have to go back," Talia admitted.

"Wow that's great! Mirlande and I missed having you here. This calls for celebration! Let's call Mirlande and see what's she's doing. If she's free then let's go out tonight and celebrate," Ally proposed excitedly.

"That sounds like a great idea but don't you think she might be busy with the wedding preparations?"

"Most likely it's Marcus who is getting everything ready and she may be just sitting pretty. Want something to drink?" Ally offered, as she texted Mirlande.

"Sure, actually why don't we walk to the café and get some coffee and sweets? I miss our café," Talia suggested.

"You know I will never say no to coffee." Ally smiled then she grabbed her purse.

The girls walked over to the café in no time since Ally lived so close to it. "Oh, how much I missed this!" Talia said, as they both walked into the café and smelled the wonderful aromas.

"I am so glad you are doing well and are here to stay. I really missed hanging out with you. Mirlande has been busy with Marcus and the wedding. I have been hanging out with Sam whenever he is free but I really needed someone to help me figure out my life," Ally stopped talking and pointed. "Hey look! Our table by the window is available let's grab it before someone else does."

"Speaking of your life, I ran into Ary when I was at my office this morning. We sat and chatted for most of the morning."

Ally raised her eyebrows but did not smile.

"You know, he really loves you and I think you love him also but you are settling for Sam. Yes, you told me what he had done to you. I know he didn't wait for you and all that, and I am sure he had his reasons but...look at him now. He could have stayed with that girl but he didn't, he let her go and he has been trying to convince you to marry him. I can tell on his face that he is getting very depressed. He truly loves you, Ally, and I think you are making the biggest mistake of your life. Sam is a really nice guy and a great doctor but will you truly be happy with him?" Talia shook her head and raised her hand when Ally tried to interject. "I get the religious thing with your family. My question to you is if Ary had waited for you in the past would you have fought to be with him?"

"I guess I would have fought with my family if I knew he loved me as much as I loved him and waited for me but the point is he didn't," Ally retorted.

"But what can he do now to prove to you that he still loves you? He let go of the girl that he was with for few years. He could have married her but he didn't...he wants you. You know, people grow up and change...give him a chance. Truly hang out with him and get to know him again, not just argue and have sex. Get this mental block out of your mind about what he did, how he didn't wait for you, etc. Look at him as the person he is now not what he was few years ago. He has changed just as I'm sure you have changed from the girl you were when you guys were together.

"Put your family aside and see if this is the guy you want to be with...is he someone you feel is worth fighting your family for? You know you always tell everyone and I know you truly believe in it that everything happens for a reason. Did you think for a second maybe Zain came into your life for a reason? He is a Pakistani, Muslim gay guy who was married and then he came out and had to face the most difficult thing in his life but he did it. I'm sure in Islam being gay is worse than marrying someone out of the religion. He somehow had the courage to face his family. I understand his father doesn't talk to him but with time he may come around."

Talia continued to press, "Look at Zain…he looks so happy even when his family is not supporting him. I know you love your parents but did you ever think about how much longer they will be in your life? I mean, they are getting older and once you are married it is you that has to live your life with whomever you marry. No matter what kind of problems you might end up having with your spouse no one will be there to understand them or live your life for you. Consider me for example, I was married to a Jewish guy that my parents approved purely because he was Jewish but they didn't live with us to experience what I went through until he almost killed me… then they started to understand that it's not the religion but it's the person that matters. If you talk to my parents about your situation I am sure they will tell you the same thing as what I am telling you now. I'm sure, if you want, they could also try to make your parents see things from a different perspective.

"I know you've made up your mind about marrying Sam solely based on your parents approval but not because you truly want to be with him, deep down in your heart. Just listen to your inner voice, which I know is telling you something else. I know you don't have that much time but somehow take a break from seeing Sam and give Ary a chance. I know Mirlande has told you the same thing I have been saying. She and I love you and want the best for you. There is only so much we can tell you because you have to decide if you want to listen to your friends or not. You are a psychologist and, of all the people in this world, you should understand how difficult it is to help someone if that person doesn't want to listen or hear what you have to say.

"Right now Mirlande and I feel the same way. We have been telling you over and over again to give him a chance and fight for him but from this point on, I don't know about Mirlande, I am done trying to change your mind. It truly is your life and your decision. I will support you with whatever you choose because I love you and because it is you that has to live your life. After today, I will no longer bring this topic up…there is nothing more I have to say. For once, I'm going to be like you. You always tell us, 'It's your life' when we don't listen to you and now I am saying the same to you, IT'S YOUR LIFE!" Talia finally finished her thoughts in a very frustrated tone.

Ally was totally shocked to see this side of Talia. Even though Talia is a lawyer, she has never spoken to her like that, ever. She was actually lost for words and just sat there looking at her in surprise. A part of her knew exactly what Talia was saying and she too would have given this advice if either one of them were in the same situation.

"I know exactly what you are saying and, yes, it's something I need to seriously think about and make a decision. Maybe what Ary did to me is an excuse I keep using to help me avoid having to face this decision and just choosing my family over him. I wish there was some kind of sign that we are meant to be." Ally sighed, shrugging her shoulders.

"Did you ever think that him coming back into your life is the sign or the fact that he chose not to stay with that girl? Come on you are smarter than that…"

Just then, Sam walked into the café wearing his doctor's scrubs. Ally looked at Talia with a sunken feeling inside…is this the sign she was asking for? Talia looked back at Ally thinking, no, this can't be the sign. While they were having these thoughts Sam noticed the girls sitting there and waved at them. He motioned to them that he was on a call and then walked out of the café as he continued talking on the phone. The girls were in a state of shock at what this "sign" could've meant.

Talia shook herself out of the reverie and realized something. "Did you noticed we have been sitting here and chatting that we forgot to order our coffee?" Talia gave Ally a silly look to try to lighten the mood.

Ally nodded, forcing a smile on her face. "I guess we should order our coffee."

"Do you want to sit here and I will get it for us? Do you want the usual? I saw they have your favorite pecan bar?"

"Sure, thanks," Ally sadly replied.

While Talia went to get the coffee and dessert, Ally sat at the table looking out the window trying not to look at Sam, who was outside the café, and hoping he wouldn't come back in.

The café wasn't crowded so Talia returned with the coffee and two pecan bars within a few minutes. She glanced outside to see if Sam was still on the phone and saw that he was.

"Here you go. Hey, did Mirlande respond to your text yet regarding tonight?" Talia asked.

"I don't know, let me check."

Ally pulled her phone out and showed it to Talia. Talia's face lit up as she looked at the text and then she smiled. There was a text from Ary asking if Ally would call him. After they both finished reading the text with shocked faces they simultaneously looked outside to see if Sam was still there but he wasn't.

"Okay, this is weird. I confess, when you asked for a sign and Sam walked into the café, I said to myself 'shit, she is supposed to choose him' but now there is this text from Ary!"

Talia looked up at the ceiling, talking to the Almighty. "Ok, God, she asked for a sign but this is confusing."

"See, even for God, it's not easy to choose. Seriously, if God can't decide who I'm supposed to be with then how can I as a human?!" Ally joked.

"Yeah, you're right. This is really confusing, but if you asked for a sign and you got one for each guy then maybe God is ok with either one of your choices. It sounds like he has given you two good guys in your life and you get to choose which ever one you want. In a way, you are lucky…he is giving you an option of two guys!"

"He may have given two good guys to choose from but how am I lucky when one of them is a choice between him and my family? Couldn't God just make it easier? If Ary is the one then have my family be ok with it and if Sam is the one then Ary shouldn't have ever come back in my life!"

"Hmm…maybe by choosing either one of them, in the future, you can't blame anyone for your decision."

The argument between a psychologist and a lawyer was something to witness. It lasted for a while and it's hard to tell who actually won since neither of them like to lose an argument. They both decided that whatever is meant to be will be and that is where they ended that topic.

As the girls were cleaning up their table and getting ready to leave the café, Ally received a text, "Oh I wonder if Mirlande is finally replying me back." She opened her purse to check her phone.

"Oh…it's Sam saying he is sorry he didn't come say hi to us. He was on his way to the hospital and thought he saw us coming in here so he stopped by to say hi, but just as he got to the door he received a call from the hospital and had to leave right away," Ally reported.

Talia teased, "Tell him that's ok…you needed a sign and that was God's way of showing it to you."

"Ha ha! You think you are so funny, don't you!" Ally snickered.

"I'm just saying!" Talia shrugged.

"I'm just so happy to see you back to being yourself. I missed you. Anyways, I don't know why Mirlande hasn't responded to my text. I think I'm just going to call her," Ally said as they walked out the café.

Ally dialed Mirlande and put it on speaker so Talia could hear.

Mirlande answered.

Ally: "Hey Mirlande! What happened to you? Didn't you get my text?"

Mirlande: "Hey! Oh, I haven't checked my texts all day, just been busy. I just grabbed the phone to call you to see if you wanted to join us for dinner but, apparently, you called me first."

Ally: "Talia and I wanted to ask you the same thing, that's why I texted you!"

Mirlande: "Talia is with you?"

Ally: "Yes, I have you on speaker"

Talia: "Hi Mirlande!"

Mirlande: "Oh My God, you are here! You didn't tell me you were already back!"

Talia: "Yeah, I came a little earlier than I had planned so I could clean up my office."

Ally: "Talia decided to stay here now instead of coming back in a couple of months!"

Mirlande: "Wow, that's great! We missed you so much!"

Talia: "I missed you guys too! And I didn't realize how much I missed my life here with you guys until this morning so I decided I'm not going back to my hometown."

Mirlande: "That's wonderful news! Yep, people complain about Buffalo when they're here but everyone realizes how great life is here once they leave."

Talia: "So I heard!"

Mirlande: "Listen you two…get your butts to my place right away. You can help us with few things then we can all go out and celebrate your return for good! I just need to relax and not think about the wedding."

Talia: "Sounds great, we will see you shortly!"

Ally and Talia stopped at Ally's apartment. Zain and Ethan were outside smoking.

"Hi you two! Being a doctor, should you be smoking?" Ally joked.

"Yeah, I know, it's a bad habit but I believe in the saying, 'do as I say not as I do,'" Zain responded with a smile.

"Done unpacking?"

"Yes, we finally finished!" Zain proclaimed.

"You know…we're going out later tonight for dinner with couple of our friends, would you guys like to join us and meet new people?" Ally asked as she looked at Talia for approval. Talia nodded in agreement.

Before Zain could say anything, Ethan chimed in, "We would love to! I think we need to take a break and just have some fun, and make more new friends."

"Ethan is a party animal. No matter how tired or busy he is, he always makes time for partying," Zain smirked.

"Fantastic! We have to go meet our friends to help them with their wedding, which is in a week then we will be going out. So, why don't you give me your number? Once we are finished, I will call or text you the time and place. Is that ok with you guys?" Ally suggested.

"Yeah, that's fine with us. We have to shower and all, so that will be perfect," Zain replied.

Zain gave Ally his phone number to add to her contacts, then she and Talia went into her apartment.

"They really seem like nice guys," Talia said as they entered into the apartment.

Ally nodded. "Hopefully, Mirlande and Marcus won't mind, right?"

"I'm sure they won't have any problems. Anyways, Marcus seems like a party guy, too," Talia surmised.

"You know, I'm going to call Mirlande to let them know in advance about the boys so there's no surprise," Ally said, as she started calling Mirlande. The phone rang.

"Oh, how come you are answering her phone now?" Ally teased Marcus, who answered.

"Hey…she will be my wife in a week so I'm already practicing. Mirlande just went to the car to get something so when I saw you calling I answered, unless you don't want to talk to me?" Marcus returned with smart remarks.

"Well, even if I don't want to talk to you, I guess I don't have a choice now do I?" The two of them laughed.

"Actually, you would be the perfect person to talk to about this. I have new neighbors and they are great guys. They are new to the city so I saw them outside and asked if they wanted to join us for dinner tonight. They liked the idea immensely. I hope you are ok with that?" Ally asked.

"I wished you would have asked us before you invited these guys. If you had, I would have said no," Marcus replied in a very serious tone.

"Oh, I am sorry! I thought you would have been fine with it. That's why I asked them but I can always come up with an excuse and tell them we are not going," Ally sounded dejected.

"Just kidding! The more the merrier!" Marcus laughed.

"Oh my God! I am going to strangle you when I see you! I was seriously feeling bad about asking them!" Ally feigned anger.

"Hey, I'm part of the gang now so I can joke around as much as I want to." Marcus continued to laugh.

"You know payback's a bitch right?" Ally winked at Talia.

"Bring it on sister! You have no idea how good I am at this."

"We shall see! So we will see you guys soon. What time do you think we will be heading out and where? So I can let them know."

"Do you want to say around 7 and at our favorite Thai restaurant, Thai Garden? If they don't like Thai food then we can plan another place."

"Ok, I will ask them and if they say they don't like Thai food then I will let you know. See you guys in a bit." Ally hung up the phone.

"Oh my God! Marcus got me good! He pretended that he didn't want the guys to come!" Ally squinched her face, as she started calling Zain.

"Hahaha." Talia chuckled.

"Hi Zain, this is Ally. Hey do you guys like Thai food?"

"Yes, we love Thai food! Actually, we pretty much like everything," Zain replied.

"Oh good, let's meet at Thai Garden at 7pm. It's not that far from here but you can look up the address. Is that ok with you guys?"

"That's perfect! We will see you guys at 7pm." Zain said goodbye and hung up the phone.

Ally looked at Talia after clicking off her phone, "There…it's all set. Do you need to change clothes or are you good with what you are wearing?"

"I think I want to change, so why don't we stop at my place before we head out to Mirlande's?" Talia responded.

"Ok, let me go wash up and change. While I'm changing, why don't you wash up here so when we get to your house you just have to change?"

"That sounds good."

After 20 minutes, both of the ladies were ready to go to Talia' house. "Should I take my car? You can drop your car off at your house then we can go to Mirlande's in my car?" Ally asked.

"Actually, I didn't get a chance to ask since we were busy talking about other things but would you mind sleeping at my place for few days? As much as I am ready to come back to live here, I need a few nights to get over my fear of being alone. I think I will be alright during the day since I really won't be there as much but at night I think I need some moral support," Talia beseeched.

"Oh, of course I don't mind sleeping at your house until you are ready to stay alone at night. Let me grab my stuff for the night. Should I bring my car also so I can come back in the morning without waking you up?" Replied Ally.

"Sure that sounds good and, in the morning, if I feel like I am not comfortable staying alone then you can stay with me during the day too." Talia said with a broad smile.

Ally had no problem helping her dear friend. It actually is a good time for Talia to readjust back into her home since Ally had taken a week off of her work to help Marcus and Mirlande with their wedding. As much as Marcus had everything planned, there were few things that were coming up and Mirlande was getting overwhelmed. She needed Ally to be her moral support and, now, having Talia there also was a great bonus for her. A week off from work meant a great staycation for the girls.

The ladies were on their way to Talia's place, in separate cars, when Ally's phone rang and it was Sam. She answered, "Hi Sam."

"Hi Ally, what are you doing?" Sam asked in a sad tone.

"Why do you sound so glum?"

"Uh, my mom just called…"

Ally interrupted, chuckling, "Yeah I can see why you are so glum."

"Yep, the other day my mom asked me if she should look for another girl for me since you have not given an answer as of yet. She is not able to understand why you need so much time to answer. To be honest with you, I can't come up with another excuse to tell her. I too don't understand what the problem is. I mean, when we are together you seem/act like you want to be with me but then on the other hand you ask me to give you some time to think. I am sorry, I don't think I can give you any more time to think. By now, you should know if you want to be with me or not. I am sorry but I just can't keep coming up with an excuse to tell my parents.

"I work very long hours during day and night and when I am off I want to spend time with you. Every minute that I am free I want to be with you. I let you know in advance when I am going to be off so you can plan it but then you tell me you can't spend time with me because you have plans with other people. You know I am going to be off later this evening and I had asked you if you want to do something and you never responded. When I saw you going into the café on my way to work I stopped by to ask you about it but then I got a call and had to go. I saw you with Talia so I had guessed that you were doing something with her tonight and you were going to say you can't do something with me, right?" He asked angrily.

Sam was correct. She understood his anger and couldn't blame him for being angry but she really needed some time away from her stressful situation. She was tired and needed some mental peace while she figured out what she really wanted in life. "I am sorry about all of this, this is life's biggest decision I have to make and I just want to…"

Before she could finish her sentence, he interrupted, "You've said this so often while I just let you be. I wanted you to have the space that you needed to think about this but what I have found interesting is that after meeting you a few times I knew I wanted to spend my life with you yet you seem to need so much time to think about it. There is one of three things happening here: either you don't want to be with me; you can't find that connection with me; or, there is someone else in your life. That's why you need so much time to think this through. I would really appreciate it if you would just come out and tell me the truth!" Sam demanded.

Wow! That was a shocker coming out of him. All this while she used to think that he was this passive guy that liked having others make the decisions for him but she had never seen this side of him before. She completely understood his anger but she didn't think he had that in him to come out like that.

"Wow, I have never heard you talk like that before." Ally was taken completely off-guard.

Sam sounded even more frustrated. "Why? Just because I am nice about things and let people be? I am not stupid, I just don't like confrontation and don't say anything to anyone unless it affects me. And right now this is affecting me. I want to be with you every minute of my life but I don't see that from you. Like I said, either you don't have it for me or there is someone else, so what is it?"

Ally had arrived at Talia's, parked the car and sat in stunned silence. Since Sam was upset and he misunderstood her silence, he thought she didn't want to be with him and that's why she has been avoiding him.

"You don't need to say anything to me. Your silence says it all to me, bye!" He growled and hung up the phone before she could respond. Just then there was a knock on her car window…it was Talia.

"What happened to you? You look like as white as a ghost." Talia moved back as Ally got out of the car.

"Hold on a minute, I need to call Sam back." Ally gestured with her forefinger as she dialed his number.

The girls continued walking to Talia's apartment as Ally waited for Sam to answer, but he didn't pick up. She hung up the phone and dialed again. He didn't answer then either.

"What's going on?" Talia asked, a look of concern on her face.

Ally told her about the conversation, or lack thereof, and Talia too couldn't believe he actually asserted himself like that…

"I didn't think he had that in him."

"Neither did I and now he's not even answering the phone," Ally said matter-of-factly.

"To be honest, I don't blame him. Either of us would have reacted the same way," Talia pointed out.

"No, I don't blame him." Ally agreed but there was a part of her that was glad he didn't answer the phone. She really needed mental peace from her situation and some time away from her life so she can just relax and enjoy her time with the girls.

"So, I wonder if this means he's going to let his mom find someone else," Talia thought out loud.

"I don't know," Ally questioned that herself too.

"Would you be alright if you lose Sam? I mean, he is a great guy and since you have closed your doors for Ary does that mean you are willing to lose this terrific man?" Talia attempted to make Ally understand how stupid her actions have been and those actions are going to make her lose someone like Sam.

"You know, I really don't know. I'm so confused about everything that I just don't know! I wish things were easier for me but they are not. I don't know if it is just me who has made it so complicated for myself or if it's just the difficulties that life has thrown at me. All I know is that I am just so tired! I wish someone could make the decision for me and I wish my nature was such that I would accept it without questioning anything, but that is not the case here. The only thing I can do is to leave it up to God and see who is in my kismet/destiny," Ally replied, in a very exhausted tone.

Talia felt really bad for her friend but this was something that had to come from within Ally. She has told Ally everything she could as a friend and there is nothing more she could do.

The girls had entered Talia's apartment while they were chatting. "I'll change my clothes quickly then we can go ok? And I am sure you need to get your mind off of all this!" Talia called to Ally as she dashed to her bedroom.

"Yep!" Ally looked down at her phone again.

As Talia went to change, Ally tried calling Sam one more time. Still with no answers, she texted him, "I guess you really are upset with me! I don't blame you for being upset but please don't shut me off either."

Just as Ally finished texting Sam, Talia was done changing. "Ready to go?"

Ally looked up from her phone. "Yep, let's go…I'll drive."

"I was just gonna ask you if you would drive so I could just sit back and enjoy the ride," Talia said, smirking.

Both of the ladies then grabbed their purses and left the apartment. As they were getting into the car, Talia asked, "Hey, isn't your car lease coming up soon?"

"Oh yeah, you are right! With all this other stuff going on I completely forgot about it. It's actually coming up next month," Ally responded.

"What are you thinking of getting?"

"I think I will get a BMW. I really like white but since you have a white car, I have to see if I want to buy the same color."

"If you really like the white one it's ok if you get it. It's not like you would be getting the same model as mine. Yours would be the latest model anyways," Talia proffered.

"If you are ok with it then I really would like to get the white model with black interior," Ally said excitedly.

"Yeah, go for it!" Talia smiled.

"Hey, you know I was thinking that you should move into another apartment. I mean I think psychologically it would be better for you," Ally suggested.

"I can't argue with a psychologist me, can I? Maybe I should look for an apartment in your building!"

Ally thought for a minute. "That would be awesome but I don't think there are any available. I think Zain moved into the last one that was open. But, I think the Luxury Lofts, a couple blocks from my place, has one available. One of my neighbors was telling me that her friend is moving out from there because she's getting married, and they bought a house. She actually told me this a week ago so why don't we swing by the leasing office right now and see if it's still available? Those lofts are really nice. I've seen them before. I wanted to move into one of them before I moved into my current apartment but there weren't any available. Just like my apartment building, it's really hard to get a place there."

"In that case, let's go see!" Talia exclaimed.

"Ok, we'll go right now. When is your lease up?"

"I still have about five months here but, you are right, it would be best for me to move out of there. It has bad memories of what my ex did and whenever I enter the apartment the entire event plays in my mind over and over again. Even though it hasn't been that long since I returned to the apartment, when I do come home I think of that day. I'm having a very hard time with it and that's why I asked you to stay with me. So, it'd be worth it for me to pay off my lease even though it's a lot of money…I think my mental peace is worth more," Talia related.

"I agree with you. It's a good thing you can afford to do that. If you couldn't move out then it would be very stressful for you to stay there for those remaining months."

They arrived at the Luxury Lofts and looked for the sign for the leasing office. "If I can remember correctly, I think the office is this way," Ally deduced, as she took a short right turn. "Yep, there it is! Let's keep our fingers crossed that for some odd reason someone hasn't taken the apartment!"

"This is a nice area. I always drove past here but never really paid attention to the beauty of this place," Talia said.

They walked up to the main door and read the sign hanging on it, 'Office Open, Please Enter'. When they entered the office, they saw that the manager was on the phone who smiled at the ladies and motioned for the two of them to have a seat. Ally and Talia smiled back and sat in the chairs across from the desk. There were brochures on the desk. Each of them grabbed a brochure and started to flip through the pages. After couple of minutes, the lady said goodbye to whomever she was talking to and hung up the phone.

"Hello and welcome, my name is Jane. I'm the office manager here. So, what can I do for you today?" She said, standing up and shaking their hands.

"Hello, my name is Talia and this is my friend, Ally. We were wondering if you had any lofts available."

Jane clasped her hands together. "What a wonderful and timely coincidence, there is one available. Just a couple of days ago, the people who were interested in the apartment called and said they needed a bigger place so they rescinded the request. The person I just spoke with made an appointment to come see the loft tomorrow but now here *you* are. I guess you may be the lucky one because these lofts go very fast and they don't become available so readily. Would you like me to show you the loft now?"

"Oh yes, please!" Talia became excited.

"Is it for one person or two?" Jane asked.

"It's for me, just me," Talia replied, as the three of them headed out of the office to see the loft.

The loft was located on the second floor. Although Talia was hoping it would be on the first floor, this would not stop her from moving in if she liked it.

"Here we are," Jane said, as she opened the door to loft #3. Talia's eyes lit up when the door opened. It was very spacious, gray and white in color, and very clean looking. The front door opened to an incredibly large living room. To the left of the living room was the dining area and connected to the dining area was a nice long galley-type kitchen with lots of cabinets and an island in the middle where there were two bar stools. The bathroom was located on the other side of the living room, right next to the bedroom. The bathroom was quite large and consisted of a shower and no bathtub, but the shower was a walk-in with pebbled flooring and a slate wall. It also had dreamy dual shower heads with one mounted to the ceiling giving the effect of a rain shower. Then, there was the bedroom, which had a connecting door to the bathroom as well as to the living room. It was an enormous room with large windows that look out over a beautiful pond and sitting area down below. There was a French door between the windows which lead to a patio. The railing of the patio consisted of built-in planters all around.

Talia fell in love with the loft. "You know Jane, I just love this! I want to take it!"

"That's great! Since I have another person coming to see the loft tomorrow, in order to secure this loft for you, our policy is that you provide a $1200 nonrefundable deposit before you leave today. Then once you sign the lease, you will need to give two month's rent in advance. The rent is $2000 per month, utilities included, and, do you have pets?"

"No." Talia shook her head.

"Ok, just that, if you did then there is pet fee involved. Do you have any questions?"

"Is a check ok?" Talia asked eagerly.

"Yes. Why don't we go back to the office and do some paperwork. When would you like to move in? The loft is available whenever you would like to move in. Our crew gets the lofts ready within two days after the tenants move out since there are great demands for them. So, the loft is ready now," Jane suggested, leading them back to the office.

"Actually, if it's alright with you, I can give a check for the two months' rent now and you can put today or tomorrow's date as the move-in date and give me the keys, that way I can take my time moving in whenever I want," Talia requested.

"Well, I can get the paperwork ready for you tomorrow morning and you can pick up the keys then also," Jane replied.

"That's fine with me. What time should I come?"

"I will be in the office at 10am tomorrow so you can come any time after that."

The three ladies reached the office. Jane walked to her desk and sat down with Ally and Talia sitting across from her.

"Alright, if you don't mind, could you please fill out these forms and I also need to do a background check, which I should be able to get done today," Jane handed Talia a bunch of papers.

While Talia was filling out the forms, Ally received a call from Mirlande. She excused herself and stepped outside to answer the phone.

"Hey, where are you guys? You should have been here while back!" Mirlande blurted out.

"Oh, sorry. I know we're running a bit late but we made a pit stop at the Lux Lofts. Talia will be moving out of her place. Will explain to you when we get there which shouldn't be much longer. We're almost done here," Ally replied.

"Ok come soon! We need your help before we head out to dinner," Mirlande urged.

"We should be there in no more than twenty minutes."

"Ok good, see you guys then." Mirlande hung up the phone.

Ally was about to walk back into the office when Talia came out of it. "You're all done?"

"Yes! I can't believe that we just came to see the Loft and, as of tomorrow, I will be living here! I don't think it's hit me yet!" Talia beamed.

"I guess it was meant for you to leave your place and come here. It's unusual for it to happen the way it did," Ally pointed out.

"I know, right?! After tonight I don't have to sleep at my place! When I sign the lease tomorrow she'll give me the keys then I can start moving my belongings slowly! Since I don't have that much stuff maybe I, or should I say, 'we' can move my things in this week. That is, of course, if Mirlande doesn't have much for us to do." Talia gave a pleading look to Ally.

"Well, you and I are off this week and I know we have to help Mirlande but we can get up early in the morning and start moving as much as we can, as fast as we can, until the afternoon. Then we go help Mirlande with whatever she wants. You don't need to pack your stuff, just put them in big garbage bags and we'll just move everything in both of our cars. We can borrow Marcus' truck to move your big items. Meanwhile, you can sleep on the floor or we can find a cot for you. I'm sure you won't mind that!"

"Oh my God not at all. I'm going to avoid being in the old place, alone. This makes it easier for me!"

All the way to Mirlande's, Talia just couldn't get over how the apartment situation worked out for her. She was really relieved she didn't have to live in her current apartment anymore since she was having a tough time there. The day her ex-husband assaulted her kept playing in her head over and over again and, of course, with Ally being a psychologist she could really see how much it impacted Talia and was happy it worked out for her.

"Hey, I forgot to tell you! I'm starting a Therapeutic Clay class. It's for anyone who needs help relieving stress so if you know anyone who might be interested give them my number to contact me," Ally related to Talia.

"Therapeutic Clay class? How did you come up with that?" Talia inquired.

"You know I love sculpting, right? When I'm sculpting I get into this zone where I feel like I'm out of this universe. When I'm sculpting I forget about everything. I don't feel any stress or aches or pain that I maybe I had been feeling. I am so relaxed! I really have this out of body experience. I know it sounds really strange but until you don't try it you won't know what I'm talking about…"

Talia interrupted, "But what about those who are not talented like you and can't sculpt?"

"You don't need to have a talent to join the class. Matter of fact, you're not actually sculpting anything per say. I will be using clay as a sensory mechanism for relaxation, and counseling techniques, too. You know I am all about positive thinking and mind over matter. Well, I love philosophy and my favorite philosopher, John Locke, theorized that our mind is a tabula rasa which means "blank slate" and as we grow we acquire knowledge through the objects in the world that our senses bring.

"Just like that, I believe that as we grow our life experiences bring stress into our mind and body. As humans, we need to learn to channel our stress in order to have a healthy life. Some are able to channel their stress on their own and some may need a little assistance. People believe getting assistance in channeling stress makes them a weak individual but that's not true. It actually makes them smart. No matter what age or gender, stress is stress. Everyone has different degrees of stress but everyone has stress whether its little children, teenagers, stay at home moms, doctors, lawyers, office managers, custodians, etc. Everyone has stress! So, I want to share with people the experience of using clay. I might be the first person in the Buffalo area who actually will be starting this. I really hope people can experience it and see how magical it is and how different they will feel," Ally clarified.

"So, I can come too?" Talia asked.

"Of course you can! Don't you have stress and don't you want to relieve it!" Ally playfully slapped Talia in her arm.

"So I can come to just one class then I will be stress free?"

"Well, this is not a quick fix. It's not a magical pill, which by the way doesn't even exist, that will relieve you from stress forever. In order, to see any difference people, need at least four sessions to help relieve stress and cleanse your mind which will then slowly help heal your body from any physical effects that may have been caused by stress. If people are looking for a 'quick fix' there are pills out there that help relieve the pain of stress but those pills do more harm to your body than help you. Anything that's good for you takes time and the long term effects are great. With the quick fix pills, the long term effects are harmful. Do you understand?" Ally peeked at Talia with raised eyebrows.

"Yeah, I think I do. Basically your counseling technique, combined with clay, will help a person to alleviate the mental pressures of life, along with easing any physical pain they may be experiencing. For example, when I get stressed, I get headaches. Then, I feel tired and not want to do anything but just lay in bed. So, if I come to your sessions you will be able to help me learn how to relax, reducing my stress and, thereby, my headaches will stop and I won't feel tired. So, I will have the energy to move around, am I correct doc?" Talia concluded.

"Yes, that's exactly what I am saying!" Ally smiled broadly.

"Sign me up! When does it start?"

"I am working on it but the class will be starting soon."

"You are a very talented woman, you know that! Always coming up with things."

"Just wait until I decide to write a book!" Ally winked.

They arrived at Mirlande's, who came running out to see them since she had become inpatient from waiting for so long.

"Oh My God! About time you guys showed up!! We have so much to do and you guys took so long to come!" Mirlande shouted.

"Sorry we took a while. We would have been here earlier but we took a detour on our way here, and…I got a new apartment!!" Talia declared.

"Yeah, Ally was telling me about it on the phone. I can't believe how quickly you were able to get the loft and, especially the Lux Lofts. They are rarely available. I guess it was meant to be," Mirlande said as she hugged Talia.

"So how is everything going? What do you need help with today?" Ally asked Mirlande as she hugged her friend hello.

"I need your help to have fun!" Marcus called out from behind them, near the door. The startled ladies turned to him.

"Marcus has taken care of everything and…" Before Mirlande could continue her sentence Marcus interrupted…

"I am the one who needs your help. I need you to get this woman out of my hair so I can do what I need to do!" Marcus came over and hugged the ladies with a big smile on his face then continued…"My lovely wife-to-be needs to just relax and who can help her do that better than her two besties? She is also driving me crazy!" He poked his fiancé in the ribs jokingly.

Mirlande teased Marcus back by hitting him in the stomach.

"I thought you guys really needed the help so I took this coming week off from work," Ally said.

"I am so glad! The three of us can hang out every day and just have fun before I marry this joker but who knows if he will allow me to hang out with you ladies like this again," Mirlande laughed.

"Hey! I am not that kind of guy!" Marcus grunted, a sideways grin on his face.

"Yeah right, that's what they all say!" Ally teased. "Mirlande is right, most likely you will not let her hang out with us as much as we do now. I know many guys who say they won't change and they do."

"Hey, you are next! Let me see if Sam will let you hang out with the girls as much as you do," said Marcus.

Ally became quiet. She thought most likely Sam wouldn't want to be with her anymore.

"Speaking of Sam, I have a surprise for Ally!" Mirlande grabbed onto Ally's arm excitedly. "Sam is actually on his way over here! We wanted to surprise you so we invited him to join us tonight! He is coming over now and, while we're doing whatever we want, Marcus and Sam will be hanging out to do some man-bonding. Then, all of us, including your new neighbors will be going out to dinner."

Talia and Ally just looked at each other. They were both a bit confused because of the serious conversation Ally had earlier with Sam. Ally stood motionless with a strange look on her face when Sam pulled into the driveway and honked his car. Ally slowly walked over to his car, Sam got out of the car and hugged her.

"Hi Ally. You look shocked," He whispered in her ears.

"I am! I thought you were upset with me and didn't want talk to me?" Ally whispered back.

"Yeah, I just said that so I could surprise you." Sam admitted.

Ally wasn't sure how true that was because the conversation between them got a bit heated… "So your mom didn't call and ask you anything?" She continued in her soft voice.

"Oh, no, she did…she did ask me about us." Sam waved off the topic, not to talk much about that conversation. He then turned to Marcus, shaking his hand. "Hey man, thanks for including me in your celebrations."

"Hey, I can't be the only man amongst these crazy women and, besides, we need to get to know each other better since you will be marrying my future wife's best friend," Marcus teased.

Ally was still confused about what was happening but she didn't say anything further…yet.

Sam turned Mirlande to face him, his hands on her shoulders. He gave her a sincere, yet mocking look, "Ready to marry this man?" He thumbed towards Marcus.

"In a heartbeat!" Mirlande gleefully hugged Sam.

Sam then turned his attention to Talia. "Hey Talia, you look great!" He gave her a big hug.

"Thanks Sam, and thank you for everything you did for me when I was in the hospital," Talia said to Sam in great appreciation.

"It was my honor. I just wished that wasn't the way of meeting you for the first time," Sam reciprocated the feeling.

Marcus knew this could go on for a while so he started directing the ladies in another direction, shooing with his hands. "Ok, why don't you ladies go do whatever it is you would like to do while Sam helps me with few things and, don't worry it won't be all work, we will diffidently have some fun too." Marcus led Sam into the house.

Talia looked at the other two girls. "So what should we do?"

Mirlande was the first to respond, "I was thinking we should get our nails done. I actually made an appointment for mani and pedi with my neighbor, whose business is right next door. It's a home-based business." Talia and Ally, who had shook herself out of her confusion, both nodded in unison.

Mirlande led the girls to the neighbor's house, the neighbor, who was expecting them, standing on the porch. "Hello ladies! I was watching you from my window and wondered when you were going to come in."

"Silvia, these are my friends, Talia and Ally." Mirlande introduced the ladies.

Silvia was a short, loud lady with an Italian accent. "I have seen you ladies several times when you come to visit Mirlande, who always talks about you. It's finally nice to meet you two ladies." Silvia squeezed each of the girls' hands in a friendly gesture.

"Mirlande has told us so much about you as well," Talia chimed in.

"Come have a seat. I know, Ally, you like very bright colors and you, Talia, like lighter colors for your nails," Silvia conveyed to the girls as if she had known them for a long time.

"Yes, that's right! I like light colors but today I actually want hot pink!" Talia declared with a broad grin.

"Wow, you want hot pink!" Ally and Mirlande both said in shock.

"Yep, it's the new me! I'm changing myself. From now on, you will see a different Talia," Talia twittered excitedly.

Mirlande put her arm around her friend and squeezed. "I don't know if I can handle this but I am glad to see you happy."

As Mirlande got her nails done, Ally and Talia sat next to the bay window. Something caught their eye so when they looked out the window they saw a very handsome, tall well-dressed Italian man getting out of a car.

"Wow, who is that? He is so good looking!" Talia intoned.

Silvia looked at Mirlande and they both smiled at each other. "That's my son Sergio and he is a lawyer, also."

Mirlande and Silvia actually had planned for Talia and Sergio to meet. Silvia was happy to see Talia's reaction since she had always thought Talia was a very beautiful woman and would be perfect for her very handsome son. Her son used to be engaged to a girl that he had dated for several years and two years ago she died in a car accident. Ever since then, he had been heartbroken and whenever she tried hooking him up with other girls he never showed any interest. This time, she was hoping he would change his mind since Talia looked very similar to his fiancé.

The door opened. "Ciao, mama!" Sergio called to his mom, as he walked through the door not realizing the girls were there.

"Ciao mio figlio (my son)," Silvia replied. When he turned to his mom he noticed the customers.

"Oh sorry, I didn't realize you had customers. I thought you were done working at this time."

Silvia introduced the ladies to her son, "You know Mirlande." Sergio smiled and nodded to Mirlande. "And these are her friends, Ally and Talia. Ladies, this my Sergio." Silvia had a proud look on her face.

"Hello," Sergio said as he shook Ally hand but when he faced Talia to shake hers, he just stood there, transfixed.

Silvia eyed the situation as Mirlande gave her a questioning but "it worked" look. Silvia finally saw her son show any kind of interest in another girl after such a long time so she was very happy that her plan may be working. Mirlande knew Sergio well since she and Silvia were neighbors, and, over the years, she had gotten to know Sergio as he came to visit his mom often.

"How are you Sergio? I haven't seen you in a couple of months?" Mirlande asked, shaking Sergio out of his trance.

"I was very busy with a case and didn't visit mom so much but when I did come over I don't think you were home. So, are you all set with the wedding?" Sergio replied, trying hard not to be obvious in his interest in Talia.

"Yes, we are! I hope you are not *that* busy that you will miss it?" Mirlande inquired.

"Nope, no matter how busy I am, I wouldn't miss your wedding for the world."

"Hey! What are you doing tonight?" Mirlande asked, knowing for a fact that he just came over for dinner with his mom.

"Well, I'm here to have dinner with my mom."

"All of us are going out for dinner tonight, why don't you come with us?" Mirlande and Silvia had planned this all along.

"Thanks, but I haven't seen mom for few days and I'm sure she has made some delicious dinner." Sergio shrugged.

"Son, why don't you go out with them, I haven't made dinner yet and I have two appointments that came up at the last minute. They are my regular customers and I couldn't say no to them. We can have dinner tomorrow." Silvia pressed her son to accept the invitation.

Sergio actually did want to go because of his interest in Talia and was glad to hear his mom give him an excuse, He tilted his head sideways. "If you are ok with it mama then I wouldn't mind going out."

Talia nudged Ally discreetly, indicating that she was happy. Ally gave her a slight side smile.

"Great! We are meeting a couple of Ally's friends at the Thai restaurant on Harris at 7pm, which really isn't long from now. Why don't you go hangout with Marcus and Sam, Ally's boyfriend, while we finish getting our nails done?" Mirlande queried.

"Sure, since mom is busy, I guess there's nothing for me to do here." Sergio kissed his mom bye and quickly glanced at Talia. Talia saw that he gave her the "look", with those aquamarine-blue, haunting eyes, and that made her heart skip a beat. Mirlande and Ally also saw them looking at each other, which made them excited to see what happens next. She had been through a lot, especially an abusive marriage and not to mention the fact that she nearly died because of her ex so she definitely deserved someone much better. Sergio walked out to meet up with Marcus and Sam.

Silvia was not a very subtle person, after all, she was Italian. Subtlety didn't exist when it came to Silvia so when Talia was getting her nails done she started to talk about her son, "You know Talia, my son is a very nice boy and not to mention successful and rich. I am not saying that because he is my son, ask Mirlande or anyone else. They will tell you what a great guy he is and, like you, he has been going through rough time after losing his fiancé in a car accident. I haven't seen him be himself ever since. But today, I saw a glimpse of my boy coming back and it's a big thanks to you. I have a feeling he likes you and, from what I can see, I think you like him also. Mirlande told me all about what you have gone through and I think that it was barbaric but I guarantee you my son is nothing like that. I raised him to be a gentleman and he is nothing less than that. He is just like his father who was a very good man, himself," Silvia continued to talk. "His father and I met when we were teenagers and we fell in love. We got married at a young age but he always treated me very well. He, too, became a very successful lawyer. He took good care me and I never had to ask for anything because he always bought things for me before I could ask him, even up to the day he died suddenly."

She didn't miss a beat, but said in a softer, more somber tone, "Five years ago we were getting ready to go out for dinner and suddenly he wasn't feeling well. I went down stairs to get him some water and when I returned he was lying on the bed, not saying a word. I called the ambulance but when they arrived and examined him, they said he'd had a heart attack and passed.

"My world came to an end! It was very hard for me to adjust to a life without my one and only love. Sergio used to live in a different city with his girlfriend but after his father's death he didn't want me to be alone so he moved back here, with his girlfriend of course. The house that we lived in was very big and I didn't want to live there anymore because it had a lot of my husband's memories. It became very difficult for me so I sold the house and moved in here. Sergio wanted me to live with him but I didn't want that. I wanted him to start his own life with his girlfriend, she was very nice too. After a few months, the two of them got engaged and, the following year, she was hit by a drunk driver. She was going home after visiting with me and died right there where she was hit. That was a month before their wedding. Since then, Sergio hasn't been the same. He comes to see me almost every day unless he gets very busy with a case and, if he can't come to see me, he makes sure he calls me no matter how busy he may be. He really is a good boy, just like his dad. If things work out between the two of you, I guarantee you, you will not be disappointed." Silvia eyes had been tearing up through the story.

Talia got up, knowing her nails were dry, and gave her a big hug. "Thank you for sharing your story. When I first looked at your son, I actually felt something inside that I haven't felt in a long time. Just being next to him made me feel happy and, if he is interested, I would definitely like to try to get to know him. It sounds like you raised a good son and I would consider myself lucky if it worked out between us. I'm glad I healed before the wedding or else I wouldn't have had the opportunity to meet the two of you. I guess everything happens for a reason!" Talia looked at Ally and smiled. For every moment of her life she is starting to believe in Ally's way of thinking…"everything happens for a reason."

The three other ladies in the room were really happy to hear what Talia said. Silvia was happy for her son. Mirlande and Ally were happy for Talia. Silvia may be a very boisterous lady but she was very nice, with a heart of gold. Although she was wealthy but she was actually quite down to earth. She chose to do people's nails, not because she needed the money, but that she didn't want to be alone during the day. She liked keeping herself busy and she loved having people come over all day long, every day, even on Sundays. She didn't charge people that much money and, on top of that, she fed them since she loved cooking her traditional Italian meals.

Although her prices were low, ladies gave her more just because she fed them and made them feel like family. Silvia's doors were always open for everyone. Neighbors also took care of her. Silvia didn't like going grocery shopping so whenever one of her neighbors was going to the store they would call or stop by to see what they could get for her. She always had her list ready because she never knew when someone would stop by and ask her what she needed. Every time she ran out of something, she would write it down on her list right away. She actually had the list on a board next to the door and neighbors knew that so when they came over instead of asking her they would just look at the list.

Every Thanksgiving and Christmas, she always prepared food for all of the neighbors so when they came for a holiday visit, she always sent them away with containers full of food. She was the neighborhood's mama.

The girls were all done with their nails and ready to go. They each gave Silvia a big hug and, as they were walking out the door, Sergio showed up.

"Hey, aren't you coming with us?" Mirlande inquired.

"Yes I am. I just wanted to check on mom and see if she needed anything before I go," Sergio replied.

That just melted Talia's heart and, deep down inside, she prayed that he would ask her out. Although she didn't know a lot about Sergio, she just had this feeling and wanted things to work out between the two of them.

"Ok, go see your mom. We will wait for you but don't be late!" Mirlande asserted.

"I won't." Sergio bowed to the ladies and went inside.

"He is so good looking," Ally declared.

Talia nodded in agreement. "He sure is! What about those eyes?! A girl could melt in them!"

The girls just couldn't get over how handsome he was. Sergio always got that reaction from people but he was never arrogant about his looks.

When the girls returned, Sam and Marcus were in the driveway waiting for them.

"Are you ladies ready to go?" Marcus asked.

"Yep!" All three responded simultaneously.

Just then Sergio returned.

"So how should we do this? Who is going in whose car?" Asked Ally.

Marcus and Mirlande looked at each other and smiled. Mirlande turned back to the group. "We actually ordered a limousine."

Marcus added, "We figured it would be fun for all of us to go together and, Ally, can you text or call your neighbors and let them know we will be picking them up also?"

"Oh wow! It will be fun going together. Okay, let me call them right now before they leave." Ally went off to the side to make the call.

Sergio stood next to Talia. It was very obvious they both were into each other. Although the two of them just met briefly, the chemistry between the two was indescribable, as if they were meant to be together. Just then the limousine pulled into the driveway.

"Wow that *is* a big limo!" Talia exclaimed.

"Marcus' friend owns a limousine business and he actually had this limo reserved for us for this entire week. He reserved the big one for us since Marcus has a big circle of friends and family," Mirlande explained.

"Marcus, you definitely are the most organized person I know. You actually beat me!" Ally snorted, with a smile of course.

"I can't help it. It comes naturally to me." Marcus emphasized this with a hand to his chest. Then they all got into the limo.

Turning to Ally, who was the second to last person to get into the limo, Mirlande asked, "Did you get word to your neighbors that we're picking them up?"

"Yes, they were about to head out when I called them. They are excited about meeting all of you and going together in the limo. Those two are like little kids but they seem like fun people. I think you will definitely like them, Marcus, they are crazy and funny like you," Ally reported, adding a smirk.

"Hey, that's the best way to be…crazy and funny!" Marcus countered. He was in a great mood.

Marcus and Mirlande sat together, across from them were Ally and Sam, next to them were Sergio and Talia. Marcus told the driver where to go then he grabbed a bottle of champagne and opened it.

"Do we have even enough time to enjoy a drink? The restaurant isn't that far, right?" Ally teased.

Marcus winked at Ally. "I told the driver to take the long way after picking up your friends."

"Seriously, Marcus you just amaze us. Mirlande, I am so glad you met him. He is the best!" Ally gave accolades when they are due.

"Glad you finally realized that. Don't forget that initially you ladies gave me a hard time." Marcus looked over at the other men in the car. "You guys are so lucky they have loosened up. These ladies were brutal, especially Ally!"

"You mean, Ally only! She is the leader of our gang and she is or, should I say, was very tough. She is tough with us also, trust me! I still remember how nervous Mirlande was about introducing Marcus to her," Talia related, looking slyly at Ally.

"Hey, I think you are forgetting something about Mirlande…" Ally began.

Mirlande was embarrassed about her past and didn't want Marcus to know what kind of guys she picked and knew Ally only saved her from making stupid mistakes, so she interrupted…. "Hey, we all grow up and learn from our mistakes right? So can we just enjoy our drinks?" Just as she finished her sentence they arrived at Ally's apartment to pick up the others.

Zain, Ethan and Lulu were waiting outside. The driver rolled the windows down and got out to let the trio in the limo. Ally saw Jeffery walking into the building and waved at him. He smiled and waved back. Ally had been wanting to talk to Jeff but haven't had the time to do so.

The three of neighbors got into the limo and Ally introduced them to everyone.

"Wow this is a big limo!" Zain gleefully exclaimed, like a big kid.

Marcus poured champagne for them and the limo drove off as they all drank, joked and just had fun. The driver took an extra twenty minutes' drive so they could enjoy themselves. They finally reached the restaurant and the limo pulled right in front. People were turning around to see who came out of the limo at a Thai restaurant. They were looking as if they were expecting some celebrity to step out but, to their disappointment, it was just a bunch of strangers. As the contingent of friends, old and new, started walking into the restaurant, Mirlande whispered to Ally, "Zain and Ethan are so good looking…too bad they are gay."

Ally replied with a devilish grin, "I know, right!"

The restaurant was busy but, lucky for them, Marcus had reserved the small banquet area. Marcus knew the owner. They had attended high school together and Marcus' cousin was married to the owner's best friend. They were escorted to the banquet area by a very pretty young Thai woman. They entered into a beautifully decorated room. On one side of the room, tables were nicely set up in rows and on the other side of the room was a handsome lounge area with silk sofas and chiffon drapes where they could sit comfortably and chat.

"Wow, this is beautiful!" Lulu exclaimed.

"Yes, it's absolutely stunning," Zain agreed, in awe of the surroundings.

While they all were standing around, chatting, the waiters were setting up the appetizers and another waiter was offering drinks. All of them were getting better acquainted with one another. Sam was glad to be part of the gang. It confirmed to him that Ally really did want to be with him. Why else would he be invited to be a part of her circle of friends?

They all made Zain, Ethan, and Lulu feel welcomed, as if they had been friends forever. There was a piano in the corner of the room. Ethan walked over to it and started to play a medley of songs while others were dancing and having a good time. They were all drinking and enjoying their appetizers as well.

Sergio seemed to fit right into the group as well but he showed a keen interest in Talia and, of course, Talia in him.

Mirlande slowly moved closer to Talia and said, "I see you guys are hitting it off. Seems to me that he likes you also." Talia just grinned back at her.

Ethan kept playing new and old songs while Zain was dancing with Lulu and the others.

"If Zain and Ethan are partners, then who is Lulu to them?" Sam questioned, with a puzzled look on his face. Ally smiled and tried to give him the short version of their story. Meanwhile, Talia excused herself to go use the restroom, which was outside of the hall.

Just as Ethan was finishing playing the song the waitress announced that their dinner was ready. She had set it up in a buffet style with the main course on one table and lots of desserts set on the dessert table off to the side so they can have them whenever they were wanted. The room was filled with the fragrance of Thai cuisine and made everyone extremely hungry

"I don't know about you guys but this smell is making me want to eat!" Marcus remarked.

"It sure does!" Zain concurred whole heartedly.

One after another, they all gathered around the buffet like flies gathering around food. Just then, Talia walked in, "Guess who I found getting take out!"...dragging Ary into the room with her. Ally felt her heart drop to her stomach when she saw Ary. She couldn't understand why Talia would bring him in here. Sam was there and she didn't want any drama.

"Hey Ary, why don't you join us?" Said Marcus.

"Thank you for the invite but I already got my food," Ary said, lifting the takeout bag to show them.

"Don't worry about that, you can have that tomorrow," Marcus added.

"Yeah, just have it tomorrow stay and have fun with us," Talia insisted.

Ally wasn't happy at all. She gave Talia that look of "what are you doing?" but Talia completely ignored her. Earlier in the day when Talia and Ally were at her house, she had texted Ary to meet them at the restaurant at 9:00pm, but at that time she didn't know Sam was going to be coming. Even after finding out about Sam, she didn't care to cancel because she just wanted Ally and Ary to be in the same room. She wasn't going to give up trying to get them together even though chances of that happening was slim to none. It was something she wanted to do so she could feel that she tried her best.

Ary looked over at Ally to get her approval but Ally was so stressed that she wasn't even looking at him. Marcus and Talia kept insisting and they weren't going to take no for an answer. Marcus even took the take-out bag from his hand and put it on the table. As much they all liked Sam, they knew Ally's true love was Ary and they all felt she would be happier with him. They didn't know how it was going to happen because of her family, but they were all hoping some miracle would happen and she would choose Ary.

Ary didn't really seem to have a choice but to stay. It wasn't like he didn't want to stay but there was a part of him that knew it was too late with Ally and, seeing Sam here with her, assured his belief even more. His jealousy began creeping in also. Ally didn't want him to be there because she knew his temper and how sarcastic he could be. She was afraid of what he would say to Sam. She was upset with her friends for forcing him to stay and couldn't understand why they would put her in such an awkward situation when Sam was there.

"Alright, since you guys are insisting this much I guess I can stay for few minutes," Ary conceded.

He was a bit confused because Talia didn't tell him anything about Sam coming but he didn't care. Part of him wanted to make Sam feel miserable so he would do whatever he could to make that happen. He really didn't know what kind of person Sam was but, to him, he was a scumbag that took Ally away from him. The more he saw the two of them together the more jealous he became.

Talia introduced Ary to Zain, Ethan, Lulu, and Sergio while they were dishing up their food.

Zain whispered to Ally, "I think Ary has the hots for you."

Ally looked at Zain in shock, her eyes darting around to see if anyone heard Zain. "What?"

"It's the way he looks at you…you can tell he has the hots for you. I'm guessing he doesn't know you are with Sam?"

Zain was definitely unaware of the history between her and Ary.

"I know him very well. He and I used to date. I will tell you about it later," Ally discreetly whispered.

Zain was very intrigued. He wanted the whole scoop but he couldn't ask more questions with everyone around. At this point, he didn't know the story with Sam. He only assumed they were dating, nonetheless, he was eager to know the whole story.

"I can't wait! Ethan and Lulu have a flight early afternoon tomorrow and I don't start my work at the hospital for two weeks so you will have plenty of time to fill me in on *everything*."

"Don't worry, I will tell you the whole *universe*," Ally assured Zain.

Everyone got their dinner and sat at the large banquet table, close to the buffet. Zain was sitting in the middle of Lulu and Ethan. Next to Lulu was Ally; then Sam; then Sergio. Next to Sergio was Talia, next to her was Mirlande. Marcus was on the other side of Mirlande and Ary rounded out the guests.

Marcus was making sure Ary was feeling comfortable and wasn't left out in any way.

"Now that we have all become friends, I would officially like to invite you guys to our wedding next week," Marcus announced to Lulu, Zain and Ethan.

"We would love to but Lulu and I leave tomorrow. I will not be returning for a couple of weeks, but I am sure Zain would love to come," Ethan said disappointingly.

"Yeah, I would love to come!" Zain said, as he stuffed his mouth with shrimp tempura.

Marcus then turned to Ary, "I'm sure Mirlande had already invited you and you are coming, right?" Marcus knew for a fact that Mirlande had not invited him but he wanted Ary to feel included.

"Actually, I didn't know you guys were getting married next week." Ary appeared surprised. When Talia told him she was here for the wedding, he assumed it was Ally and Sam's.

"You didn't invite him?" Marcus turned to Mirlande, who knew what Marcus was doing so she played along.

"No, I'm sorry I didn't. You were the one that was taking care of everything so I assumed you invited him." Mirlande shrugged.

"I thought you had invited him, so I didn't. Sorry about that man! We actually didn't hand out any invitations or anything, we just called our friends and family. I would really like you to come, even if you have something planned you need to cancel it and be with us on our special day. I am not planning to get married again so you better come," Marcus bantered.

Ary was so glad to hear that it wasn't Ally that was getting married next weekend. For someone reason, there was still a part him that was hoping she would change her mind. "I would love to come. I wouldn't miss it for the world." Ary couldn't hold back his glee and looked at Ally with a smug smile.

Ally just couldn't believe this was happening. How could her friends do this to her. They knew Sam was coming to the wedding so how could they invite Ary? Sam had become quieter ever since Ary arrived. Sam may be a subdued person but that didn't mean he was dumb. He saw how Ally changed once Ary walked through the door and he could see how Ary was focused on Ally, even though she was trying to avoid him. It wasn't like Ally not to talk to someone. He noticed that she didn't even say hi to Ary. She was the one who had introduced him to Ary when Talia was in the hospital. Something just didn't seem right to him and he couldn't ask Ally anything at that time so he became a silent observer.

The evening just became very interesting to Ary since he found out Ally wasn't getting married next weekend, it meant the game was still on for him and he started having some evil thoughts in his mind.

Ally could see it in his face that he was up to something and she didn't like it a bit. She excused herself and as she got up asked Talia if she would accompany her to the restroom. Talia could tell Ally wasn't happy and didn't want to go but she deserved whatever Ally had to dish out to her, so she also excused herself. Both of the ladies started walking toward the ladies room.

Ally was angry, she quietly seethed…"Why did you ask Ary to come?"

Talia was trying not to say anything to her until they got into the restroom which was not far. "Listen, I had texted Ary earlier in the day when we were at my house to meet us here. I had no idea Sam was going to be here. Remember, he was supposedly fighting with you?"

"But why would you do that?" Ally was exasperated.

The two ladies stopped just inside the bathroom door.

"Because I love you and I know you, as much as you know me! I know its Ary who you want and will be happiest with. I am not denying the fact that Sam is a nice guy…not at all, but I think you would be happier with Ary," Talia countered, then started fixing her make-up in the mirror.

"I know you mean well, Talia, but we have been over this many times. It's just not going to work out between me and Ary. It's not going to happen. The sooner you and Mirlande accept that the better it will be for us, and for me to be able to move on. By you continuing to bring him in my life, it makes it harder for me. Can you please understand that?"

"If you really are that serious about it, then there is nothing that I or Mirlande can do. If this is the choice you have made then that's fine. But what I don't understand is if you want to be with Sam then why haven't you told him you will marry him? He has been waiting to hear that from you for some time now. I think you haven't said that to him because you're not sure."

"I have decided to tell him sometime tonight. You're right, if he is my choice then there is no reason for me to wait."

"Well, I will believe you when that happens! Now let's get back to everyone." Talia grabbed her purse from the counter and started to walk towards the door with Ally following. One would think that after a discussion like this, friends would be upset with each other and not talk but that wasn't the case with these ladies. They always kept it real with each other; always spoke what was on their mind because they knew they loved each other and always looked out for the best interest of the other.

They both were heading back to the others when they saw Ary coming…"Talk to him." Talia said and winked at Ary as she walked away.

Ary and Ally walked towards the bar together. Ally turned to face Ary, placing her hand on Ary's arm. "Listen, I need to get back to Sam, I don't want him to get suspicious."

"So when is your wedding?" Ary inquired sarcastically.

"It will happen when it needs to happen," Ally replied with a touch of arrogance.

"You haven't even said yes to him yet."

"We were busy, but I am planning to tell him tonight."

"I just don't understand why this has become like an ego thing with you? I know you, if you want something, you never wait. You just go for it but you haven't done that in this case." Ary tried to reason with Ally.

"I didn't say yes to you either! Now I need to get back in there. I don't want Sam…"

Just as she was about to finish her sentence, she saw Sam coming in their direction but, apparently, he didn't see them so Ally told Ary…"If he asks, I'm in the restroom."

Then Ally rushed back to the ladies room. Ary went the other way to avoid running into Sam but Sam was approaching the restrooms. As he got to the ladies room, Ally came out. "Hi, using the restroom?" Ally asked with a nervous smile, hoping he didn't talk to Ary.

"No, I came to see if you were ok," replied Sam.

"Oh, that's sweet. I actually had to take a call so I told Talia to go ahead." Ally lied.

"While we're alone I wanted to ask you…" Unfortunately, at that moment, Mirlande showed up…

"Hey you two, what are you guys doing here? Everyone is having dessert and teasing each other, especially of Zain and his unusual habits," Mirlande inquired of her friends.

"We were on our way back." Ally was about to grab Sam's hand...

Mirlande interrupted again, "Sam, would you mind if your lovely comes to keep me company in the restroom?"

"No, not at all but make sure you bring her back with you. She has been spending more time in the bathroom than us." Sam chuckled.

"Will do." Mirlande waved at Sam and pulled her friend into the bathroom.

Mirlande stopped inside the bathroom and turned to Ally. "Hey, I came out here to ask you what was going on. It must be weird for you to have Sam and Ary here?"

"Yes, it is! Talia invited Ary not knowing you invited Sam without asking me. She is trying to get me to choose Ary," Ally conveyed in a frustrated tone.

"You know she just loves you and wants to see you happy."

"I know, but I told her I'm going to give Sam my answer tonight."

"You are?!" Mirlande was shocked.

"Yes, I think it's time for me to settle down."

"Ok, as long as you know what you are doing."

"Really? That's it? You won't try to convince me to be with Ary like Talia did?" Ally had a look of disbelief on her face.

"Like you tell people, you are an adult, you know what you want. In this case, you think you want Sam because of your family. Talia and I have been telling you to be honest with yourself, not your family, and fight for Ary but you're not listening so I am done telling you. I think I know exactly how you used to feel when I would make stupid decisions about men and you would get tired of constantly tell me not to be stupid. The only difference is that I eventually listened to you and look at me today, I am so happy that I found Marcus. If I didn't listen to you I wouldn't have him. Just like you used to talk with me about my relationships, Talia and I have been doing the same with you but you are so stubborn that you won't listen. If I was stubborn like you, you would have given up on me also and would have told me your favorite line, 'it's your life'. Now I am telling you that it's your life. If you want to marry Sam, then go ahead. He is a very nice guy but we know you don't love him. Now, let's get back to everyone. Wow! I never thought I would talk to you the way you talk to us and it feels good!" Mirlande was done and went to the sink to wash her hands.

Both of the ladies returned to the group who were eating dessert and laughing. As Ally sat between Talia and Sam she looked around and noticed Ary wasn't there. She whispered to Talia asking her where he was. Talia replied that he had left...

"He said that if you had made up your mind to tell Sam tonight then there was nothing more to do and, before he left, he told me to tell you that he is done trying to convince you and you won't hear from him again. He decided to move out of Buffalo as soon as he can so he never runs into you again," Talia conveyed the message to Ally. Ally was relieved to hear that he was gone for good.

Everyone continued to enjoy their night with great dessert, drinks and dancing. Talia and Sergio were really enjoying each other's company. They were so comfortable with each other as if they had known each for ages. Zain, Lulu and Ethan also were enjoying themselves. Marcus and Mirlande made them feel like they had been part of the gang forever.

Chapter 13

Ally's Decision

It was Sunday afternoon and Sergio had come to see his mom. "Hi mama." He called out as he opened the door. There was no response so he repeated it, looking around.

"Ciao mama…where are you?!"

"I'm back here!" She finally responded to his calls. Sergio dashed over to his mom, with the look of a little kid on his face. She was watering her plants on the patio. He gave her a hug and a kiss on her cheek, with a beaming glint in his eyes.

Silvia hadn't received that kind of hug from her son in a long time. He always hugged her but the feeling that she got in this hug was like the old hugs he used to give her when he was a happy go lucky kid, before his fiancé's death.

"Wow mio figlio! I haven't seen you this happy in a long time figlio!" She exclaimed, gleaming with pride at seeing her son.

"It's been a while since I have felt like this, mom." Sergio stood behind her and wrapped his arms around her.

Although Silvia had a hunch of why he was so happy she had to confirm, "So, tell me, what has made mio figlio so happy?"

"I think I found someone mama…Talia. But I feel guilty about being so happy, mama. I feel like by finding someone else I'm letting go of…"

Silvia interrupted him, she knew what he was going to say… "It's time for you to let Olivia go figlio. God put her in your life for the amount of time necessary. God gave her a short life but it was happy because she was very happy with you. I think I would rather take a short wonderful life than a miserable, unhappy long life. You should be honored you were chosen by God to make her life joyous and, now, God has given you someone else. A person who is supposed to be with you. Embrace it and enjoy, figlio. Don't think of it too much, just let things fall as God has chosen for you. Remember, figlio, everyone comes into your life for a reason. Either they are there to help you or you may be there to help them. In your case, you were put in Olivia's life to help her have a good life. Think about it, she was so happy with you and died suddenly so she didn't feel any pain. I am sure she is looking down and thanking you for the wonderful life you gave her. I'm also sure it hurts her to see you unhappy," Silvia explained to her son.

What his mom said made a lot of sense to him. He always trusted her but the guilty feeling was still there. He knew it was something he had to work on but talking to his mama made him feel a lot better about letting someone else come into his life.

"I wish Olivia could somehow let me know she is okay with this, mama."

Just few seconds after he made this statement, his phone rang. It was Talia. His mom looked at him with a broad grin.

"There you go, mio figlio, there is your answer."

It was hard for any educated person to understand this but Sergio, being well educated, was also a religious man who strongly believed in God's strange ways of making things happen. This was a proof for him to accept what's happening in his life.

"Thank you, mama, I don't know what I would do without you." Sergio hugged her tightly.

"Oh, mio figlio, I am so glad God has kept me in your life for this long to be there for you and to feed you as much as I can." Silvia chuckled.

"Mama, if it's alright with you, I asked Talia to come over for lunch here. She was going to her new apartment leasing office to sign some paperwork and get the keys. She must be calling me to let me know she's done. What time would you like for her to come over?"

"She can come over anytime she wants. She can even come over now. So why don't you call her while I go in the kitchen and make lunch." His mom walked back into the house.

Sergio was so happy to hear his mom liked Talia, not realizing that she had set this up with Mirlande…mom knows best!

He looked at his phone and pressed on Talia's name, feeling excited like a teenage boy who just got hooked up with a girl for the first time…there was something cute about that.

"Hi, sorry I missed your call. I was talking to my mom. Are you all set with your apartment?"

"Hi yes. I just got the keys and I can move anytime. Since I'm off this week, I'm planning to use the time to move. It will be hectic with Mirlande's wedding prep but I don't want to be in my current apartment anymore."

Talia had told him the night before about her life as they were becoming better acquainted. Sergio felt really bad about what she had gone through and wanted to do whatever he could to make her life better from this point on.

"I don't blame you for wanting to get out of there fast. After lunch, I can come help you pack and move your belongings for however long you need me. This coming week I just have light work since last two months were chaotic so I can take some days off and help you," Sergio told Talia.

"I would love that! It will also give us more time to be together." Talia was quite excited. She was very grateful and couldn't believe she actually met someone amazing like him.

"Mama is getting lunch ready so do you want me to pick you up?" She could have come over on her own but he wanted to spend as much time as he could with her.

"That would be wonderful!" Talia exclaimed.

"Great! I will be there in ten minutes." Sergio hung up the phone.

He then walked into the kitchen where his mom was singing and cutting onions.

"Hey mama, I'm going to pick up Talia from her apartment. I will be helping her move some of her belongings into her new apartment after lunch so I figured instead of us driving around in separate cars I would just pick her up."

"That sounds great figlio. I'm glad you are taking some time off because you have been so busy lately. I will be busy this week making lots cookies for Mirlande. She and Marcus asked me if I would make my famous cookies for the dinner night before their wedding and, you know, how much I love to bake so I said yes. That doesn't mean I won't be making lunch and dinner so whenever you and Talia want to eat, give me couple of hours of notice and I will have it ready."

"Do you need me to pick up any ingredients for the cookies, mama?" Sergio asked.

"Nope! The Wales, down the block, were going shopping the other day and they stopped by. They saw my list and picked up everything for me. You know how great these neighbors are. As soon as I put items on my list, someone is always going to the store and getting it for me. They have all become my children." Silvia washed her hands and wiped them on a kitchen towel.

"I'm so glad you have so many people that love you mama and keeping an eye on you every day when I am not here. I'm going to go pick up Talia now and will be back in a few." Sergio grabbed a carrot and walked out of the kitchen.

Meanwhile, Talia was on the phone with Ally, waiting for Sergio.

"How was your night with Sergio?" Ally asked.

"It was incredible! He did things that I didn't know was possible," Talia excitingly replied, still in a dreamy state.

"You naughty girl!" Ally tsk'd.

"What? Can't a girl have fun?" Talia laughed, impishly.

"Have all the fun you want! Hey, did you pick up the keys to your new apartment?"

"That's what I called to tell you. I went and signed the papers and got my keys."

"That's great! I know we had planned to go together but since you chose to have Sergio spend the night with you instead of me I couldn't go with you," Ally teased.

"You're saying that as if you didn't have fun with Sam sleeping over at your place? By the way, did you tell him you are ready to get married?" Talia needled Ally back.

Ally was about to respond but then Talia's doorbell rang. "I think Sergio is here. I'm going over to his mom's for lunch and then he is going to help me move some of my stuff. I'll call you back later. I want to hear an update." Talia said goodbye and hung up the phone. She went to answer the door.

Ally was sitting on her bed while she was talking to Talia. After she hung up the phone with Talia, Sam walked out of the bathroom, showered and dressed. He was in a very good mood.

"So what's the plan for the day?" He asked enthusiastically.

"I thought you said you had to go to work?" Ally questioned.

"While I was in the bathroom, I called in to say I will not be coming in today."

Ally was shocked. "Really? You have never done that before. Wow, this a first!"

"I know, I just feel very different today. I just wanted to spend time with you." Sam began getting dressed, wearing jeans.

"Uh...you do realize I have crazy friends and, with Mirlande's wedding right around the corner, nothing is going according to any our plans. Even with Talia, now that she met Sergio, she is going to his mom's for lunch and, just yesterday, we had made plans to go sign the papers and get the keys for her new place. Not only that, I was supposed to sleep over at her place last night but things had changed. So, I would love to plan something with you but I have a feeling it's not going to work out the way we might want," Ally reminded Sam.

"Ok, how about we don't plan, just go with the flow, and if things come up with your 'crazy' friends which I'm sure will happen, then I don't have a problem with that. I like how all of you get along so well and, because of you guys, I feel like I'm not as reserved as I used to be. I'm starting to like the new me." Sam danced in a kid-like way.

Ally was really surprised to see him like this. He really seemed to have changed overnight. He's much more flexible than previously. "Ok, then that's great! I'm glad it doesn't bother you if plans get changed. I think I can actually relax and not worry about you in that sense. So, do you want to go grab something to eat at the diner?"

"Sure!" Sam was finished getting ready.

"Great! Let's go get something to eat…I am starving. We woke up late and missed our breakfast." Ally jumped out of the bed, giddy as a child.

Ally had showered and was ready before Sam finally got out of bed so there was nothing more for her to do than to grab her purse and leave.

"I guess you have to drive since my car is at Mirlande's?" Ally said.

"Well, you can drive my car so I can just sit and relax." Sam smiled and threw Ally his keys.

As they walked out of the building, Zain was coming back from the airport, looking very sullen.

"Hi Zain," Sam and Ally said at the same time.

"Hey, guys." Zain's voice seemed gloomy

"Hey, why so glum?" Ally inquired, putting her hand on his shoulder.

"I just dropped Brett and Lulu off at the airport and I already miss them." Zain's face showed his sadness.

Sam looked at Ally for a second then turned to Zain. "Why don't you come to the diner with us?"

"Oh, thank you but you guys go ahead," Zain replied, waving them off.

Sam and Ally could see that Zain wasn't the cheery self he was last night so Sam gestured for Ally to ask him again.

"Come on, Zain come with us. You look like you need to be around friends and we are not going to take no for an answer." Ally locked her arm into his.

Sam had no problem with Ally being touchy with Zain since Zain was gay and a very nice guy too.

"Are you guys sure? Don't you already have plans?" Zain asked.

"Zain, if you are going to be friends with Ally, Talia and Mirlande, learn that with these ladies there is no such thing as plans. I have learned that these ladies are wacky and they just do whatever they want. Marcus is no different than these women and that's why they all get along so well. I had to change myself so I could fit in," Sam told Zain.

Ally smiled. She didn't know what had happened to him over night but she liked the new Sam.

"No, I meant the two of you having plans right now," Zain replied.

"No, nothing like that. We were getting hungry so decided to get something to eat. I'm sure we will hear soon from the others about doing something," Sam surmised.

"Ok, in that case, I'd rather come than be alone. I hate being alone!" Zain mustered up a grin.

"Then why were all the drama? I think I should call you drama queen," Ally teased.

"Go right ahead, Lulu and Brett already do," Zain laughed.

The three of them got into Sam's car. Ally drove car since he wanted to relax. It was actually his way of getting used to her being a part of his life. It was a beautiful day and the three of them were enjoying the drive as they listened to the music.

It was a twenty minute drive to the diner, so they had enough time to enjoy some top 40.

At this same time, Talia and Sergio were both lying in bed after making love. Talia had her head on Sergio's chest and he was gently running his finger down her cheek.

"Your mom must be wondering where we are," Talia quietly guessed.

Sergio looked down into Talia's eyes. "I suppose we should head out but first I want to ask you something very important."

"Go ahead, ask me anything you want," Talia said, as she held his hand.

"I know this might be crazy but ever since I met you I just feel like we have known each other for ages..."

"I know what you mean. I have been feeling the same way," Talia quickly chimed in.

"So, would it be weird if I asked you to marry me?" Sergio gave Talia an innocent but questioning look.

Talia bolted up surprised. "What did you just say?!"

"Will you marry me?" Sergio gave Talia a sincere look and took her hands into his. "I know it sounds crazy to ask you to marry me when we just met yesterday but I really feel like we are meant to be. My mom is a wise woman and even she feels that we are meant to be so why waste time when I feel like it's eventually going to happen."

Talia was just shocked. "I don't know what to say. I mean I haven't felt like this about anyone else either but I feel like we really don't know each other yet."

"What's there to know? I told you everything that has happened to me and I promise you I will never hurt you in anyway. I will always protect you and keep you safe. When my dad met my mom he knew right away she was the one. He wanted to spend the rest of his life with her and they had a very happy marriage. My mom tells me I am just like my dad so, just like my dad kept my mom happy, I will always keep you happy. As far as getting to know each other, we have all the time in the world to do just that. I just don't want to be alone and neither do you. I have a nice place that would be perfect for you and I. So, what do you say?" Sergio asked in a tenacious but sincere tone.

Talia trembled with emotion. "Wow! This is all crazy and it's happening so fast...I don't know what to say!"

"Say yes!" Sergio pleaded.

"Yes!" Talia was elated, which could be seen in her eyes, tears of joy flowing down her cheeks.

"Really? Yes?" Sergio exclaimed excitedly.

Talia nodded her head so Sergio grabbed her up in his arms and kissed her, tasting the saltiness of her tears.

"What about my new apartment? I just signed the lease, what if they won't let me break the lease?"

"We will go there right now and ask the lady about breaking the lease since you just signed it this morning. You haven't even moved in so if she says you can't break the lease then I don't care, I will buy out the lease. I make great money so it won't hurt me financially. Even if I didn't make that much, I am an only child of rich parents who won't even think twice about giving me the money. Come on, let's put some clothes on and go see the lady about the lease." Sergio lifted Talia, twirled her around and then gently lowered her to the floor.

"I need to call Ally and Mirlande and tell them! They will be as surprised as I am!" Talia giggled in delight.

"Let's get dressed and on our way to the leasing office. We'll call my mom and the girls from the car," Sergio said as he started grabbing up his clothes.

"Ok!" The two of them started getting dressed fast.

Meanwhile, Ally, Sam and Zain just arrived at the diner. Ally was parking her car when her phone rang. She asked Sam to answer the phone for her.

"Hello?" Sam answered.

"Hi Sam, how come you are answering Ally's phone?" It was Talia.

"She's parking so I'm the answering service." Sam grinned.

"Can you put me on the speaker real quick?" Talia asked. Sam located the phone in between him and Ally, pressing the speaker phone icon.

"Hey Talia, what's going on?" Ally asked Talia.

"Sergio asked me to marry him and I said yes!" Talia announced in a lively tone.

"What? Oh My God, are you serious?!" Ally responded shockingly.

"Yes, you heard it correct, we are getting married!" Sergio yelled into the phone.

"Wow, that's great! I'm still in shock but that's great! Congratulations you guys!" Ally shouted.

"Wow, congratulations to you both!" Sam added his kudos.

"Thank you!" Talia and Sergio replied together.

Zain offered his congratulations to the couple also.

"Where are you guys right now?" Sergio inquired.

"The three of us just arrived at the diner for lunch," Ally responded.

Talia blurted out, "No, don't go in! Meet us at Sergio's mom's house for lunch. She wants to celebrate! We are on our way also and as soon as we are done talking to you we are going to call Mirlande."

"Ok, we will see you there in twenty minutes or so." Ally hung up the phone. She then turned to Sam and said, "Wow,

I can't believe they are getting married, they just met yesterday!"

"I guess when it's meant to be, it's meant to be," Sam said, shrugging.

"They met yesterday and they are getting married? Holy cow!" Zain exclaimed.

They were all surprised by Talia's news, especially Ally.

"I guess, no diner for lunch. Let's head over to Silvia's." Ally drove the car out of the parking lot.

Sam turned to Zain and said with a wink, "See what I mean about planning with girls, get used to it!"

Zain smiled, "I have no problem with it…I'm pretty easy going. I just love how all of you have a great relationship."

Ally slapped the steering wheel. "WOW, I'm still in shock that she is getting married!"

"You know, they probably are just getting engaged but I am sure the wedding isn't going to be for a while," Sam guessed.

"I know, but I just can't believe she did that just a day after meeting him."

"Well, if you really think about it, it's really no different from the concept of an arranged marriage in our culture. People meet for the first time, the family agree to the marriage, and then a few months later they get married. With us it's a bit different because you were able to convince your parents to give us time to get more acquainted," Sam analogized.

"Yeah, I agree, but now parents hook their kids up and let them get to know each other right?" Zain chimed in.

"Most so-called 'modern' parents are doing that but there are also conservative parents like ours that don't allow that. The only reason we done anything yet is because of Ally. Trust me, otherwise neither of our parents would have been ok with it. Actually, a week after we met my parents started asking me about our decision because they felt that was long enough," Sam clarified.

"So how long has it been since you guys have been together?" Zain asked.

"I think about almost two months now," Sam replied, looking at Ally for confirmation.

"So how much longer do you think you guys will take or should I ask how much longer will your parents allow you to…" Before Zain could finish asking they had arrived at Silvia's.

"Here we are but I don't see Sergio's car. Looks like we got here before them. Let's go next door to Mirlande's and wait until they get here," Ally suggested.

"Whatever you say, you are the boss." Sam nudged Ally teasingly.

Ally smiled at him then the three of them stepped out of the car. They rang the doorbell but there was no answer. They tried again and waited for a couple of minutes and still there was no answer.

"Strange…I thought they were supposed be here. Mirlande said she and Marcus were going to be home doing some work. I will call and see where they are," Ally said, as she pulled out her phone and, just when she was about to dial, Mirlande opened the door.

"Hey, we thought you weren't home so I was about to call you." Ally held up her phone and then greeted Mirlande with a kiss on her cheek.

"Sorry, I was in the shower and when I heard the doorbell that's when I got out. Marcus isn't home because he went to the airport to pick up his aunt. I'm surprised to see you guys here, I thought you were going to the diner for lunch?" Mirlande explained as she let them in.

"We came over to go to Silvia's for lunch. Didn't Talia call you?" Ally asked in a surprised tone.

Mirlande gave Ally a puzzled look. "No I haven't talked to her. When I came out of the shower I realized my phone battery was dead so I just plugged it in to charge. Why are you guys going there for lunch instead of the diner?"

"So. . you don't know that Sergio asked Talia to marry him and she said Yes! And, Silvia invited everyone for lunch to celebrate," Ally related to Mirlande.

"What?! He asked her to marry him?! Wow that was fast." Mirlande replied in a surprised tone.

"I know, I'm still in shock!" Ally exclaimed.

"I'm really happy for her. Sergio is one of the nicest guys I know and I have known him for a while now. Silvia always liked Talia, although she had never met her, she said she always used to watch her when you guys would come over here. I guess she knows her son and his taste very well. I am just surprised Talia said yes. I thought she would be more guarded because of her ex-husband but I am happy for her, she really will not regret saying yes for sure," Mirlande said.

"Knowing Silvia, she probably started preparing for the wedding!" Ally joked.

Just as they all were chatting the doorbell rang and Mirlande went to answer it. "Oh my God, congratulations you two!" Mirlande yelled after opening the door and saw Talia and Sergio standing there. She gave Talia a huge hug and then Sergio.

Talia and Sergio walked inside and they were greeted and congratulated by the rest of the group. Handshakes and hugs all around.

"What is all this commotion about?" Marcus asked as he entered the house a minute later. He saw the excited faces on everyone and came by to stand next to Mirlande who placed her arm through his and gestured toward the couple.

"Sergio asked Talia to marry him, she said yes!"

"Wow, I thought I was fast in proposing to Mirlande but you beat me by far man!" Marcus barked, slapping Sergio's back and shaking his hand. He gave Talia a kiss on the cheek also.

"Well, thank you guys. I guess I knew the moment I met Talia that I want to spend the rest of my life with her. We are not getting any younger and I didn't want to waste my time trying to impress her. You know what I mean? We are not teenagers anymore, now I have the cash to buy me love." Sergio teased Talia. Everyone fell extremely silent and then they all burst out laughing.

"We decided to think of it like having an arranged marriage, first get married then learn to love," Talia finally said after the laughter died down. She looked over at Sam and Ally to make her point.

"Funny thing is Ally and I were getting arranged and look at us, we are not even married yet. Looks like you two are following our culture and we are following yours," Sam needled, giving Ally a squeeze around her shoulders.

"Hey, you didn't have parents matching you guys up," Ally countered, looking at Talia.

"Now, wait a minute that's not true, his mama got a hand in this one. It was her idea to get these two together so mama knows best." Mirlande nudged Sergio.

"My mama always knows the best," Sergio agreed, as he pointed to Talia with a big smile on his face. Talia was confident she had made the right choice or else her two best friends would have told her otherwise.

"Mirlande, I tried to call you but it went straight to your voicemail and I did leave you a couple of messages to call me be back so I could tell you. I didn't want to leave a voicemail about it. Now that you know, did Ally tell you guys that his mom has invited everyone over for lunch to celebrate?" Talia asked.

"Yes, I found out everything when these guys got here. My phone's battery died so I didn't get any calls. I'm not sure if we'll be able to come for lunch because Marcus' aunt is here, he just picked her from the airport and dropped her at her brother's house so we have to go there after we run some errands." Mirlande replied, looking at Marcus hoping he would say they could go to his uncle's later or something.

"Oh, I know that puppy-eyed look but I am afraid we will not be able to go for lunch. You don't know my aunt, she will never let me hear the end of it," Marcus turned to the others. "I hope you guys can understand, I know these three are buddies and I would have canceled my plans with my aunt if it wasn't for the wedding. I just don't want her to be upset and she had planned it before she came here." Marcus explained, hoping Sergio and Talia understood.

"Hey, no problem! I know it's your wedding and I know I should have waited to ask her until your wedding was over. It's a very important week for you guys but I was so jazzed up about my feelings that I couldn't stop myself from letting it happen," Sergio expressed.

"No, don't apologize man. We are very happy for you guys." Marcus put a broad grin on his face and turned to Mirlande. "How about I take care of the errands and you join them for a little bit and, when I'm done, I will come pick you up?"

"Will you be able to get everything done by yourself?" Mirlande asked, squeezing her fiancé's arm in appreciation.

"You guys really don't worry about it, we can celebrate later tonight or after your wedding. This is your special time and we don't want to take that away. You guys go ahead and do the things as you had planned, we completely understand," Talia said.

"Are you sure, Talia? You know I love you and I am happy for you, these errands have to be taken care of today and it will be a lot for him to do. As a matter of fact, I was actually going to text you guys to come help and maybe the three of you can help do few things for us after you are done with the lunch?" Mirlande asked, looking at Ally, Sam and Zain with a coquettish smile.

"Yes we can, I told you I've taken time off to help you whenever you need it. I am your servant for the week," Ally bowed to her friend.

"Of course, I'm off also to help you guys," Talia chimed in.

"Aww, thank you guys so much. I couldn't have asked for better friends," Mirlande said starting to cry. She pulled her friends into a group hug and then picked up a tissue from a nearby table.

"Oh no not again, I don't know what is wrong with her. She has been crying about everything today," Marcus said as he rolled his eyes, but not in a mean gesture.

"She is probably just getting the usual pre-wedding jitters," Ally joked.

"Ok, let's go to my mom's now and you two go do what you need to and text us to let us know where to meet you guys, in, say, a couple of hours? Then we can help you finish whatever needs to be done today. Is that ok with everyone?" Sergio asked, eager to go see his mom.

"Yeah, that sounds great!" Marcus replied.

The men started to head out of the house. Sergio led the way with Zain following, and then Sam. The girls hung back briefly to talk to one another.

Talia had her hand on Mirlande's arm, looking apologetically at her. "I am so sorry this is taking the attention away from your wedding today Mirlande, I really hope you don't mind. I promise you, after today, it will be all about you. I had no idea my life was going to turn out like this! Now that the guys can't hear us, do you think I made the right decision? I really don't even know Sergio and I said yes purely because of how he makes me feel. He makes me happy! I feel like I have known him forever and it really hasn't even been twenty four hours. Please you guys, tell me I am not making a mistake."

"You are not!" Mirlande and Ally simultaneously cried out.

"Sergio is such a sweetheart, I know he will keep you happy. I have known him for a while now and he's just wonderful! You are the first girl he has liked since his fiancé, think about it, he remained single for this long and when he met you he instantly knew you both had a connection with each other. Like Ally always says, when it's meant to be it will happen and it happened to you now. Don't think about it too much and enjoy him, enjoy life," Mirlande told her friend, flailing her arms wide for emphasis and broadening a smile of encouragement.

"Hey, you know me if I didn't feel like he was a great guy I wouldn't even have left you alone last night with him. I must say, you must have rocked his world last night that he wants it for rest of his life," Ally said, giving a bit of a chuckle at the thought.

"Thanks guys, I really needed to hear that from you two. I love you so much," Time for another group hug.

"We love you too, now go meet up with that future mother-in-law of yours!" Mirlande ordered Talia as she gently pushed her friend out of the door.

Ally and Talia joined the guys as they were waiting for them in front of Silvia's house. As everyone started to go up the stairs Silvia opened the door and excitedly ran out to hug Sergio and Talia. "Congratulations you two!" She looked at her son with happiness in her eyes. "You have made me very happy, mio figlio." Silvia gave her son an extra squeeze and kissed his cheeks.

"Thanks Mama, I am very happy also." Sergio smiled back at his mother.

They all walked into the house.

Silvia handed Sergio a small box and told him to put it on her, pointing to Talia. Sergio turned to Talia, got on his knees and opened the box to show Talia. Talia's face beamed and tears welled up in her eyes.

"This engagement ring has been passed on in my family for many generations and every woman, including me, who has worn this ring had a very happy marriage and I wish the same for you," Silvia said fondly.

Talia held out her hand and Sergio put the ring on her, the ring was a bit loose but the ring was custom designed so it could be adjustable. It was a beautiful ring that was fit for a queen. It was an 18k white gold 8ct Emerald Cut diamond engagement ring.

Silvia stepped toward Talia and gave her a big hug. "I promise you, my son will give you all the happiness you deserve. He is a very good boy and he will treat you very well like his dad had treated me. I cannot express enough how happy I am!"

After Talia pulled away from Silvia, she gazed at the ring circling her marriage finger, put her face into her hands and started crying.

"Hey hey, are you ok?" Sergio asked while reaching out to his wife-to-be with a concerned gesture.

Talia was crying so hard that she couldn't even speak, she just held up her palm and shook her head. Sergio took a step back as Ally came over to her girlfriend because he knew Ally would know what to do.

Ally held Talia tightly and whispered, "Accept what you have now and appreciate it, your past is your past, your future will be nothing like your past. Sergio is not like your ex so enjoy it."

Talia wiped her tears, looked at those around her, and slowly smiled. "I am so very lucky to have all of you in my life. You see, I *am* very happy but also a bit scared so please don't mind me, it might just take me a little time to get used to your love after what my ex did. He made me lose trust in men but you…you are so wonderful that I just can't believe you are for real," Talia said, turning to Sergio, grasped his hand, and held it along with Ally's. Silvia and Zain had tears in their eyes while listening to Talia.

"If you are done making everyone cry can we get on with the celebration?" Ally teased, to lighten up the environment.

Talia got the hint and teased back, "Jeez, you never let me have a moment, will you!"

Everyone laughed which lightened the mood a great deal.

"Alright, now that we all are done crying, let's enjoy a nice meal. The weather is gorgeous so I am going to set the table out in the back, would you girls mind coming and helping me?" Silvia asked as she started to walk towards the kitchen.

"Of course we will help setup," Ally replied as she and Talia followed Silvia to the kitchen.

Silvia's house was gorgeous, she had converted her living room into a salon. On one end of the room she had set up her salon and at the other end of the room was where she had very comfortable sofas and chairs along with an antique table that had a coffee maker, small plates, cups and napkins set on top of it. She always had dessert on the table, either homemade or the ones people brought for her whenever they came over. Her table was never empty since she also had people coming to her salon or just visiting her. Attached to the living room was a small beautifully decorated bathroom with a soft light. At the center wall of the living room there was a door leading to the dining room to the left and kitchen to the right. The kitchen was impressive and spacious in a classical style. It appeared to come straight out of a page from the Home and Garden magazine. It had a mahogany island in the middle big enough to sit at least seven people. There were French doors in the back of the kitchen which led to a deck and a breath-taking garden beyond that she worked very hard to maintain. The deck had opulent furniture and lots of trees surrounding it. At night, the deck looked like paradise with beautiful lighting. Silvia's house wasn't that big but it was elegant. Money was never an issue so she had the taste for designer furniture that she was used to for most of her life.

"We'll also come help so the table can be set fast, I *am* starving," Sergio declared, motioning to Sam and Zain to follow him outside.

Talia turned back and smiled, she liked the idea of him helping because it gave them an excuse to spend more time together. They were all joking around, tasting food and just having fun. In no time, like working ants they all worked together and set up the table.

They were halfway done with their lunch when Sam heard Ally's phone ring. He whispered to Ally letting her know that someone was calling her. Ally wiped her mouth with the napkin that was set on her lap.

"It might be Mirlande and Marcus, remember they were going to let us know when they were ready for us to meet them."

She excused herself and ran into the other room. By the time she got to her purse the phone stopped ringing. She opened her purse to get her phone out, she had five missed calls from her sister and had a voicemail asking Ally to call her back right away and it was regarding their father.

Ally quickly called her sister back, "Hello Appa, you called?"

"Yes, I have been calling you forever, where have you been? Baba is in the hospital, he had another heart attack and was taken to the emergency room, and all of us are here," her sister replied, sounding worried on the other end.

"Oh, is he ok? Which hospital?"

"He is at the Suburban and they are still doing tests on him, get over her quickly," her sister said.

Ally hung up the phone then went to let everyone know. As she walked out on the deck, Talia turned to her and asked, "Mirlande and Marcus ready for us?"

Ally put her hands on the back of Sam's chair. "Actually that was my sister, my father had a heart attack and he is in the hospital. I am sorry but I need to go." She looked down at Sam.

"Oh, don't be sorry, go to your father and make sure he is ok," Silvia said, getting up from her chair and coming around to Ally, giving her a hug.

Sam stood up, "Come on, I will take you." Looking at Sergio, he asked, "Sergio, would you mind taking Zain back to his place whenever he's ready?"

"Absolutely! Don't worry about anything. We will let Marcus and Mirlande know, go take Ally to the hospital and keep us posted," Sergio agreed.

Talia got up to walk Ally and Sam to the door. Sam could tell Talia wanted to have a moment with her friend so he told Ally that he would wait for her in the car. Sergio was going to walk Ally out also but Talia gestured him not to come. He understood that the two friends needed to talk so he just stood up gave a quick bow to the girls as they walked around to the front of the house.

While they were walking, Talia put her arm around Ally and said, "Sorry to hear about your dad. I also know this puts a lot of pressure on you and will force you to make a decision that I don't think you are ready to make. Before you say anything to anyone just think about it and you make sure it's what you want."

"Ugh, I don't know." It was all that Ally could say. She was really stressed, yes it was sad her dad had a heart attack but this also meant that the family will be putting pressure on her to get married. History repeats itself, last time her father had a heart attack her mom blamed her for it stating that her father was very stressed about her relationship with Ary and now it's going to be because he wants to see her getting married now. Of course, her sister the "the perfect daughter" will not help. She too will be putting in her two cents, but her first priority now was to make sure her father was alright.

The twenty minute car ride to the hospital was a very silent one. Sam tried to cheer her up but she had a lot going on in her mind that she stayed mum. They arrived at the hospital and parked. Sam was about to get out of the car to go open the door for Ally but she put her hand on his hand, he stopped and looked at her with a questioning face.

"I am ready to get married," She told him, but she couldn't look at him in the eyes. Sam was very shocked to hear her say that. It came out of the blue and he wasn't expecting that, at least not at this moment.

Sam's eyes opened wide. "Really?"

"Yes, I wanted to tell you last night but it got so late and we were so very tired. Then I was going to tell you during our lunch but then we invited Zain so it would've been after lunch then Talia announced that she was getting married. One after another, something or other was interfering and, now, with my father in the hospital…I wasn't going to try to wait for the right time because I just didn't know when that right time was going to happen and I just didn't want you to wait any longer and felt you deserve an answer soon," Ally explained, feeling exhausted at just listening to herself.

Sam gave her a tight hug and their lips met in a brief but passionate kiss. Sam pulled back and gazed into Ally's sultry eyes. "You have no idea how happy I am to hear that. To be honest I thought you were going to say no to me but I didn't want to stop seeing you until you came out and said no. I'm so glad I hung around."

"I am glad you didn't give up," Ally smiled.

"Let's don't say anything to anyone yet until your father gets better."

"He might feel better right away hearing that." Ally may have been joking but deep down inside of her that's what she actually believed, she was actually hoping.

Sam laughed not realizing what she was saying.

Ally continued, placing her left palm on Sam's chest, "But we will wait to tell the girls because it's Mirlande and Marcus' time to celebrate and I don't want to take away that attention from them. Talia was feeling bad about announcing her engagement but she had no idea Sergio was going to ask her to marry him and that she would agree."

"You are right about that but won't they get upset if you tell them later?"

"I think they will understand and besides it's not like they didn't know I was going to say yes to you…I had told them last night during dinner when we were in the bathroom that I was going to tell you I would marry you, I think they were surprised that I didn't tell you last night," Ally said, but inside of her she knew that the girls must have been relieved she didn't say anything since they both want her to marry Ary and might even be disappointed in knowing that she finally gave Sam the answer he wanted.

The two of them got out of the car and started walking towards the elevator holding hands. They had to go to the fifth floor. While they were in the elevator Sam was holding Ally in his arms since no one else was there. He then nuzzled her on the neck. He was feeling that familiar warm sensation as blood flowed to his manhood with the excitement of her finally saying yes to him. If he could, he would love to rip off her clothes and make love to her right there in the elevator but he couldn't so he needed to wait.

When they reached their floor, the nurses said hi to Sam since they all knew him. He responded to them with nods and then told Ally to go ahead and see her father while he went to reads his chart. As Ally entered at the waiting room there she saw so many of her relatives including her sister gathered around talking. When anything happened to anyone in the family all the relatives would drop everything to be with the family member. Ally walked around and greeted everyone then her sister came up to her and gave her an imperious look like a mother does to a misbehaving child.

"Where have you been? Everyone but you came to see Baba right away and you, being his daughter, does not come until now?"

"I came here as soon as you told me," Ally replied, with her own look of disdain and trying hard to control herself from exploding in front of everyone.

"You know he is in the hospital because of you again, he is stressed about you not getting married. I don't understand what your problem is and why you keep torturing that man that loves and cares about you and only wants to see you settle down..." Her sister wasn't done with what she had to say when she was interrupted by her brother.

"You need to seriously stop being selfish and think of your parents. They have done so much for you and this is how you pay them back!" Her brother bellowed angrily.

Ally was getting attacked by her sibling, one after the other, and they weren't even giving her a chance to say anything. It was making her more and more upset towards them. This is what she had gone through the last time their father had a heart attack.

As Ally was about to say something, the doctor came out of the surgery room to update everyone on their father's condition. He spoke to everyone in the room.

"Hello, I'm Dr. Washkins. We have successfully performed the surgery on your father, he had two blockages in his arteries. We did an angioplasty and put two stents in to help restore the blood flow. He is currently in the Recovery room so they will only allow his wife to go see him for now but, so you understand, he is still unconscious. He will be shortly moved to the ICU. Do you have any questions for me?"

Ally saw Sam coming into the waiting room so she went towards him while her siblings were talking to the surgeon.

"Hey, just saw your dad's chart and didn't get a chance to speak to the surgeon because he was finishing up with the procedure," Sam said, putting his hand on Ally's arm.

"The surgeon just came here and is talking to my brother and sister." Ally gestured towards her siblings.

"Oh great, let me go talk to him then." As Sam was about to walk towards the other side of the room, the surgeon was coming their way, followed by Ally's brother and sister. Sam knew the surgeon so when he saw him he called out his name, "Hi Greg, got a second?"

"Oh hi Sam, I have to go to another procedure, would you mind walking with me and we can talk on the way?" The surgeon replied, looking up from his phone.

The two of them walked out of the waiting room together talking medical jingo. Ally was standing there and then her siblings came over.

"Oh, is Sameer working?" Her sister asked.

"No, he and I were out together when you had called so he came with me and now he is talking to the surgeon about Baba." Ally's tone was not a friendly one. She was upset with her brother and sister for attacking her the way they did.

"Oh you guys were together, you didn't tell me that!" Her sister pointed at her in a chastising way.

"How could I've said anything when the two of you were just attacking me?" Ally was just disgusted with them.

"Hey, everyone just wants to see you get married to a nice MUSLIM guy, is that wrong?" Her brother added in that same condescending manner.

Ally was very nauseated by her siblings' attitude but she didn't want to create any problems by saying something, so she kept her mouth shut. Their mom was sitting and talking to their relatives but she was also glancing at her kids to see what they were doing. Sam then walked back into the waiting room.

"Hi Sameer," Ally's brother and sister echoed each other.

"Hello," Sam nodded to Ally's siblings and then looked to everyone. "I just spoke with the surgeon that attended to your father and he said that your father should recover without any issues. In a few minutes, the nurses will allow visitors beyond just the wife. I told them that you guys were my family so they will allow everyone to go in one by one, but just keep in mind that the less people who visit him the better it is for him because of infections. You don't want him to develop anything so it's best if we could just limit it to maybe just the four of you, and other relatives should just wait until he is out of the ICU. We really don't want him to develop any complications so please try to explain it to everybody that we're not trying to be mean or anything but it's just better for him and, then, the sooner he gets better the sooner he can go home and they could see him as much as they want."

Just after he finished explaining everything to them, the nurse came and said that Baba had been transferred into the ICU and they could come to visit him one at a time. Ally's sister walked over to their mom to let her know they could go visit their father while Ally, her brother and Sam walked towards the ICU. Ally just didn't want to be there because of all the bullshit with her siblings, she wished her siblings were more supportive of whatever she wanted but she felt that because their marriages were arranged they couldn't understand anything.

Ally's mom was the first one to go into her dad's room, then her sister, followed by her brothers. Ally was the last one to go see her dad. She actually went in with Sam to see him to avoid any conversation with anyone. She had asked Sam to stay with her for as long as she was going to stay at the hospital. She didn't want to deal with any of her relatives but of course they all had the same question on their mind, surprisingly though, they didn't say anything to her as soon as she arrived to the hospital. Ally kept herself busy by getting food and drinks for everyone. As the day went by, more and more relatives were coming from out of town to visit.

After a couple of hours, Ally's dad was up. The doctor and nurse, along with Sam, examined Baba to determine his recovery status.

After few minutes, Sam returned to the waiting room and told all of Ally's relatives, "Uncle is up and doing well, he is still groggy so he might not be able to comprehend what's going on around him but all vitals are good and by morning, if all goes well, he should be transferred to a private room. Since he needs his rest the ICU will no longer be open for visitors so it's best for everyone to go home and rest up yourselves. You should be able to come visit him in the morning once he is transferred to his own room but, sorry, not before that."

Surprisingly, all of Ally's relatives understood and listened to Sam because, knowing them, they all would have just stayed at the hospital, worrying about Baba. Everyone decided to go home with the exception of Ally's two brothers, who decided to stay at the hospital just in case if there were any issues.

Ally said her farewells to all of her relatives and, when she was saying goodbye to her mom, her mom insisted that Ally come over to their house since all the relatives were over. She lied and told her mom that she had to go to work in the morning when, in fact, she had taken the week off.

Of course her mom couldn't help herself, cupped Ally's cheek with her hand, and said, "Sam has taken care of all of us so well today. He is such as nice boy. When are you going to make your decision so your Baba doesn't have to stress out about you and end up in the hospital again! You know how he strongly he feels about you not being married yet and that's why he had a heart attack. When are you going to make him happy? Why are you so selfish?"

Ally was furious about what she was hearing from her mother so she blurted it out, "I didn't want to say anything right now because Baba is in the hospital but I have decided to marry Sam!"

"Oh, that is wonderful beti (daughter)! I have to tell everyone and your father so he can get well quickly." Her mother's mood changed suddenly and, gleaming with happiness, she went to tell her other kids. Ally just stood there, her shoulders sagged a bit in absolute defeat. She watched her mother speak with grand gestures and pointing towards Ally. Her mother turned around and came back to Ally.

"You and Sameer need to come home now so we can tell everyone," she said

"No Ammie, Baba is in the hospital and I don't want to do anything until he comes home. If you want to tell people go ahead but I just don't want to deal with everyone right now and I have work in the morning so I am going home," Ally responded to her mother in a somber tone.

"Beti, why do you always have to make it so difficult, this is the time to be happy once your Baba hears the news I know him, he will get better so fast and will have a party. He had a heart attack because he was so stressed out thinking about you," her mom repeated again to Ally.

Ally was getting very upset and just needed to get away from everyone so she glanced around to see where Sam was and saw him talking to one of her aunts. Sam looked like he needed rescuing too, so she went up to him and her aunt and said, "Excuse me auntie, the nurse wants to talk to Sam, and auntie Ammie is waiting for you over there so you can go home with her. " Ally grabbed Sam's hand and pulled him away, out of the waiting room and down towards the exit.

"Thanks, I needed that. She kept asking me when we were getting married and I didn't know what to say," Sam said.

"I know how these aunties can be, that's why I had been avoiding them as much as I could this evening. I did end up telling my mom about me wanting to marry you though."

"I thought you wanted to wait?"

"I know, I did, but my mom kept harassing me so I told her, then she wanted us to come over tonight so she could announce it in front of everyone but that's where I drew the line and told her that Baba was in the hospital and I don't want to deal with this right now. I said I had to work in the morning so I needed to go home. Let's get of here before we get trapped into something else with everyone." Ally dragged Sam behind her and made a beeline for the stairs…she didn't even want to take the elevator for the fear of being that her relatives would be in there too.

Sam was actually enjoying this. He was getting turned on by Ally and was trying very hard to control himself. Once they got into his car he turned to her. "If you don't mind, can we call and tell my parents so they don't hear from your mom first?" He asked.

Ally completely understood what he was saying. His parents would feel bad not hearing from him so she nodded. "Yes, of course."

As soon as he got the green light from Ally, Sam dialed his parents' number. His mom answered but he asked her to hold for a second so he could pay for the parking. After he finished paying the attendant he got back on the phone.

"Hi mom, I'm in the car with Ally and I have you on the speaker. We wanted to tell you that Ally is ready to get married…" Before he could say anything further, his mother screamed with excitement and called her husband over so he could be part of the conversation.

"It's Sameer and Aliah, and they are ready to get married!" His mom shrieked to her husband with excitement, then returned to the conversation with her son. "Beta, that's the best news I have heard all day! Congratulations to you both"

"Aliah, I am sorry to hear about your father, how is he now? Does he know yet?" Sam's dad asked.

"Thank you and no he doesn't know yet. He was still a bit groggy so we didn't say anything to him but I am sure Ammie will tell him first thing in the morning," Ally related.

"Oh ok. Why don't you guys come over right now so we can have some sweets?" His mom asked, wanting to begin celebrations at that moment.

"Actually mom, I'm taking Ally to her apartment then I have to go back to the hospital. I have a 24 hour shift so we will see you after I'm done." Sam lied but had no regrets as so wanted to get Ally alone.

"Ok beta, I will call your mom, Aliah, and talk to her. Bye!" His mom hung up quickly so that she could call Ally's mom to discuss wedding preparations.

After they hung up, Ally smirked, "You bad boy, lying to your mom!"

"Hey, I just want to spend time with my soon-to-be wife, is that ok?!" Sam exclaimed cheerfully. He started the car, put it in gear, and left the hospital parking lot.

They reached Ally's apartment and, as Sam parked the car, Ally checked her phone and saw that she had missed calls from Mirlande and Talia. They also had texted her asking how her father was doing. Ally responded to both of their texts updating them on her father's health and letting them know that she is back at her apartment.

Ally's phone rang, as soon as she answered it Mirlande spoke, "Hey, you ok?"

"Yes, we just got home. Baba is out of surgery and recovering. Hopefully, there won't be any further problems."

"Glad to hear your dad is doing better. What are you guys doing right now?"

"Sam is parking the car and then we're going to get something to eat."

"We haven't had dinner yet, Talia and Sergio are meeting us at the brewery so come join us!"

"That sounds good, what time are you guys going there?" Ally looked over at Sergio, who had just turned off the car after parking it, her eyebrows raised.

"Marcus and I are just finishing up some stuff, Sergio and Talia are finishing up moving some of her belongings into Sergio's place so about an hour from now is what we had decided."

"Ok that sounds good, I need to go take a shower and just relax my mind a bit so we will see you guys in about an hour then," Ally said as she and Sam were exiting the car.

"Ok, great, see you guys then, bye." Ally ended the call after she heard Mirlande say goodbye. She put the phone back in her purse and by that time, she and Sam were walking into her apartment. As Ally put her purse on a chair, without looking at Sam, she ran the plan by him.

"We're meeting the gang for dinner at the brewery in an hour, hope its ok with you?"

"That sounds good and I wanted to surprise you, while we were at the hospital. I had changed my schedule around and took few days off also so we can spend time together," Sam replied.

Ally had taken off her coat and turned to Sam. "Oh that's great!"

"I am just so happy right now that you have agreed to be my wife and I am so glad I took time off because I know I will not be able to concentrate on work at all. And, I am not going to tell my parents I have taken the week off because you know what will happen once our families know that!" Sam happily declared as he took off his coat and laid it on the back of a nearby chair.

"So, does that mean you will be able to stay with me for the week?" Ally asked with a smile.

"I will be able to stay tonight and might have to go home tomorrow night since I live at home with my parents but I am sure I will come up with something to stay with you for the rest of the week. Maybe I will have to tell them I am going out town for a seminar just in case they ask for me at the hospital when they go to visit your dad." Sam took Ally into his arms and both looked at one another.

"Wow, look at you lying to your parents, sneaking out and staying with me, you bad boy," Ally teased Sam, poking him in the chest.

It was a side of him that she really started to like. Lately, he wasn't asking her for advice on anything and was making decisions on his own and surprising her with one thing after another.

Sam just couldn't control himself anymore, he started kissing her lips and then moved his lips all over her face, grabbing her ass and pulling her into him. She could feel his swollen organ through his slacks and pushed her hips further toward him. Sam picked Ally up and carried her into the bedroom, her legs wrapped around him. He gently threw her on the bed and playfully jumped on top of her, he quickly unbuttoned her jeans and slipped his hand inside her jeans, feeling the wetness of her soft spot. He knew she was ready but he wanted to tease her more and make her see that he is in control now so he pulled his hand out and slid her top off, throwing it on the floor. Sam cupped her breasts and suckled her nipples as she moaned in agony. As he made his way down her stomach with his tongue, he slowly pushed her pants down to her ankles and when he reached her inner thigh, he yanked them off. He moved her legs over his shoulders so that they were straddling his head and he buried his face into her essence. Ally moaned with pleasure, her fingers winding around his hair, she would've reached her pinnacle had Sam not abruptly pulled away. She saw the look in his eyes, a look of dominance but also of desire, she knew what he was asking for and moved to help him take off his shirt. She loosened his pants and pulled them off, along with his boxers. Ally could see his engorged organ at eye level and took hold of it with both hands, engulfing it with her lips and using her tongue to create a rapturous moment. Sam couldn't take it anymore and needed to be inside her so he pulled her up and turned her so that she was kneeling on her knees, on the bed Bending over her he grabbed her breasts and fondled them, thrusting deep inside her, a gasp escaping her lips. After several thrusts, he pulled out of her and then turned her onto her back, bringing her to the edge of the bed while he remained standing and plunged back inside of her wetness. His thrusting quickened, her moans escalating, both moving in a rapid dance of pleasure, finally culminating in a burst of brilliant sparkles. Both of them spent, their breathing labored, Sam collapsed beside Ally on the bed.

Sam smiled down at Ally with leery eyes and kissed her hand. "I have been wanting to do this all day."

Ally gave a half-hearted grin but snuggled into his arms.

"I must say, for someone who has never slept with any woman you seem to know exactly what you are doing," Ally commented, forgetting that he is not aware of her past experiences.

"So how many people have you done this with that you know how to pleasure a man?" Sam asked, lifting one brow.

"Thousands," Ally joked, trying to avoid the topic.

Just then Ally's phone rang, her phone was in her purse in the other room. "Let me go see if it's one of the girls calling." Ally said, getting up from the bed. Sam dropped his arms to the bed, looking up at the ceiling.

"If it's either of our families, please don't answer."

He really didn't need to say that to her, he had no idea that, more than him, she was trying to stay as far away as possible from the families. When she opened her purse and checked her phone it was actually her sister calling and of course there was no way she was going to talk her. She had been meaning to assign ring tones for everyone so she knows who is calling but for some reason or the other she hadn't gotten around to do that.

While she was checking her phone, Sam had gone to the bathroom and by the time she was done he had returned to bed.

"Who called?" He asked.

"It was my sister so I didn't answer," She replied, laying back on the bed, on her side next to him, her hand supporting her head.

"I'm glad you didn't answer, you and your sister are so different. She is so religious and you are not even close to being religious. Even your personalities are so different, it seems to me that she likes to please everyone and be that perfect daughter," Sam reasoned.

"Yeah, she and I are very different. She wasn't religious like this though. Her husband made her become religious and she didn't standup for herself and let him know how she felt about the whole thing but instead she got brainwashed into becoming what she is now. I really hope you don't expect me to be religious later in life because I am not my sister and I do have a big mouth. That's one thing I would fight with you about. If you ever change and impose that on me and, believe me, even if we have kids I am willing to walk away from you with the kids because I can financially take care of myself and my children," Ally asserted in a very serious and clear tone because that was something she could not tolerate.

"Don't worry, I won't be like your brother-in-law, you have my word and if I do then you can leave me," Sam said, looking at Ally confidently.

"Good, I am glad that's one thing you accept where I stand but what if your parents impose that on me?"

"I am not planning to live with my parents and they won't have the right to say anything to you and, if they do, I will take care of it."

"Do I have you word on that? I really don't want any unpleasantness between the two of us in the future because of this. This was the main reason why I took so long to think about agreeing to get married. I have seen so many of my family members becoming very religious and, to me, religion is within me, I don't need anyone telling me what I should believe or how I should live my life. I hope you really have realized what type of person I am. I hope you know that I am a very strong, independent woman and I can walk away from anything or anyone if that's the choice I make. My parents may be my weakness but I don't think anyone else will be if they try to control me. I hate being controlled, please know that and if you want to think about it go ahead because I will not change who I am for anyone, not even for you," Ally declared forcefully.

Sam could tell that she was uncertain about her decision from the look on her face. To allay her fears, he said, "You don't need to worry about that. You can be who you are and there is no need to change. I will follow and do what I need to and you may follow and do what you need to and when it comes to kids I am sure we can come to a mutual agreement."

When he said "we can come to a mutual agreement" about the kids she didn't like the sound of it. Just as she was about to ask for clarification, her phone rang and it was Mirlande.

"Hi Mirlande," Ally answered it.

"Hey are you guys ready for dinner?" Mirlande asked on the other end.

"Almost, are you guys on your way there now?" Ally replied.

"We're on our way to pick up Talia and Sergio. I forgot to tell you, remember Marcus had booked the limo for this entire week? Well, we are in the limo picking everyone up so be ready, we should be there in half hour."

"Oh yeah, I forgot about the limo, ok we'll be ready by the time you guys get here, bye." With that, Ally hung up the phone and got up from the bed. She turned to Sam and signaled to him with a wave.

"Come on, we need to get ready fast, they will be here in half hour. While you wash up and change I will take a five minute shower." She ran into the bathroom naked.

Sam followed her. While she was showering, he peed then washed his face and a quick once over his body with a washcloth, then he went into the bedroom, made the bed and straightened a few things that were out of place from their rocking sex. By the time he was done, Ally came out of the bathroom naked, looking very sultry, water dripping down her breasts.

"You are turning me on again. I feel like going for round two." Sam eyed Ally seductively as he put his arms around her waist.

"Control the wild dog in you for later, I need to get ready quickly." Ally chuckled, pulling herself away from him and towards the closet to get clothes out for herself.

While she was changing, Sam had a few texts to answer so he was busy doing that. Many of his relatives were texting him after the good news of him getting married to Ally. His parents had spread the news like wildfire to his relatives so now he was getting calls and texts from them. Ally too was getting them but she wasn't interested in returning any of the calls or texts. After a few minutes Ally came out of the bathroom. Sam turned around when she walked into the bedroom.

"You look stunning!" He exclaimed.

Ally's was wearing a red spaghetti strap dress and black heals, her hair was flowing beautifully, she looked gorgeous as always.

"Thanks, hope after marriage you won't have a problem me dressing like this," She said as she put her earrings on.

"You can wear whatever you like but I must warn you, I might get jealous of other men looking at," Sam replied, pointing his index finger at her.

"They can look as much as they want but they won't be able get any," Ally joked, putting her arms around him and giving him a quick kiss.

Just then the doorbell rang. "Looks like they are here, could you please get the door while I use the bathroom really quick?" Ally ask Sam and then rushed to the bathroom, closing the door behind her.

"Sure."

Sam went to the door and opened it. Mirlande, Talia, Sergio and Marcus were all standing there.

"Hi Sam, is it safe for us to come in?" Marcus teased.

"Well, you already disturbed us so I guess you can come in now," Sam laughed, making way for everyone.

The friends walked in just as Ally came out of the bathroom.

"Wow, you look gorgeous!" Marcus exclaimed, giving Ally a big hug.

"Watch it, I am right here!" Mirlande teased.

"Yeah, me too," Sam added to the tease.

"Ha ha! Hey you guys!" Ally smiled and went around kissing each one on their cheek.

"How is your dad doing?" Sergio asked.

"He is doing better now, we are hoping he will be transferred from ICU to his private room tomorrow morning if all goes well with him tonight," Ally replied.

"There is nothing to worry about, he should recover without any problems," Sam assured, wrapping his arm around Ally's shoulder.

"That's great!" The friends chimed together.

"I am surprised you were able to escape from all the relatives. We thought we might not see you for a while," Talia said.

"Oh my God, tell me about it! Especially after I told them I am ready to get married!" Ally blurted out, not realizing what she had just said.

"What? You guys are getting married!" Mirlande exclaimed with a shocked look.

After seeing Mirlande's reaction, Ally realized what she revealed. She looked at Sam quickly then to Mirlande and Talia. "I said yes to Sam then told everyone about it. I didn't want to say anything to you guys until Mirlande's wedding was over because this is your special moment and I didn't want to take that away from you," Ally explained, holding Mirlande's hand.

"Don't be silly! Congratulations to you guys!" Mirlande proclaimed as she put her one arm around Ally's waist and the other around Sam and gave them a squeeze.

Talia was also shocked and was trying her best to hide it because she really was hoping Ally would marry Ary but she too congratulated them.

"So when is the wedding?" Asked Marcus.

"With my father being in the hospital we haven't had time to discuss anything with the family. Once he is feeling better, hopefully by tomorrow morning, I am sure my mom will tell him about it and, knowing them, they will start planning it from his hospital bed," Ally joked.

"Correct me if I am wrong, Indian weddings are a week long celebrations right?" Sergio asked.

Sam replied with a resounding "Yes!"

"So we will be partying for a week?" Marcus questioned excitedly.

"Yes, but it won't be any drinking type of party though," Sam said.

"Doesn't matter, a party is a party!" Marcus laughed.

Ally could tell Talia didn't seem that thrilled about the announcement and Talia couldn't pull her to the side and talk to her either but her look was enough to let Ally know how she was feeling about her decision.

Mirlande glanced at Talia and could see the same reaction that Ally was seeing on her face. Mirlande was happy for Ally so long as that's what she really wanted. With Talia, though, it was a different story because she knew Ary and how he truly felt about Ally and she also knew deep down inside Ally really would like to be with Ary and she was just compromising with Sam so she could please her family. Talia was so upset with Ally and felt really bad for Ary because ever since Ally told him she had made up her mind about Sam, he was having hard time letting her go so Talia had been calling him every day talking to him to help him get through this since he had no family member to help him. Talia and he had become good friends.

"Well, it seems like all of us have so much to celebrate so why don't we get the party started!" Marcus exclaimed, doing a jig and leading everyone out of the apartment to the limo.

Marcus grabbed Mirlande's hand, Sergio then took Talia' arm and followed them, Sam held out his hand for Ally who accepted it and grabbed her purse from the table. The two of them were a little behind the others since Ally was locking her apartment.

Marcus stopped and said, "Hey, let's see if Zain is free to join us."

He then turned around and knocked on Zain's door. There was no answer so he took his cellphone out of his pocket and called him. Since there was no answer to that he led the way out of the building.

The limo was parked right in front and one by one they all stepped inside. As they were driving, about a block away, Mirlande saw Zain walking. "Hey there is Zain!" She exclaimed.

Marcus then asked the limo driver to pull over. They pulled up alongside Zain, Marcus yelled out of the window, "Hey Zain, here you are! We tried looking for you at your apartment and called you on your phone."

Zain stepped over to the limo and leaned in. "Oh sorry, I left my phone for charging."

"Hop in, we all are going out for dinner," Marcus offered.

"You guys go ahead, I'm a bit tired." Zain replied, showing some wear on his face.

"What?! You don't want to go out? That's not like you…you love going out. We don't care how tired you are, you are coming with us," Marcus declared, getting out of the limo to compel their friend in joining them.

Zain knew Marcus wasn't going to take no for an answer so he capitulated, "Alright, I'll come."

"Hey guys." Zain waved to the others as he sat next to Ally in the limo. Ally, in turn, looked at Zain and could see it on his face that he wasn't himself. Something was bothering him but she didn't want to ask him in front of everyone just in case he didn't want to talk about it.

They were all chattering and enjoying themselves when they arrived at the Brewery. As they pulled into the parking lot, Zain was surprised at the size of the building and, when they walked into the restaurant, he was blown away.

"Wow, for a small city I can't believe how great the restaurants are here," Zain commented.

Ally decided to be the advocate for Buffalo. "Yep, people have no idea what a gem Buffalo is. They hear about the snow in the news and people avoid it like the plague but Buffalo has many terrific restaurants that are equivalent to or even better than most restaurants in the bigger cities. I feel like I do a commercial for the city when I tell people it truly is a wonderful place for dining out. Western New York is well known for great schools and it is a safe place to raise kids. The seasons are so beautiful!

"Yes, it gets cold but climate change is happening everywhere and it's getting cold everywhere. Ironically, Buffalo's winters are actually getting warmer. Yes, we have snow but it really depends on where you live. If you live in the South towns, that's where most snow fall occurs, matter of fact, people who love the snow move to the South towns. Here in the North, where we live, we barely see any snow. Buffalo is also incredibly equipped to handle even seven feet of snow.

"Here, schools are open even if there is two feet of snow on the ground because the roads are cleared so fast that one is surprised at how that could be possible. Even when there is a snow storm you will see kids playing in the snow, people going to the mall, work etc. Snow will never stop the Buffalonians from going on with their everyday life. There are many winter activities for those who love the snow. And just like the winter, summers are gorgeous here. With beautiful clear skies and nice hot days, you will always find people outside enjoying the weather and there are many outside events that take place during the summer. Autumn season is to die for here! The colors of the trees are breath-taking, it's picturesque. The kids enjoy apple picking and hayrides at the nearby farms. The farms have so many activities for kids and adults to enjoy from morning until night. So far, you have only been experiencing a few restaurants, wait until we show you the things to do and places to visit when it's autumn and winter."

"Wow, I guess I am glad I moved here and can't wait until I visit more places," Zain concurred.

The friends were standing around the restaurant lobby, waiting to be seated. The restaurant was in the style of a very big warehouse that had three floors with a bar in the center of the first floor and four giant television screens. The décor of the brewery was very minimal with old style lights and chairs, brick walls with posters that were a 'blast from the past'. The restaurant was busy tonight so they decided to wait at the bar, it took about thirty minutes for them to be seated. The view from the third floor was great, they could see what was going on all the way to the front of first floor. Mirlande, Marcus, Sam and Ally sat on one side of the table and Talia, Sergio and Zain sat across from them. The waiter, wearing black t-shirt and khaki pants which was their uniform, arrived to take their drink orders. Since they had already brought their drinks over from the bar, the waiter took orders for appetizers. They ordered the fried pickles and Bavarian style pretzels, which was a huge pretzel, hung on a metal rod served with three different types of dipping sauce. Along with that they ordered the soup of the day which was slow cooked chicken in garlic, tomato, basil broth.

Ally noticed that Talia was trying to avoid her and seemed a bit unsettled. She let her be for most of the evening thinking that she will get over whatever was bothering her. Mirlande noticed the tension between the two girls so she decided she needed to talk to them.

"Excuse me guys but I need a little girl time with my ladies here. Talia and Ally, can you two come with me to the bathroom so you can advise me on something?"

The three girls got up and went to the restroom while the guys sat around chatting. As the girls entered the rest room, "Ok you two, what is going on?" Mirlande firmly asked, with her hands on her hips.

"I have no idea what is wrong with Talia, I thought she was just upset about something so I was giving her some space," Ally began.

"You know exactly why I am upset! How could you go ahead and tell everyone you are ready to marry Sam? I know you, this is not what you want. You give people advice all the time and it's sad you can't following your own advice," Talia admonished Ally angrily, crossing her arms in front of her.

"I am just fine with the decision that I have made, I don't understand why you just can't accept it and be happy for me. Well, anyways, it's not about me right now. Mirlande's wedding is only in a couple of days and we need to be upbeat and have a good time," Ally countered.

"Seriously Ally, that's what you have to say? Why couldn't you wait a little bit longer before telling everyone about marrying Sam? Let me guess they all accused you of causing your father's heart attack again and this was your solution?" Talia turned to look in the mirror, checking her make-up, trying to distract her anger.

"Why do you sound like Ary? You are supposed to be my friend who should understand me and be happy for me but from the way you are reacting you sound like he has brainwashed you into his way of thinking!" Ally was losing her calm.

Mirlande just stood there listening to the two of them and staying out of it. She felt this was between her two friends and they needed to get it all out.

"If this is his way of thinking then how is he wrong? I can bet you a hundred dollars that's what exactly happened at the hospital, you were cornered and that's the reason why you made that decision," Talia claimed.

"I had made my decision few days back and just didn't get a chance to tell Sam and it just so happened that earlier today I was able to tell him before I told everyone else," Ally replied, looking off to the wall of the bathroom that had a picture of a couple in an old jalopy.

"So, why did you say anything to your family about it when your dad went into the hospital? Shouldn't you be more concerned about your dad getting better?" Talia turned back to Ally, noticing that Ally avoided her gaze.

"Ugh, you know I really don't need this from you right now, if you can't be happy for me, that's fine! This is not the time nor the place to have this discussion. This is a happy occasion and I don't want to ruin it!" Ally demanded as she grabbed Mirlande's hand.

"Whatever! We will go back to the guys but I am not done with you," Talia answered, walking out of the restroom.

The girls were great at poker faces. They returned to the table as if nothing just happened between the two. The men stood up.

"I was telling the guys that we need to get used to the three of you hiding from us to have some girl time. I told them about the time I went looking for the two of you when you didn't return from the bathroom at a restaurant," Marcus wisecracked while putting his arm around Mirlande.

"Yeah, sorry guys, that's just how it is with us. Don't get offended by our behavior. Sometimes we get these moments where we just need time for each other," Mirlande explained with a smile for her future husband.

Ally looked around the table and noticed that Zain wasn't there. "Hey, where is Zain?" She asked.

"He had a phone call so he stepped out to talk...he wanted to have a cigarette also," Sam replied.

Ally looked out the window of the patio across the room and saw Zain standing there on the phone while he was smoking. She watched him as he finished his conversation and noticed that he looked a sad so she excused herself to go talk to him. Zain was standing on the patio leaning against the wall smoking.

"Hey, everything ok? You haven't been yourself since we picked you up. What's wrong?" Ally asked, walking up to him, she had a concerned look on her face.

Zain took a deep breath and just let it out, "Remember I told you that my father hasn't been talking to me ever since I told him I was gay, etc.? Well, I guess my father has been very ill and was even admitted into the hospital a couple of days ago because he has been so stressed and sad about me. I called to see how he was doing and if I could see him. My mom finally talked to me after Lulu went over there to convince her to talk to me, even she has been very upset with me and accusing me of making my father sick. She told me it will be best if I didn't come to visit him." Zain eyes were becoming wet with tears.

"I am so sorry, but I know exactly how you feel. Trust me, my family blames me for my father being in the hospital too," Ally said, trying to console her friend.

"What do you mean?" Asked Zain puzzled. To help Zain understand that he was not alone in this type of situation, Ally started telling him everything about her family and Ary…

While Zain and Ally were in deep conversation, the rest of the gang were chatting and eating the appetizers. Sam was about to get up and go see what was taking the two of them so long but he saw from his seat that they were having a serious conversation so he stayed seated and joined the conversation with others. After few minutes Zain and Ally returned. Although they all looked up, none of others questioned them and everyone just enjoyed their night out with each other.

Chapter 14

Change of Plan

It was 10am, Sam was in the shower and Ally had just ended her phone call with her mom. She went into the bathroom to talk to Sam.

"Hey I just finished talking to my mom. She said my father is doing great and she told him about us. She said he was so excited that he told her as soon as he gets home they should have the engagement party and wedding next month."

"I agree with your dad. They should be planning for our wedding next month!" Sam shouted over the running water, eager to marry her.

"I don't understand how they can plan an entire wedding in a month!" Ally exclaimed.

"Knowing our mom's, they probably already have a hall reserved."

As they were talking, Ally's sister texted her about what was going on with the family…

"Actually, I guess your parents were at the hospital this morning and they are planning to have the wedding in my parents' backyard since it's so big. They are planning to set up tents. They really do have the entire wedding planned out already!" Ally said to Sam.

"I'm actually happy they have everything planned out, which means we can be husband and wife in a month's time…I like that!" Sam couldn't contain his excitement.

"Yep, most likely than not we will be married in a month's time. That sounds weird doesn't it?" Ally did not sound excited

"Not weird at all to me. I can't tell you how excited I am about us getting married. If our family says 'let's have the wedding tomorrow', I would be more than happy to."

"Yeah it is exciting…it's going to get very busy and crazy! Mirlande gets married in a couple of days then I'm sure Talia will be getting married soon too. I just hope not within a week because I don't know how we could have a week-long ceremony for our wedding and be able to give our hundred percent to Talia. You know, she will need that after her previous marriage experience. So, where are we going to live? Will you be ok living here? I mean, this is a great apartment with central location. What do you think?" Ally's speech was very rapid, almost nervous-like.

"I think living here is a great idea! I like this apartment and it's only five minutes to the hospital for me. When we decide to have kids, we can think of buying a house then unless you want to buy a house now?"

"You know I never thought of buying a house. I guess we can think about that later but, at least for now, we can live here. This apartment is big enough for the both of us without a problem. Wow! I can't believe this is actually happening!" It was really sinking in for Ally.

"I know, finally! I really thought you weren't going to say yes to me. I mean, it was taking you so long to think about marrying me, whereas, I knew right away I wanted to marry you."

"Yeah, sorry about that. I told you that I just wanted to make sure you weren't going to be like my brother-in-law, who became so religious and forced my sister to follow him. Just the thought of someone being able to control me scares me. I really hope your parents don't expect that from me and if that causes problems between the two of us I don't know how I would handle that. I am *not* my sister. I know me, if you side with your parents, then divorce it is." Ally covered her uncertainty by teasing Sam. She should be happy because it's a special occasion but she felt like the conversation wasn't making her happy so she decided it was time for her to take a breather.

"I told my mom I have an hour before my next appointment so I will stop by the hospital. Why don't you finish up your shower while I go visit my father? You can't come since you told your parents you're at a seminar," Ally proposed, as she stood in front of the mirror and applied lip gloss.

Sam peaked out of the shower, "Don't be late, I don't want to spend any of my time away from you. If anyone asks, tell them that I'm ready to get married next week, if they want. I don't care for a big wedding so we can just have a small family ceremony."

Sam was trying to be funny but Ally knew that deep down he meant what he said. Ally smiled, gave him a kiss and walked out of the bathroom.

Meanwhile, Talia and Sergio were at her apartment packing her belongings so she could move into his place. They both were dressed very casually, she in a tight green t-shirt and capri yoga pants with her hair tied in a ponytail and he in a fitted blue t-shirt and gray sweat pants. They both actually looked like Barbie and Ken. They were very good looking and tall, with perfect bodies.

"If we keep working without any breaks, I think we should be done in three hours," Sergio announced.

"I Hope so, I really want to get out of this place as soon as possible. I just get the chills being here and I'm glad we were able to get some empty boxes from the grocery store or else we would have been making many trips to the car. Hopefully, we don't have to meet anyone for lunch or else that will delay us further," Talia said, as she lifted a box and put it by the door, next to the other boxes.

Sergio stopped packing and looked at Talia. "Can I ask you a question?"

"Of course, go ahead, ask me anything you want. We *are* moving in together so we need to really know one another," Talia replied, putting a book in one of the boxes and straightening up.

"Last night when we were at the restaurant it seemed like something was on your mind. You were trying to be yourself but, to me, it seemed as if something was bothering you. Are things alright between us? I mean, I know things happened so fast with us but I just hope you are sure about all of this."

"Oh, of course, I'm sure about us! Yes, it did happen fast but maybe it's meant for it to happen that way and I'm ok with that. I am just very upset with Ally," she told him.

"Why are you upset with her? Did you guys have a fight or something?"

"I guess I have the time to tell you her entire store while we pack. You see…" Talia began telling the story.

While Talia relating everything that's happened to Sergio, Ally was at the hospital meeting her father. Her father was awake and seemed to be doing well. Her mom had told him about Ally's decision and, of course, he was very happy and couldn't wait to get home to plan for the wedding. The doctor told him he would have to remain in the hospital for a few days more so they could monitor him closely.

Half an hour after she arrived at the hospital, Sam's parents came to visit her father again. Her mom actually had called Sam's mom right after Ally told her she was going to the hospital and asked them to go over also so they could discuss the engagement. Relatives were still in town so they needed to get everyone's availability for the engagement party and wedding. Her father was so happy that Ally agreed to get married that he didn't want to waste any time and wanted to plan the party while he was in the hospital, before she changed her mind.

Ally was starting to feel rushed. She wasn't surprised her mom would start planning in the hospital but the reality was hitting her. She was happy but, also, scared. As she was visiting her father, Sam kept texting her to come back soon and that he missed her. Ally stayed at the hospital for about forty-five minutes but it seemed like hours to her. Getting texts from him aided her in an escape plan. She told everyone that her work was texting her and that she needed to go. They all understood that she had busy schedule so they didn't give her a hard time, especially now that she had agreed to get married. Ally was really feeling claustrophobic with her aunties hugging her, asking her what she would like to wear for the engagement…it had to be Indian of course. The atmosphere was too much for her to handle.

She said goodbyes to everyone and told her father she might not be able to visit him in the evening because she has evening appointments but will call him whenever she is free to see how he was doing. Her father was so happy he kept saying to her, "Beti, now I will get better very fast. You will see that I will be home very soon. You have made me very happy."

Ally didn't know what to say so she just smiled and said goodbye to everyone again. With her family, there was no way anyone could leave after saying bye, once people kept talking and talking, so there would be two or three goodbyes before anyone could walk away.

She finally left the hospital and as she was going into her car, she texted Sam letting him know she was on her way home. As she was driving by herself she started to think about her engagement, then her wedding, and then how her life would be with Sam. For some reason, she was having a hard time envisioning her life with Sam. Ary kept coming to her mind. She couldn't understand why she couldn't see Sam. Could it be because deep down inside, subconsciously, she wished it was Ary? That worried her a bit because she somehow was able to foresee what might happen…one could say that she was able to see the future. It sounded as if she was crazy but, yes, she would get these visions in her head of what was going to happen before it happened. For her, it was like watching a movie about the future. She had these, one can say, psychic visions that just came to her out of nowhere and they usually came true.

In the past, she only had shared those visions with Ary because she had told him things that were going to happen and they did happen. So, when they were together he wouldn't make decisions about anything until he confirmed with her that they were good for him and, if she said they were not good, he wouldn't go ahead with his decisions. He believed in her visions that much. She would never get any visions if she was under any stress, only when her mind was clear. As she was driving and thinking why was she having a hard time imagining her life with Sam, the only thing that made sense to her was that she was perhaps nervous or scared of the next chapter in her life. As she continued with her thoughts, her phone rang. Since her phone was connected to her car via Bluetooth, she could see Talia's name displayed on the screen.

Ally: "Hi, Talia."

Talia: "Hey, what are you doing?"

Ally: "I was on my way home from visiting my dad at the hospital, what's up?"

Talia: "How is he doing now?"

Ally: "He's actually doing well. Already planning the engagement and wedding."

Talia: "Actually that's what I wanted to talk to you about. Are you sure this is what you want? I know deep down inside you can't let Ary go and he really loves you also. I really haven't told you this but I still talk to him. I see him at the office when I go there but he calls me on daily basis because he is having hard time letting *you* go. He made a mistake once and you won't forgive him. He even left the girl he was with when you came into his life again. I told him about you getting married to Sam and that it's going to happen soon. He really wants to talk to you, he really needs closure. I told you that he is even thinking of moving out of this city because he doesn't want to run into you and Sam. Why don't you go see him? He looks really sad. I have never seen him like that."

Ally: "I can't stop you from talking to him. Being my best friend though, I can't believe you still talk to him about me. Why can't you be happy with whatever decision I make? Don't you think I know him more than you know him? I can't believe you would want me to be with a guy who wasn't there for me when I needed him the most. He didn't even wait for me!"

Talia: "Yes I know, I have heard this story many, many times, many times from you. But obviously you didn't hear what he said to you about why he did what he did and you obviously still mean something to him if he told the girl he was with that he wouldn't marry her because he loved you. I can't do this anymore! You know deep down inside of you that you are ruining three lives. You won't be happy. Sam won't be happy because you won't be happy with him and Ary will not be happy once you marry Sam. Ugh! I just can't take this anymore, I no longer want to be a part of this. You are my best friend and I can't be part of the celebration that I don't agree with. Please understand that I will not participate in any of your ceremonies, including your wedding. Just have the decency to tell him in person and let him have the closure that he needs so he can accept it and move on. I personally think you may need that closure also, that's all I have to say to you."

Talia was so upset with Ally that she hung up the phone without saying bye. Ally, too, was upset with Talia and didn't know what to say to her. She just wanted her friend to be happy with the decision that she has made. There was no way Ally was going to meet Ary. She felt that since she had decided to marry Sam, she didn't feel it was right for her to go see Ary and, besides, she didn't think she owed Ary anything for her to give him that closure.

Ally had arrived at her place. When she pulled in she saw Sam standing there waiting for her with a big smile on his face as if a dog was waiting for his master to return. Ally parked her car, took a deep breath, pulled herself together, and stepped out of the car with a semi smile. Jeffery was looking out the window and could see that fake smile on her face. He stood at his window watching as the two of them entered the building. Once they entered the apartment, Sam started kissing Ally on the back of her neck.

Ally knew exactly where he was going with that and she wasn't in the mood so she turned around, kissed him on the lips and said, "I am starving."

"Me too." Sam concurred while kissing her breasts. Ally was about to say something to him when her phone rang. Her phone was in her hand so she quickly answered it, but that didn't stop Sam from continuing to kiss her breasts.

"Hi Mirlande, what's up?" Ally answered, pushing Sam away from her with a look that said not now. He stopped and sat on the sofa like a little boy who was disappointed that his toy was taken away.

Mirlande was crying hysterically on the phone.

"Hey, sweetie, what's wrong?" Ally was very concerned.

"I'm at the hospital. Marcus got into a really bad car accident!" Mirlande reported, between tears.

"Oh my God, is he ok?!"

"I don't know yet. The doctors are with him. All they said to me was that he was unconscious when he was brought to the hospital by the ambulance. I wasn't with him. He had gone to run a few errands while I was entertaining his family. An hour later, when I called his cell phone, one of the nurses picked it up. They didn't know who to call and figured they could get the information from his phone."

"Ok, we will be right over! Which hospital?"

"Buffalo General."

"Ok we're on my way right now!"

Ally quickly hung up the phone and turned to Sam. She told Sam what happened to Marcus and the two of them rushed out of the apartment. Sam drove while Ally tried to reach Talia, but she didn't pick up. Ally figured Talia wasn't answering because she may still be upset with her so she texted her instead.

A minute later she received a text from Talia stating, "just hung up with Mirlande we r on our way also."

Buffalo General Hospital was in downtown so it took them about thirty minutes to get to the hospital. On their way, Ally tried to call Mirlande but there was no answer. She then tried texting her several times asking her what was going on…still no response. She was very anxious not knowing why Mirlande wasn't answering her. Sam kept trying to comfort her and telling her that they'll get there soon. He said that maybe Mirlande wasn't answering because she was busy talking to the doctor.

They finally arrived at the hospital. Sam dropped her off in front of the emergency room exist and told her to go in while he parked the car. He'd be there in a few minutes. Because Sam worked at that hospital at least once a week, he parked in the doctors' lot. Ally ran into the ER and she saw many of Marcus' family members there but didn't see Mirlande. She asked one of Marcus' cousins, whom she knew, how Marcus was doing. The cousin said that they didn't know and that Mirlande went in a few minutes ago. They were waiting to hear from her or the doctors.

A Few minutes later Mirlande and a nurse came into the waiting room. Mirlande was crying hysterically and couldn't speak a word. The nurse told them that Marcus suffered severe internal injuries. The doctors couldn't control the bleeding and he passed away. Everyone in the room was in shock and started crying. Ally just held Mirlande in her arms and, just then, Sam walked into the waiting room but there was no need for him to ask anything. From everyone's reaction he knew Marcus didn't survive. He walked over and put his arms around Mirlande and Ally.

Within a couple of minutes, Talia and Sergio arrived. Sam looked at the two of them and shook his head, letting them know that Marcus didn't make it. Talia covered her mouth to stifle a cry and tears ran down her cheeks as she walked over to Mirlande and Ally. Sam moved away and let the three friends be together. He walked over to Sergio and gave him a hug. In the last few days they all had become very close, like a family. It was hard to tell that they had only known each other for such a short period of time. They were all in shock. Marcus was so full of life and was so excited about getting married. He had planned every detail of the wedding but now, instead of a wedding, everyone will be attending his funeral. Mirlande was so devastated...she truly had found a great guy who was so genuine and who loved her unconditionally. He made her feel beautiful. The waiting room was full of Marcus' and Mirlande's relatives who had come from different cities for the wedding and there was no dry eye in the room. He was sincerely a nice guy who helped anyone he could. The kids in his neighborhood looked up to him. It was hard for everyone to accept he was gone.

Chapter 15

The Funeral

It was a dark, rainy, and somber Saturday morning. The morning of Marcus' funeral and it was also the day he and Mirlande were to tie the knot. Talia and Ally had stayed with Mirlande since the day Marcus passed away. She was in very bad condition. She had stopped eating and speaking with anyone. She did nothing but cry and just lay in her bed. Ally and Talia understood how devastated she was and couldn't even imagine the pain she may be feeling. They just let her cope with her loss the way she wanted. The two of them provided support for her by just being there and not leaving her sight, even for a minute. One of them was always in the room with her making sure she was not alone.

The day of the funeral was the worst. Instead of helping their friend get ready in a white dress for a beautiful wedding planned by the man who loved her dearly, they were helping her put on a black dress for the funeral of that same wonderful man that she would have to say goodbye to forever. Talia and Ally were doing their best to stay strong for their friend. Mirlande refused to get out of the bed and say goodbye to her love. He was supposed to be the man she would wake up to every morning and say goodnight to every night. She thought they would grow old together and she would die before him so she never had to feel the pain of losing him. That, apparently, is not what life had in store for her.

It took Ally and Talia two hours just to get Mirlande up and dressed (or ready) to go. Mirlande just sat in her chair lifeless, crying and not saying a word. The two of them felt so bad for her, they both did their best to hold their tears back so they wouldn't make it worse. Of course, the tears just rolled down their cheeks involuntarily.

The funeral procession was at least four blocks long. It consisted of Marcus' friends, neighbors, business people, family, and guests who were in town to attend the wedding. The Church was filled with so many people who loved him that there weren't enough benches for everyone. Mirlande looked around with tears raining down her cheeks. She was so moved to see how many lives he had touched.

At that point, Mirlande was very upset with God for taking Marcus away from her. She couldn't understand why he was brought into her life if their relationship was so short-lived. She didn't know how she was going to go on with her life without him. The pain inside of her was unbearable. The service took hours as everyone came to the casket, which was placed at the altar of the church, to say goodbye to the man who was full of life. Mirlande, Talia, Sergio, Zain, Ally and Sam were all standing next to the casket. After four hours of everyone saying goodbye, the guests left to go to the cemetery. Then there was one last person that arrived to pay his respects…it was Ary. He came and hugged Mirlande very tightly.

"I am so sorry, Mirlande." He just held her. Mirlande felt great comfort in his arms and wouldn't let him go.

Seeing how Mirlande reacted to Ary, Ally couldn't hold her tears back and began to cry. Talia put her arms around Ally, hugged her and whispered, "Life is short, and everyone comes in your life for a reason." At that moment Ally just hugged Talia tighter and knew exactly what she was trying to say.

After a few minutes Ary, noticed that the priest was ready, so he whispered to Mirlande, "It's time to go, Mirlande."

She began to cry even harder and asked him if he would accompany her. Ary nodded his head yes.

Ally couldn't believe how close Mirlande felt to Ary that she could speak only to him after days of silence. They all started walking out. The cemetery was actually only a block away so they all walked there. Since it was still raining, everyone broke off into couples, with umbrellas to protect them: Sergio and Talia; Zain and Silvia; Sam and Ally. Mirlande and Ary were walking together in front of the others. Ally watched the closeness, the comfort Mirlande felt with Ary and couldn't believe it, but she could understand exactly why Mirlande felt that comfort with him. Ary always treated women with care and respect. He always made women feel very special. The rain came down harder but no one cared. In the cemetery, you could see nothing but black umbrellas everywhere. Most people stayed outside of the cemetery and allowed the family members to go in since there were so many people and not enough space to accommodate everyone.

After the burial, everyone went to Silvia's house. She hosted a gathering for all of Marcus' and Mirlande's family in her backyard. She had a big backyard so she had tents put up and they served as a great shelter from the rain. Silvia was great at arranging events since her husband always entertained people but this was one gathering she wished she didn't have to plan. The neighbors knew she was hosting the gathering for the family after the funeral, so they all brought a dish and dropped it off at Silvia's house earlier that day. The gathering was only for family and limited friends. There was so much food that three long tables were filled.

The family members were sitting around remembering Marcus Few members left town after the funeral was over. They found it hard to stay when he longer was there. He used to be the center of all the parties and he just wasn't there anymore...that was hard for them. One by one, the families were departing since there was no need to stay longer. By 8pm all of the relatives were gone and it was Silvia, Sergio, Talia, Sam, Mirlande, Ally and Ary left. They all helped Silvia clean up. Mirlande looked so sad, just sitting there with puffy eyes from crying so much. Thanks to Ary, she actually ate a little bit. She didn't want to but he wasn't going to take no for an answer and, for some reason, Mirlande listened to him. His charming personality is what she loved about him. Ally t watched how the two of them interacted. As much as she didn't want to see Ary, she realized he was good for Mirlande so she just let it be.

They were all very tired. They hadn't rested for the past few days so Silvia told Talia and Ally that she was going to have Mirlande stay with her and that they should all go home to rest. Mirlande's parents had passed away when she was in her twenties, coincidentally in a car accident also, and she was the only child so she really didn't have family that she was close to. Her aunts, uncles, and cousins came for the wedding but they too had to leave because of work. One of Mirlande's aunts, whom she was close to, was going to stay with her but Mirlande asked her to go because her aunt was the only bread earner in the house and she needed to go to work the next day. Silvia was like a mother to Mirlande so she loved spending time with her. In turn, Silvia treated Mirlande like a daughter so she loved taking care of her. They all said goodbye to each other for the night. Everyone had to return to work the next day since it was the end of their week-long vacation they took for the wedding. Talia and Ally told Mirlande to call them anytime she needed them and they will come over after work tomorrow for sure.

Ary said goodbye to Mirlande, who thanked him for coming and caring for her. He then said bye to the others. It bothered him to see Ally and Sam together but he tried hard not to pay much attention to the two of them since he was there to pay his respect to Marcus. Ally did thank him for taking care of Mirlande. His only response to Ally was that he considered Mirlande a friend and would do anything for her. He then walked away.

Ever since that night when they all were out, Sam sensed tension between Ally and Ary. He wondered if there had been something between the two of them but was afraid to ask. Besides, she was going to be his wife now so even if something was there between them it's not there now. Then, he thought, he would probably always have that question in the back of his mind. This will continue to bother him whenever there's a chance they might run into Ary again. That's why he wanted to question her just so he could have that peace of mind. He was confused as to what he wanted or perhaps he was just was afraid to know if there was something between them? He could sense that he was starting to become possessive of Ally since she was going to be his wife and didn't want any man looking at her.

A few minutes after Ary left they all said goodbye to Mirlande and Silvia. They knew she was in good hands and didn't need to worry about her.

Chapter 16

Saying Goodbye

Life was starting to get back to normal for most of them after Marcus' funeral but Mirlande wasn't who she used to be. She kept herself busy at the boutique so she wasn't alone at home. She had lost that glow and clearly had sadness on her face. She didn't have that desire for life like she used to when Marcus was in her life. She wasn't spending much time with Talia and Ally either because when she saw them with Sam and Sergio she missed Marcus even more so she tried to avoid them as much as she could by keeping herself busy. Talia and Ally sensed that it was hard for her to be around couples so they did their best to spend time with her without the guys. Talia and Sergio had moved in together and day by day they were getting to know each other more and more. Ally and Sam were busy with their work since they both had taken so much time off but their families were busy planning their engagement now that Ally's father was home from the hospital and feeling better.

It was Friday and Ally only worked half a day so she could take care of few things at home. She wanted to relax a bit before meeting her and Sam's family for dinner at her parents' house. There was a part of her that was uncomfortable about the two families getting together tonight. They were meeting to plan for their engagement party and the wedding. On her way home from the office, she picked up lunch for herself. She really wasn't hungry so she just got a salad to would have something in her stomach. She always lost her appetite whenever something bothered her. As she was walking towards her apartment she ran into Jeffery.

"Hello my vicious vixen. What are you doing home so early?" He asked.

"Hi Jeff. I have to go to my family's for dinner tonight so I just wanted to relax my mind before I deal with the chaos," Ally replied.

"What chaos?"

"Oh, I'm sorry I haven't had the chance to update you on what's going on in my life. With you being gone out of town for a few days and with all the things that were going with Mirlande, I didn't get a chance to talk to you. When you were out of town, Marcus got into a car accident and passed away so, instead of the wedding, we had a funeral for him. Mirlande is devastated and rightly so...."

Jeff interrupted her, "Oh my God that is so sad! He was a great guy. I feel horrible for Mirlande. How is she doing?"

"Well, you can imagine what a wreck she is! She stays busy with her Boutique. Plus, she tries to avoid us but Talia and I visit her as much as possible and, also, give her the space she needs so she can accept and cope with her loss,"

"Poor girl, I will definitely go visit her either today or tomorrow."

"I think she might like that. She might not say it but I think she would definitely appreciate you stopping by."

"Here, since you have some time why don't you come in and chat. I'll make some coffee for us," Jeff suggested.

"You know, I think I would love that! I have been meaning to sit and talk with you. Now is the best time." Ally followed Jeff into his apartment.

Jeff made a gesture towards the dining table. "Have a seat at the table. I'll make coffee and get something to eat for us."

"I actually have a salad here if you want to share?" Ally offered.

"Salad is not enough so why don't I warm up some stew to go with it."

"Let me come help you. I'll make the coffee while you nuke the stew." The two entered the kitchen.

Jeff quickly warmed up the stew in the microwave while Ally put coffee on for brewing and got out the bowls and utensils for the two of them. Everything was ready in a snap so they both sat down at the table with their food and coffee.

"Sooo…what's going on with you?" Jeff wanted to hear the story.

"Well, I think I had told you in passing that I decided to marry Sam but never had the chance to further explain how things happened," Ally began.

"Yes, you did. Now, is this what you truly want or is that what your family wants?" Jeff knew what she was going to say but asked anyway.

Instead of replying, Ally started playing with the bowl of stew that was in front of her. Jeff sat there quietly waiting for her to answer. He knew deep inside her heart this was not what she wanted but had no choice...correction...everyone has choices but this was a choice she made to please her family. After a few minutes, he noticed that her eyes were starting to water.

Ally knew he wouldn't say a word until she answered so she tearfully spoke, "You know, if I want to remain in my family's life, this is what needs to happen. Mirlande and Talia have been telling me the same thing that you are going to tell me but I think it's best for me to marry Sam. Talia is even upset to the point where she's not talking to me about it at all. She's also upset because she feels I should meet up with Ary in person and tell him seriously that it's over so he can have closure and move on with his life. Why can't she understand that would be hard for me to do that? Sam is a great guy and he has been so happy ever since I said yes to him."

Jeff gave a thoughtful but severe look. "There is no doubt that Sam is a very nice guy but you need to do what's right for you. I know all of us have been telling you the same thing over and over again and at the end of the day it's really your life. The choice you make will impact three lives. Your parents have lived their life and they will continue to live as long as God wants them to, and then what? They are not going to live forever you know! They might be around for few more years, and you? You are still young and have many more years to go, so the only thing all of us are telling you is make too sure you choose what's best for you and, to be honest, I too think it would be best for you to have closure with Ary.

The closure is not just for him, it's also for you. I would strongly advise you to meet with him before you go for dinner tonight. I really think you also need it as much as he does. If you've made up your mind about marrying Sam then you don't need to worry about anything when you see Ary. You just need to say goodbye to him. You will thank me and Talia for telling you do so. Once you have said bye to him then you will be able to move forward with *your* life and will be at a better state of mind when making all of these wedding plans with your family"

Ally looked at her watch. "I don't even know what time he would be home."

Why don't you call or text him saying you want to meet with him."

"I don't want to do that. I will stop by his house and, if he is there, I will say bye. If not, then I'm fine with that and done with all of this."

"Ok, that's your choice. You are an adult and there is only so much we can do for you. You, being a psychologist, should know one can only help those want to be helped. You know life is short...who knows what tomorrow holds? Look at Mirlande and Marcus, they were ready to tie the knot and now he is gone."

"Yes, I know and I really am thankful that I have great friends in my life."

The two of them sat and spent some time together catching up on everything. It was something Ally needed, talking to Jeff always made her feel better. They not only had serious talks, they also joked around quite a bit. What Ally liked about Jeff was that he was like a father figure to her. Someone she can go to if she needed fatherly advice and he was so very honest. He didn't say things just to make her feel better, he always spoke his mind.

It was early in the evening and Ally was getting ready to go to her family's. She dressed conservatively as she always did every time she went to visit her family. She wore an Indian salwar (loose harem type pants) kameez (long top). It was yellow with fuchsia embroidery. Ally loved bright colors and it suited her personality. She looked beautiful in yellow. With her suit, she wore big gold earrings with a simple gold chain and she wore hair down as always. She was very nervous and even had butterflies in her stomach for two reasons. First, she had to go to her family's for the engagement and wedding planning. Secondly, she was also going to stop by Ary's to say goodbye to him. She couldn't figure out which made her more nervous.

On her way to Ary's, she could feel the butterflies in her stomach and she had a lot on her mind. She didn't know what she was going to say to him. Ary lived about fifteen minutes away from her. The drive to his place felt so long to her, yet was quicker than she wanted. As she got closer to his place, she started to feel the heat in her face and lots of knots in her stomach. She parked her car outside Ary's place and sat there for few minutes. She could feel her heart beating fast, weakness in her legs, and her palms were sweating. She started doing her yoga breathing, trying to calm her nerves. She sat there with her eyes closed as she took deep breathes. She did the best she could to calm herself. She realized she couldn't sit in her car for long so she gathered herself, got out of the car, and started walking towards his apartment. As she got closer and closer her heart beat faster and faster. She took deep breaths again and rang his doorbell. She waited a few seconds but there was no answer so she rang it again, waited again for few more seconds, yet still no answer. She rang the doorbell for one last time, waited for a couple more minutes. There was still no answer so she turned around and started to walk away slowly....

Just as she was about a few feet away, the door opened. She turned around. There stood Ary, with a bath towel around his waist.

"Hi," Ally nervously uttered, as she walked towards him.

"Hi. Sorry, I was in the shower. Surprised to see you here, everything ok?" He asked, leaning on the door jamb.

"Can I come in?" Ally gave him a hesitant look, as she stood a foot away from his door.

"I'm sorry but I can't have someone else's wife visit me alone, especially when I'm in my bathrobe. Unless you want to become my wife?" Ary respond very seriously.

Ally turned and looked at her car, then turned and looked at Ary. As she looked at her keys in her hands and with tears coming down her cheeks… "I just came to say bye."

Ary didn't say a word and just stood there. He was feeling a lot of pain and anger inside of him, so he didn't dare move.

Ally couldn't control her tears. "Please say something, I need to go!"

"Then go,"

"That's it? That's all you are going to say?"

Ary crossed his arms in front of his chest. "What is it that you would like me to say? You came to say goodbye and you did that. If there is anything else you would like to say, go right ahead."

"Can we please go in and talk?" Ally was practically begging Ary at this point.

"Honestly, what is there to talk about? You have decided to get married to someone else and there is nothing I can do or say to you that will make you change your mind. If I allow you to come in then I will never want you to leave. I truly love you and it really hurts me to see you become someone else's. You are more than welcome to come in only if you are going to stay in my life forever. If not, you said your goodbye so you need to leave please."

Ally started crying even more. She could see the hurt in Ary's eyes. As much as it was killing Ary to see her like that, he realized it was her choice. Ally slowly turned towards her car and walked away crying.

That just broke Ary down even more. He was hoping she would come in but instead he watched her get into her car. He walked inside his apartment and slammed the door shut. Once inside, he leaned back against the door and started crying. He knew it was over for good. He sat down in a chair with the towel still wrapped around him, lamenting his loss.

The doorbell rang. He couldn't care to see who it was and just sat there. The doorbell kept ringing but he didn't get up to answer it. Then there was a loud banging on the door. He kept trying to ignore it but the banging didn't stop so he wiped his tears away and went to answer the door, annoyed....It was Ally

"I can't imagine my life without you. I will never leave you ever. Can I come in now?" She declared, with a big smile. He couldn't believe it. He blinked his eyes then picked her up and carried her into his apartment.

THE END *for now...*

CPSIA information can be obtained
at www.ICGtesting.com
Printed in the USA
LVHW111309030221
678255LV00030B/136

9 780578 845029